RED
WARNING

MATTHEW QUIRK is the *New York Times* bestselling author of *The 500, The Directive, Dead Man Switch, Cold Barrel Zero*, and *The Night Agent*, which is in production as a limited series for Netflix. He spent five years at *The Atlantic* reporting on crime, private military contractors, terrorism prosecutions, and international gangs before turning to fiction. An Edgar Award finalist and winner of the ITW Thriller Award for Best First Novel, he lives in San Diego.

Follow Matthew on Twitter @mquirk
matthewquirk.com

By Matthew Quirk

RED
WARNING

MATTHEW
QUIRK

An Aries Book

First published in the US in 2022 by William Morrow,
an imprint of HarperCollins Publishers

First published in the UK in 2022 by Head of Zeus Ltd,
part of Bloomsbury Publishing Plc

9 7 5 3 1 2 4 6 8

A catalogue record for this book is available from
the British Library.

ISBN (HB): 9781803284507
ISBN (XTPB): 9781803284743
ISBN (E): 9781803284484

Printed and bound in Great Britain by
CPI Group (UK) Ltd, Croydon CR0 4YY

Head of Zeus Ltd
First Floor East
5–8 Hardwick Street
London EC1R 4RG

WWW.HEADOFZEUS.COM

To Dean and John

1

SAM HUDSON LOOKED at the clock. The second hand ticked forward: 10:05 p.m.

"How do you know we can trust this guy?" the young man behind him asked.

"I don't," Sam said, and stepped closer to the window.

That was intelligence work: waiting half the night in a bland corporate apartment in Geneva, not sure if your date for the evening was going to kiss you or kill you.

A rhythmic scratching drew his attention, and he turned to face the other man, Eric Finlay. All wiry muscle with sharp features, Fin was on his first overseas tour as a deep-cover officer. He was picking at the cardboard package of a Toblerone with his thumbnail.

Sam eyed the candy, and Finlay glanced at it, then held it up, offering it to his partner, who only shook his head slowly. *No.*

Finlay looked at his thumb. "Sorry," he said.

"It's all right, Fin."

Sam watched his charge, studying the smile lines around the eyes. Fin was the kind of guy you want to tell your best stories to. It made him a good case officer. But now his face was grave.

The nerves were out of character but understandable. This was a crash meeting, and they hadn't cleared it with headquarters. There was no time, and HQs had been shooting down or slow-walking every approach in Europe—you can't get in trouble for doing nothing, was the bureaucratic code—so Sam had gone ahead on his own. People were dying. He couldn't afford to wait.

Tonight they were pitching a potential source, a man who went by the name Alex Clarke. Sam believed that was a cover but had little on the target's true identity. Clarke moved money for a holding company called Gemini GmbH that Sam suspected of being a front for a foreign intelligence service, likely Russia's or one of its proxies'.

Sam had linked Gemini to illicit flows of cash that connected to a series of murders in the United States and the United Kingdom— the victims all bankers and intelligence sources. The killer, he believed, was a legendary deep-cover operator known as Konstantin. Alex Clarke was the way into his network.

"But Clarke could be Russian intel?" Finlay asked.

"If we're lucky. He's ready to turn."

Fin checked the clock. Clarke was supposed to have been here by nine thirty. No call. No text. No answer when Sam rang him.

"And if someone got to him? Or he's setting us up?"

"If you have a bad feeling, you can step out and keep watch up the street. I wanted you to be here for the pitch, but I understand."

"He's worth the risk?"

"Absolutely," Sam said. "But you know me."

"Trust your instincts."

"Right. We've been trying to get inside this network for decades. It's fine if you want out, Fin. But this is the real game, and you're ready. You've earned it. I wouldn't have brought you otherwise."

Fin was the best new officer Sam had seen in years. He wanted to show him how the dance went, and the only way to learn was to be in the room with the target. Real human espionage was a dying art in the age of drones and the all-powerful NSA, and he had a duty to pass it on. Someone had taken a chance on Sam once too. If it made the job harder tonight, so be it.

"I trust you," Fin said, almost casually, his confidence coming back.

Sam went back to the window so he could watch the main street. The clock's ticking, hard and sharp, was the only sound. He peered out at the countless unlit buildings. Looking over the steep roofs and dormers of Old Town, he had a narrow view of the Mont Blanc range, still white in summer, jagged against the stars. He never quite trusted Geneva, despite its carefully tended gardens and postcard-perfect cobblestoned squares. There was always a complicit feeling about these Swiss cities where Europe kept its secrets, so formal with their quiet luxuries and hidden wealth.

Tick. Tock.

A shadow lengthened on the street below. A woman in a white blouse passed by and then disappeared around a corner.

"Did they have a place with a louder clock?" Finlay asked.

"We couldn't afford it."

"I'll go—"

Three hard knocks at the door.

Sam smiled. He moved past Fin, tapping his shoulder with the side of his fist. "It's on," he said, his voice low, and went to the peephole.

Alex Clarke stood just outside, looking slightly downward, not crowding the entrance. He was six feet tall with dark hair swept back. Sam opened the door. Clarke's eyes, large and blue, met his. The face was so calm and full of understanding that Sam had almost checked the man's collar the first time they met. There was something priest-like about him.

"Alex," Sam said as he let him in and shook his hand.

Alex clapped him on the arm. "Great to see you, man."

"You remember Thomas, right?" Sam said, gesturing toward Finlay. Thomas was an alias. Both men used cover identities in their work with Clarke.

"Of course." Alex gave Fin's hand a pump.

Sam was operating undercover as a tech consultant for private financial markets. Alex claimed to be an investment adviser and ran with the hundred-millionaire-and-up crowd: horse auctions in Saudi and summers on the Med. It gave him an excuse to go anywhere, see anyone, and say little—a good front.

Sam had spent months slowly getting close to him, starting with drinks and dinners at investment conferences. Looking at him now, Sam couldn't help but be impressed by the quality of his cover. Alex spoke in unaccented, idiomatic American English and had the manners nailed, right down to the bro half-hug, yet there was no record of him ever entering or living in the United States. He had come back clean on a search through all the U.S. and partner intel databases. It was some of the strongest identity work Sam had ever seen.

This evening they would head to the Bar des Bergues, a wood-paneled jewel box inside the Four Seasons overlooking the lake. That was the story, at least, but Sam doubted they would make it out of this apartment. He was going to turn Alex in this room.

Something was off, though, as Clarke strolled past the windows, seeming to admire the view. His eyes were moving too fast, subtly scanning Fin and Sam for weapons. The relaxation was forced, with a tightness showing in the shoulders.

Fin looked to Sam; he saw it too. Alex could simply be a money-man in over his head, a go-between who was terrified about the gravity of what he was about to give up and just wanted to sell his secrets and get out. Or he could be a foreign intelligence officer calculating a way to leverage Sam, to turn him and sway him to treason. Or he could be one of the killers.

Sam liked the game, liked playing it against someone as skilled as Clarke. But there was no safety net here. He and Fin were operating under nonofficial cover, commonly called deep cover, which meant they were on their own with no diplomatic immunity and no backup.

"What are you drinking?" Sam asked as he opened the refrigerator.

"I'm good," Clarke replied, the tone clipped, a military succinctness. There was an urgency in Alex's posture, something lethal, the training showing now. This wasn't the same man Sam knew from those hotel bars.

Sam shut the fridge. "Held up in traffic?"

Alex cocked his head as if to say, *C'mon, man.* No bullshit small talk this time.

"I need to speak with you one on one," Alex said, then looked to Fin. Sam felt the night accelerating, his heart pumping a steady beat against his breastbone. This was it.

"He has my absolute trust," Sam said.

"He must be good. I thought you always worked alone. Couldn't let anyone slow you down." Alex's gaze was cool, measuring. That was the closest he'd ever come to calling out Sam as CIA. "You should go," Alex said to Finlay. "It's for your own sake."

Fin looked at Sam, the kid doing a good job hiding his nerves, and Sam gave him a nod.

"I *could* use some air," Fin said with an easy expression on his face. He walked close to Sam and paused by his side. "It's fine," Sam said. "I've got it." Then, turned slightly so that Alex couldn't see, he mouthed, *Keep your distance,* to Fin.

The young officer walked out. As the door clicked shut behind him, Alex took a step to his left, between Sam and the exit. His face was pale. It looked like fear, but Sam kept his eyes on Alex's hands.

"I know you're onto these killings," Alex said. "I know what you want. I can give him to you."

"And who's that?"

"Konstantin."

2

SAM DIDN'T BETRAY any emotion.

Most of the old hands at the Agency dismissed Konstantin as a folktale, a convenient specter that could explain decades of encrypted radio bursts and dark-money flows. But Sam believed he was a real human being, an agent who could slip invisibly into the United States, the linchpin of a secret Russian network that posed the greatest threat to the West since the end of the Cold War. Sam had dedicated his life to hunting him down.

Konstantin would be an irresistible lure for a setup, so Sam disguised his interest even as he felt his heart rate tick up.

"That's what you people call him, right?" Alex said.

Sam crossed his arms. Silence was best; it would draw Alex out without Sam having to reveal anything. Alex had all but confirmed he was foreign intel.

"'You people'?" Sam asked.

"I know enough. You don't have to say a word."

"If you know so much, why the dance?"

"To see if I could trust you and if you were good enough to handle this."

"How'd I do?" Sam asked.

"I'm here."

Sam wondered if every move over the past three months had been a trap. Alex could have been developing Sam the whole time, building rapport to turn him. It had been Alex who'd made the first approach, a casual introduction at a hotel bar in Zurich. They talked about skiing, going on about the pleasures of Wasatch and Hokkaido powder until, without realizing it, they had shut down the bar. The conversation always seemed to flow naturally, never a misplaced word or awkward silence. That was the mark of a good case officer: the ability to make everything seem natural, though Sam had recognized the encounter as an approach from the beginning.

Alex was fast in getting close to Sam, always down for another drink, another spot. Sam questioned from the first contact whether Alex had a sense of Sam's real identity as CIA. If so, how? And what was he after?

Alex always knew someplace open late where the locals liked to hang out, and Sam would roll with him through the night in the back of a cab to a part of town he barely recognized. The last time, in Lucerne, they'd ended up in a basement club with ten tables where everyone seemed to know each other and a Swiss-German girl sang like Billie Holiday until the small hours.

At every moment with Alex, Sam couldn't be certain if he was the predator or the prey. It was a contest between the two men to see who could stay in control as the liquor flowed and who could keep up the patter, spinning out stories, real but false. When operating undercover, you always started from a grain of truth, fragments of yourself that you adapted on the fly to fit the persona. It was strange; there were times in this confidence game when Sam, going by a false name, was more honest than he ever would have been in real life, like the story Sam had told Alex, as he tried to draw him out on a predawn walk back to the hotel, about the last words his father had said to him.

As those nights grew late, and the booze seemed to accelerate time, Sam would feel the pleasure of the game, of the edge of control, wondering who might make a fatal slip first and show too much behind the mask.

This was the most treacherous moment. Sam would meet his sources undercover and feel them out, looking for those who might be inclined, because of greed or grudge or glory, to help him get inside the networks that fueled proxy wars and state terror. At some point, he would drop the cover, make his pitch, and ask them to betray all they knew.

"Are we in danger?" Sam asked.

"Always. That's the job. But I'm clean. No one followed me."

"You're on edge," Sam said.

He laughed. "Of course. You know what I'm going up against."

Sam watched him for a moment. "Better than anyone."

"Konstantin. Why have you been running him down so hard? Half your people don't even think he exists. You know the risk you're taking just coming here?"

"I do," Sam said. "I have my reasons."

"Why don't you clue me in?"

"I owe it to someone. Leave it at that. You work for Russia?"

"There are many Russias. Konstantin is real. I can give him to you. But on my terms."

"Which are?"

"I help you stop him. And this doesn't go up the chain."

"That would be a hard promise to make."

"That's the deal."

"*Stop* him?"

"Yes."

"What's he planning?"

"I need your word."

"And what do you want?"

"Peace."

Sam almost laughed. That gauzy notion was the last thing he'd expected to hear. But after a long look, he saw that Alex was absolutely serious.

"Arrangements can be made—cash and maybe a house in the States—but peace is a tall order," Sam said.

"It's what I'm offering, not what I'm asking for."

"Lay it out for me. Starting with who you really are."

"This stays between us. I approve everyone you run it past at your office?" Alex said.

"You know I can't promise that without a good reason. Give me something to start with and we'll talk."

Alex examined his face with a hard, unsettling gaze. Sam knew he was looking for signs of deception.

"I can't tell you who I am, not yet. But I can lead you to Konstantin. I'd heard about you. I thought it was a lot of hype until you tracked me down." He opened his eyes wide for an instant. "Gemini. How did you find it? How'd you find me?"

"Call it luck."

Alex shook his head.

"It's what I do. You hurt our people, I find you. You're part of these killings." Sam put it out there as a statement. He wanted to read his reaction.

"No," Clarke said. A liar would have been more defensive. "But I can get to the network behind them. You're on the right path."

"Where do I go next?"

"You need the courier, and there isn't much time." He took a long breath in through his nose, weighing what to say. Then his eyes went unfocused for a second, as if he were looking through Sam.

"Who is the courier, Alex?" Sam asked slowly, a shadow of a threat behind the words. "Tell me where I find him."

Alex didn't answer. He was concentrating. He was listening.

An engine hummed outside, growing louder, coming from the south.

Alex's eyes went to the window to his left. Had he stood in that spot specifically so he could watch the exterior? To set the geometry of the meeting so that Sam wouldn't see anyone approach?

Sam filled his lungs and exhaled with deep, even breaths, getting ready. He stepped back and to the side to look out the other window. The engine cut off. There was no sign of anyone on the street, but there were countless places to hide in Old Town's maze of narrow lanes, alleys, and squares.

"Waiting for someone?" Sam asked.

"No. Who knows we're here?"

"I didn't tell a soul besides Thomas." Alex shifted his weight to the balls of his feet—the fight-or-flight physiology kicking in.

"Who is it?" Sam asked.

"Listen," Alex said, coming closer and putting his hand out to Sam. Sam seized the wrist and twisted the palm to the side, squeezing the bones like a vise while his face remained utterly calm.

"I didn't set you up," Alex said.

Sam let his hand go. "Raise your jacket."

"Come on."

Sam stared back.

Alex lifted his jacket and turned. No gun. He tugged up the legs of his pants to show he had nothing in an ankle holster either.

"What is this?" Sam asked, glancing toward the window.

"Someone doesn't want me talking."

Sam's phone buzzed in his pocket. He looked at the screen and saw a message from Fin. "At least two cars watching building. West exit clear."

"We have to go," Alex said.

Sam cocked his head toward the door. "Downstairs and turn left." He wasn't letting Alex out of his sight or showing him his back.

Alex nodded and walked out of the room, Sam right behind him. Halfway down the stairs, Sam heard a door open. He pressed against the banister and looked toward the entryway, scanning the main hall on the ground floor, dimly lit by sconces set against the paneled walls.

The yellow light silhouetted a figure ahead, coming from one of the side halls that served the ground-floor apartments. As the man turned to them, Sam saw it was Finlay.

"Thomas," Sam said as he and Alex hit the landing.

"They're closing in from the south and east, at least four—" Fin said. He looked to his right, bringing his hand up, gesturing for Sam to stop.

A crack. A flash of white from the side. Fin took a long staggering step, then hit the floor. Sam felt it shake and ran to him.

3

CROUCHING DOWN, SAM neared the line of fire from that side corridor. Fin's eyes were open wide. His lips parted twice as he let out hitching breaths.

Sam dropped lower, grabbed Fin's shirt, and dragged him back over the smooth tile. Two gunshots cracked, booming down the hall, the bullets hissing over Sam's head as he hauled Fin to safety.

He kept going around the stairs, then into the recycling room, which led to a rear exit. He laid Fin down on the worn marble tiles. The bullet had entered near where Fin's neck and trapezius joined, and Sam pressed his hand down on the wound. He glanced over his shoulder to see that Alex had followed him in and was stepping closer. Sam's body tensed for an attack, but Alex only looked down at Fin, his face twisting in anger. "What do you need?" Alex asked.

Sam brought out a set of keys with his free hand. "Lock that and break off the key," he said, nodding toward the door leading to the main hall. He looked back down while Alex secured the door, the ping of snapping metal sounding through the room. Sam tore off the sleeve of his shirt, balled it up, and pressed it against the wound in Fin's neck. Warm blood seeped through.

Fin reached out, laid his hand over Sam's wrist, and held it for a moment, eyes on his. "I'm sorry."

"You've got nothing to be sorry about. Nothing." Sam thought back to their last real conversation and pushed down harder. "Remember what we talked about? Acadia. We'll get you back there. Just hang on. Hang on."

Fin tried to speak, his chin trembling, but no words came. His hand slipped away.

In the moment, Sam nearly spoke Fin's real name, but caught himself. "Tom," he said. "*Tom.*" He fought the urge to shout it, to try to shake him awake. He could hear footfalls pounding on the marble floor outside, men approaching. "Get that arm," Sam said to Alex.

Sam lifted most of Fin's weight with an arm around his waist, reaching up to keep pressure on the wound. Alex took the other side, draping Fin's arm around his own neck, and they moved to the rear exit.

Sam wanted to trust Alex, to believe he was on his side in this, but some part of him was still playing the angles, calculating whether Alex was trying to keep up his cover as an ally.

They stepped outside and took shelter in the doorway. It was set back from the narrow cobblestoned lane that passed behind the hotel and ran downhill to Sam's right.

Sam edged out, scanning in both directions. About twenty feet down to the right, there was an intersection with another narrow street. A half a dozen spots offered concealment: around the corners, in the doorways on the opposite side of the street, or in the deep stone archways of the older building next door.

"I have him." Alex wrapped his arm around Fin's torso, supporting his weight, then put his hand on the cloth compress.

Sam let go of Fin and leaned into the street. He wanted a clear exit or to take a gun off one of the attackers so he could get Fin and Clarke out of here. The light shifted near the intersection—someone moving slowly, attempting to keep cover.

A carefully controlled rage burned in Sam, clearing his mind of all but the urge to strike. "Stay here," he whispered to Alex. The cool, damp air closed around Sam as he stepped out and slipped along the limestone walls.

Sirens sounded in the distance, the up-and-down horns of European police. Sam passed the archways and pressed against the next-door building's exterior as he neared the corner.

A fountain murmured down the street, and Sam heard the quiet grind of grit against the cobbles, someone approaching. He dropped low as a man emerged from the side street, something bearlike in his movements, leading with a gun that passed just over Sam's head. As Sam rose, he shot out his left hand and closed his fingers around the man's hand on the grip. Driving with his legs, Sam threw his right fist into the man's chin; his attacker took a step back but managed to hang on to the pistol. Sam seized the gun with both hands and they fought over the weapon, standing side by side, the man tilting the barrel toward Sam's face.

Sam pressed him against the wall with his body and slammed his wrists against the corner of the building once, then twice. The gun clattered to the ground in the dark.

Sam dropped his right foot onto the man's ankle and felt it give, and as he fell, Sam threw an open-palm blow to the side of his head, knocking it into the worn stone. The man dropped, and Sam took a step forward, looking into the dark of the side street for the pistol.

He saw the other shooter too late, approaching from below, at the far end of the lane. A gun rose in front of him, the muzzle aimed straight at Sam's head. The air cracked and the buildings' facades flashed red.

Sam threw himself down the side street. The bullet slit the air above him. A miss. Another shot sounded as Sam hunted for the gun that had fallen there. He heard footsteps growing quieter, moving farther off. It sounded like the shooter who had just missed him was retreating, perhaps fleeing the police.

The sirens called out, louder now but impossible to locate in the labyrinth of curving streets.

Sam saw the dropped pistol, a compact SIG Sauer, lying against a drainpipe. He picked it up, the grip still warm from the man's hand, and checked the brass and magazine—ten rounds.

He went back to the intersection. The gunman Sam had fought with was still down; the one who had fired the shot was gone, but his face stayed with Sam: the lifeless eyes, the close-cropped gray beard, the boxer's crooked nose at odds with the sheen of his expensive suit.

As Sam turned back the way he had come, he heard a grunt. Two men, both armed, flanked the doorway up the lane where Fin and Alex had taken cover. One of them struggled with Alex, grabbed his collar, and pulled him into the street.

Sam raised the gun and moved in. He paused on the cobbles, holding his breath for a split second as he aimed at the man fighting with Alex. He fired. A clean hit. The man fell back as the other took aim straight at Sam.

Sam jumped to the side, pressing into one of the archways. Four shots popped, and the stone beside his head exploded. Sam saw only black as he felt himself falling; his knee slammed into the curb as he crashed into the road. Pain raged through the back and side of his head. The world spun. He opened his eyes, just barely, his cheek against the cobbles.

It all happened in an instant. Up the street, one of the men threw Alex to the ground and stepped over him, moving with a brutal efficiency. Sam could make out the man's face by the streetlamps—deep lines ran along the sides of his mouth, there was a scar near his temple, and a heavy brow hid his eyes. Russian. Southern Slavic.

Alex raised himself up, lifting his hand as if it could stop the bullet. "No. How could he—" Alex said, anguish in his voice before the gunshots cut off the words. The man fired twice. The muzzle flare lit up Alex's face like a camera's flash. He fell and lay still against the curving pattern of the cobbles.

Sam was already rising, fighting against the vertigo, lifting the gun in his unsteady hand. He moved as fast as he could, though it seemed impossibly slow, like running in a nightmare. The attacker turned and shot before Sam could. Fire tore up Sam's ribs, the bullet breaking bone. He stumbled to the side and went down in the archway. Another shot sailed past. Sam's head struck the ground. Blackness pressed in like desperately needed sleep.

Sam was out, but eventually an image—Fin's face, his shaking chin—pulled him back. He dragged himself up into a crouch, pain arcing up his right side, and leaned out. The lane was clear.

He rose, steadying himself against the limestone with his left hand, the SIG in his right, and worked his way up the lane toward the rear exit of the apartment building. There was no trace of the gunmen or Alex Clarke's body. As he came to the doorway, he saw Finlay slumped in the corner.

Trust your instincts.

Sam dropped to one knee beside the young officer, Fin's eyes open in the night like two blank coins. Blue and red flashes filtered down the alley, lighting up his pale cheeks.

"Fin." He placed two fingers to the side of his throat, searching for a trace of life. He came back with nothing but blood on his hands as white light flooded the street and the police called out for him to drop the gun.

4

Six weeks later

THE MAN WALKING down the steps of the World War II Memorial went by many names: Karl Stadler on the Continent, George Malek in the Middle East, and here in the United States he was Michael Lange. There was something old-fashioned about Lange's manner, with its unrushed pace, relaxed shoulders, and the classic looks of a 1950s actor. His hair was black going silver, though on a closer view, he seemed too young for that, with his strength easy enough to discern under the light coat and open-collared shirt he wore.

The circle of American flags behind him hung down, barely stirring in the muggy night as he headed for the trees along the Reflecting Pool. A family passed on his right, the boys bickering, likely sapped by a long day marching under the sun. The Mall was a mostly empty expanse, patches of dirt and ill-tended lawns once used for overflow parking. High summer was over, but the DC heat had a way of sticking around. He paid the tourists little mind as he watched the path ahead through the trees.

Something cut in at the edge of his peripheral vision. He spun toward it, fists rising. One of the kids nearly crashed into his legs. Lange checked his instincts, relaxing his hands and softening the look on his face as he stepped to the side, dodging the boy and slowing him down with a gentle palm on the shoulder. He had long ago mastered his outward self and could use it to be anything he wished: a kind tourist or a walking nightmare.

"Ethan, I told you!" a woman in a blue tank top called out in a soft North Carolina accent. "I'm sorry, sir."

"It's fine," Lange said with a quiet laugh and kept walking as the kid ran back to his mother. The warmth of his shoulder stayed with Lange. He reminded him of another boy, another country, another time, and for a moment a shade of doubt pressed in about the remote trigger in Lange's coat pocket and what was to come next.

His eyes searched between the elms that lined the paths beside the Reflecting Pool. Finally, they fixed on a runner.

The man's legs moved like pistons firing. He kept his arms low, no wasted movement, flying down the path, muscles standing out with every stride. He didn't look like he was out for a run. He looked like he was chasing or being chased—both true.

The sight of him erased any doubts in Lange's mind. He reached his hand into his pocket and felt the smooth plastic of the trigger. Measure for measure.

He watched Sam Hudson race past him, eyes forward, unaware that the man he sought so desperately now stood fifty meters away. Hudson knew Lange by another name: Konstantin.

Lange watched him often and could recognize him even in this half-light: the hair trim, the blue eyes so often narrowed with amusement, the relaxed bearing that stood in contrast to his eyes, which were always on guard.

Hudson was on administrative leave from the Central Intelligence Agency after the bloodbath in Geneva. He would rather die than sit still, and now he was forced to pause, unable to strike back, his hands tied by his own superiors, cut off from the work that gave his life meaning. There's no worse torture for men like Hudson than stasis. They go insane.

Of course Hudson was running. He was always moving, exercising for hours every day, anything to vent the anger and frustration, channel that desperate need for retribution. Lange knew the feeling well.

The fighter in him admired how intensely and how quickly Hudson had thrown himself into regaining his strength after the concussion and a fractured rib from a bullet graze. Constant exercise had hardened him, and his face had the hollow look of a soldier at the end of a long deployment.

Lange felt the blood rising in his body, his pulse working in each fingertip. Hudson was right there. He felt the animal need to close and kill. He could do it now, but Lange had plans for Sam. Tonight was only the beginning.

He turned and looked to the steps of the Lincoln Memorial and the bushes that lined its approach. In the shadows beneath lay a brown bag, by all appearances just a bit of blown trash, inside of which was a kilogram of plastic explosive and the board from a cheap walkie-talkie for a simple remote detonator.

He kept moving under the trees, a calculated path that hid him from the view of any cameras. Lange's eyes went to the statue of Lincoln, the Emancipator's face serene in white marble. They built this temple, an American Parthenon, for the victim, but it was the assassin who had made him a hero.

This nation never failed to impress him with its fetish for faultless martyrs, the beautiful forgetting, the way history was rewritten to make it as palatable as a morning show. His own country had a different, darker amnesia.

He thought of John Wilkes Booth and the dramatic call he made from the stage after he killed the president. One man. One bullet. One instant. And with that, he ultimately undid nearly everything that six hundred thousand had died for in the Civil War, undid everything that Lincoln had won. The South would go back to its ways for another hundred years, though the schoolbooks here didn't talk much about it. The assassin triumphed in the end. When Lange looked at this memorial, he saw a monument to the power of one man to destroy a fragile peace, to bend history to his own desire.

The Americans thought they were so independent—a country of cowboys on the range—but there had never been a more overfed group of sheep in the history of nations. Fear. These people ran on fear, and he would use it to control them.

Booth's weapon was a six-inch pistol made by Henry Deringer. Lange's was Semtex and bright copper wire.

He reached into his pocket and watched Sam Hudson flashing between the trees, racing toward the memorial.

5

YOU HAVE TO go fast to outrun the dead. Sam usually managed it by mile six or seven, keeping himself at his old college pace, five-minute mile after five-minute mile. Eventually the steady beat of his heart and the endless one-two rhythm of his stride would take over, clearing his mind of the last words he'd heard from the fallen, the images of Finlay's face as the life left him and the flashes in the alley as the gunman executed Alex Clarke.

He'd been around death before, with the Rangers prior to the CIA. But it being part of the job didn't make it any easier. Clandestine work, the life of pretending you're a normal man while you're joined in a secret war, made the violence so stark when it came. That meeting had been his call. The deaths were on him, riding him every minute he was awake, giving him a crazy amphetamine feeling that only movement could allay and only temporarily. He knew it wouldn't leave him for good until he had made it right.

It was nine p.m. The heat had barely broken. A dull ache pulsed in his ribs on the right side. He often ran here in the dark, past the monuments, the quiet dead. He came out from under the elms and slowed to a walk as he approached the steps to the Lincoln Memorial. Even this late, a clutch of people stood there, some chatting, others staring at the statue in awe. The place always felt like church to Sam, though he hadn't been to one in years.

His phone rang with a tone he didn't recognize and as he drew out the handset, he saw no number. He raised it to his ear and heard light static and then a calm baritone voice:

"Remember Geneva, Sam?"

"Who is this?" Sam growled.

"It isn't over. This is on you."

That night flooded back in an instant. He was kneeling on the marble tiles as Finlay's hand closed on his wrist, then slipped away.

He felt his throat tighten, and he swallowed as the line went dead.

Sam checked the phone's log, but there was no record of the call. He turned, scanning the trees and shadows. He had been picking up signs that he was being surveilled ever since he'd come back to the States. He assumed they were watching now.

Even on leave, he'd never stopped searching, hunting down the trail that Alex had given him that night before he was killed: Follow Gemini. Find the courier. He'd traced every contact and started tracking the handful of Russian "businessmen" around DC with ties to foreign intel.

None of the Geneva shooters had been caught, nor was Alex Clarke's body recovered. The killers had had the grit and the skills to stage an ambush in the heart of Geneva and escape the police without leaving a trace.

Sam moved toward the steps. *This is on you.* Something was about to happen. He wanted higher ground.

He lifted his phone as he went and called his old boss, Greg Jones, the Russia group chief. The Agency would have the tools to trace the call he'd just gotten. The phone didn't ring, just went straight to voice mail.

"Greg. It's Sam. I don't care if I'm in the doghouse, call me back. It's big."

He disconnected and searched the crowd as he moved. A man stood with his hands in his pockets near the bushes, then turned and joined his wife and daughter. A red-haired young woman lifted a dark object—an old 35 mm camera—and focused on the monument. The wind pushed east to west, the gust a darkness spreading over the Reflecting Pool. It chilled the sweat on his neck.

A white flash swallowed the world like a sudden dawn. A pressure wave hit and tore at the hollow spaces in him—his lungs, his ears—as it drove his body sideways. His vision tunneled, leaving him disoriented in the chaos. It felt as if the earth beneath his feet had been knocked over like a game board.

Sam knew instantly that it was an explosion, strong and close. He lived with the ghosts of blasts like this one—a dusty road at the edge of Kabul, the torn steel of an armored personnel carrier, a burning wind of diesel and sand—but here on the familiar paths of the Mall, the violence seemed unreal. Even as a vicious rain, small pieces of shrapnel, dug into his skin, the whole scene felt false, like a memory or a dream.

He planted his foot to keep his balance. His legs tried to freeze in place, some instinct, but he forced them to move—a few inches, one step, then another. The flash had whited out his vision, but he reached forward and touched the low wall that ran to the side of the main steps to the memorial. He steadied himself and then felt his arms and his legs, checking for injuries or missing limbs. The adrenaline was going full on now, pumping through him, a superhuman drug. He'd seen men try to walk on broken bones and worse without realizing it. But he was good.

He choked on a breath of smoke as his vision returned. A high ringing noise—like a knife scraping a plate—filled his head, and through it he heard a voice cry out. As the fumes drifted past, he saw a camera smashed on the ground, the back plate open, film sticking out like a tongue. Through the smoke he saw the red-haired woman lying on the ground beside it.

She raised herself on her elbow and looked down at her right leg, the fabric and skin ragged, her eyes wide.

Sam moved closer. "Please," she said and reached her hand out to him. Her breath cycled in and out at the edge of shock. He knelt beside her and checked the wound. It was bad, an arterial bleed. He unclipped the leather strap from her purse. The movements were almost automatic, his long training taking over, channeling the wild energy into action.

"You know what you're doing?"

"Yes," he said. "It'll stop the bleeding, but it will hurt. Okay?"

"Yes."

He slipped the strap under her leg, then knotted it, his fingers shaking slightly. "What's your name?" he asked.

"Abby."

"I'm Sam. You're going to be all right. Ready?"

She bit her lower lip and nodded.

He twisted the makeshift tourniquet tight as she closed her eyes, and her body shivered against the pain. Her fingers stretched toward him and he took her hand, holding the knot with the other. Sirens whooped toward them.

"Help's coming."

She nodded, her eyes welling, but still she kept the panic at bay. "Thank you."

He scanned the park, looking for signs of a secondary attack. Emergency lights flashed through the smoke. By their red strobes he saw people staggering through the night, one of them a woman in a blue tank top carrying a boy in her arms, and others on the ground, unmoving.

He looked at his hand, painted red once more, and the warning words of Alex Clarke came back to him—*Konstantin. Stop him. Peace*—the dead man's voice mixing in with the cries in the dark.

Lange's fingers cradled the smooth plastic of the remote trigger, still in his coat pocket. He stood there, all-American in his black Levi's, boots, and worn white oxford button-down, the thumb of his other hand hooked into the pocket of his jeans. A cloud of black smoke unfurled toward the sky as the ripples from the blast turned the Reflecting Pool into a wavering mirror. He took a last look, listening to the screams, the sirens, then turned and started walking. He had a long night ahead.

6

SAM SAT ON the edge of a hospital gurney and braced his palms against the cool linens. The blast lingered in his ears, a high-pitched drone. After they stitched him up, the staff had tried to park him in a side hall at George Washington University Hospital with the others from the attack. This was a mass-casualty incident, and doctors flooded the emergency department, their faces solemn and focused.

He eased himself down and looked around the bay. He had to get out of here and he needed a shirt. An eager EMT had sheared his off during triage. The frag had cut his chest and neck, both now covered with fresh dressings. With the local anesthetic, they weren't giving him much trouble, but a headache had set in like a nail behind his right eye. He'd had one just like it for weeks after Geneva.

He walked toward the nurses' station, searching for a phone. He wanted to call in what he knew to his boss, and he didn't trust his own cell. After a few feet, he noticed a man approaching from his right. He wore a tucked-in polo shirt, a Glock on his waist, and a Metropolitan Police Department badge clipped to his belt.

"Mr. Hudson?" he said.

"Can I help you?"

It was habit—answer without confirming anything. Always hide yourself.

"I'm Detective Morales with the Metropolitan Police Department. I wanted to talk to you."

"I gave a statement to Officer—"

"Benedetti. I know. I had a few more questions."

"Shoot."

"What sort of work do you do?"

"Software consulting," Sam said. He wasn't going to blow a cover that had taken years to build. He needed to connect with Greg Jones or whoever was working this at the FBI.

"People saw you move toward the blast after it went off."

"I wanted to help."

"A witness said you seemed agitated beforehand."

Sam waited.

"Did you see something, a sign of a threat?"

"No," Sam said. He had no choice but to stonewall this guy. The detective wasn't cleared for anything Sam knew.

"What's the name of your company?"

"Aspera Systems."

"Did you ever serve in the military?" The detective spoke quietly, calmly. He had the tired, implacable face of a man who had spent a couple of decades wading through bullshit.

Sam weighed his answer as Morales's right eyebrow rose a millimeter or two, barely noticeable unless you knew what to look for. He suspected that Sam wasn't who he said he was.

"Yes . . ." Sam said, then looked past Morales at a man with bushy hair, salt-and-pepper gray, and a beard to match coming toward him. Sam knew him well. It was Greg Jones, his boss.

Jones walked up to them as relaxed as a guest at a house party and stood to Sam's right.

Morales checked out Jones from the corner of his eye. "Can I help you?"

"Your chief wants to talk to you," Jones said and thumbed down the hall. A cluster of police brass stood in the distance. Jones must have already talked to the detective's supervisor and played his agency card.

A woman in a white dress shirt with two bars on each shoulder—a Metropolitan Police Department captain—waved him over.

"Who the fuck are you people?" Morales asked.

"You should talk to your chief," Jones said.

The detective looked down the hall, then let out an angry breath—bigfooted by a couple of mystery feds. He locked eyes with Jones for a moment, then walked away.

The pissing contest didn't seem to faze Jones. He carried himself with the air of an affable uncle. He listened more than he talked and always reminded Sam of a guidance counselor or 1970s psychologist. He came from Boston Brahmins, one of those families that seemed embarrassed by their wealth, or pretended to be, and did penance through philanthropy, public service, and PhDs in obscure disciplines. But underneath the worn flannels and sport coats, Jones was all steel.

He leaned over to check out Sam's shoulder and neck. "You all right?"

"It's not bad. I wasn't in the direct path." Sam looked around, then cocked his head down the hall. He walked away from the nurses' station, found an empty admin office, led Jones inside, and shut the door behind them.

"The bomber called me right before it happened," Sam said. "He said, 'Remember Geneva' and 'It isn't over.'" He put his hand down on the desk. "And that this was on me."

"The bombing?"

"What else could he have meant?"

"None of this is your fault, Sam. Where's the phone?"

He pulled the phone, wrapped in a torn piece of Mylar blanket, from his pocket and unlocked it.

Jones took it. "You're worried it was compromised?" The metallic blanket would stop anyone from listening in or scrubbing the phone by a remote signal.

"There's no trace of the call in the log."

Jones scrolled through, the corners of his mouth drawing down, then folded the Mylar around it again and put it in his own pocket. "I'll get it checked out. You think the attack was targeting you? And they missed?"

"Possibly—I run that route three or four nights a week. Or he's fucking with me. Which would explain the phone call."

"Who's 'he'?"

"Konstantin. Or one of his people."

Jones sighed. "You don't even know if he exists. This is all speculation."

"You can say that after Geneva?"

"That could have been a trap."

"If it was a trap," Sam said, "why did they kill my source before he could talk? Have you tracked down anything from that night?" He took a half step toward Jones, the anger rising. The bomber was out there, the trail getting colder by the minute.

"You know I can't discuss any of that," Jones said and ran his fingers along his beard. "You're sure someone called?"

"Say what you mean, Jones."

"You got pretty banged up that night, and I know you've been under a lot of strain. You've reported seeing surveillance on you in the States?"

"Yes."

Jones watched him for a moment. Sam knew how he looked—stronger now, lean and hungry and weathered by the sun from all the time running, and maybe obsessed. With Fin gone, he was the only witness to what had happened in Geneva and to this phone call tonight. He could guess what Jones was thinking: that Sam had to believe he was close to something big so that Fin wouldn't have died in vain. Maybe Sam wanted to believe it so badly that he wasn't seeing things clearly.

"How are you doing, Sam?" Jones's voice was soft.

Sam saw the look, the slight forward lean and raised brows, like a doctor on his rounds. Sam knew the game he had to play—he had to seem appropriately troubled but not a lost cause. He ran it with the CIA counselor he was required to report to biweekly. He regarded the Agency human resources staff—a team of well-dressed lawyers and shrinks on the sixth floor—almost as warily as he did a threat in the field. Their job was to figure out if you were too crazy to work or too dangerous to fire, if you might talk, if they had to "protect their equities." The Agency was happy to buy off the troubled ones, place them on leave indefinitely or give them some bullshit job in an annex and never bother to check if they showed up. The rubber room. Purgatory.

How was he doing? The question brought back the past six weeks in a flash: the pacing, the restlessness, the bloodletting in Geneva playing on repeat every time he shut his eyes to sleep. He remembered the counselor's office full of Andean and Buddhist trinkets, the soft sell on pills that Sam couldn't even pronounce—"It's very common. It takes strength to ask for help"—that sounded like they would turn him into a zombie.

Doing fine, he would say, and he was, as long as he kept moving constantly, working the case on his own, lifting until the calluses tore off his palms, and running until he could come home and collapse into a dreamless sleep.

He was happy with his performance with the shrink; just another cover, whatever it took to get him back on the job. He didn't want to numb himself or forget. He knew the cure, the one thing that would make this right: to take out Konstantin and the men who had murdered Fin and Clarke.

Hell-bent on revenge wasn't a particularly good answer to the *How are you doing?* query, so Sam just looked at Jones squarely and said, "Fine. Getting through it."

"That's what I hear," Jones said and seemed to peer through him. Was it a look of doubt?

"You think I'm cracking up?" Sam asked.

Jones set his jaw. "No. I believe you. But there are plenty of people on the seventh floor who are looking for any excuse to get rid of you." The seventh floor of the old headquarters building was home to the clubby mahogany-paneled executive suites, a stronghold of the old-school Yalie CIA. They still looked down on the military types who had started to fill the Agency after 9/11.

"The Swiss want someone to fall for what happened that night. And now this . . ." He shook his head. "I'm trying to figure out what's going on and how to keep you out of a courtroom."

The Geneva police could have gotten him for murder that night. Sam said nothing to them after they took him into custody. He'd spent six years of his life building that cover, and he would keep it, no matter the cost. He requested a phone call and sent a message to Jones through an emergency line. Jones eventually managed to get him out and placate the chief of station in Bern. The Agency was careful with the Swiss authorities. It pumped a lot of money through numbered accounts.

Sam rolled his shoulders back, drawing a stab of pain from the cuts. Jones had always protected him from HQs. He was an ally, and Sam needed him if he was going to have access to the investigation. Sam was hunting down leads to find the killers by himself, but it was nothing compared to what he could do with the full resources of the Agency behind him.

"I'll call and have the techs trace anything that went to your phone. We'll find them."

"Appreciate it," Sam said. "Was there anything on the cameras?"

Jones weighed the question for a moment as if wondering how much to give up, then shook his head.

"Jesus," Sam said. "All those targets and they don't have coverage?"

"There are ways around them. He's good."

"I've known that for a long time. I'll come back and work it. I'm ready."

Jones drew his hand through his hair and looked down for a moment. "They don't think you are, Sam. And after tonight . . . it's tough, but I'll make the pitch. What else do you need?"

Sam opened one of the office cabinets and looked inside. "A shirt."

7

JONES PUT IN the request to have all communications to Sam's phone traced, and Sam, while searching the admin office, told Jones what he had seen that night, anything that could help them track down the bomber.

He found a green scrub top in a cabinet and had just finished putting it on when a tech walked in and jumped back, startled by their presence.

"All yours," Sam said with casual authority, then led Jones back out into the hall.

An older man with a bandage over his cheek and ear and a lost look in his eyes passed by. Sam paused outside a trauma bay. It was where they had rushed the young woman he had helped after the bombing, though all he could see through the window were multiple gowned figures around a gurney.

Heat built up in Sam's face and neck as he looked around at the victims. His fingers curled into fists. His heart beat harder and harder in his chest, going like a kick drum.

Jones put his palm on Sam's shoulder, and Sam flinched, right hand starting toward him. He caught himself and gave Jones a neutral look, doing his best to cover the anger overpowering him.

That wasn't like him. In the field he'd learned to control every instinct, every gesture.

"Come on," Sam said and continued toward the lobby. He needed air.

They stepped outside through the automatic doors, and Sam looked down Twenty-Third Street toward the Lincoln Memorial. Red and blue lights flashed in the hazy night like a carnival.

He turned back to see Jones staring at his phone.

"What's up?"

Jones's eyes met his. "The tech got back to me. There was no trace of any call to your cell."

Sam had expected to hear as much. "So it was hacked."

Jones did a good job hiding the doubt, but the signs were there, a slight tightening around the mouth.

"The phone was clean?" Sam asked.

"He pulled the whole disk image remotely and scanned it," Jones said. "That's how it looks so far."

"I'm already in the middle of this. Let me in on the investigation off book. Pass along what you have. I was so close in Geneva."

"We've been following up on everything you had and everything you've given us, Sam. It's gone cold."

"Christopher Dimos. He's a business consultant, or claims to be. Former colonel from Cyprus. He's the best lead on Gemini. He's back in Washington."

"You're still working this?"

"I pay attention."

"That's funny. A couple of the FBI boys have noticed that someone else seemed to be tracking their Russian counterintelligence targets. Would you know anything about that?"

"I'm on leave."

"Good. Because it's not like the old days here. The rule book is out the door. Intel, organized crime, the oligarchs and their arm-breakers—it's all one, and they're getting bolder by the day. Tangling with them could get you killed. You'd just disappear." He snapped his fingers.

"I can look out for myself. Put someone on Dimos."

"We have. He's clean."

Sam pressed his lips together and looked back to the Mall. "He'll attack again. Are you just going to sit—"

"Sam," Jones said, a flint edge to his voice. It was a warning.

"Listen to me. They killed my source before he could help us stop this, and—"

"There was no body, Sam."

"I saw the shooting."

"Sometimes people see what they want to see."

"You think it was a setup to draw me out?" Sam asked. It was possible he had been getting too close to the killers and the whole meeting with Alex Clarke had been engineered to take him down. The Russians were getting more aggressive, targeting deep-cover officers like him. But they had seemed more focused on silencing Clarke than killing Sam.

"I don't know. I wasn't read in. You went on your own."

"Don't. There wasn't time. It was a judgment call."

"There's a line between trusting yourself and overconfidence."

"You're saying I crossed it? You think I got Fin killed to—what, serve my ego?"

"No. But I need you to be careful. I know this Konstantin thing was personal, even before Geneva."

Sam's right hand balled into a loose fist, and he covered it with his left. His mentor had put him onto Konstantin and had been pursuing it himself before he died.

"It's admirable, but don't let it warp your judgment. You can fool the shrinks, but I see it. The anger. That fixation. The white whale. Just be careful. Don't let it get the better of you, put you on tilt. I've seen it happen too many times. I'll get you in again. We'll do this the right way. You need to back off for a while before someone else—"

He stopped himself and clenched his teeth. *Before someone else gets killed.*

Was Jones blaming Sam for the bombing? For Fin? Sam remembered Finlay's words that night: *I trust you.* The muscles tightened along Sam's spine, a surge of fury he welcomed. He wanted to go off on Jones, to burn this whole fucking thing down. They hadn't listened.

"I'll take the heat for what happened to Fin but not for what happened tonight. They sidelined me. I could have stopped this."

Jones didn't say anything for a moment, then nodded slowly. "Sorry. That was too much. Long day."

Sam looked to the sky, then back at Jones. "I get it."

"Let me give you a ride home."

"I'm set."

Jones put a hand on his shoulder. "You're a good officer, Sam. You'll be back. I'll put a word in."

"I appreciate it."

Jones walked off. Sam waited for him to disappear around the corner, then stepped back into the hospital. He walked down the corridor, looking over the crying families, the dazed victims, the stained dressings.

He wanted to see it all, to sear into his mind what was at stake. He paused near the hall that led to the trauma bay. A couple in their late fifties sat side by side in a waiting area nearby. On the man's lap lay a broken 35 mm Nikon camera, the back open, the film gone. He was holding his wife, his eyes closed, as she cried softly, her head resting against his chest. Sam assumed they were the parents of the woman he had helped, Abby.

He turned and walked back to the exit. He stepped through the sliding doors into the night, and the humidity weighed on him like a blanket. He went down the sidewalk, each step longer and faster than the last. He needed to move or the rage would shake him apart. He began to run. The pain from the cuts braced him, helped him focus as he raced toward the Mall and the marble columns of the memorial, now pitted from the blast.

8

SAM RAN HOME along the Potomac, then uphill on Wisconsin Avenue through Georgetown.

He lived in a one-bedroom brick cottage behind a large Federal town house that was rarely occupied—the family who owned it also had places in New Mexico and Florida, giving Sam a lot of privacy.

At home, he went straight for the shower and cleaned himself up, standing in the claw-foot tub.

He reached for the taps and turned off the hot water. The cold was its own kind of burn, but he didn't react, just let it wash over him as his skin and muscles tightened. The shock wore off, and eventually he felt nothing at all.

The shower left him centered and calm as he went to the closet and pulled on a pair of jeans and a V-neck tee. He walked through the living room to his grandfather's credenza, a couple of dozen bottles of liquor on top, all covered in a fine layer of dust.

Bookshelves lined three of its walls, and a few nylon gig bags leaned in a corner. The drums were out in the shed. He hadn't touched them in years. He'd been traveling nonstop, his life a false front, and this place had become a glorified storage unit, somewhere to leave his belongings and crash when he was in DC, usually in back-to-back meetings with HQs.

He turned on a small television that sat on a shelf and flipped to CNN. They played different clips from the bombing: the massive police cordon, then a cell phone shot of a plume of black smoke rising into the air. The talking heads poured out speculation, but there was no news other than the casualties—two confirmed dead so far. He muted it and put the captions on.

His laptop sat on his kitchen table, and he opened it and checked his e-mail. There was one message—a voice-mail transcription. He had his cell set up so that any messages were transcribed and sent to his e-mail with a recording. It helped him keep track, as he was always switching phones undercover.

He hit Play and heard a relaxed voice. "What's up, man. It's Ryan. We just got back into town and were wondering what you were up to. Give me a shout if you want to come by for dinner or to jam or something. Been too long."

Sam smiled. Ryan was a high-school friend from Pennsylvania. He'd played in an indie band for years, been pretty successful at it, then opened up a couple of bars on Fourteenth Street and Bloomingdale in the District and settled down in Takoma Park. Sam would go over and they would play in his basement, and sometimes on Sunday nights Ryan would bring the kids over and they would do camp songs around the firepit here. Sam hadn't been able to keep up with a lot of his friends outside the life, but he could see Ryan after a two-year break and they would get back into it as if it had been a few weeks.

He remembered the last time he'd been over there, on a couch on the porch with Ryan's three-year-old climbing over him, hanging off his neck in a halfway decent choke hold while Sam tried to tune a vintage Rickenbacker. Ryan's wife sat down with a can of pale ale and joked that sometimes she thought that Sam was a hit man, the way he was always traveling for work. Sam had just laughed, maybe a hair too loud, and strummed a chord.

Now he looked out the window into the backyard. The firepit sat with rust eating away at the bowl.

He thought of calling Ryan, but that didn't seem wise if there were people following him, and besides, he remembered with a quiet laugh, he didn't even have a phone. Jones had kept it.

He'd been off work for weeks, but the instruments were untouched, and his backpacking gear was still stowed. It all felt like an indulgence. Any time off the clock was time when the enemy was gaining. The only things here that he used these days were the rowing machine in the bedroom and the weights on the patio.

He remembered one of the last conversations he'd had with Fin. They were heading to the apartment in Geneva, looking at the Mont Blanc range, and they got to talking about climbing and hiking, how Fin missed it, how whenever he had leave, he'd disappear into the forests up in Maine for weeks. His favorite was the Hundred-Mile Wilderness, the hardest stretch of the Appalachian Trail, a hundred miles without a chance to resupply. "It keeps me sane, you know?"

Sam understood. He'd spent a couple of years as a rafting guide in Colorado before he joined the army. But he hadn't been on a serious trip in years. The job took over.

"You've never been up there?" Fin asked.

"No."

"Tell you what—after we find these guys, I'll take you, show you Acadia and the Knife Edge route to Mount Katahdin." He shook his head. "Just awe."

"Deal," Sam said. "You may have to slow down the pace for the old man, though. Too many hotels and surveillance posts."

Fin took a look at him. "I'm not buying that."

He was dead four hours later, and as Sam watched the life drain out of him on the checkered marble tiles, all he could think was that the kid would never see those trees again.

Jones's words came back to him: *Warp your judgment. Fixation. White whale.* His life had narrowed down to nothing more than work, nothing more than the hunt.

The ringing from the blast still sounded in his ears, softer now, and the images from the Mall mixed in with scenes from that night six weeks ago, flickering across his vision like windblown pages.

Remember Geneva? It isn't over. He heard that voice in his head again, the way he sometimes heard Fin's. The call he received before the bombing seemed as fragmentary as the rest of the memories, more and more like the dreams that so often pulled him from sleep.

There was no trace of any call, just like there was no trace of Alex Clarke's body.

The doubts pressed in. He ran his finger over the aluminum edge of the laptop. Then he closed it.

No, Sam thought. The call was real. And he had seen that man shoot Alex Clarke. He had to trust himself, even if no one else did.

He walked back to the living room and sat in his reading chair. The guitars leaned to his right, and he zipped open the Martin's case a few inches. He ran his thumb over the strings on the headstock, felt the corrosion. He should take a break. Play for a while, some old Neil Young he could just disappear into. Or sleep. His whole body was heavy with fatigue. He shut his eyes for a moment and felt his breathing slow.

But the thoughts wouldn't leave him alone—the promises he made to his mentor and Clarke's warning that Konstantin was coming, that they were running out of time. The violence had already begun.

Someone was killing NOCs—pronounced "knocks"—CIA officers working under nonofficial cover. Most field officers used official cover overseas, which meant keeping their real names and holding a diplomatic cover position like "cultural attaché" at the U.S. embassy while doing their spy work out of the embassy's CIA station. That gave them resources and diplomatic immunity if anything went wrong. Real deep-cover work was vastly more dangerous and done by NOCs, officers like Fin and Sam who worked on their own using false identities with no diplomatic protections. They could easily end up in prison or dead.

One NOC, Jeff Parker, working undercover as an energy trader had been shot to death the previous summer at his home in McLean in an apparent burglary, and another NOC, Sarah Hassan, supposedly died of heart failure in Minsk a month later while doing advance for an agent meeting. Sam suspected that Konstantin was behind both deaths, and now this bombing. Konstantin was in Washington. He was watching. Sam could almost hear the footsteps coming closer.

Sam was moving without even thinking about it, leaning forward, hands on his thighs, eyes open. He went to the bedroom and opened up a safe in the back of his closet. He pulled out a metal box, brought it to the kitchen table, and opened it up. Inside, there were papers and a few bundles of cash: Swiss francs, euros, and fifty-dollar bills. A nylon case held a Heckler and Koch pistol and two magazines. He pushed it aside and picked up one of a half a dozen cell phones and a manila folder.

They'd scrubbed him of all classified material and access while he was on leave, but a good field man always squirreled away gear. He hated waiting on HQs. And they couldn't take away his memory. He opened the folder. It contained sheets of printer paper drawn on with a mechanical pencil mapping out the network that had brought him to that apartment in Geneva. He'd reconstructed it all.

He laid them out on the table, one page after another, then stood and looked it over: a constellation of lawyers, wealth managers, banks, and shipping and logistics firms connected to Gemini GmbH. This was the bland face of evil, wearing a trim suit and credentialed with degrees from the best schools, chasing the dollar like everyone else.

Would it lead him to Konstantin? Alex had told him as much before he was killed. Sam had been tracing a river of black money and shipments coursing through safe havens around the world. It left behind trails, but they came to dead ends: a messenger killed in a hit-and-run in Guernsey, a lawyer drowned in chest-high water at the end of a private dock in the Caymans. And Alex Clarke on that cobblestoned street.

Gemini was a holding company incorporated in Switzerland with connections to a handful of Panamanian shell corporations and no true physical base. Before Sam was put on leave, he'd had enough resources from the U.S. intelligence community—travel and financial info and phone metadata—to track down a handful of real people behind the front.

The night Alex Clarke was killed, he'd told Sam to find the courier, which narrowed the search. By working his sources over the past six weeks, he'd zeroed in on three possible suspects; two were Europeans who often traveled back and forth to Asia, but it was the third figure who captured his interest. His name was Christopher Dimos. He was a Greek Cypriot, though his mother was French, and he had risen through the ranks of Cyprus's military intelligence staff before becoming a consultant on business intelligence and data mining, a job title that, to Sam, a connoisseur of vague titles, screamed typical cover bullshit.

Dimos's life for the past decade was far too opaque, and he frequently traveled a circuit between Cyprus, Panama, and the United States. The pattern suggested a messenger or paymaster.

Sam had checked on a home Dimos used in the District's Wesley Heights neighborhood and stealthily taken a few surveillance shots with one of the phones in this box. He picked up the handset, powered it on, and scrolled through the photos. There it was, a shot of a brick Tudor mansion with two black Mercedes SUVs parked outside. Dimos was back. He'd arrived in Washington two nights before the bombing.

Could Dimos be responsible? Be the man behind all this? Possibly, though his movements were so open that it was unlikely he was the shot-caller. At the very least, he was a lead. Sam looked at the pistol case. He had done all he could from the street. The next step was actually going into the property, searching, and setting up surveillance.

Back off for a while before someone else . . . Jones's words came back to him. Sam had always run ahead, done his own thing, but there were bodies on the ground, and more tonight. He could still taste the smoke.

Leave it, he told himself. *Get some sleep. You're running on anger. Maybe the fucking suits are right, and Alex and Fin would be alive if you'd been willing to slow down and jump through a few hoops for the bosses.*

But if he'd done that, he wouldn't have known about the courier or that this was all connected to Konstantin. He looked at the gun.

Two knocks sounded on the front door. He swept the papers together, locked them in the box with the phone, and grabbed the pistol.

He moved along the wall toward the door. Two more knocks. He tightened his grip as he circled to the narrow window beside the door and peered out, the gun hidden by his right thigh.

A woman stared back at him.

9

EMILY PIERCE LET out a breath, her face filled with relief. Sam had been ready for almost anything, but the sight of her threw him. He'd always had a soft spot for her.

Her expression changed, more guarded now, the way Sam remembered her when she was working: focused, hair up, looking slightly down, in control. The flashes of pure emotion, like the relief he had just seen, were rare. They always felt stolen somehow. Emily was connected to everyone, went everywhere, one of those outgoing, high-achieving people whom you never felt like you really knew.

She was seven years younger than Sam. They'd come up together through training and had the kind of bond that only comes with going through hell side by side for nine grueling months. After a solid five-year career in the field working under nonofficial cover, she'd joined the Russia group at HQs as the seventh floor's favorite. Her family had been Agency going back decades.

Her light brown hair was shorter now, falling at her neck in a wavy bob. It suited her. She had a patrician face, and her weary eyes gave away the stress of her work. Her beauty was a strange thing. She always seemed indifferent to it, like some fussy luxury she'd inherited that she'd never asked for. She played it down; it made her job more difficult when it came to disappearing into a crowd or being judged on merits at CIA. She'd told Sam once that she'd been a tomboy all the way to college.

He gestured for her to wait a moment, put the gun back in the lockbox, and opened the door to let her in.

They stood there, facing each other, not quite clear on the next move, the little tango you get into with an ex, or whatever the hell they were.

She came in closer suddenly, put her arms around his waist, and pulled him in. He felt the soft skin of her cheek against his neck, and it carried him back to the last night they'd spent together. A kind of hunger stirred in him. "I heard about the bombing," she said. She squeezed him and then broke away just as suddenly. "I know it's late, but I thought you were dead. Why weren't you answering your phone?"

"They took it for evidence."

She walked in, head turning. She couldn't help but examine the interior; analyzing him, Sam knew.

"Are you okay?"

"Nothing too bad."

She eyed the bandages on his neck doubtfully.

"How are you doing?" he asked.

"Solid. You know."

"Surviving HQs?"

"You're worried about *me*?"

"Sure."

"It's a thrill a minute. I nearly went blind helping out on that massive IT audit."

"I'd rather get blown up."

She tilted her head and made a face as if to say, *Fair point.* Her eyes went back to the bandages. "Were they targeting you?"

"You're just here to check up on me, Emily?"

"What else would I be doing?"

"I don't know, but it's been a while." The last time he'd seen her, they'd been down the hall in the bedroom. It was hard to believe they'd been together only that one night. They had been growing closer for years before it, circling each other, but the timing was never right. And after they slept together, she drifted away. It wasn't meant to be, and that was for the best. They were too different, too committed to the work.

"I should have come earlier, after you got back, but I was on the road."

"It's all good," Sam said. Emily always had her own agenda. He didn't doubt her concern, but he suspected there was something behind it. Maybe she wanted information. Maybe she was after something else. "They were targeting me," Sam said. "I got a call just before it went off. He said it had something to do with Geneva."

Pain flickered across her face. She'd known Fin since high school, Deerfield Academy in Massachusetts, where he'd been tight with her little brother. Emily was a Deerfield third-generation legacy, and Fin was a townie from outside Kingfield, Maine, who was so scary-smart and fearless on skis the school gave him a full ride. She and her family looked out for Fin, a kid from an A-frame in the woods with a serious Maine accent, and that connection helped bring him to the Agency after his second tour with the Eighty-Second Airborne. Fin had always looked up to her like a high-school freshman to a cool older sister. They were Agency true believers. Emily was more careful about the rules than Sam, and Sam taught Fin all the street-officer standards—never give HQs everything up front; ask forgiveness, not permission. Emily and Sam were the angel and devil on Fin's shoulders.

"What were you doing out there tonight?" she asked, a trace of suspicion in her voice.

"Running."

She considered him for a second. She'd never approved of the way he would go ahead on his own, and he assumed that she blamed him, at least in part, for what happened to Fin.

Sam guessed that their differences in style were why she kept her distance after they finally got together that night, though he couldn't be sure. It was odd, how she had pursued him and then disappeared. It had felt like so much more than a casual thing. They had been close since training, building to it, then it happened, and then nothing. He definitely wasn't a good match for a career creature of headquarters, but that didn't seem enough of a reason.

With one long inhale, she pushed down any hint of emotion, back on the job in an instant. "It's the same attacker?"

If she wanted to stick to business, that was fine. He was looking for information, and she was close to the investigation. "Yes," he answered. "Konstantin or his network."

"Well . . ." She pursed her lips just slightly, the same face she always made when she heard something she didn't like. She could never resist a correction. "That wouldn't fit the profile. It's too much attention."

"And if he's done hiding?"

"There are easier ways to kill you," she said.

"And quieter. Though it's nice to know you've given it a lot of thought."

She rolled her eyes. "So . . ."

"I don't think he wanted to kill me," Sam said. "He wanted me to see them suffer. Or make me look like I'm losing it."

"How's that?"

"There was no trace of the call."

"That's hard. You want us to take all of this on faith?"

"No. On my word."

"What were you really doing there, Sam?"

"Running, I told you."

"You've been pursuing this on your own here in DC?"

"It's better you don't know about any extracurriculars I might have going."

She began to say something, then stopped herself, shaking her head.

"It's fine, Emily. I can handle it."

She hesitated for a moment, but then the impulse seemed to get the better of her. "You were always the golden boy, Sam. Doing whatever you wanted. Just clapping your hands together and plunging ahead—'It's on. Let's go'—every time. And they let you get away with it because you got the job done and you can do the charm act. But eventually it catches up with you. You go off on this Konstantin thing. And you're meeting solo with Russian sources no one's heard of. And Fin . . . and now this."

"What are you saying?"

"You need to stop. Maybe you got played. Maybe it was a trap, and Konstantin was just bait, a prize you wouldn't be able to resist."

It made sense, in a way, if the Russians were trying to take out NOCs like Sam, and they wanted to draw him out. But they'd killed his source. That didn't square with it being a setup.

"And now I'm just making shit up because I can't admit I got Fin killed for nothing?" he asked.

She looked down and to the side.

"Is that the word on me at headquarters?" he asked.

"Not with everyone."

"With you?"

She looked at him. No answer.

"This is all just me chasing glory?"

She shook her head slightly, though he couldn't tell if that was an answer or frustration.

Emily turned away and took a step farther into the living room. She tapped her fist against the arm of the couch twice and looked at the muted TV. "Then what is this bombing about tonight?" she asked, turning and facing him. "Revenge?"

Her tone was different now. She seemed open, or at least ready to listen.

"That's what it sounded like, but that doesn't scan. It's not like I did a hit in Geneva. I shot back, caught one of their guys. This doesn't make sense for a soldier taking down another soldier."

"And why the Mall?" she asked. "It's so high risk."

"The attention, the fear."

He could see the case drawing her in, the analysis going on behind her eyes.

"That means there's a goal," she said.

Sam dipped his head. That's what most misunderstood about terrorism. The violence may seem pointless, the victims random. But it was calculated to spread maximum panic through a population, to break the people's spirit or trigger a reaction from their leaders. Konstantin wanted to use the fear.

"He's building to something. 'It isn't over,' he said."

She still wasn't convinced. "Have you told all of this to Jones?"

"Everything. But I'm still locked out."

Emily walked to the kitchen, put her hand on the door frame, and looked at the well-used knives and the All-Clad pans hanging over the stove and then out the back door to the garden.

That's where they had spent most of that one night together. She'd met Sam and Ryan at Madam's Organ, a rowdy bar in the

Adams Morgan neighborhood that had dangerously cheap drink specials and an open bluegrass/acoustic session on Wednesdays that had been going for decades. By midnight, Sam was on the drums and Ryan a twelve-string. Sam pulled Emily onstage. He knew she could sing. He thought she might freeze up, but she asked them if they knew "C'est la Vie—You Never Can Tell," the old Chuck Berry song that Emmylou Harris had covered. She started out gripping the mic stand for dear life and by the end she was burning the damn place down. That was the night he realized he had no idea what Emily had going on behind that professional mask.

Her gaze went to the bedroom and then back to Sam. She looked him over, her eyes pausing on the bandages, then his face, perhaps measuring the change from when she had last seen him, all muscle and focus now, with no time for those long Sunday cookouts she used to drop by for, the yard crowded with friends.

"Jones is trying to protect you. You should back off this for a while. You're burning yourself out, man. I've seen it too many times."

"I'm not going to sit here, Emily," he said.

"Because you think you can help? Or because *you* need it?"

Sam let the sting of those words pass. "I can't hide here in the dark." He did need it. If he didn't move on this, he knew, he would break.

"When is the last time you took your mind off it? For a minute?"

"I run. I row."

"A real break."

Sam couldn't remember. Once he'd started after Konstantin, it had consumed him, and the string of deaths only pushed him harder.

"Sam, just stop. Go somewhere. Get on the road like you used to, find some mountains, disappear for a while. You need it. Don't let this take over your life."

She reached out and held her finger gently to his temple, near a scratch from the blast. Her breath was coming faster now. He didn't say a word.

Still, some part of him kept wondering why she was here, why the softness. Was she looking for answers? She had every reason to be leery of him. Sam had met off book with a Russian source, and death now seemed to trail him like a shadow. Fin had been like family to her, and both of the NOCs who had been taken out were in her division. She'd been especially close with Jeff Parker, the NOC who'd been killed in McLean. Surely Emily was as hungry for answers and a culprit as Sam was.

A buzz broke the silence—her phone. She dropped her hand and took out her cell as she stepped away.

"Hello? . . . Nothing . . . I can be there in ten . . . sure."

The other speaker's voice was low, but Sam could make it out: Jones.

Emily hung up, then turned to him

"Did they find something?" he asked.

Her posture changed, wary now, as if she were facing off with an armed man. She took in the room as she weighed what to say.

Sam knew her well enough to guess. Was she picturing herself trapped in purgatory like he was? What if he pulled her down with him?

"Don't do that to me. You're not cleared. I'd lose my job."

"I had to ask. Go. Find him."

Her hand tightened on the phone. "You're all right?"

"I'm fine. For real."

"I meant what I said, Sam. Be careful. Just leave it be."

"I heard you."

She kept her eyes on him for another moment, then went to the door and stepped out. Sam locked it behind her.

He stood there, shifting slightly from foot to foot, feeling the fatigue weigh his body down. She was right, for tonight at least. He needed rest.

He walked back to the table to put away the lockbox. But he just rested his hand on top and looked at the television. It showed the Lincoln Memorial, cell phone footage taken just before the blast of a family standing at the end of the Reflecting Pool. Sam didn't have to watch. He knew what was coming. But he did anyway.

He opened the lid of the box and picked up the dossier on Dimos. He looked at the man's face, a Roman nose and a skeptic's smile. Then he picked up the gun.

10

SAM PARKED HIS Jeep on a narrow street in Wesley Heights and sat back. He killed the engine, his eyes fixed on Dimos's house down the block. This neighborhood was a lesser-known DC enclave, hemmed in by parks on three sides and filled with half-acre lots, a favorite refuge of socialites, corporate heavyweights, and the senior diplomatic and espionage set. Police and Secret Service often patrolled the area. He didn't have much time to wait here in plain view.

The gables and timbered facades gave Dimos's house, set back among the trees, a fairy-tale quality. The windows were dark, the driveway empty. From past visits, Sam knew that Dimos was often out for hours in the middle of the night.

Sam wore a light jacket, and he pulled a yellow utility vest on over it. That and the Washington Gas ID badge clipped to it would give him cover if necessary, though he didn't plan on running into anyone. He kept a stock of badges and plastic credentials. They were easy to mock up with a photo printer. On break-in jobs overseas, he even carried a vial of methyl mercaptan when he used a gas-inspector cover, though he had none tonight. Natural gas is odorless, and mercaptan is added for safety to give it that distinctive funky-cabbage smell. A few drops gave the gas man carte blanche to get in anywhere he wanted.

He reached into the glove box, took out the HK pistol in a nylon holster, and slipped it onto his belt. He'd already put a SIM card into one of his spare phones, and he carried that in his right jacket pocket, along with a zippered nylon bag that held the gear he would need to deal with the security system and set up surveillance.

Sam had already cased the property. There was a camera at the front door, but that was it; there wasn't a full suite of pro-grade equipment and motion detectors around the perimeter. Security cuts both ways. If Dimos was concealing a criminal or intelligence connection, then having his house locked down like a fortress would give away that he was no ordinary businessman.

A glance up and down the street confirmed that no one was coming. Sam could feel his pulse beating strong. This was a direct violation of orders. He had no authorization. Going after Dimos was just a crime.

He ran his fingers over the cut on his ribs, pressed down, felt the sting. He remembered that wave of heat, that young woman's face tight with pain.

He stepped out, his jacket falling to cover the gun. There was no hiding the approach, so he would make it fast. Walking confidently down the street, he stuck to the shadows, then crossed and went along the side of the front yard, staying close to the trees that separated it from the house next door.

He started in the backyard. High brick walls surrounded the rear of the property, giving it the feel of a courtyard, and a dry fountain stood at the back, a brass lion's head set above it.

Sam stepped onto the bricks, then paused. He kept still, breathing slowly through his nose, examining the windows for any signs of an occupant, the calm settling through his body until he felt as invisible as the wind passing through the trees. He loved this feeling, this thrill.

He moved on, past a wrought-iron patio set, then stopped at the back door to double-check the locks. Schlage Primus. Same as in front. That could take anywhere from five to fifteen minutes, depending on his luck. The window in the door here offered a view straight through to the front of the house. The interior was decorated like a boutique hotel, with angular low-backed sofas and abstract art on the walls, much nicer stuff than the Russian power-player standard he'd expected—marble columns, gold window dressings, and knockoff Renaissance nudes.

A few motion detectors hung in high corners inside, their faint green lights glowing, good consumer-level security. One was aimed straight at this back door. Looking along the walls, he located two more sensors for the alarm system. He'd already determined it was a popular brand with glass-break detection, which meant microphones, which meant if he could get on its network—usually Wi-Fi with a cellular backup—he could take control and use it to eavesdrop. That would let him tap into the front door's camera and see when Dimos came and went and who he met with.

Such hijackings were a recent CIA specialty. People no longer needed to be bugged; they bugged themselves, filling their houses with devices and technology that could easily be turned against them. The average bedroom had three or four microphones in it at all times. Smart TVs were prime targets, and even a Wi-Fi-connected speaker could be taken over and used in reverse to pick up audio.

The easiest way to do this job was to just hack the Wi-Fi from outside, but there was no way he could crack the encryption Dimos was using without parking on the street for days. He needed to get inside and actually have his hands on the networking equipment. That would give him a chance to search the premises as well. He saw the router, its LEDs flashing behind a wall-mounted TV.

Down the road, an engine hummed, getting closer. Sam pressed against the house and waited as the vehicle drifted off to the north. He went back to the window and looked toward the front entrance where the base for a security system was usually mounted. No sign.

Walking up the side of the house, he checked another window that gave him a different view of the entryway. The base was mounted on the wall just to the right of the front door. It was set to Away, not Night. No one was here.

A denial-of-service attack would let him bypass the alarm system—he'd just blast out a strong radio signal that would stop any of the sensors from communicating with the base unit and jam it using a small tool he carried in his kit.

He went to a side door about ten feet away, closer to the front yard. The landscaping offered decent cover at this entry, and if he went in here, it would put him close enough to the base unit to jam it before he opened the door.

He pulled out the nylon bag, unzipped it, and took out a USB thumb drive and the jammer—a black plastic box about the size of a pack of cigarettes with a switch on one side and three stubby antennas sticking out of the top. That would hold off the security system, and then all he had to do was plug the USB drive into the router inside. It would inject malware into the machine so he could access the cameras and microphones remotely later.

He pulled out his tension wrench and pick, slid them into the lock, and began feeling his way along the pins. Number four set almost immediately with a subtle, satisfying click.

The work absorbed nearly all of his attention, but something broke him out of it—a drone in the distance. He let the tumbler fall, pulled his picks, and listened. A car was moving fast through the neighborhood, approaching the house.

Blue-white beams strobed between the trees near the front of the property—halogen headlights, swinging his way. He slipped back and pressed against the inside angle of the chimney for cover as the beams passed over him, lighting up the brickwork and the bushes to his side.

A car pulled in the front drive, the engine idling thirty feet away.

Welcome home, Dimos.

The headlights hit the wall across from him, throwing a faint reflected gleam onto Sam. He waited, listening, while his body grew warmer, readying for a fight. Car doors slammed, three of them, as people exited the vehicle, so at least three threats now. The headlights turned off. No voices. No footsteps coming his way. He didn't hear any steps at all, but caught the sound of the front door opening and closing.

A drop of sweat ran down the side of his neck.

After taking a step forward, he noticed a shadow moving along the front yard—someone approaching. He edged back the other way, ducked, and moved fast and low along the rear of the house. He wanted to go around to the other side of the property. From there he could reach the front and then cut through the trees and the neighbor's lot.

The windows were dark. If there were people inside now, they were watching, hidden. Two flashlights flooded the backyard from the way he had come, beams bouncing as the men approached, casting a silhouette of one of them, and Sam could make out a gun in his hand, held low.

He could use his gas-worker cover, but these guys didn't seem very trusting. It would be a last resort. Sam kept going across the rear of the house. He thought he could make it around to the far side before they turned the corner, and he was almost there when a pair of French doors opened and a towering man stepped out, less than a yard away, a forward lean to his walk. Sam stopped short, then moved away from the house, turning so he could keep an eye on this man and the pursuers. They came around the side of the house and their lights fixed on him. He squinted against the glare.

His hand almost went to the gun by reflex, but he was covered and that would only get him killed. His vision narrowed, focusing on the weapons, as the edge of every shadow sharpened.

The utility-worker cover was still an option. The drawn guns would justify his attempt to flee. He raised his hands, but before he could say a word, the man who had exited the house spoke up.

"Sam Hudson," he said slowly, voice full of disbelief. "Well, damn."

So much for his cover. Sam turned away from the gunmen and looked at him. Christopher Dimos stood twelve feet away. His hands were empty. His face seemed kind.

"I was hoping we could talk. I'm a friend of Alex Clarke."

Sam said nothing. Dimos took a step toward the open door, then looked back at him. "Come on in."

11

SAM DIDN'T MOVE. His hand hovered a few inches from his gun. He noticed the two guards' postures changing, leaning forward. He wasn't about to hand himself over to these men.

"If we were going to kill you, we'd have done it by now," Dimos said, a trace of his native Greek coming through in the hard *R*s of his speech. "Do you want to know what you're in the middle of or not?"

They could have tried to take Sam, sure, but it wouldn't have been quiet.

"Or maybe you are just checking the meter?" Dimos said, and smiled.

"Tell me here," Sam said.

Dimos walked a few paces past him and stood by the wrought-iron table, slowly taking in the trees and a three-quarter moon behind them. The other two men moved by some unspoken choreography, covering Sam, maintaining the angles to keep each other and Dimos out of the line of fire.

Sam couldn't make out their faces, just the outlines of heavy builds under their shirts, a navy polo on the right and a black button-down on the left. The guy in the polo was a southpaw, and the one in the button-down seemed more aggressive.

"It's all right," Dimos said, and the two lowered their weapons.

Dimos put his phone on the table and worked the screen. White noise streamed from its speaker, a measure to prevent audio surveillance.

That augured something worth telling. Sam moved toward him.

"Closer," Dimos said, his voice low and his eyes on Sam's. "You never know who's sneaking around in the middle of the night."

Sam took another step, a foot inside normal speaking distance, and tilted his head back slightly. Dimos was maybe six six, as solid as his guards if not more, with black hair parted on the side and gelled. The hooded eyes gave the impression of weariness, and he wore an expression somewhere between suspicion and amusement.

"There are easier ways to get in touch with me," Dimos said.

"How do you know who I am?"

"Alex."

"You worked with him?"

A slow nod.

Sam thought back to the night when Alex was killed. *You need the courier,* he'd said. Sam thought that meant he had to track him down as an adversary, but perhaps Alex was planning to bring Sam to him as an ally after they worked out the terms in Geneva. Were Alex and Dimos on the same side in all this? It was possible. They were both associated with Gemini GmbH. All the evidence suggested that they worked for Russian intel, but Alex had said there were many Russias. They could be operating against their own service or a rival faction within it. There was a chance that Sam could turn Dimos just as he had been planning to turn Clarke. "Why should I believe you?"

"Because he told you to look for me," Dimos said. "What else . . ." He circled his hand in the air as if trying to recall something. "Oh, yes. You and he talked about your father's last words. Your father was at death's door, but he never let it show. You asked him how he was, and he said, 'Top of my game.' I guess he would always say that. Sounds like a good man." Dimos looked to him for confirmation.

"Okay," Sam said. "You know Alex was trying to help me, then."

"I do. He went to you, and now he's dead."

"Who killed him?"

"Didn't you?" The words hung in the air. Dimos's eyes drilled into him, and Sam looked to the guards.

"No."

"Given the circumstances"—Dimos glanced down at Sam's hip, where the gun hung—"I'm not sure how much I credit that, Sam."

"I almost died that night trying to stop it," Sam said. "I can show you the scars."

He turned his head to the side and pointed to the raised lines of skin behind his ear where the stone frag had hit. Dimos's cool wavered for a moment. He had no clever response.

"Konstantin," Sam said. "Alex warned me about him. He wanted to stop him."

"Yes, he did."

"Tonight. The Mall. That was him."

"Yes."

"What is he after?"

"Tonight was nothing," Dimos said. "A first step."

"So help me. I can take him down."

"I'm going to need something if you expect me to trust you."

Sam brought his shoulders back. There it was. The ask. Sam knew the strategies well, but he wasn't used to being the target. He admired Dimos's ballsiness. He was putting Sam on trial, reversing the suspicion, when Dimos was the one running a foreign-intel op on U.S. soil.

"What do you want?"

"DEMETER," he said, tilting his head slightly as he studied Sam's reaction.

Sam waited, but that was it. He heard the two guards move closer, quietly, across the bricks. He glanced over and saw that they'd brought their guns up to low readies. Dimos kept his eyes fixed on Sam as he raised his hand, signaling for them to hold off for a moment.

"You don't know that name?" Dimos asked, his voice rising with skepticism; he was a practiced interrogator. This was some kind of test. He was looking for tells. Sam had no idea what DEMETER was, but he had a sense that the wrong reaction could be fatal.

"It's from myth, but I don't remember the story. Enough with the games. Tell me what you want."

"I think you're very good at this, Sam," Dimos said, rocking back on his heels. "An intel file in the Russian section classified with the code name DEMETER? Nothing?"

Sam raised his shoulders. "Come on," he said. If Dimos knew anything, he'd know that Sam would never give up information like that, or even confirm it existed.

"How about two American NOCs who turned up dead in suspicious circumstances after getting on Russia's bad side? McLean? Minsk? Is this beginning to sound familiar?"

Sam stayed calm, but Dimos's questions chilled him as much as the two guns aimed in his direction. Was Dimos testing him? Fishing for what Sam knew? It was all too easy to target someone for information and end up being turned yourself, betraying your country one small step after another, so slowly you never even noticed crossing the line.

Dimos seemed to be confirming Sam's suspicions that one man was behind all of this violence, a mounting campaign against the West. "Konstantin had a hand in that?" Sam asked.

"Yes. But he's not alone. Officers are dying on both sides. I have no idea who I can trust. And you should be careful, Sam." Dimos talked with his hands always moving, pointing back and forth between them, underscoring points. Now he rested his right hand on the table. "There are wars between nations and wars within each."

"What does that mean?"

"There might be a traitor in your house, and it cost Alex his life." He looked down and tapped his fingers on the iron, weighing his words, as if thinking he'd said too much. "Maybe it's you. You drew him out and tipped the killers. I don't know. That's why I need that file."

Was there a leak? A mole? Sam immediately tried to think of who else knew about the Geneva meeting, but he had told no one but Fin. "What do I get in exchange?"

"I can put you onto Konstantin. I have a source who can lead you to him." Dimos crossed his arms. "Of course you don't trust me. But you're going to need all the help you can get. You only have a few days."

"Until what?"

"Sunday night. An attack that he's been building up to for decades. It will happen on Sunday by ten o'clock. The memorial bombing is just the opening move."

"How do you know? What is it?"

"Not yet, Sam. Not yet."

"Help me stop it. Give me something."

"I have. Now it's your turn." Dimos waited, a daring look in his eyes, letting the cicadas fill the silence.

Sam wasn't offering him anything, no matter how badly he wanted the information being dangled in front of him.

Dimos nodded, then took a few steps away and paused by the open door to the house. The guards kept still, both with their backs to the moon.

The Cypriot made a gesture toward them. They retreated, lowering their pistols.

"I understand how difficult this is," Dimos said. "But these are strange days. I'll be in touch. Any meeting will be three hours late."

It was an offset, a standard bit of tradecraft when connecting with a source. You would prearrange a certain amount of time to be added to any instructions about a future meeting so that if the communications were intercepted, the meeting still wouldn't be discovered.

"I'm not your spy," Sam said, and Dimos responded with a look: *We'll see.* Sam stepped away, never showing them his back as he made his exit.

He returned to his car and drove to his apartment, feeling the adrenaline ebb, the muscles in his neck and shoulders relax as he cruised the quiet streets.

He needed sleep, but instead of going inside, he stopped at the end of his block, killed the lights, and waited, watching his home, studying every shadow.

Dimos wanted information from within CIA. With that, Sam had to reconsider all he knew. What if everything Dimos said was a trap? An extension of a long con that started with Alex Clarke in Switzerland?

Hinting at a mole was a good way to plant doubts, isolate Sam, and even turn him against his own service. And dangling a ticking bomb and a lead on Konstantin was perfect bait to get him to swap secrets—something he would never consider doing unless countless lives were at stake. Dimos had set the hook just as Sam had so many times when drawing in a source.

Getting caught and having guns on him had put Sam on edge, but that wasn't the worst threat he faced. Violence was simple, straightforward. What worried him more was that he felt part of himself turning. He needed those answers, and he wanted to trust that man.

12

MICHAEL LANGE WALKED through the shin-high grass of the field toward the forest ahead. He felt the damp soak into the toes of his boots as he moved through the dark. Cirrus clouds streaked the night sky. Dawn was still a couple of hours off.

A water tower loomed to his right. He traced the low Virginia hills rising to the north and noted the flashing red light on top of a radio tower. The two landmarks gave him his bearings. He had a description of this place and military grid coordinates that should have brought him within a hundred meters of his target. But they had come half remembered from a dying man.

A treasure hunt.

He wore a canvas work jacket, long enough to cover the Smith and Wesson .40 on his hip. A deep inside pocket held a spade, a thin metal rod, and a length of cord.

He reached the edge of the woods and picked his way through the undergrowth. Then he saw it—a retaining wall loomed ahead of him, holding back the hillside above. His reference point. The description fit.

Lange touched his fingers to the smooth concrete of the wall. He began to walk beside it, trailing his left hand along its surface, feeling for the hidden sign. The action reminded him of a boy walking home from school, dragging his fingers along a picket fence.

A memory rose in his mind: A nine-year-old kicking a ball against a brick wall in a courtyard, wearing a blue and white Moscow Spartak football jersey for his hero Valeri Karpin. The fabric hung off his thin frame as he raced back and forth, keeping the ball in the air, his breath labored and his face red. Even after Lange called down for him to go slow, to take it easy on his heart, he didn't listen, just kept going faster, nonstop, until it was almost too dark to see, though he could still hear the *thock-thock-thock* of the ball.

The image warmed him like an embrace, then he felt a tightness growing in his chest and his throat. There was no time for that. After a deep breath, he cleared his mind and pressed on.

He picked his way around the ragged trees and fallen branches, and every ten meters or so, he felt a vertical seam in the concrete.

He must be getting close now. A light sweat beaded at his temples. How long had it been hidden? At least thirty-five years. The earth didn't give up its secrets easily. Neither did the past. But Lange was patient. He would find it.

He didn't risk a light. His eyes had adjusted by now, and he was comfortable in the dark. His fingers felt a seam, and then another, and he froze. The two seams were only a half a meter apart. That was the sign.

He took the cord from his pocket, two meters long exactly, and ran it out perpendicular to the wall. The rod he carried was a probe with a sharp tip, folded into three sections. He extended it, locked it straight, and drove it into the dirt near the end of the cord again and again, working methodically in a grid pattern.

It hit on the fourth stab, something solid and, he discovered after a few more touches, perfectly flat. A warm rush ran through him.

It was here. After carefully surveying the area for anyone watching, he set to work with the spade.

Fifteen minutes later he was brushing dirt off the weathered stainless-steel surface of the cache. He found its edges and pried it out, a box thirty centimeters square and five centimeters deep. He had been looking for this for almost ten years, yet he resisted the overpowering urge to open it. He stood and studied the darkness for a long minute to be certain he was in the clear. Then he pulled back the clips on the side of the cache and pushed up the top. It opened with a gasp—it had been vacuum-sealed—which meant it had remained untouched all this time.

A thin sheaf of what looked like papers lay in the bottom. He ran his fingers over them. They were sheets of printed nylon covered in maps and routes, chosen to withstand the elements. Underneath them, sealed to the bottom of the box with wax, was a key. He pried it up and examined it. He'd never seen one like it before. It was eight centimeters long and hexagonal in cross section with bits of various heights running along each face. The six-sided key.

He lifted the nylon into the moonlight and saw the word HYACINTH.

It was real. Code name HYACINTH, a weapon concealed for decades, a last blow from a dead empire. Russian military tradition reserved the gentlest code names for the most devastating plans. These were the final pieces that he would need, and the most crucial. Now that he had them all, he could shove this country onto its knees.

13

AFTER FILLING IN his spadework, Lange headed back to his car, holding the cache box under his arm. A few porch lights shone on the other side of the valley: houses, sleeping families.

It took ten minutes for him to reach the access road where he had left the car he was using tonight, and as he stepped onto the rough asphalt, he noticed a Toyota pickup parked farther down, in view of his vehicle, close to where this access road met the two-lane public byway. Its lights were off. He scanned in both directions and saw no one.

He'd been carrying his keys in his right hand, and he put them into his pocket now to free it. The Smith and Wesson was in easy reach as he walked toward his vehicle, though he gave no indication of any hurry or reaction to a potential guest. He'd gone about fifteen meters when he caught the sounds of steps echoing his own, crunching gravel. Someone was coming up behind him from the direction of the truck. Had the other person been in the woods waiting for him?

"Hey there," a man called in a commanding tone.

Lange turned about three meters from his car. A figure with a stocky build approached, step by slow step. He wore an untucked flannel shirt and work pants and stopped six meters away. Good tactics. That was the standard distance police used to face off against a potential threat. It gave them enough time, a second and a half, to draw and shoot if the suspect charged.

"Hello," Lange said. Fear was the correct reaction, and Lange drew back and kept his voice hesitant. He didn't have to think through his cover. He'd lived as his various different personas for so long that they felt as natural as his real self, maybe more. He didn't say another word. The guilty explain.

The man had a broad, friendly-seeming face, though now it was tense. Lange noted the man's posture and the way his hand hung near his side. He was armed, with some training—a local cop or ex-military. The wedding ring was a good sign. Husbands and fathers were more hesitant on the trigger.

"What are you up to out here?"

"You are?" Lange asked, matching the slow country cadence of the man's speech.

"A police officer with the county. This is all the water company's land."

The Toyota must be a personal vehicle, then. No law out here would use an import. He was off duty, which meant there was no radio in that truck, and there was no cell signal along this ridge, so he could assume the stop hadn't been called in.

"Oh," Lange said and let relief show in his face as he moved a little closer.

"What were you doing back there?"

"The Perseids," he said, pointing up. "Meteors. I grew up nearby. On Fox Hollow Road. My grandparents used to own some of this. We would stargaze in that meadow."

It didn't particularly matter how believable the story was. He wasn't desperate to convince this man. He was more interested in reading him.

"Did you see any?"

"Not tonight," Lange said, his tone bittersweet.

"And that?" The officer gestured to the cache box under Lange's arm.

Lange glanced down at it. "For taking notes," he said. He moved his hand toward it, a little faster than necessary. The cop's body went tight in response.

"Okay, then," the man said, and hitched a thumb into his belt. "You have a good night."

Lange nodded even as he picked up something off about his tone; it was just slightly too open, forced, a man seeking to reassure. He'd noticed the cop looking at his fingers, the nails lined with dirt, and the contours of his jacket near the holster.

Fear. He was suspicious. He would call it in.

You're right, friend, Lange thought. *You should have been like every other clock-puncher and driven straight home to bed. But no.*

Lange put the box on the hood of his car so that both of his hands were free. Then he turned around and raised one finger as if he'd just thought of something. He looked over the officer's face. "Did you grow up around here?" he asked.

"Sorry?"

"You seem so familiar."

"Yes, I did."

He moved nearer to the man and watched him turn away slightly, putting his gun hand and hip farther away.

Lange kept an amiable expression on his face. "Maybe I know your family." He took another step. Just a couple Virginia boys who could remember the time before the developers came, when it was nothing but farms out here.

"Hold it there," the officer said, raising the forward arm now.

"What's your name?" Lange asked. Even as the adrenaline fired in that man's system—his hand betraying a faint tremor, his breath coming fast through an open mouth—the alarm probably wasn't enough for him to shoot a friendly middle-aged white guy driving a Mercury sedan. And either way, Lange was already too close.

Before the officer could answer, Lange was in motion; with a startling quickness, he rushed inside the man's guard as he drew his gun, an honest-to-God revolver.

Lange twisted. The man's outstretched hand slid across his chest while Lange moved in and shot his knuckle into the front of the cop's shoulder, lighting up the nerves of the brachial plexus. The gun arm dropped, though he managed to keep a grip on the weapon somehow. The blow gave Lange time to seize the man's outstretched hand and pull him forward as he blocked his legs. As the cop tumbled, Lange wrapped his arm around his neck in a guillotine choke and jumped, tightening the grip and snapping the man's head sharply back, using his falling momentum against him like a hanging.

A muted crack sounded from his cervical vertebrae. The pistol fell from his hand. His arms and legs spasmed, feet dancing along the asphalt, then went limp. This way was quieter than the gun.

Wrapping his other arm around the officer's torso, Lange hauled him up into a chest-to-chest embrace and dragged him to the Mercury.

He unlocked the trunk, lifted the cop on his hip as one would a toddler exhausted after a long day, and laid him inside. His eyes were open, still seeing, but everything below his chin, even his heart and lungs, were now still. It wouldn't be long.

Lange slammed the trunk shut, climbed behind the wheel, and drove off.

From the glove box, he pulled a handheld scanner and began to search for any police communications. He drove past the man's Toyota. That could be taken care of with a phone call.

He turned onto the public road. The only radio traffic he caught was a state trooper working a speed trap eight miles away. A bit of sweat dampened the hair along Lange's neck. He watched his mirrors as he worked the unlit country lanes but saw no one. He was clean.

Heart pounding, hands chill, every sense magnified—but it wasn't fear. He leaned and looked at himself in the rearview. After decades of self-control beyond measure, he was coming out of the shadows, activating, starting the final orders. His eyes were wide, but it was pure exhilaration.

What good is a weapon you never use?

14

SAM RACED ALONG the river trail on the Virginia side of the Potomac. After five hard miles, he came to a stop and looked to the east, squinting against the morning sun. He was still sore from last night, but movement kills pain, overrides the signals. His first sergeant taught him that. It's why you shake your finger after you hit it with a hammer and hop around after you smash your toe.

This was always how he thought things through, moving fast until the answers and the next steps settled in his mind. He had a Russian agent offering him a way to stop a killer, and all it would cost was Sam's soul—giving up secrets from his own side.

He cut right onto a narrow trail, picked his way among the boulders. The river ran ahead of him with a low rushing sound, and as he stepped out onto a wide outcropping, he could see the water flowing between walls of granite on either side. Off to his left a haze rose over Great Falls, where the Potomac dropped seventy-five feet through a series of rocky cascades.

Sam put his hands on his hips and took a deep breath, tasted the mist in the air.

"How are you doing, Williams?" he asked the water as he lowered himself onto the ledge twenty feet above the surface and watched two fallen leaves circle in a whirlpool to his left.

Joseph Williams had been Sam's mentor in the CIA, had brought Sam over from the Rangers into the Agency after they'd worked together on ops outside Jalalabad. He had died a little less than a year ago, a few months after having a stroke, and his family had scattered his ashes here. It was a small ceremony, held after the funeral and a memorial service in the Bubble—the main auditorium at HQs. Sam was honored that the family had reached out to him through the Agency, and he'd flown back to the States for the day. Williams's daughter had emptied the urn. She was a surgeon now living in Ann Arbor, his only remaining child, and she shared her father's knock-you-on-your-ass laugh. Williams had lost his son in Afghanistan.

Williams had liked to walk here as the sun came up, especially when he was hung up on a tricky bit of analysis. "Sometimes you need to get out in the fresh air and quit banging your head against the damn thing for a while. Then you'll see," he would tell Sam.

"Good game last night. Nats beat the Braves five to four," Sam said. "Zimmerman had a sac-fly in the bottom of the ninth and Turner scored." Sam had checked the highlights on ESPN this morning before he rolled out to the river. Williams had grown up in Maryland, his parents West Indian immigrants, and like so many Washingtonians, he'd developed a fast and profound allegiance to the city's restored baseball team, even in the early years when the Nationals were awful, playing out at RFK Stadium. Sam remembered him listening to the games late at night in the office. With every loss, he would repeat the old line about the previous DC franchise, the Senators—"Washington: First in war, first in peace, last in the American League."

After Williams had the stroke, whenever Sam could, he would visit him in the nursing facility, put the Nats game on Williams's old pocket radio, and sit with him. Williams had been able to speak with difficulty for a few months, slowly regaining strength. Whenever Sam asked how he was doing, his answer was always the same. "Top of my game," he would say and manage a smile. Those were the last words Williams had ever spoken to him; a second stroke took away his speech for good. When Sam was undercover and told stories about his dad to Alex Clarke on those nights in Switzerland, he was actually talking about Williams, the closest thing he'd had to a real father.

Some people blamed the smoking for killing Williams—a few Winstons a week when working late—because it was easier than blaming the stress. Konstantin had been Williams's cause, and by the end of his career, it had made him an outcast at the Agency. When Alex Clarke asked Sam what drove him so hard to go after Konstantin, the answer was Williams. Sam owed it to him.

Williams believed that one or more sleeper agents, possibly dating from before the disintegration of the Soviet Union, were plotting violence against the United States. The Russian Federation had used other deep-cover agents in the U.S. over the past thirty years—they were known as *illegals* in Russian intelligence lingo—but they seemed to be focused more on information gathering, influence operations, and economic espionage. Konstantin and his network were different, a potential holdover or continuation of the sabotage plans that had been drafted by Soviet intelligence in case of an all-out conflict with the United States, trained killers designed to bring America down from the inside.

After the collapse of the Soviet Union, some illegals simply gave up their ties to the homeland and took their cover identities for their true selves, happier as Americans. The temptations of the U.S. had always been a threat to Russia's long-term sleeper operations, and the Russians often kept a child or spouse at home as leverage. Williams believed that Konstantin and his crew, disgusted by the breakup of the KGB and Russia's kowtowing to the West, had stayed behind in the U.S. for a darker purpose and might be formulating their own plans independently or perhaps in concert with a select handful of hard-liners in the Kremlin. Konstantin was a ticking bomb, hidden away, that could go off at any moment, and Williams was determined to root him out.

As the Agency shifted its focus away from Russia and then dedicated itself to counterterrorism after 9/11, Williams's warnings were dismissed as outdated thinking—the old Cold Warriors kept seeing Communists under the bed, probably as a way to protect their budgets. The defectors who fed them hints about such a network were simply trying to inflate their own value and resettlement deals. And even when Russian aggression grew impossible to ignore—after the invasion of Crimea and a series of killings by poison in Russia and the UK—Williams found little support for the Konstantin theory. Russians were interested in disinformation and influence, not all-out war with the West. They wouldn't go that far. Their main goals were getting rich and shoring up their own power. The U.S. had no political appetite to confront them. Every administration thought it could "reset" with Russia.

And then Jeff Parker and Sarah Hassan died. Their deaths were never proved to be assassinations, but many suspected they were. It came out later that Williams had brought the two officers into his hunt for Konstantin and had asked them to follow up on leads in the field. For those who did think they had been murdered, blame fell on Williams for pushing it so aggressively and for tasking NOCs outside of official channels, perhaps exposing their identities and getting them killed. Though now Sam had to question if their deaths had been the work of a mole, as Dimos had hinted.

Williams went even harder after Konstantin, since he believed he had killed two American officers. The seventh floor wouldn't listen, and Sam could remember finding Williams in his office, pacing back and forth, fuming after a meeting upstairs.

"The truth will set you free," he said, and shook his head. "By getting you canned."

He couldn't hide his anger and disdain at the brass for not following up on Konstantin. He didn't care. His bridges burned. And Williams never complained about it, but Sam knew that part of it had to do with the color of his skin. Even though he'd made it to a leadership position, he was never fully allowed in the club.

He doubled down on Konstantin, trying to track down who had killed Parker and Hassan. He stayed late every night, living off snacks and the vending machines in the basement. It took over his life, just as it had taken over Sam's. Williams worked himself into the ground, and one night the stroke hit. The cleaning crew found him on the floor beside his desk, trying to drag himself up to reach his phone.

The execs came to visit him at the nursing facility and told him his job would be waiting as soon as he was better. Sam would go by whenever he was back, and after a few months, he noticed that there were no more notes, no more gifts from the Agency. It forgot about him and Konstantin. The bureaucracy was full of survivors, and they knew to avoid the whole affair like a plague house. Sam always brought him a bag of Pepperidge Farm Milanos. Williams had kept a sack of them in the top drawer of his desk, and Sam could remember him dialing open the combo lock on the drawer—standard at CIA—and pulling out a cookie like it was a state secret.

Sam made it back to DC by game six of the World Series that October and went to the facility. Williams had been deteriorating after the second stroke and was on oxygen. Sam noticed there was already a bag of Milanos on his bookshelf. Someone else had been visiting.

Sam sat late with him to listen to the game. The nurse came by and told him that visiting hours were over, as she always did, and Sam said, "Sure, I'll get going," as he always did, and then she would smile and leave them in peace for hours more. Sam was with him the next night, too, when the Nats brought the title home. Sam pumped his fist in the air after the final strike, then put his hand on Williams's shoulder, the bruiser frame down to skin and bones now, and wondered if he even knew what was happening. He died four days later, while Sam was on an operation in Spain.

Sam watched a red-tailed hawk skim over the surface of the river. If he played this wrong, he could go down as a traitor. He could *become* a traitor.

He thought about how good it would be to have Williams here, to walk these trails with him and talk it through. Sam had loved watching his mind work, the way he would sometimes turn and stare through you, unsettling you with his bright eyes, while he crunched through a thousand angles, then come out with a laugh, as startling as a shotgun blast, when he had his solution.

But Sam knew the answer. People might say he was doing it because he always went alone, or because he had to take down the big prize, or because he was so damn stubborn he couldn't resist doubling down on a mistake. But Sam knew what moved him, and it was none of those things.

He pictured Williams coming back from one of his standoffs with the execs and giving him an easy shrug of the shoulders. "Fuck 'em," he'd say, then get back to the case. Good advice, then and now.

Sam stood and dusted off his hands. There might be a way to hook Dimos without crossing any lines. He remembered his cell number from the dossier. Sam took out a phone and tapped out a message to the Cypriot.

15

SAM WAS WALKING back from his car toward his house when he saw it a second time—a gray Infiniti sedan. He'd clocked it right before he parked too. The driver could be lost or looking for a spot, but after last night, Sam wasn't taking any chances. The skin under his collar prickled as the day's heat seemed to ratchet up.

He continued south past his house, and started going through one of his normal routines, trying to draw out any pursuers so he could identify them. He said a quick hello to Daniel, the man who had a shoe repair and dry-cleaning place down the street. A fourth-generation Washingtonian armed with an inexhaustible supply of dirty jokes, Daniel liked to hold court on the corner just outside his shop door.

Sam glanced up the street behind him as he ducked into an ivy-lined alley. A man in his forties with short blond hair was walking slowly behind him, looking at a phone—a potential watcher.

Sam stepped into a small coffee shop that kept a few wrought-iron tables on the alley. The woman behind the counter leaned her head to the side and stared at him. She had straight black hair and an expression as if she'd just been told something she didn't quite believe.

"You look skinny."

"Thanks, Tovah," he said. "Black coffee, please."

She turned and filled up the cup while Sam's eyes went to the window facing the street.

"Why aren't you ever at work?" she asked.

"Working from home," he said.

She looked him up and down. "Are you rich?" Her eyes went to the ring finger on his left hand.

"No."

"Hmm," she said, as if that were a shame. She'd come to DC from Tel Aviv about ten years ago. Sam stopped by here a couple of times a week and loved her bluntness, though he hadn't been able to rule out the possibility that she just didn't like him until his second week of leave, when she started slipping him the odd free pastry and then tried to set him up with her sister.

"You don't seem like a lazy man," she said. "But you're always around in the middle of the day. You should get a real job. A routine."

"I agree," he said, watching a pair of college students pass on the sidewalk as she put the coffee and a doughnut on the counter.

"Eat that too."

"Thanks," Sam said. He paid and gave her a tip to more than cover the doughnut. The café was painted sunshine yellow, and framed inspirational sayings and dancing folk-art figures in metal hung on the walls. It looked like a blissed-out Sonoma hippie had decorated the place, yet Tovah was one of the most endearingly grim women he had ever met.

"Did you pick all this out?" he asked, pointing to the art.

"You have a problem with Kokopelli now?"

"Just asking," he said. He raised his coffee and headed out, taking note of the camera over the door.

As he circled back to his house, Sam evaluated every passerby as a potential threat. He saw no obvious signs, but he most likely wouldn't, not at first glance.

He put the coffee down beside his laptop. Daniel's and Tovah's places were among a half a dozen stops he would make regularly, the seemingly normal rounds of a sidelined spy, but like all surveillance-detection routes, known as SDRs, every step was deliberate. He wasn't able to have a whole team watching his back, but he had slowly gained access to seven exterior cameras along his routes. They were all on Wi-Fi, and he had breached them months ago, which allowed him to review their footage over the web at any time.

He had installed a few others, well hidden, around the house, though experienced surveillance crews would be aware of that and know to avoid straight sight lines from his residence.

While he went about his day-to-day—the long runs, the errands—he was dragging any tails in front of those cameras.

Sam pored over the footage, looking for any of the telltale signs of pursuit. Clothes could be swapped easily, so he focused on faces. Gaits were another giveaway. Only the most dedicated street operators could put on different postures and ways of carrying themselves.

Scrubbing through the video, he noted this student on a run, that homeless man heading down to the river park, each of them a possible watcher with his own seemingly natural routine. As he went, he captured clips of any suspects who were too regular, too focused.

He looked over them now, zeroing in on the eyes. He wondered if Konstantin would be so bold. From the way Konstantin had talked to him last night just before the bombing, Sam believed he'd been at the scene, watching. There was something personal about how he'd reached out, the hate in his voice. Sam could be staring at his face right now.

After another ten minutes, he closed the laptop and pushed back his chair. He had to stop him. He knew who he needed to call: Emily. She'd been close to the two NOCs who'd died and she was inside the Agency. She would be able to use its facial-recognition tech and, more important, she would have access to DEMETER.

16

SAM SHUT THE door of his Jeep and walked down the gravel driveway to Emily's house, perched at the edge of Scott's Run Nature Preserve. The trees formed a canopy of pale green overhead, and the air dripped with humidity. These little valleys that fed into the Potomac felt like they were in the middle of nowhere, but he was only a couple of miles from CIA headquarters.

The house was a two-story Victorian, tiny by the McMansion standards of McLean, the surrounding town. He climbed the front porch and knocked. He and Emily had texted before he came by.

It took her a minute to answer the door. Her hair was still damp, and a shoulder bag sat in the front hall, clothes visible inside. She looked like she'd pulled an all-nighter at the office. That was fairly common. She would come home to shower and change, then head back to work. The Agency was well stocked with cots and everyone kept an eye mask in a desk drawer. There was nothing unusual about living out of the office for days or weeks when a crisis hit. Her group must have been mobilizing in response to the bombing, which meant they were searching for a Russian connection. The attack had been the lead story on all the news stations as he drove over, and speculation about the culprits—foreign terrorist, domestic militia, crazed loner—had gone into overdrive, but no one knew the truth.

The DEMETER file belonged to Russia House, the informal name for Emily's group at the CIA. Sam always found it odd that HQs staffers used the nickname, since it came from a John le Carré novel in which, as always, the Americans were the duplicitous villains, and they were outwitted by an alcoholic amateur.

He had to be careful with her. She was already primed to distrust him, and he was skating dangerously close to the line here, looking for answers to a question posed by a Russian agent. Emily had been a good street officer, though she had been behind a desk for a long time now. Getting information without burning himself would be quite the dance.

"Come in," she said. He entered and she shut the door behind him. She glanced at herself in the mirror and quickly fixed her hair as Sam walked into the foyer. He pretended not to notice, though the scent of jasmine he picked up as he passed her flooded him with a memory of their one night together.

She was carrying a zippered toiletries case that she dropped into the bag before she led him to the kitchen. "Sorry if I was a little prickly last night," she said without looking back.

"It's all good," he said.

The house was all worn-in DC establishment inside: old hardbacks on shelves everywhere, with the hallmarks of generations of foreign service tossed in among them—jades and vases and a Japanese officer's sword.

She asked Sam if he wanted something to drink. He was fine, he said, and she picked up her glass of water and led him onto the back porch. The smell of the woods was stronger there—damp earth and grass. Someone must have just mowed.

She went to the porch railing, rolled her shoulders back and stretched her neck, then turned around and rested against the rail.

"Feeling cooped up?" he asked.

"I've been at work from when I saw you last until now." Intelligence offices didn't have windows. They were like casinos—you never knew when the sun went down, and you might come out to find it was a new day and there was three feet of snow on the ground.

Sam looked over the garden. The dahlias were blooming, and near the shed, the squash was ready in raised beds. "How do you have time for all that?" he asked.

"Headlamp. Moonlight. Get up an hour or two earlier on the weekend. You can't let the job be your whole life." She peered down at the blooms. "Though I do like to pretend I'm snipping off my nemeses' fingers as I prune."

She faced him and took a sip of water. "You remember those cookouts you used to have? People actually having fun at a party in DC. It was a revelation. Gillespie, from NSC Europe, what did he end up singing?"

"'Rock You Like a Hurricane.' He was hilarious. I probably wouldn't have given him all that punch if I'd known he was the director."

"It was funny. Nobody ever asked 'And what do you do?' at your place," she said, seemingly still in disbelief.

Sam saw where she was going. What happened to the guy who used to throw those parties? The job happened. A twenty-three-year-old bombing victim named Abby had just had her leg amputated at GW Hospital. Sam had called for an update that morning. But he kept that anger hidden now.

"Did you pick up any leads?" he asked.

She tilted her head to the side, her lips pursed.

Sam raised his hand. "I get it." He took a folded sheet of paper out of his pocket and passed it to her. "Take a look at these guys. Maybe it'll help."

She opened it and scanned the page. They were Sam's courier suspects, a list that included Christopher Dimos as well as a few Russian moneymen that Sam had his eye on. He wasn't going to sit on good leads, not when the Agency was going full bore on this, and it might surface something on Dimos that could tell Sam whether or not to trust him.

"These are all associated with Gemini?" Emily asked.

"Yes. First- and second-order links."

"And you think it connects to the bomber?"

"My theory."

"And Geneva?"

He nodded slowly.

"If I find something, I can't share it with you, Sam."

"It's not a trade, Emily. I want to help."

The corners of her mouth curved up just slightly. "This is how you hook them, huh?" She shook her head. "All those sources. I'm not so easy, Sam."

"Oh, I know."

She drank some more water and looked out over the woods. "Why was Finlay there that night?"

That threw him for an instant.

"I need to know the truth," she said. "Did you push him into going?"

"No. What do you think happened in Geneva?"

"I don't know. He was impressionable. Gung ho. The young officers idolize you. You know your rep."

"I don't. Fill me in."

"The cowboy stuff."

"I didn't ask for any of that. I don't talk to anyone at HQs. I'm just out there doing the job."

"I tried to warn him."

"Against me?"

"I grew up around all of this. I've seen it before. Obsession. Losing perspective."

"I'm that way?"

"You weren't. I don't know, Sam. But he would have followed you anywhere."

"What did you hear?"

"You needed backup and couldn't wait for headquarters. So you brought him in."

"Because he wouldn't know any better?" Sam looked down, his lip curling. He gripped the railing with his left hand. "Fin pushed *me*."

She didn't say a word, only watched him.

"He found out I was going, and he insisted."

"How did he find out?"

"I don't know. He was good. We were out that afternoon. He might have noticed I was nursing a drink or that I had a game-ready vibe going. He knew something was up, and he followed me out to my car."

"You hadn't planned to bring him?"

"I'd thought about it. He'd been in on a couple of early meetings, and I wanted him in on the big pitch, to learn. But I wasn't going to risk it that night. Everything was moving too fast. I'm not sure how he figured out I was up to something, but it all just confirmed that he was ready. He was even messing with me about it, said it would be a shame if anybody found out I was running some off-books meetings."

"He shook you down?"

"Not seriously. He wouldn't do that. But I respected the grit. Reminded me of myself. It was his call, his idea. I did want him with me that night, for sure. If he hadn't stood watch and sent up a flare, I might not have made it out, and we'd have no idea who was behind all this."

She was concentrating, weighing what he'd said. He could see her fighting with her pride, wondering if she'd been wrong.

"He had your back." Her fingers went to her necklace, a simple gold cross. "He was always that way." She didn't say anything for a moment, then went on. "You know he was honored that you gave him a shot with Alex Clarke."

She held the cross between her thumb and index finger and looked down at it, the gold glinting in the sun.

"What's that?" Sam asked, gesturing toward it.

"I never told you the story about this and Fin?"

"No."

"It was my father's. He wore it every day and left it to me after he passed. My senior year of high school, Fin and I were up at Sunday River for the ski races one weekend, hanging out with a bunch of friends crashing all over this condo. There were some college kids around too, total maniacs, drunk and high all weekend. My bag went missing. It was one of those Kate Spades that were big then. I really only cared about the necklace.

"A girl I was staying with told me that one of the college guys had taken it, this huge dude staying at the other complex. He pinched it for his girlfriend, I guess, just because he could, a power thing.

"Fin asked me about it. He could tell I was upset. And I think he was worried I was going to go get myself in trouble."

She ran her finger across her glass, wiping aside the condensation.

"He took off without a word. A half hour later he was back with the bag in his hand, his knuckles all banged up, and his eye already going red."

"He didn't say anything?"

"Just that he had to skip the party that night." She looked at Sam and squinted slightly, then went on with a Maine accent: "And that he was about three minutes ahead of a half dozen Colby lacrosse bros who were out for *fakking* blood."

Sam let out a quiet laugh. The impression was dead-on.

"We got out of there. He took me to some diner he knew outside Oxford. Everything came in those red plastic baskets. We got burgers and then went home on the back roads, him driving, me picking CDs out of this old case he had."

She smiled, then looked down and closed her eyes tight.

He took a step closer, put his hand to her elbow, watching her fight back the emotion.

"It's all right, Emily."

She bit her lip, nodded, and moved toward him. Sam put his arms around her.

She didn't make a sound, her chest rising and falling against his. She lifted her chin and looked into his eyes, pressing against him. His hand rose to the back of her neck. After a moment she stepped away and gave him a smile as if they'd come this close to falling for an old trick.

"Why did we decide that . . ."

"I think you decided, Emily."

"Right," she said, and her eyes went down for a second, as if she were searching for the reason again.

"You never did tell me why."

She didn't respond but didn't look away.

The day after they'd gotten together at his place, Sam was called to a crash meeting in Malta. He was out of contact for ten days, and when he came up for air, he reached out to her, but she was on the road too. He kept trying, but something had changed. After a few back-and-forths, it was clear enough that she didn't want to pursue it and he respected that. Though he never did understand why. Maybe it was because that night was so intense and so comfortable, as if they'd already been together for years, and she wasn't ready to make that leap. Maybe she didn't like how he did things on his own and knew he'd be bad for her career.

Agency relationships are all or nothing, either empty hookups or sudden, deep, and intense pairings. It's the pressure, the secrecy. The leadership encouraged them. The fewer attachments to the outside world, the better. She and Sam had grown close early on at Camp Peary, the former Navy base, nicknamed "the Farm," that housed the Agency's training grounds. She was younger than Sam but sharper about Agency politics, and he helped her out with his field experience from the army. He remembered working with her on the range one morning, just after dawn. She could shoot an expert grouping at twenty-five yards, but she kept biting her lower lip on one side when she fired. He tried to help her break the habit—it could interfere with the smooth breathing necessary for consistency—but her aim grew worse, so in the end he told her to just keep doing it and tearing out bull's-eyes. It was always a funny juxtaposition to see her put ten rounds in a paper target's heart, as cold and lethal as any door kicker, then beam and pump her fist like she was at a pep rally.

A lot of the officers in training would get blitzed on the weekends and pair up as a way to blow off steam. The only places to go around Camp Peary were awful chain restaurants and hotels in strip malls. But for all their attraction, Sam and Emily never crossed that line.

She'd had a marriage fall apart not long before she went to NOC training, and she was still rocked by it then. The guy was a major in the British army. It was an Agency marriage because of an Agency rule: you want to share a bed with someone foreign-born, you'd better be married. They had priests who'd come out and do a ceremony on a few hours' notice. They'd push people together before they were ready, and between that and the pressure of the job, the relationships would often blow up. Sam never got the full story. By the time she'd gotten over it, they were both on assignment undercover—new countries, new names, new lives. He didn't really get to see her again until the past couple of years, when she was at headquarters and he was back and forth to DC giving briefings to Jones and some of the brass. Then that one night together. Then it was all over.

Emily stepped away, went to the railing, and looked out at the woods. They stood there in a comfortable silence.

Something snagged in Sam's mind, something she'd said just a moment ago: *He was honored that you gave him a shot with Alex Clarke.*

She knew about the Alex Clarke meetings. Fin must have talked to her. He looked up to find Emily watching him. "What is it?" she asked. She was sharp enough to see that something was troubling him.

"You said Fin was honored that I brought him in on the Clarke case. Did he tell you about the work we were doing?"

"He mentioned it."

"Anything about Geneva? The meeting?"

"No." She denied it quickly and surely, without overemphasis. Perfectly natural. Or deliberately made to look that way.

Dimos had warned him that there might be a penetration at CIA, and Fin had told her about Clarke. Sam steeled himself and put aside any feelings to weigh the question: Could Emily be the leak? She'd worked with Parker and Hassan too.

He could press, but if she was concealing something, she wouldn't just give it away, and it was better for him to keep any suspicions hidden for the moment. He wasn't done here. He needed information from her.

His phone buzzed in his pocket. He took it out and glanced at it. A new encrypted message. Dimos had written back.

Emily was watching him now, not revealing any suspicion, but she wouldn't in any case.

Sam put his hand on the white-painted wood of the railing and looked at her. He'd try a blitz.

"DEMETER," he said, borrowing a move from the Cypriot, examining her face as closely as Dimos had his. He wanted her reaction.

"What?"

"It's a cryptonym. For a file, maybe an operation."

"And?"

"It could be a lead on who killed Fin, who did that bombing, and who's responsible for the deaths of Parker and Hassan."

"Fuck, Sam." She shook her head, her lips pulled into a bitter smile. "The Fin stuff. Memory lane." She gestured back and forth between them. "This. Are you working me?" The smile disappeared.

"Were you, when you came to my place last night?"

"I was worried about you." She let the hurt into her voice.

"I need your help on this, Emily."

"Why?"

"Because I saw a girl get her leg blown off last night. And they're only getting started." He thought of Dimos's deadline. Sunday. Three days left.

"I can't, Sam."

"We can stop this."

"What the hell were you doing meeting with a Russian source? Why didn't you tell anyone about it? And now you're asking me about crypts?" The shorthand for cryptonyms. She looked at the papers on the table. "Parker and Hassan are dead. Someone got their names. Someone hunted them down. You know what that means."

"A leak," he said.

"Right. So why are *you* here asking me for classified information?"

He didn't argue, just measured her reaction. How much of it was justified anger? How much suspicion? And how much was deflection and fear that Sam was too close to something?

"What is this, Sam? Did someone get to you?"

She stood with her hand tight on the glass, breathing fast, real anger showing in her face.

"No, Emily. You know me."

"I thought I did."

"I'll go."

"I think you should."

He took the steps down to the yard and circled around the house to his car. He started it up and looked back at her place. It was hard to see her in the shadows behind the drapes, but she was there, watching him from the living-room window.

17

SAM STOOD AT his dining-room table. The lockbox was open in front of him. His gun lay by his right hand on the dark-stained maple.

DEMETER. A file that might solve the murders of two CIA case officers. He had tested Emily with that one word, and it had triggered something in her. She was the only person besides Fin who might have known about the Geneva meeting in advance. He didn't want to believe she was the leak, but he would go where the facts took him.

He looked at his phone. Dimos was in play. Sam needed more from him. Meeting with a Russian agent was a dangerous move, but that didn't matter anymore. He had to know what he was in the middle of.

There was a chance that Dimos was working him, trying to use doubt as a weapon, driving him away from the people whose help he needed to solve this, but Sam had to trust that he could outplay him.

He didn't have DEMETER, and he wouldn't have given it to Dimos if he had. But he had something. "Don't give them what they want," Williams used to say. "Give them what you want."

He unlocked the phone and pulled up Signal, an open-source encrypted communication app that let you reach out privately to anyone whose phone number you knew as long as that person had the app as well. It was used in intel circles and far beyond. Once, encrypted comms had required months of training and classified gear. Now they were everywhere.

Sam's first message to Dimos had gone out this morning when Sam was at the river: "Good meeting last night. I have something for you."

Only Dimos would know the identity of the sender. The app worked as easily as texting, but it ran the message through a modern cryptographic gauntlet—a double ratchet algorithm, a triple Diffie-Hellman handshake, and 256-bit encryption—that was, for all practical purposes, as good as what the Agency used.

"What was on the table?" Dimos had written back while Sam was at Emily's. He was double-checking Sam's identity, a detail only he would know.

"Your cell phone," Sam wrote.

The reply popped up a moment later. "You already have what I want?"

"Not all of it, but a start. It's worth your time."

He put the phone down and lifted a printout he'd taken from one of the folders in the lockbox: a black-and-white image of a man's face. A closer look revealed something strange about it. The contours were too smooth and perfect, making the subject look like a high-resolution digital avatar. It was an EvoFIT image, a computer-generated facial composite. The Agency used this now instead of a sketch artist to allow a witness to create an image of someone from memory. Sam had done it in the hospital forty-eight hours after the Geneva ambush. This was Alex Clarke's killer, frozen in Sam's mind by a pistol's flash. In Sam's write-up of the attack, he went by the bland name of Shooter Two. Sam had done a composite for the first shooter as well, the one who'd sent a bullet just past his head, but he'd managed to get a copy of only this one during the rushed return from Switzerland before he was locked out of the Agency files.

If Dimos was who he claimed, an ally of Alex Clarke, then he would want to find this man as badly as Sam did. Sam just needed something to get him talking, to start the dance.

The phone vibrated on the table.

"Hains Point, 4:30 p.m. Leave your gun at home this time."

Dimos had said that any meeting would be three hours late, which meant the actual time would be 7:30. Sam pulled up a map on his phone and switched to a satellite view. During training, he'd spent three months scouting drops and rendezvous locations in the District and could draw a map of most of the city from memory. His eyes traced a body of land like a curved blade along the southwestern edge of town, with water on both sides: Hains Point.

It was at the end of an island that sat between the Potomac and the Washington Channel, a narrow waterway that fed the wharves and marinas of Southwest DC. The land was a man-made strip of park a third of a mile wide, built up from Potomac dredge in the nineteenth century. It was mostly golf courses, woods, playgrounds, and trails along the water. There would be people, but not too many. He would have liked more exits, but there was decent cover and several ways out if something went wrong.

"I'll be there," he typed, and hit Send.

He'd always run sources. Now he was one.

18

YOU LEARN A lot as you become a case officer but there is one lesson that takes the longest to drill into someone new to the field: Go slow. The stakes and the nerves will push you to rush, but you have to fight against it. It was funny, given Sam's reputation, that he respected as much as anyone the central fact that intelligence was 95 percent drudgery—hours spent casing sites and developing backup, emergency, and contingency plans. In hard-target countries, Sam would run a two-hour surveillance-detection route every time he left his apartment. And when you operate as a NOC, you actually *do* your cover job. You have to live it, spending fifty to sixty hours a week toiling away like any other drone, keeping up appearances to justify a few real source meetings a month. It's maddening, but if you're a good NOC, you do it gladly, because one shortcut could get you or your source killed.

Sam made his first pass by the site ninety minutes before the meeting and started his serious scrutiny an hour before. He parked on Ohio Drive, the road that ran along the entire perimeter of the island on the Washington Channel side, then did a slow survey of the site on foot, figuring his exits, looking for cover and spots for potential ambushes. It was a few hundred yards from where he parked to Hains Point at the end of the island. It was almost sunset by the time he finished, with fifteen minutes to go until the meeting time.

Gray clouds hovered low in the sky to the east, bringing darkness earlier than it would have come on a clear night. Stands of trees dotted the dried-out lawns of the park, and they grew thickest to the north, with dense underbrush at the edges of the golf course. There were a few picnic tables and playgrounds, empty now, near the center of the park. In the lot, teachers chaperoned a crowd of school kids onto a last tour bus.

The roar of a jet filled the air. Reagan National Airport lay just across the Potomac to the east. A black Mercedes approached the parking lot, and Sam stepped behind a cottonwood tree to watch as it parked.

Dimos stepped out of the car, wearing a dark suit and no tie. A guard exited from the passenger seat, straightening his jacket over his left side, a habit when you're carrying and getting out of a car. It was the lefty from last night, the mellower of the two.

So one armed guard, and neither he nor Dimos had waited or appeared to do any sort of communication from inside the car that would suggest coordination with other watchers, and Sam had seen none. Having the guard approach in the open was a good sign. Dimos was being straight, bringing protection. If this were an ambush, he'd be trying to hide. That inspired confidence, as did the fact that Dimos and his crew had had a good chance to kill Sam last night but didn't.

Sam's Heckler and Koch was in his glove box. He'd already rolled up on Dimos's house with a gun, and it was time for a show of good faith. It would be clear enough that he wasn't carrying; Sam wore a black T-shirt and a pair of jeans. He'd seen people carry concealed with that kind of outfit, but it usually meant wearing a shirt the size of a hockey jersey, and the contours of the pistol's grip were still apparent to anyone who knew what to look for.

He stepped out from behind the tree and began walking, hands loose at his sides. Dimos paused, met his eyes, and then looked to the right, toward the Potomac, and started strolling slowly enough that it was easy for Sam to come up next to him.

"You mind if I see your ankles?" Dimos asked.

"On the first date?"

"Second."

"Then sure." With his hands in his pockets, he drew up his pant legs enough to show, over the next two strides, that he was clear.

The guard trailed about fifty feet back, near enough to close and kill before Sam could pull from a concealed carry.

"Nervous, Sam?"

"Nope," he said. "And you can skip all the Psych 101 bullshit."

"Oh, good. So what do you have?"

"Do you want to know who killed Alex Clarke? I can show you."

"And DEMETER?"

"Please. I can't get your file if I have no idea who I can trust. You said there was a leak. Who do they have on the inside?"

"You're trying to steal home," he said, smiling at his Americanism. "Step by step."

"If you're really on Clarke's side, surely you want to know who murdered him."

"I'm interested. And what do you want from me?"

"A lead on the mole you hinted at or on Konstantin. I want to stop him. So do you, right?"

"There was one camera on the street that night and it was taken out. How did you get a photo of Clarke's shooter?"

A police car cruised down Ohio Drive and started to round the point. Sam didn't react. "I saw him, and the Agency put together a sketch, a composite made by computer."

"But you don't know his name."

"No."

"So that's the trade?" Dimos said.

The park narrowed as they approached the tip of the point. A cool wind slapped waves against the seawall. Sam turned, scanned the water, then looked across the channel to the campus of Fort McNair, a historic military arsenal of stately brick buildings that was now home to the National War College.

Sam stopped. McNair was most famous as the site where the coconspirators in Lincoln's murder were tried and hanged in the courtyard of the Old Arsenal Penitentiary. Traitors.

"The fort?" Dimos asked as he put his hand on a picnic table under a stand of trees. "Are you getting morbid, Sam?" He did a quick mime of raising a rope around his neck. "I'm not the enemy."

Sam had traded information before but usually with the careful vetting of the analysts at HQs. He'd even given up secrets, but artfully. The CIA would let an officer be "turned" to leak or sell weapon plans, although with some crucial technical details changed. Then a nuclear centrifuge would tear itself apart two months later and four thousand miles away. But this was different. He was on his own here.

Dimos slid his hand into the pocket of his suit, and Sam stepped closer, hands rising, eyes darting quickly between Dimos and the guard now moving in.

He came out with a piece of candy wrapped in cellophane. "Caramel?"

Sam lowered his hands as Dimos smiled.

"I'm good," Sam said.

"Greeks and gifts, huh?" He unwrapped it and waved away the

guard. "They're from Costco," he said. "Dark chocolate sea salt caramels. I was trying to quit smoking and now I'm addicted to these." He popped it in his mouth and sat down.

"It's a deal," Dimos said. "I'd like to see that sketch."

Sam came around the other side of the table and sat. "And?"

"I'll give you a lead on Konstantin's network here. A meeting site."

"You said you had a source who could lead me to Konstantin. Introduce me."

"I do. But we're not there yet. Take it slow."

"Slow? We only have a few days left." Dimos had said the attack would happen on Sunday night, and Sam wondered if the ticking clock—he had been so specific about the time—had simply been a way to hook him.

"We do. But you tried to break into my house last night with a gun. So allow me a little caution. This is much better," he said. He looked to the river and took a deep breath. The air smelled like wet leaves with a hint of the pre-thunderstorm scent of ozone.

He took out another caramel, and Sam extended his hand. It was nothing, but Sam knew that in this game, it was everything, those moment-by-moment bids for trust—a drink, a meal, a confidence.

"How good is that?" he asked as Sam took a bite of the rich chocolate, then nodded. He finished it, then reached slowly into his pocket. He took out the composite image and slid it across the splintering wood of the picnic table. Dimos unfolded it and examined the man's face. He brought his knuckles to his lips.

"Distinctive features?" he asked.

"Scar near the temple on the right. Though it's hard to make out; it's mostly behind his hairline."

"How close were you?"

"Thirty feet."

"And you just, what, gazed at each other?"

"No. It was dark. Except for the muzzle flare."

Dimos looked at him. "You got all of this from a flash?"

"That's him."

Dimos checked the composite again and any doubt seemed to resolve.

"Who is he?" Sam asked.

"I need time on that."

"You've seen him before."

A nod.

"Where?"

Dimos folded up the sketch and put it in his pocket. "Here's what I can give you. Ready?"

Sam did a quick scan around them. The guard had fallen back, and there was no one within earshot. The roar of a jet engine built in the distance, and Dimos leaned in slightly, holding off for a moment until the plane noise covered them from any audio surveillance.

Then he gave an address on Washington Boulevard in Arlington.

"What is it?"

"A Peet's Coffee."

"What kind of meeting? In-person? Drop?"

"We don't know."

"Repeating?"

"No. Signaled."

"How?"

"A unique phrase posted on the internet."

"Where?"

"Anywhere. You pick it up with a Google alert."

"The phrase?"

"*Messi miracle god on earth. Messi* with an *i*, as in the football player."

"Hard to argue with that. And the time?"

The sound of the plane retreated and Dimos lowered his voice to match. "Six digits follow the username of whoever posts it. They correspond to date, hour, and minute, in that order."

"You've seen the system before?"

"Variations."

Sam looked to the left. Dimos's bodyguard was gone. He craned his head around, then stood.

"What is it?"

"Your man. Where is he?"

"What?"

Sam circled around the table, moving closer to the Cypriot, wary that Dimos might have used the moments when Sam was focused on his information to allow his guard to move into position. Dimos got up and backed away, searching for the left-handed shooter. "What the hell is this?" he demanded.

Dimos certainly looked threatened. His guard should have been here and on Sam by now, but there was no sign of him. Either Dimos's surprise was genuine or he was a better actor than Sam had ever encountered.

"Come on," Sam said and started moving toward the Potomac. Dimos followed a few yards behind, uncertain, it seemed, whether Sam was a threat or his only protection. Sam circled around the trees to the stretch of grass that ran along the river's edge. He looked both ways, searching for the guard.

"He didn't just fucking disappear," Dimos said.

Sam reached the railing on top of the seawall and looked over. The sun had set by now and the water was all shimmering blacks and grays.

"What is it?"

"Nothing," Sam said. He scanned the other way, and under the light from a lamp near the end of the point, he caught it: the arms out to the sides, the wet black hair, the back of a head bobbing in the river. A man floated facedown, bumping along the breakwater with each wave, turning slowly like a piece of driftwood as the current pulled him farther south. There was something off about the angle of his neck. His throat had been cut.

19

SAM PIVOTED AWAY from the railing and sidestepped left toward Dimos, searching the line of trees for any attackers.

"Come on," Sam said, forceful but calm. The trees were clear.

"Did you see him?"

"He's dead. We have to move."

"What?" Dimos reeled back.

"He's in the river."

"But—"

"The plane noise covered the sound. They're coming. No one kills security and then leaves. We need to get to your car." Sam put his hand on Dimos's back and pushed him behind the thick trunk of an elm. He leaned out, searching among the other trees and shadows for an attacker. Another roar built from the airport as a jet climbed into the sky.

Dimos pulled away. "You're setting me up."

"No. Listen. We need to get—"

Red flashes went off to Sam's left, cracking twice in quick succession. He drew back behind the tree and brought Dimos close beside him as two bullets ripped by, feet away.

"Christ," Dimos said. The shots seemed to convince him. If Sam had been setting him up, he wouldn't be a target himself. On the far side of the island, a tourist jumped in his SUV and took off. Sam looked across the road to the lawn at the center of the island and the lot where Dimos's Mercedes was parked. It was much closer than Sam's Jeep.

Sam's mind emptied of all but the scene before him, the crystal-sharp focus of combat. "Your car. Ready?"

"Okay," Dimos whispered.

Sam scanned the trees, then put his hand on Dimos's shoulder to urge him forward in case he froze. "Stay low," he said. He slipped the toe of his boot under a stick by the roots of the tree, then kicked it in a low arc toward the river for a distraction. "Go."

He pressed on Dimos's shoulder and they sprinted in the other direction, toward the parking lot, crossing the road and then the lawn.

Double snaps sounded from the trees. Sam took it for a suppressed pistol or subsonic rifle rounds. Dimos was faster than Sam had expected, and when they reached the car, Sam guided him around the hood, and they both dropped near the front tire on the driver's side, taking cover behind the engine block. Dimos did it without a word. This wasn't his first gunfight.

"Keys," Sam said.

"No chance." Dimos hauled open the door and climbed behind the wheel. A shot. A high punching sound rang out as the car shook, taking a bullet. Sam wanted to drive, but there was no time to argue or drag him out.

The back door locks thunked open, and Sam climbed into the back seat and stayed low as Dimos raced the car out of the spot in reverse. Another shot blew out the rear passenger window, showering Sam with tempered glass. Dimos put the car in drive, hit the gas, and screeched toward the one-way road that would let them off the island.

The acceleration rocked Sam back against the leather. He kept low, but there was no more gunfire. Dimos's breath was coming fast, in and out, audible over the roar of the engine.

As the cherry trees whipped by, Sam weighed the next steps. He had a gun in his car, but depending on the number of attackers, that might not be enough.

The U.S. Park Police headquarters were on the northern side of the island, close to the Jefferson Memorial. At least one bystander had seen the shots. The cops would be here soon. He and Dimos just needed to get off the X.

"Faster," Sam said.

The car surged forward.

"No one followed you?" Sam asked, pushed back in the seat, the glass digging into his legs.

"We were clean."

Sam's eyes went to the trees ahead along the river, thick enough to offer good concealment. He caught motion in the shadows, a man's face among the low branches on the side of the road, his arms rising.

"Get down!" Sam shouted as a gunshot flashed from the woods and the driver's-side window blew in. Dimos slumped to the right, and the car swerved. Sam reached forward between the seats and grabbed the wheel as the car jumped the curb and clipped a thick branch from a cherry tree. He turned the wheel hard to the left, but it was too late. The tires skidded over the grass, and the car slammed into a lamppost. Sam was thrown forward between the two front seats, his shoulder and head crashing into the side of the airbag as it blew. It sounded like a gunshot inside the car.

He slit his eyes against the dust. It took him a moment to focus. He was lying across the center console and he pulled himself into the passenger seat.

Dimos hung against his seat belt behind the wheel, his neck and shirt a mess of blood.

Sam reached over, felt for the wound to try to stop the bleeding. He scanned the windows. Veering off the road had put some distance between them and the shooter, but they didn't have much time.

"TRIBUNE," Dimos whispered.

"What?"

"The source who will lead you to Konstantin. That's how you'll know him."

"Who is it?"

Dimos licked his lips and took two pained breaths. "Don't trust a soul—" He broke out into a hitching cough, then closed his eyes.

"The attack. Sunday, by ten p.m. Where is it? What is it?"

A rasp escaped from the back of Dimos's throat. "I unseen," Sam heard him say.

"What does that mean?"

He formed the words again, shaking with strain, and this time it sounded different.

"HYACINTH?"

Dimos nodded once.

"Where?" Sam asked as Dimos's head fell forward. Sam grabbed his shoulder, trying to rouse him. "Tell me where!"

The tone went from his muscles. Sam threw his door open, reached over, and popped Dimos's seat belt. He'd have to carry him.

The rear window to Sam's left blew out—another shot. Then another. Dimos's body jerked with each one. Sam looked up and ground his teeth together. Dimos was gone.

He pulled back and climbed out of the passenger door. He used the car for cover, then bolted at an angle toward a stand of trees along the edge of the golf course, running as fast as he ever had, arms pumping, ducking branches.

He dropped low as he neared his Jeep, which he had parked in one of the turnouts along the Washington Channel. He came up on the passenger side, opposite from where the shooters had been, unlocked it, and climbed in and over the console to get behind the wheel.

He punched it and took off, opening the glove box and grabbing his gun as the speedometer climbed.

Police lights flashed on the far side of the island, shining through the woods of the golf course as Sam sped north.

The sirens grew louder and then quieter, the pitch dropping just slightly as the cruisers went past him. He kept on, flying under the freeway overpasses, then crossing the narrow bridge over the mouth of the Tidal Basin, the Jefferson Memorial glowing like an ancient temple to his right. Sam looked in his mirrors, scanning for police or the attackers in pursuit, then glanced up and saw the CCTV camera mounted on a light pole ahead, recording him as he made his escape.

20

SAM STOOD BEFORE his hallway mirror and pulled down the collar of his T-shirt. He checked the cut along his neck from last night. It had pulled open slightly during the chaos on Hains Point, but it wasn't bleeding anymore. His shoulder was sore, but he had no vertigo, no nausea, no symptoms of a concussion. He was lucky the curb and the cherry branches had slowed the Mercedes down before it hit the lamppost.

He went to the kitchen, opened the drawer next to the stove, and took out a bottle of ibuprofen. He shook two into his hand, then decided on four and swallowed them with half a glass of water. Putting one hand down on the counter, he faced the kitchen windows, eyes open but unfocused. All he could see was Dimos jerking in that seat as the bullets hit. He set his jaw, and the water glass shook in his hand.

"Motherfucker," he growled and threw the glass down. It shattered on the tile, sending fragments skittering along the floor. Three dead—Finlay, Clarke, and now Dimos. Three who had trusted him. He'd just finished washing the blood out from under his nails.

There had been no sign of a tail on Sam, and he would have picked one up during the hourlong surveillance-detection run.

They must have been tracking Dimos and filled in for the ambush quickly. They were good. Still, Dimos had managed to get across two leads on Konstantin, the Peet's meeting and a source close to the network: TRIBUNE. It sounded like a recognition signal, but it could have been a code name as well. Sam could use it in a search if he could find a way to access the Agency databases. Men had given their lives to get him that information. He would do those sacrifices justice.

Sam walked into the living room and started to order his next steps. He had already set up an alert on the phrase that Dimos had given him, so if it appeared in a post anywhere on the web, Sam would instantly get an e-mail and know that the meeting was coming. He needed to go case the coffee-shop site so he would be ready for the next rendezvous.

Through the window, he caught movement under the streetlight outside. A tall man approached on the sidewalk. Sam wouldn't have been surprised if it was a detective or an FBI agent who had already connected him with Dimos's murder, but he was taking no chances tonight. His gun was holstered on his right hip. He drew it and stepped toward the window.

Greg Jones was walking up to the front door, holding a cell phone in his hand.

Had the Agency already put Sam at the shooting at Hains Point? When the execs did their worst, they sent a friend, someone who could manage you, work you. He'd been trading with the enemy. There was another body on capital soil. Jones could have come to bring him in. "Don't trust a soul," Dimos had said.

Sam grabbed a broom and dustpan and swept up most of the glass. He was dropping the shards into the trash as the doorbell rang.

He put the gun in the credenza drawer, walked across the living room, and studied the street behind Jones, who was alone, as far as Sam could tell.

He opened the door. "Hey, Greg," Sam said.

"I hope it's not too late. I know you had a hell of a night."

Sam didn't give him anything and assumed he was talking about last night, the bombing on the Mall. "No worries."

"I wanted to get your phone back to you," he said. "I would've called, but . . ." He pointed to Sam's cell in his hand.

"Of course." Sam smiled. "Come on in."

Jones stepped through and Sam shut the door. Sam watched him casually taking in every detail, reading Sam's state from his environment. No clutter. No indication Sam had been off work for six weeks. It was a safe house, not a home.

"It's clean," Jones said as he handed him the phone.

"The caller?"

"No trace."

Jones was still giving him information. That was a good sign. Sam looked down at it but didn't power it on.

"I'd get a new one, just in case."

"Sure."

Sam looked up to see Jones peering into the kitchen, where a few small shards of glass glinted under the lights. His eyes went to Sam's hands, where the faintest lines of red still edged his cuticles. It took days, he knew, for it to wash away completely.

"Everything all right, Sam?"

"You're just here to bring me my phone?" Sam asked, letting some playful doubt into his voice.

"And checking in, yes. Last night was rough. Anything I can do for you?"

Sam thought of asking him if the FBI was waiting in two vans on the street, but that didn't seem like a great way to put him at ease. "Not beyond what we talked about at the hospital. Any movement?"

"I put a word in. We'll see." He noticed something on the shelves, went over, and pulled out a hardcover of Tennyson's poems. "Did Williams turn you on to this?"

"He gave that to me."

"He loved this stuff. All those blood-and-sinew rhymes." He riffled through the pages. "'Theirs not to reason why / Theirs but to do and die.'" A warm look to Sam. "He was the one who told me to watch out for you at the Farm," Jones said. "The Republic of whatever the hell it was."

"Vertania," Sam said. When you train as a NOC, the CIA turns half the facility at Camp Peary into a fictional country—the Republic of Vertania—where you work undercover. "He never told me that."

"Mysterious ways," Jones said. One of Williams's old lines. "You remember that?"

"Of course," Sam said. "I turned you."

Jones laughed. "You did. You just had it. I could tell from the jump. Williams had told me the same, said you were indestructible too."

NOCs were trained separately from the regular clandestine service folks in order to protect their identities. Everyone was there under a false name, known as a work name, and the final test was a full-on field exercise operating as case officers behind enemy lines in the imaginary Republic of Vertania, modeled on the most dangerous countries in which the CIA operated. The trainees ran countersurveillance, recruitments, agent meetings, and the occasional pursuit or gunfight—a lifetime's worth of bad days in the field rolled into two months.

CIA personnel playacted the parts, posing as potential agents to be recruited. Most were burned-out NOCs doing an easy turn back in DC after a misstep abroad had earned them a one-way ticket home. But you had to be careful in training, because often a division or group chief would come down for a few days' fun and play the role of a disgruntled Vertanian schlub looking to sell secrets as a way to find the best of the class to recruit to his or her team. So even while you were trying to spot tails and stay alive in the wilds of Vertania, you were also trying to figure out who the real-life players were, since they could make or break a career. The place was head games inside head games.

Sam was supposed to recruit Jones, who was playing a debt-ridden Vertanian bureaucrat in the defense ministry who ate lunch at the same spot three or four days a week. Sam read his dossier and zeroed in on the fact that he liked classic rock. Blasting Led Zeppelin would have been too obvious, so he found a copy of Keith Richards's memoir and started showing up at the same cafeteria.

He said nothing on the first day, just made his presence seem normal and familiar. On the second, on his way out, he asked Jones if the lentil soup was any good, and Jones said it was. On the third day, he kept the memoir beside him while he typed on his laptop and worked his way through a bowl of that soup. Jones approached him with a simple "Not bad, right?"

They got to talking about the Stones. Sam mentioned that he had some signed memorabilia at home, Jones said he would love to see it, and bam—second meeting in private secured.

As soon as Sam said that he'd be glad to have Jones over to his house, Jones broke character, transforming from a wary post-Soviet apparatchik to relaxed New England gentry, his normal self.

"Great first meeting," he said as they strolled out into a drizzly Virginia Tidewater afternoon.

"Too slow?"

"No. It was perfect. Ideally, they approach you. I like the bumps too."

"Bump?"

"Asking about the soup, showing up again, just making your face familiar. It's called a bump. The approaches before the approach that seem like chance run-ins."

Sam nodded along.

"No one taught you that?"

"Just made sense."

"My name's Greg Jones," he said and shook Sam's hand. "Drop me a note around assignment time."

Sam had recruited an imaginary Vertanian and been recruited *by* the real deputy chief of the Russia group.

He and Williams put Sam to work on hard targets in arms trafficking and state-sponsored violence. It was a world where somebody with combat experience would be useful. Russia and its satellites were, once again, some of the riskiest environments for recruitment in the world, and those in the weapons trade didn't abide by the gentlemanly rules of espionage. They didn't swap spies— they executed them. As Williams rose to senior leadership, Sam operated more and more on his own, and Jones gave him cover on day-to-day matters at headquarters. Sam started working his way closer to the Russian president's triggermen around the world and the flows of cash that supported them. He found a dark conspiracy of oligarchs, organized crime, and state power, all working to enrich and strengthen the president, a man who had risen to become a new czar by swapping the Communist ideology for a new cult of personality, wealth, and ultranationalism.

The work suited Sam. He'd loved the ass-kicking camaraderie of the Rangers, but he wanted to be more than a finger on a trigger. He liked to put together his own intelligence, set his own priorities, and chase down his targets. That was what brought him to Williams's attention while they were both working in J-Bad—Sam spent months on a task force and hunted down a Russian-backed Taliban leader who'd killed dozens of allied soldiers. Sam led the team that crossed him out in a tunnel complex near Chaparhar.

He thought back to that overbright cafeteria where he'd first met Jones, playing as though he were behind enemy lines, his first recruitment. But now, as they stood in the living room, the stakes were real. Why all this sentiment? Building rapport? He could trust no one. He had to assume everyone was turned.

This kind of flattery is a basic part of the tool kit. You'd be recruiting a scientist and you'd mention some great paper you read, and he would say, "Oh, that was mine." Maybe Jones already knew what had happened on Hains Point, and he was here to talk Sam down and bring him in quietly. During the conversation, Sam stepped to the right so that he had a view out the front window. He took in every detail of the night outside, watching for Jones's backup.

But it wouldn't be out of the ordinary for Jones to check in. He was an exception to HQs' backstabbing culture, where all too often a mistake made you toxic and where peers were always looking out for weaknesses, some means to climb over you to a more senior position, the way getting narrower and more desperate the higher you went. Jones was an old public service Yankee. He never seemed to have much to prove, and Sam had heard stories from other officers of Jones appearing from out of the blue to offer help, then acting almost embarrassed by gratitude, because that was just what one did.

"I know how close you and Williams were. I know he put you onto this Konstantin thing. I respect it, you trying to honor him. But I want you to be careful, Sam. You didn't see what it did to him."

"I saw some."

"In meetings up on seven, he wasn't himself. His judgment was off. He'd become so rigid in his thinking, and I was open to what he was saying. Then the stress. The stroke. I'd talk to him about all this stuff, about Konstantin. You know, it's so comforting to think there is one man behind everything. One villain, one network that you can pull down to stop it all. But these threats, this evil, it's everywhere, and you just do your best to hold back the flood. He didn't want to hear that. He thought I was a damned idiot for not seeing it, but I would still go sit with him every so often, bring him some of those cookies, read to him."

Sam pressed his lips together. Jones had been the other visitor, there all the way to the end, even after the others stopped coming.

Jones took out his phone and glanced at the screen. Headlights shone through the front window, and Sam braced himself. But the car kept going, and Jones simply stood there, the phone hanging by his side.

"We all lose people, Sam. I have."

"Parker and Hassan."

"No one knows what happened there." He ran his thumb along his beard. "Not a day goes by when they're not on my mind."

"What do you think?"

"Accidents. A leak. I don't know. If you have something on it, you can talk to me." He paused. "I'm worried about you. I know what this does to an officer. I've been through it. If there's anything you need, anything I can do, I'm here." Jones waited.

Sam looked up slightly; his eyes moved over the paint drips on the molding near the ceiling. Jones wasn't here to bust him, and there was no hard sell. Sam wanted answers. He wanted to share his leads and stop this fucking thing, but if a source gives up his life to tell you that no one can be trusted, you trust no one.

"DEMETER," Sam said, and brought his gaze back to Jones. There was surprise, sure, and, more than that, a mournful look.

"Who are you talking to, Sam?"

"What is it?"

"Whatever you're doing, for the love of God, be careful. We've already lost good men and women on this. It's so easy to slip. I've seen it. I've come close myself. They use your best instincts against you." He shook his head. "I don't need to tell you. You know the game."

Another long look. He seemed to understand that he'd get nothing out of Sam. He took a few steps toward the door, then turned back as if wondering if he'd left something behind.

"You didn't kill him, did you?" Jones asked.

Sam was surprised by how little the straight question shocked him. "Who?"

Jones's grim smile said *Nice try*. "Dimos. They pulled his body out of a Mercedes on Hains Point. Shot to death."

Sam froze and glared as if the news were fresh. So Jones knew. That was why he had come. "No."

"I can't hide that we talked about him last night, Sam."

"I understand," Sam said, steeling himself.

"But I don't have to volunteer it."

Sam took a moment to absorb what Jones was saying. The weight in his stomach lightened, and he gave him an appreciative nod. "You connected it to me based on what?"

"Inference. But if you know anything, you should come forward. Get ahead of this."

"You're right."

Jones waited for more. But nothing else was coming. He clasped his hands and looked to the door. He knew when to press and when to back off. "Think about it, okay? And get some rest. You need my help on this or anything, you let me know."

"I will. Thank you, Jones."

"Sure." He went to the door, stepped out, and closed it behind him. Through the window, Sam watched him disappear into the shadows under the trees.

Jones's sympathy was genuine. Sam was sure of that. But he was on his own until he was absolutely certain whom he could trust.

The killers were close. Sam had one of their meeting sites and the code they would use to trigger it. It was all he needed to start the stalk.

21

LANGE WATCHED THE drop of metal hang from the tip of his soldering iron like a ball of mercury, then traced it along the bare copper wire, leaving a thin coating connecting it to the board. He put the iron down and studied his handiwork, a time-delay detonator.

At the Lincoln Memorial, he had used a simple design, almost the Platonic ideal of a bomb. Lange could wear a mask even as he stoked terror, hiding his true self, employing the microwave trigger of the late-period IRA car bomb or the rocker switches favored by the Palestinians. But here he wasn't trying to hide his identity or sophistication. Both the Semtex, with its distinctive orange color, and the design could easily be traced back to the last days of the Soviet Union and its proxy fighters. He wanted America to know what had hit it, to understand that the empire lived on. The war had never ended. Men like him had guided the homeland from the shadows since its founding. They were the steady hands, Russia's forever state. They went by many names—NKVD, KGB, SVR, FSB, GRU—but it was all one tradition, and they thought of themselves simply and proudly as chekists, as the secret services had been known during the revolution.

The workbench was bare plywood, and the walls behind it were covered in peeling floral wallpaper. The Smith and Wesson lay to his right. The window was open. A warm breeze carried a hint of motor oil along with the smell of evergreens. Through the screen, he could see the rusting tower of an old windmill.

He did a last check of continuity and resistance across the circuits, then put away his tools and pressed Play on a CD boom box on the desk. Patsy Cline's voice filled the aging cabin.

Lange had first heard this kind of music during his indoctrination courses at the Red Banner Institute. He spent three years living in a model America, learning every facet of the culture, down to how to count on one's fingers. (An American extends each finger out one at a time, ending with an open hand when he counts to five; a Russian curls each finger down, ending with a closed fist.) Then two years in Canada, living under the name of a child who had died at age three, and only then was he considered clean enough to enter the United States, the main enemy.

He hated so much about this nation—its ignorance of its own history and the world's, its smug hypocrite smile, the way it wiped away the blood of its meddling and domination around the globe, again and again, and dared called it virtue.

But you have to find things to love or else there is no way to pass, to survive the double life. Cline started to sing "Just a Closer Walk with Thee," and he turned the volume up. A neat stack of CDs sat on the shelf beside the boom box—Hank Williams and Buck Owens and Johnny Cash. He looked out the window at the lines of the gentle Virginia hills, their beauty in sharp contrast with the falling-down outbuildings and junk cars that dotted this property.

He listened for a while, then unzipped a bag to his left on the workbench and pulled out a file folder. He opened it and began paging through a stack of eight-by-ten photos. The first showed Sam Hudson entering a café in an ivy-lined alley in Georgetown. A second showed him leaving a few minutes later with a paper bag in his hand. He pushed them to the side and spread out a few others. They were telephoto shots and showed Hudson as he pulled down the blinds in his bathroom last night after the Lincoln bombing. Another showed him entering his house. He could read Sam's life through a few photographs: the drive, the hunger.

Lange arranged five of them on the rough surface of the plywood, his best views of the interior—the living room, the bath, the bedroom. He reached out and laid his palm on the textured grip of the Smith and Wesson. He put himself in that house, that room; felt the carpet give under his feet as he trailed silently behind him, blind spot to blind spot, dark to dark.

The United States was, of course, the most dangerous hunting ground, but it was also where the officers of the CIA were most vulnerable, far from the concrete barriers and armored SUVs that they hid behind overseas.

He could get to Sam whenever he wanted. He had done it before.

Lange remembered the day he'd killed Jeff Parker, the American deep-cover officer. Parker had picked up a thread on Lange's network—the lifelines of money and matériel that let Lange survive and slip into different countries as different men, one of the same threads that Sam Hudson later pulled. Parker threatened everything. His work was flawless, and he would have been nearly impossible to track down, but Lange had a way to get inside the Agency's secrets: DEMETER. That gave him Parker's true name.

Lange traced him to his Northern Virginia home—if you could call it that. Parker was divorced and lived in a rented house at the edge of McLean, stretching himself thin so he could be close to the kids when he was in the States and they could have a yard to play in.

It was a long weekend, Parker's turn with his boys, eight and twelve years old, when Lange started hunting him. He watched his target, an easygoing Californian, standing with his arms crossed beside the bleachers next to the baseball field, getting a few introductions to the other dads. Afterward, he brought the boys to the Silver Diner, where they ate mostly in silence, the older one barely glancing up from his phone, as Lange looked on from the counter. It was odd how seeing that pained Lange more than anything that was to come with Parker.

He trailed them toward his ex-wife's house, the old family home, a four-bedroom in West Langley. As they drove down the tree-lined streets, he saw Parker look up in the rearview mirror and smile. The boy in the back must have said something, and all three of them broke out laughing.

Parker walked the kids up to the front door, where his ex-wife and her new husband waited. It was obvious he wasn't welcome inside.

Undercover work takes your whole life, every moment. Spouses learn soon enough what the priorities are, and divorces are all too often just a formalization of what's been clear for years—that one partner's gone, physically half the time and in his or her head for the rest. It's the sacrifice they all make.

There was only one note of grace to the fact that Lange's own wife passed after she gave birth to his son: Lange never had to do this to her. Her mother raised the boy, and Lange saw him grow by leaps and bounds in the rare moments Lange was home, dropping into a real life that felt as put-on as any cover.

It was hard work, giving up all he had, and the privileged life that came with being a third-generation chekist, his grandfather a hero of the Great War. But Lange didn't care for privilege. He left his family behind. No photos. No mementos. Some brought a snapshot or two, but that only made it harder. You had to let go of every thought of them. When you were here, only the cover existed. The man you had been was dead.

He watched as the younger boy hugged Parker on the stoop. The older son stood by the door while Parker held his arms out, but after a moment, he stepped over and gave his father a long embrace.

Lange would leave Parker with that. He could have taken him earlier, but he gave him that day.

He waited inside Parker's condo that night, standing in the dark next to the front door for thirty-five minutes in a house that spoke of a life so much like his own. It looked as though it was staged for sale, with the generic furniture, barely used; the only signs that someone lived there were the stacks and stacks of books overflowing the shelves and piled on top of them.

The front door opened, and Parker entered, takeout in one hand, a gym bag over his shoulder, coming back from pickup basketball. As he put the bag down, Lange closed on him with three unhurried steps, near enough to smell his sweat. Lange came down hard on the last footfall. Parker turned, dropped the food, and threw a fist. Lange seized his wrist in his hand and felt the bones bend under his grip as he sprayed him in the eyes and nose and mouth with an aerosol paralytic. Parker tried for another blow, but he was already growing weak; Lange held on to his wrist, caught him as he fell, pulled him close, and eased him to the floor.

Parker's eyes were open, desperate and full of hate, while the drug spread through his body, leaving him unable to move. Over him stood the man he might have seen sitting at the counter at the diner, flipping through the pages on the tabletop jukebox. Nothing about Lange stood out. He was invisible, your next-door neighbor.

Lange made quick work of the staging, pulling Parker's wallet, trashing the bathroom, scattering pill bottles, and dragging out the drawers of the desk and nightstand in the office. All the signs would speak to a rushed home invasion. He came back and drew his gun, a cheap Taurus purchased from an online listing, a private-party sale in Annandale with no records required. He returned to the living room and stood over Parker, the tendons in his neck straining weakly as he tried to speak.

Lange crouched over him. "It was nothing you did wrong," he said. "You were so close." Parker's eyes went to the side, where a dozen framed photos of him and his boys hung on the wall, the living room's only artwork.

Lange hauled the man up by his collar and propped him against the sofa so the last thing he saw would be those photos.

He fired four times, the fatal shot to the head first, a mercy, and then three strays to give the impression of a rushed amateur. After a few minutes, he set in on Parker, delivering hard blows to the face of the dead man. A burglary. A struggle. A panicked shooting.

The story had sold. The Agency liked to keep its secrets, even in death. He'd expected some kind of repercussions, but the CIA seemed content to let the killing go, with far less scrutiny than Lange had anticipated. He found it strange later, given how much this country liked to parade its fighters as heroes at every football game and in every car commercial and how accustomed he was to Russian culture, where there was no greater hero, or martyr, than the spy. But the Americans didn't seem ready to accept that the enemy could find them in their homes, or maybe they weren't willing to take up the fight, to see it for what it was: the first shot in a war.

Lange got up from his bench and walked across the garage. He jumped up and gripped an overhead beam, his fingers wrapping over the top, and lifted himself slowly. His chest came up to his hands, and he kept going, pushing himself above the beam until it came to his waist, then lowering himself down for another round.

Focus. Discipline. Strength. They kept him alive in this world. The pressure was building, and the exercise brought him calm, centered him. Sam Hudson was getting closer. But he could handle him, just as he'd handled Parker and Hassan. Or, better, put him to good use. Lange had DEMETER. He was already inside.

22

A PEN SPUN across Emily's fingers like an airplane propeller, rolling from one knuckle to the next, whipping around her thumb and back.

Russia House was almost empty at ten p.m. The sun had gone down outside its windowless walls.

Emily loved these moments when time ceased to exist, when everything disappeared but the job, as she put herself at the center of dozens of streams of information coming into the Agency about the Lincoln bombing, tasking case officers and NOCs around the world with questions to put to their sources.

She tapped out a message on her computer to an officer in Kiev. She'd worked the other side, her only connection to the CIA a modified laptop that seemed completely unremarkable, but if you held down the right combination of buttons, it would pop up an encrypted-messaging program that allowed you to send covert communications back to HQs.

One thing troubled her focus, though. Sam Hudson's words about DEMETER stayed with her. A leak. Parker and Hassan. Ever since he had raised those suspicions, she felt like she was being watched, like a spy. Her head turned left, then right. No eyes on her. She went back to a set of FBI files and began to skim, losing herself in the work.

Movement to her left. The pen clattered to the desk. A smiling man in his early thirties stood outside her office door holding two hot dogs in his left hand and a stack of papers in his right.

"Matt, come in," she said.

Matt Wilkinson was a classic national security Mormon, an FBI agent detailed to Russia House, gorgeous in an oddly sexless way, like a Ken doll, and so good-natured and straightforward that Emily could barely manage a conversation with the man without worrying that she had said something to scandalize him. The Latter-Day Saints could all sail through background checks, had incredible language skills because of their missions—Matt had done his in Siberia—and were vastly overrepresented in the upper-security clearances. They were known as the Mormon Mafia.

He held the hot dogs out to her. They'd come from an automated vending machine in the basement, just another oddity of this strange bubble where they spent most of their waking moments. "You want one?" he said with a laugh.

She stood and raised her shoulders. "Sure."

"Seriously? I thought you were going to give me the 'Do you know where those come from?' veggie speech."

Emily ate a lot of salads, grains, and homegrown vegetables she brought in Tupperware, but hunger had her stomach clenched like a fist.

"I barely ate today. I'm not above a vending-machine dog."

He handed it over with a smile.

"Thanks, Matt."

"I had a feeling."

She glanced down at the pen she'd been spinning. That was one of her tells for stress. There were advantages and dangers to working with a hyper-observant crew of mind readers.

"I heard back on the explosives," he said and ate half his hot dog in three bites. He was well over six feet, a former center for UCLA.

She held her hand out, and he gave her the file. It was from TEDAC, the FBI's bomb-identification lab, which kept a library of thousands of devices. They'd matched the explosives used at the Lincoln bombing. Emily looked over the results.

"This doesn't make any sense," she said and glanced up to see Greg Jones walking toward them.

He stopped outside her door. "What's up?"

"We have the explosive trace from the Lincoln bombing," Matt said.

"And?"

"It doesn't add up," Emily said. "They used untagged Semtex. The original Czech manufacture. The nearest matches for the bomb were from decades ago—the Popular Front for the Liberation of Palestine, the National Liberation Army of Colombia."

"So it's homage?" Jones asked. "A greatest-hits album? What?"

"They're all proxies of the Soviet Union."

"Soviet? Russia doesn't use Semtex anymore."

"No. And all of it produced since 1990, after Lockerbie, had chemical taggants added so it can be traced. Those explosives are at least thirty years old."

"The USSR?" Matt said. "You're saying we were hit by a country that doesn't exist anymore?"

"Someone could have gotten into one of the old stockpiles," Emily said.

"Give me a write-up on this I can get to the Bureau and a distro in-house," Jones said. "Track down any thefts. Anyone selling this. You know the drill. I have to head out."

"On it," she said as Jones walked off and Matt followed him.

She started in on her write-up as she ate. Jones headed out the main door of the Russia House suite about fifteen minutes later.

Sam Hudson was already arguing that the Lincoln bombing was Russia-linked, and now there was proof. As soon as she sent her report, she went back to the list of leads Sam had given her: Christopher Dimos, a Russian playboy named Markov—an oligarch's son who kept a house in Virginia—and a few other possibilities. She had put alerts in the database for news on all of them, and now she saw that she had a hit on Dimos.

It was a report from the Park Police that had been passed on by the FBI. Christopher Dimos had been shot dead on Hains Point, and another man had been found in the river with his neck cut. She read over the dry cop talk and felt her throat tighten. "Jesus," she whispered as she went through the details. The Mercedes crashed and was lit up with small-arms fire. It had been a full-on barrage. No suspects identified.

DEMETER. Sam was already onto it, talking about a leak. She had seen the cryptonym once before. It referred, not to a person, but an operation, its details hidden away in a compartmented file, open only to a select few. She knew the contours but not the specifics. Russia House was developing a human source with high-level access inside the Russian government, possibly even within the Kremlin. In reports she had worked on, she saw DEMETER referenced as a source of intelligence on Russian operations abroad. Sam had connected it to the deaths of Parker and Hassan. Emily knew nothing for sure, but they could easily have been involved with the DEMETER activities. They had years of experience recruiting hard targets in Russia's sphere.

Her hands felt clammy, and she ran them down the legs of her pants.

"Heading out," Matt called from near the cubicles outside her office. She looked up at him as if startled out of sleep. "I'll pull anything I can from the Bureau on sources of that explosive."

"Great," she said and forced a smile. "Thanks."

She went back to her work until she heard him leave the suite, then she stood and went to her doorway. Russia House was empty.

DEMETER. That name appeared in a half a dozen documents she'd seen over the past year as a source of information with no further explanation. There was a danger in even searching for it, drawing attention to it, linking it to herself, but she had to know.

She went back to her computer, brought up the local network, and went to the work-group files that had referenced DEMETER.

She searched for it. There were no results. She pulled up a planning document on counterintelligence that she knew had used DEMETER as a source and scrolled through. The reference was gone. She searched the document. Nothing. She pulled up another write-up, then another. All the references to DEMETER had been deleted. An appendix that would at least list it as a source had been removed entirely. Every trace of it had disappeared.

Emily sat back and laid her palms on the cherry veneer of her desk. The screen was a haze; her eyes were unfocused. Her face felt hot, and she took a deep, slow breath.

Someone had gotten to it first.

23

A SWITCH HAD been flipped. She was operational here at her own desk, in the heart of the Agency. She looked at the photo of her father standing next to the mast of his 1951 John Alden cutter, then pushed back her chair and got up. Through the open door, she scanned the suite once more. The lights were out in all of the workspaces.

Emily logged out of her machine and left, locking her door behind her. She walked the length of the office past all the cubicles to confirm that no one else was here.

She took the elevator down to the lobby and offered a polite nod to the guard stationed by the man-traps near the front doors, making sure she wasn't moving too quickly, wasn't betraying any signs of alarm. She had to be careful here. One wrong step and her career, her life, was over. This wasn't the kind of decision you make after eight hours behind a desk in an office like a submarine.

The scraping of crickets filled the night. Looking out over the wooded hills that surrounded headquarters, she felt like she could breathe again.

The auditorium rose to her right as she walked by the CIA Memorial Garden, with its cherry trees and footbridges over a peaceful stream.

She wanted a moment to reflect, sure, but also the high ground.

She scanned the senior intelligence service parking lot. Jones's Volvo wagon was gone. The few cars left belonged to the ops folks working in the hastily assembled buildings between the old and new headquarters put up after 9/11.

She cursed Sam Hudson under her breath. It would have been better if he had just been cracking up, with all this talk about leaks and murder plots, but now she had seen it herself—someone had wiped out any mention of that program. Sam seemed to suspect her when they'd last met, which had infuriated her at the time. She was no traitor and had nothing to do with the deaths of Parker and Hassan. At least he had shown her what to look for: DEMETER. Someone inside had scrubbed it. If Sam didn't trust her, that meant no one could be trusted.

Now she was roped into his damn crusade. These penetration cases often brought down the careers of whoever got near them, even innocent bystanders. Three officers were already dead: Finlay, Hassan, and Parker. Parker had been like family, and she'd been even closer to Fin. She would find whoever was responsible.

There was a way. She thought it through, calculating the risk. Not totally reckless. She would have decent cover if she was caught. She turned back to take in the old headquarters building. Inside was a statue of Wild Bill Donovan, the founder of the Office of Strategic Services, the maverick precursor to the CIA. The Agency had built itself up through power plays and by concealing its true motives from its political masters when it wasn't outright blackmailing them. It was the one part of the U.S. government dedicated to breaking the laws of other countries. A deep breath, and she started walking. Forget the rules; she was CIA.

Three minutes later she was striding back through the marble foyer and casting an approving glance at Wild Bill as she made for Russia House.

She swiped her key card at the door and punched in the combination to unlock it. The whole office was a sensitive compartmented information facility—a SCIF—essentially a large vault that was soundproof and impossible to bug.

After turning on the lights, she started walking across the suite, looking to the far corner, where the networking equipment sat in a closet. The good news about the hard perimeter of the office was that, once she was inside, she was implicitly trusted.

CIA's computer network was a lot of twenty-first-century patches on top of a 1970s mainframe-era information system. From her desk she couldn't see who had tampered with the files. She didn't have access to DEMETER and there was no way to guess or hack passwords, and in any case, attempting to do so could get her fired or indicted or both.

But if she hooked up to the servers directly through a physical USB connection she could see the logs that should have recorded any deletions or alterations to the files. She couldn't see inside DEMETER, but she might be able to see who had messed with it.

She picked up her laptop from her desk in her office, slipped a USB cord from the top drawer into her pocket, and headed to the closet.

Cover for action was second nature. If you meet with a source undercover as a real estate agent, you better have some glossy listings on the table in case anyone busts in. Emily's cover was simple enough: the local network was acting up and she was going in to check the status on the router before she called it in to IT. The network was buggy enough that it was plausible. Although it would still be a nightmare if she was caught rooting around in the files, looking for dirt on a program to which she had no access.

She regulated her breathing, trying to slow down her heart rate.

When she reached the closet, she pulled the door open and stepped in, no hesitation. She shut the door behind her. The air was hot and close among the server racks. The only light came from their indicators, pulsing green glows.

She plugged in the USB cable, opened a terminal on her computer's screen, and navigated to the logs on the server, which were generated by a program called ArcSight. One of the joys of moving into middle management was that she had been tapped to do a turn on the audit committee that every department was required to have after the Edward Snowden catastrophe and subsequent leaks. One of the ten commandments of cybersecurity had stayed with her: if someone gets physical access to your hardware, it's no longer yours.

First, she checked the appendix file mentioning DEMETER that had been deleted. The username for the person who'd done it was five letters: *Local*. Normal CIA computer IDs were always a first and last name. She guessed those letters might have been picked because they blended in easily with the text *local* that showed up often in Unix paths, making it easy for people to miss it when skimming through the code.

She did a lookup and saw that user Local had existed for only two hours, from 1:30 a.m. to 3:30 a.m., six weeks ago. There was no trace of him or her otherwise. The only person who might be able to do that was someone with system administrator rights, and it would be nearly impossible to audit because that was the highest level of control. An admin could easily cover his tracks. That was how Snowden managed to rob the NSA of its secrets.

She searched through the logs for any file named DEMETER. Text flashed next to her cursor, the line changing rapidly, too fast to read clearly. The search yielded a list of disk images—snapshots of the system at a certain time. The last one was six weeks ago, that same early morning. She clicked on one, but the underlying file had been deleted too.

She searched again. Again text streamed past. She managed to make out a few commands in the code as it flashed by and a set of numbers—the IP address of this machine. It was being logged.

Her search was triggering a routine. Someone had set it up to report back when anyone did a scan for DEMETER. He or she was watching her now.

Her hand lifted to the cover of the laptop to close it. But she was already here, and if she had been detected, the damage was done. She ran another search on Local and listed every file he or she had changed. There were a few dozen, many she recognized as having been sourced to DEMETER, but then her breath caught and stopped scrolling. The first two files that Local had deleted belonged to Parker and Hassan.

She copied the text to a file and saved it on her laptop's hard drive, then killed the terminal and pulled out the USB.

She felt the sweat on the back of her neck. Holding the computer in her left hand, she put her right on the door handle, then hesitated. She had no idea what was on the other side. Security Protective Service, CIA's police force? The mole that had given up Parker's and Hassan's identities, ready to come for her?

Whatever it was, the last place she wanted to be was trapped in a dark room with one exit between two racks of classified servers she'd just breached.

She opened the door, believing her cover story as the full truth, the only way to do it.

The room was empty.

She relaxed her shoulders, breathed, and made for her office. She passed the cubicles and a pillar with a framed 1989 photo of Gorbachev raising his hands in amazement at the frozen-food section of a Texas grocery store. As she went around a row of file cabinets, marked with a red flag to show they'd been locked, she saw a slant of light coming from an open office door.

Jones was back.

She kept going, forcing her eyes to stay straight ahead, however much she wanted to check to see if he was waiting, watching her. It hardly mattered. He knew now she was the only one at the office.

She left her door open about a foot when she returned to her desk. She started looking over the files that had been changed while her mystery user was on the network, but her attention kept going back to the room outside and that splash of light. Had he come back because he'd received an alert about her searches? He couldn't have gotten here that quickly. Her fingers paused on the keys. But he could have made it back if her first queries about DEMETER, from her desk, had triggered some kind of alert.

The light shifted, and she heard footsteps across the thin gray carpet. She continued working, switching over to possible sources for the Lincoln explosives, but she had to force herself to keep going on as if she weren't trapped here alone at night with a potential traitor who knew she was digging into his secrets.

The steps grew quieter, and she heard the familiar working of a combo dial and the sound of a file drawer opening. He was just going about his work, as was she.

Nonalerting, they called it in the trade. It was the reason why spy movies always made her roll her eyes. Even if they're tailing you, you don't run. That would give away that you know and who you are. You would be burned, years of work wasted. The greater the risk, the more you act like nothing is happening. She knew it. Jones did too. He'd taught it to her.

A shadow crossed her open door. Jones stopped just outside, then stepped back, peering in as if noticing her for the first time. The door creaked all the way open.

"They loved the write-up," he said. "Thank you."

"Great. Let me know if you hear anything else on the bomb attribution. I thought you were done for the night."

"So did I," he said with a little laugh. "But I need to get some of this over to the director of national intelligence staff to get into the president's brief." He tilted his head to the side slightly. "The bad guys will be there tomorrow, Emily," he said. "You should get some rest."

She gave him a weary smile, thinking, *Not a fucking chance,* as she said, "Thanks, I will."

24

SAM LOCKED HIS Jeep, pulled the brim of his Nats cap low over his eyes, and started walking down Washington Boulevard.

The Peet's Coffee was ahead on the right, closed now, in a two-story brick building with a gleaming tower rising behind it.

He'd circled it twice in his car, looking for surveillance, finding none. But there was always a risk when you rolled up on part of an adversary's network.

This was Clarendon, an Arlington neighborhood that consisted of a hodgepodge of expensive condo towers stacked next to 1960s Colonials, all developed without rhyme or reason. Halfway between the Pentagon and the Agency, Arlington played host to dozens of anonymous intelligence offices and safe houses, and Sam knew it well. NOCs usually operated out of front offices to obscure their connection to HQs. They settled in among the thousands of consultants and contractors who plied their trade outside the capital.

Clarendon, like a lot of these neighborhoods, had always seemed to him more of a convenience than a real place, a bed along the Metro. It was known for a string of sports bars and hard-partying former frat brothers. In his cap and flannel, Sam wouldn't draw much attention.

He walked into a 7-Eleven that he'd already flagged as having a good view of his target. Standing next to the shelves full of cold pills and single rolls of toilet paper, he examined the coffee shop. He ID'd two cameras inside the Peet's. It had large picture windows and tight tables, a bad choice for a face-to-face meeting between two agents. That suggested a brush pass of some kind. The classic moves of trading identical bags or simply dropping a memory card in a pocket were still very much in use by the Russian services, though they had been tending toward more high-tech approaches recently.

For cover, Sam needed to justify a trip into the 7-Eleven and a slow walk outside, so he went to the front and looked at the cigarettes on display behind the clerk. He stepped up to the counter, with its single bananas and the heated rack of pizzas and chicken wings, and asked for a pack of Marlboro Reds and a lighter. He paid in cash and stepped out.

Waiting for the light to change so he could cross, he lit up and took a drag. The heat in his lungs instantly brought him back to Afghanistan, kneeling behind a mud wall in that superfine white dust as he and his squad ripped Marlboro Reds to keep from dropping dead asleep in the twenty-eighth hour of combat.

That day he ended up tracking the insurgent leader he'd spent six months hunting into a half-collapsed tunnel complex and shooting him in the heart before a grenade took down the ceiling. Sam's squad mates had had to pull him from the rubble.

The major spent a few weeks deciding whether to write Sam up for an award or demote him for going in on his own, but there had never been a question in Sam's mind about what to do. That insurgent had been killing his guys. Williams had been working with the intelligence arm of the task force, and he made Sam an offer to come over to CIA. The army wasn't big on independent thinking, but Williams was. Sam didn't want to be someone else's gun for his whole career, and Williams showed him the way. He'd never be able to repay him for that.

His heart beat a little faster. Another war. Another time. So different from the hidden violence circling him now on these familiar streets.

He crossed and walked past the Peet's. The Russians usually preferred to meet in parks and woods. When they came inside to a site like this, Sam suspected the meeting would be all nonpersonal communication, as it was known. The most likely means would be via computer. Someone would set up with a laptop inside, and someone else nearby would have another machine. They would create a private Wi-Fi network between them. Because the data didn't travel over the regular internet, the NSA couldn't get to it.

Sam took a phone out and glanced at it as he walked close to the Peet's windows, just checking texts or Instagram by his appearance, but he actually was pulling up a suite of security tools that would let him hack into the store's wireless networks and access its cameras. He needed eyes on the street in all directions and inside the shop. He didn't have a countersurveillance team, but once he got access to those video feeds, he would have all the coverage he needed. Dimos's home Wi-Fi setup had been locked down with strong encryption, but these were typical consumer-grade networks. Getting inside the coffee shop's system took less than a minute, giving him credentials that would let him view the video feeds later from anywhere with an internet connection.

He kept going toward the office building that looked down on the main entrance to Peet's, noted the security camera near its doors, and cracked its network. He crossed the street, moving toward a dry cleaner's and a gastropub that had once been a sticky-floored sports bar where he vaguely remembered meeting up with some Ranger buddies when he was in his twenties. He'd noted they both had cameras on his drive-by casing, and he pulled wireless credentials for them too.

The work was done before he finished the cigarette. Sam walked quickly back to his car. A meeting site like this usually wouldn't be under continuous surveillance, but there was a chance that he wasn't the only one watching.

25

LANGE STEPPED OVER the fallen branches and paused at the edge of the woods. "Here?" the man beside him asked.

Lange nodded. He was on a high hill on the Virginia side of the Potomac, just across the river from the District. To his right lay Arlington National Cemetery, with its endless rows of American dead.

He carried a nylon map in his hand and tilted it to catch the moonlight. Two birds fluttered overhead and flew off.

The other man raised his gun and did a slow survey of the trees around him. After a minute, satisfied that no one had startled the birds, he looked in the direction they'd flown.

"Whippoorwills," he said quietly and stretched his neck left and right.

This was Lange's deputy, and while operating in the United States he went by the work name Richard Cole. He was a Black Earth farm boy from Kursk, raised with the simple but necessary brutality of the land. A trained illegal, he could speak fluent unaccented English and blend in well, feats of such subtlety they always surprised Lange coming from a man like Cole.

He usually didn't say much in any language, and his habit of constant movement, the twisting of his neck, the cracking of his knuckles, was an annoyance that Lange gladly put up with in exchange for Cole's talents with a blade. He was a veteran of the Chechen wars, and like so many soldiers of that fight, there was a certain blankness to his eyes. He was able to perform any act of violence with utter calm.

"Keep watch," Lange said, and Cole took off to the south, moving silently despite his size.

Lange went forward slowly, his eyes adjusting to the dark. Ahead was the river, and beyond it, peeking out above the trees on the District side, were the icons of Washington: the White House, the Lincoln Memorial, the Washington Monument, and the dome of the Capitol.

He lifted the map again. He was at the center of a grove of trees set in the parkland that surrounded the Marine Corps Memorial, a statue of three Marines and a navy corpsman raising the flag on Iwo Jima.

Just down the hill rose a steel tower fitted with fifty bells. The carillon was a gift from the Netherlands to the United States for its efforts in the Second World War.

This country had built its whole myth of the twentieth century around winning that war and defeating evil, but it had played only a small part. Eight and a half million Russian soldiers died in that fight, almost twenty times the number of Americans lost. Seven and a half million civilians perished, resisting from house to house, starving to death in the brutal winters while under siege by Hitler's forces. Russian blood had saved the world from domination, from endless war. The enemy was different now, but the fight hadn't changed.

He took sight lines on the carillon and the memorial, then walked three meters southeast, moving easily through the shadows, a nocturnal animal. He stopped, took a few steps back, then felt it underfoot.

A stone, a block of light granite with a crack running through it, lay half buried in the earth, the roots of a birch tree twining along one edge.

This was his reference point. He crouched and ran his fingers over the rough stone. Thirty-seven years ago, the authors of HYACINTH had stood in this exact spot, undercover in the enemy's heart, as he was.

He raised his map and rotated it until it was oriented, lined up with what lay before him in real life. Then he reached into the pocket of his work jacket and took out a second sheet of nylon. It was transparent except for a jagged line marked with text notations.

He laid it over his map and turned it, matching up landmarks. He slid it a centimeter forward, then held it still.

He traced its route, then looked up over the tops of the trees and followed the same path with his eyes among the lights of the capital.

The bombs he had built were only a small part of this plot, and its crux lay at the end of that path.

HYACINTH. He could finally see its target. A sense of lightness filled him.

There would be pain, so much pain, when the moment arrived. The Lincoln attack was only the opening bid. It was one of the strange truths of his profession: the greatest commitment, the greatest capacity for violence, came from love. There was no other word for it.

The Americans would call him a murderer, but everything he did, he did to protect. Lange had known loss so profound, he'd have preferred death, though that wasn't saying much for an old soldier who'd long been prepared to die. It justified any retribution. The war had already begun. The Americans had set it off.

It had been difficult, on Hains Point, to control himself, to not risk everything to take down Sam Hudson. But there would be time, step by step. Hudson would know loss. He would know how it felt to be an enemy within, to be hunted by both the adversary and his own people, as Lange was.

A figure approached. "All clear" came Cole's voice. He walked to Lange's side and looked down at the stone. "This is it?"

"Yes. We have all we need."

The other man nodded his head solemnly, then listened as Lange gave him instructions on what was to come. They had to be meticulous. It had been decades. Cities change. The earth moves. Buildings rise and fall. There were two days left, and they had only one shot.

26

SAM PARKED AROUND the corner and walked toward his house. As he reached his street, he took the block in from the corner of his eye, not giving away that he had noticed movement behind him.

He pocketed his keys to free his hands and watched the light from the streetlamp for shadows following as he moved along the brick sidewalk.

Footfalls now, coming up fast. A shadow stretched toward him. This wasn't a follow. Any decent watcher would do a better job covering his tracks. It was an approach.

Sam turned, pivoting his gun side back as his right hand drew near his weapon. A woman walked straight toward him, then stopped, her eyes narrowing as they focused on his hip.

It was Emily. She held her hands out to the sides, no threat.

"Jesus, Sam," she said, eyes fixed on the outline of his gun. "It's me."

"What are you doing here, Emily?"

She brought her fingers to her temple. "A massive mistake, probably." A glance up and down the street. "Can we go inside?" She looked shaken up.

"Sure. Come on."

He led her in, and when he flipped on the lights, he could see that her face was pale and heavy with fatigue or fear. That worked against the wariness he'd felt outside, but he wasn't letting his guard down.

"Are you all right?" he asked. "What's going on?"

A dark laugh. "Do you have anything to drink?"

She sounded like someone who was ready to talk. Sam walked to the living room, and she eyed the bottles. "Besides old-man liquor?" she asked.

Sam looked into the kitchen, where a bottle of wine sat on top of the fridge. She pulled it down and ran her thumb over the glass, streaking through a fine layer of dust. She found the corkscrew in the utensil drawer, slammed the drawer shut with her hip, and had the cork out a few seconds later with a low pop. She took out two drinking glasses and poured them each a few inches of red.

Sam had his questions. He had his doubts. But he had dealt with enough sources to know that when they were in confession mode, you just sat, raised your glass, and listened. The sorting of fact from fiction came later.

"You asked me this afternoon what I knew about the Geneva meeting."

"Yes."

"Do you think someone gave it up? That there's a leak?"

"What happened tonight, Emily?"

"You thought I betrayed Fin?"

"If you knew in advance about the meeting, I had to consider it."

"So you think there's a threat inside Russia House?"

"What did you find?"

She drank the wine, then grimaced. "How old is this?"

"I have no idea. I haven't been doing a lot of entertaining."

She put it on the counter, looked at the bottles in the living room, and nodded at him. Sam fixed two short pours of bourbon with some ice from the freezer for hers. She clinked his glass, took a sip, then put her hand to her chest and exhaled.

Sam took a drink. "It grows on you."

"Do you have any information on who it might be? Besides me?"

"No."

"Why were you asking about DEMETER?"

There it was, Sam thought. Her chain of questions seemed to confirm that the DEMETER file existed and that it pointed to a mole.

"Where did you hear about it?" she went on.

"You understand why I can't tell you that."

"You don't trust me."

"I don't talk about my sources and I don't trust anyone. Neither should you."

She took another sip.

"You came to me," he said. "Just tell me what's going on and we can take it from there."

"The DEMETER file is gone, along with any reference to it. Like it never existed."

"Someone deleted it."

A nod.

"Who is it, Emily?" he asked. He was still suspicious. There was a chance that this was all misdirection, that she was trying to pin the blame on someone else when she was suspect, but if so, it was a hell of a performance.

"Greg Jones."

Sam hid any reaction and finished his drink. He had to suspect Jones, as he suspected everyone, but it still shook him. Jones did make some sense as a possible penetration agent. He'd had lots of contact with Russians over the years, though Sam couldn't imagine a motive. Everything about Emily's affect seemed genuine. He wanted to believe her, but he had to be careful with that instinct. He was too close to her.

"What was DEMETER?" he asked.

She looked down at her glass, then back up. "You don't know?"

"Give me your version," he said. He wasn't going to reveal that he was in the dark on it.

"I wasn't read in on it. I can't give it to you."

"You know enough. I saw how you reacted this afternoon. If you're not read in, there's nothing to withhold. So why don't you color it in for me?"

"It was an operation to develop a highly placed source in the Russian Federation. I don't know who was developing him or if it's even a him. I just know it was promising and very closely held. I heard the crypt only once or twice and then it seemed like they tightened up access."

"Who did you hear it from?"

"Jones. Some of the intelligence from DEMETER informed work I was doing. It was cleaned of any information on who the source was. And when I went to check it tonight, all of it had been deleted."

"You're sure that's not normal housekeeping?"

"No. No one would go back and purge like that unless they were hiding something. And an anonymous user account was created to do all of it, then the account was scrubbed."

She shouldn't have access to that kind of information about a program she wasn't part of. Sam hadn't figured her for a rule-breaker, but that was only one of a dozen questions he had about the Emily he thought he knew.

"How did you get access to all this?" he asked.

"I'd rather not say."

"Who else knows?"

"I've told no one, but . . . Jones may be aware of my suspicions."

"How?"

"When I was searching for DEMETER, I noticed a routine in the system that was logging everything I did, watching me. Jones had already left for the night, but by the time I finished, he was back."

"To see who was looking into DEMETER?"

"That's my conclusion."

"And he clocked you?"

"Yes. I was the only one there."

"Reaction?"

"None, but that's to be expected. He's a pro."

"What else, Emily?"

"That's not enough?"

"For you to come here like this? No. Is there more?"

"What did your source tell you about the leak, Sam?"

"What do you want to know?"

"Hassan and Parker. Did it have to do with their deaths?"

"Yes," he said.

She looked around the table—for a coaster, Sam guessed—then put her glass down on a place mat and crossed her arms as if she were cold. "Whoever deleted DEMETER also scrubbed something from Hassan's and Parker's files."

"Were they part of the DEMETER operation?"

"I can't be certain, but it's their area."

Sam felt the urge to move and started pacing. "Let's say Jones is leaking to Russian intel. He can explain those contacts by claiming that he is recruiting someone from their side—"

"The best way to cover making a deal with the Russians is by making a deal with the fucking Russians," she said. "The DEMETER op. But instead of collecting intel, he's giving it up."

"Parker and Hassan found out and he had them killed?"

"Or the Russians just took them down once he leaked their true identities."

"I can't see it, Emily. That doesn't mean it isn't there, but what's his motive? Career's great. Family's great. I don't think he's ever needed money."

"You never know. Could be ego. Was he working alone?"

"You want to know who you can trust over there?"

She nodded.

"No one."

"Your source told you that?"

"Yes. 'There are wars between nations and wars within each.'"

"That's pretty cryptic. Makes it sound like there's a whole faction inside we need to be afraid of."

"And factions on the Russia side. Alex Clarke claimed he wanted peace."

"So you think the people who killed him wanted war?"

"The bombing was a good start. Go after a national icon."

"How do you know you can trust your source?"

"I know." It came out harder than he'd intended. He knew because Dimos had died to get him that information.

"All right," she said, then waited.

"All right what?"

"I gave you everything I have, Sam. So help me figure out what is happening here."

"Emily."

"You still don't trust me."

"Would you?"

"He could be coming for me, Sam."

"I won't let that happen. But I can't give up my source or what he told me. Not yet."

"Fine. What do you expect me to do in the meantime?"

"Keep your eye on Jones. And if we are going to stop this, I need access."

"Inside the Agency? Through me?"

"I'm cut off. But if I could get back into the Russia House files, we'd be miles ahead on this thing."

"You think I'm going to give up info to the man who's been doing God knows what with off-book Russian sources?"

"No. You'll need time. And so will I."

"To do what?"

"See for myself."

She rapped her knuckles softly on the table. "I should go."

"Are you in danger?"

"I'm fine."

"I can look out—"

"I'm fine."

He nodded. "Take some time. Think about it. If you want to help me with this, you should know you're risking the job, maybe more."

"There's *no one* inside I can trust?"

"For now, no."

She let out a long breath, then walked to the door.

"Thank you, Emily, for coming to me. Are you sure—"

"I'm sure," she said. She opened the door and stepped out. Sam walked with her to her car and stood as she pulled out. Once her taillights had disappeared around the corner, he crossed the street and doubled back to his Jeep.

He started it up, rolled his shoulders back, and glanced at the clock. She was part of this or she needed protection from it. Either way, tonight he was on watch.

27

THE GRAY LIGHT of predawn filtered through the windows of Jones's home office. He sat at his desk, the blotter clear, four generations staring back at him from silver-framed photos.

He had deleted the DEMETER files from the world, but he couldn't push the images out of his mind: Jeff Parker slumped against a sofa, eyes open, black blood caking his skin; Sarah Hassan lying dead on the white-tiled bathroom floor of an apartment off Independence Square in Minsk.

Jones shut his eyes tight and clasped his hands, fighting back the nausea. He turned away from the desk and went to the closet, where he pushed aside some formal wear still in its dry-cleaning bags and opened the safe.

A sound came through the window, an engine starting. He stepped over to check and saw his wife's Mercedes SUV backing out of the driveway; she was on her way to the six a.m. class at Orange Theory. He went back to the safe. From the bottom shelf he slid out a Beretta pistol with a cable lock running through the ejection port. CIA folks all used Glocks now, but Jones had come up in an earlier time and was accustomed to the double-action dinosaur. He took out the accessories case and brought it all back to his desk.

It had taken him twenty-five minutes this morning to find the keys. He fished them from his pocket, undid the cable lock, and loaded the magazine with fifteen rounds. His fingers shook at the beginning but over time grew steadier.

He inserted the magazine, then racked the slide back and let it snap forward, chambering a round, the stainless-steel cold under his fingers.

His hands now seemed to work on their own. It never failed to astonish him how it all came back, the automatic motions drilled in under years of stress.

He didn't like sitting here alone with the gun. He put it in a holster on his belt, covered it with a light Patagonia running jacket, and headed for his Volvo.

The sun still hadn't risen, though the clouds to the east were brightening as he drove the winding roads of McLean. This little stretch of Northern Virginia around headquarters was a small town, really, especially for Agency people. There were some cul-de-sacs where every single house was CIA. The owners would pass them down to younger officers by word of mouth, have their own little secret suburb with backyard barbecues where you didn't have to pretend you worked for State or Commerce.

He passed the mouth of Emily's street and kept going, onto a park road where he could stop without being seen and still have a good vantage of her house and driveway.

This was not his first trip past Emily's home. He'd come last night after he left work, and her car had been gone. It was back now. The bedroom light was on, the shades down.

Late night, Emily? he thought and saw her shadow moving. The light came on in the bathroom.

He tapped the button for the air conditioner and wiped the sweat off his palms as he considered what he needed to do.

The holstered gun dug into his ribs. He ran his hand back and forth across the steering wheel, then gripped it hard and looked down at the cell phone on the console.

He had prayed this moment would never come. It was time to make the call.

28

EMILY WALKED THROUGH Russia House, her eyes on Jones's office. It was empty. He hadn't come in yet this morning. That wasn't unusual. He spent half his time in meetings around the campus and in other parts of the intelligence community. But after last night, everything seemed like an omen.

She reached the door to the hallway outside, stepped out, then saw him. Jones was a hundred feet down to her right, talking to two people, one she recognized from the office of policy.

She turned to the left and walked away quickly, although not quickly enough to attract suspicion, making for the intersection with another corridor ahead. She powered up her phone, and a moment later it vibrated in her pocket as it picked up the cellular networks. She kept it turned off inside the Russia House SCIF, where it wouldn't have a signal anyway. Mobile phones only worked in some public areas and outside.

The Agency actually jammed signals near the entrances to the campus to avoid them being used for eavesdropping or even detonating explosives. Commuters had long ago learned not to be on the phone while cruising by the entrance on Route 123.

She made it around the corner and took out her phone. A text was waiting: "How'd you like the red wine?"

It was Sam. She turned again and exited into the courtyard, the sun warming her skin.

"I don't have time for this," she wrote back and took a seat on a bench under a poplar tree.

"Make some" came his reply. "Important. I can meet you where you like to go running. I only need 10 mins."

She put the phone down. There was a local park just down the highway from the CIA entrance. Emily would drive out and run its fields whenever the HQs claustrophobia got too bad.

"Okay. When?" she typed.

"Now," he wrote back.

She stood up and started walking.

Sam saw Emily park in the lot near the basketball courts, and he moved toward her along the trees that edged the soccer fields.

She met him, and they kept going, heading for the fields in the back of the park.

"What is it?" she asked.

"I shouldn't have doubted you," he said and held his phone out. The screen showed a photo of Greg Jones's Volvo parked on a tree-lined street looking down on Emily's house.

She studied it and walked a little faster, hands stuffed in her pockets, doing a decent job of hiding the fact that it had shaken her. "When was this?"

"Five forty this morning."

"How long?"

"About ten minutes."

"Were you watching him or tailing me?"

"Him," he said, but he wasn't sure if she believed it.

Sam had wondered if Jones was watching Emily because he suspected her of being the mole, but that didn't add up. If Jones had had real suspicions, he would have passed them on to counterintelligence. A group chief doesn't run around in the dark watching subordinates on his own for any legitimate reason.

"Did he do anything else?"

"A phone call from the car on his way out of your neighborhood."

"And then?"

"He headed back toward his house, some twists and turns. I pulled back before he could make me."

"You believe me, so now, how about some answers? What happened to Christopher Dimos?"

Sam played it off. "What about him?"

"He died last night, Sam. Right after you told me to check him out."

"How?" Sam said.

She watched him for a long moment as they walked through the grass.

"No," she said. "You knew, Sam. Start making sense or I'm out."

Sam thought it through. Dimos was already gone. He couldn't protect him anymore. And Emily had put herself at risk to get to the bottom of DEMETER.

"Was he your source?" she asked. "On the leak?" She'd always been good.

"Yes. He was working with Alex Clarke. How'd you put it together?"

"Last night. When I asked if you could trust your source. You responded so emphatically. He'd just been killed. I could see it was raw."

"He risked that to get me this info."

"So what do you have?"

"He said an attack was coming. Something major. It's Konstantin."

He could see it almost pained her to hear it, but she nodded slowly.

"What did you give him, Sam?"

"What?"

"Come on. You didn't get something for nothing." She was still suspicious of him, and he couldn't be angry. She was right to be.

"A sketch of the man who killed Alex Clarke and probably Finlay. I wanted his help in finding him and the rest of Konstantin's network."

That seemed to satisfy her. "We have a match on the explosive from the Lincoln bombing. It's untagged Semtex, and the closest matches for the detonators were the PFLP and Colombia's National Liberation Army."

"Soviet proxies. Soviet tactics," Sam said. "That follows. It could actually be Soviet gear."

"It was old enough to be."

"Cached. Williams used to talk about the possibility of Konstantin activating one of these plots. It was real doomsday shit, plans the Russians had been working on since the height of the Cold War, the Cuban Missile Crisis. Some defectors he recruited talked about there being caches for sabotage hidden around the United States in case the war ever went hot. We don't have a lot of time."

"According to Dimos?" she asked.

"Yes. He said whatever happens will happen by Sunday night at ten."

"What do you have?"

"A meeting site. Part of Konstantin's network. Dimos gave it to me before he was killed."

"You were *there*?"

Sam nodded.

She put her hand to her temple. "Where and when is the meeting?"

"We can't give it to anyone inside the Agency, Emily. You trust the wrong person with this, and your life is in danger. I've already lost three people. I'm not losing anyone else."

"You can't take them all down on your own."

"We'll see."

"So what do you want from me?"

"I have some leads, footage of suspects, and I want to run them past the Russia House files on illegals working in the States and anything the FBI has. And for this meeting, I could use some satellite tracking. We won't have enough people for a proper watch team."

She shook her head. "You want the nuclear codes too?"

"I don't think it'll come to that, but it couldn't hurt."

She didn't respond. Sam thought of something Williams used to say: a lot of case officers are willing to die for their country, but not many are willing to give up their careers.

He put his hand on her shoulder, and she faced him. "I understand how hard this must be," he said. "I don't want to pressure you. I know how much your job—"

"Sam, honey. You don't know shit about me. Now I have to get back before anyone else gets suspicious."

"Are you in?"

"Call me when you have more on the meeting," she said and walked away.

29

MESSI MIRACLE GOD on earth.

Sam was halfway home, crawling through traffic on M Street, when he saw the alert pop up in his e-mail.

He pulled over. Those words had appeared in the comments on a Portuguese soccer forum, triggering Sam's Google alert and sending him this notice.

He went to the site and scrolled through the comments until he found it. It had gone up ten minutes ago under a compilation video of Messi penalty kicks. The username was Fozdorio. Sam looked at the numbers that followed it, which would give the date and time for the rendezvous. He thought he'd misread it at first, but no—the meeting was today, in less than an hour.

Sam cursed, pulled out, and cut left across traffic at the next light, then worked his way back around to the cars stacked up heading outbound over the Key Bridge.

He would barely have enough time to get there and set up. As he inched across the bridge, the Potomac threading far below, he called Emily's cell. It went straight to voice mail, which probably meant that she was at her desk at HQs.

"It's on," he said. "Call me as soon as you get this."

Sam made it to the site with twenty minutes to spare and worked his way in carefully, checking for surveillance. It was clear as far as he could tell. A Mini Cooper pulled out of a spot ahead, and Sam parallel-parked in the space, which was less than a block from the Peet's. He opened his laptop, clicked on the video software suite, and one by one brought up the camera feeds he had hijacked last night.

He did a scan to check for any watchers outside the shop, but found none. The shots inside Peet's showed that all but one of the tables were occupied. A family of tourists had spread out across two of them, now covered with what was left of their lunch. At the next one, a young woman wearing a large pair of headphones sat hunched over a notebook. None of them jumped out as operators, and there were no laptops. In theory, it was possible to set up a wireless link from cell phone to cell phone, but the range would be short, and the Agency had never seen the Russians do it.

He checked the time. Anyone in the meeting would have been in place by now. He was tempted to just go in, but Konstantin's people surely knew his face. This was his one chance, and he couldn't scare them off.

He looked up the street. If they were using a private Wi-Fi network, they didn't even have to be in Peet's. The range could be up to a hundred feet, strengthened by an antenna hidden in a bag close to the machine. The people in communication could have been anywhere on that side of the street, in a car or an office nearby. That was why these networks had superseded the old brush pass. The two parties never even needed to see each other. He checked inside the shop once more, looking for an old-school pass, and then noticed the Wi-Fi sniffer on his laptop. One Wi-Fi channel was spiking, pulse after pulse. Someone was transmitting on a private network.

He checked the feeds for vans or anyone in a car that might fit the profile. From the camera in the dry cleaner's, he could make out a man sitting in the lobby of the office building past the Peet's, leaning forward, his head slightly down. Sam could see him only from the back, but the posture suggested he might be working on a laptop.

Sam stepped out of his Jeep and started down the sidewalk. He needed a better look.

Another office building, a glass and steel tower, rose to Sam's right, and he examined the windows, looking for anyone on the lower floors who might be sending out a signal. He kept on, faster now, past the Peet's. He was losing them. A glance confirmed that there was still no one on a computer inside.

He neared the intersection, eyes on the office building ahead where he had seen the man. The door to the building opened and a wiry guy in a black polo shirt stepped out. He had a beard and carried a laptop bag over his shoulder.

Sam felt the urge to close in and grab him, but he checked it and kept walking calmly. This man would be low level. Sam needed to keep him unsuspecting, to follow him to his masters.

Sam's phone hung in his hand, and he turned his wrist slightly so that the rear lens pointed straight ahead as he thumbed down on the volume button, snapping off five shots without looking. The man turned to his right, away from Sam on the sidewalk, and kept moving.

The face was familiar, but Sam couldn't immediately place it. His gait, a purposeful stride, drew Sam's attention. The left arm swung slightly more than the right, common with those used to carrying weapons. The man reached the crosswalk for the side street next to the office building, waited for a delivery van to stop, then trotted across.

Sam had it—he'd seen him on video, passing the café where

Sam had stopped yesterday morning. His beard had been longer and lighter then. That was easy to change, as were clothes and even, to a degree, someone's face—cotton stuffed around the gums could give a watcher an altogether different appearance. But his walk betrayed him.

This man had been watching him. He was part of Konstantin's crew.

Unidentified surveillance targets usually get nicknames based on their appearance, and Sam dubbed the guy Blackshirt and watched as the man pulled his keys from his pocket and stepped off the curb behind a gray pickup truck.

The mark would look around before he went into the street, for cars and probably a tail, so Sam turned away, checking his phone as if he'd just received a text, then walked back to his Jeep.

Blackshirt took a moment before he pulled out, and Sam was ready behind the wheel. He forced his way into the slow-moving traffic in front of a Tesla and followed it up with a wave to the driver. He didn't need any honking to attract attention.

As he followed the curve of North Highland Street, he caught Blackshirt's truck ahead. Sam wanted a long tail, eight cars back in this kind of traffic. This man had been running surveillance on Sam, quality work. He surely knew the game. Tailing a professional without being seen usually required a twenty-person team. Sam didn't know how long he could keep it up solo. He called Emily again, left another message, and hung up. "Come on," he growled. The Agency had tech that could track this guy without spooking him.

Sam hung back, and the truck disappeared around the corner at the intersection ahead. The natural urge was to lock onto his bumper, but Sam had to give him space. Konstantin had survived in deep cover for decades. That required a serious network. Each layer would be insulated, and Blackshirt would lead him to the real players only if he thought he was totally clean.

The gray pickup pulled into a subdivision and slowed down. That was how it was done, fast and slow, commercial district and then a quiet street—he looked like he was doing a surveillance-detection route, and doing it well. There were no sudden accelerations or turns without signals or four rights in a row, nothing to give away that he was suspicious. He just made smooth, nonalerting moves, one after another. The best SDRs are subtle, almost invisible. They look like a normal routine so the tail doesn't realize he's being drawn into the open, but Sam had long ago learned to see through them.

He pounded the console. He'd have to either fall back and risk losing him or just take him now.

He gave it more gas and closed in.

30

EMILY SPENT THE afternoon at her desk looking for any traces of DEMETER and any leads on long-term illegals that might connect to Konstantin. Jones's office remained empty. At four, she headed down to the lobby, where a crowd was gathered, filling half the space. She slipped along its edge.

Her phone shook in her pocket as it picked up a signal. She glanced at its screen—two missed calls and two new voice mails from Sam. She couldn't check them in this crowd, and she was already late.

A lectern stood against the windows facing the courtyard. It was a retirement ceremony for the general counsel, and Emily needed to be here—and not just to keep up appearances. The senior leadership, Jones included, would be present. She wanted to see them for herself, watch them like a Kremlinologist poring over shots of the Central Committee to see who was down, who was up, and who was in league with whom. Sam had asked her to go against the chiefs, against every rule of this place, her home. It wasn't a decision she could make lightly.

Matt Wilkinson smiled and made room for her near the wall. As she took a spot beside him, she had to consider if he was part of it as well. It seemed impossible, but she would have said the same about Jones.

She stood there as the formalities wrapped up and everyone applauded the outgoing general counsel, a rail-thin widower who'd given the Agency forty years of his life.

Emily noticed that one of the senators from the intelligence committee, an old family friend, was standing by the lectern, then she spotted Jones a few feet away. She kept her eye on him, watching as he met the deputy executive director and then shook hands with the general counsel.

The staff had put out some coffee and soft drinks, and people gathered in small knots with their office mates, a rare all-hands moment when the employees were out of their little vaults. The real power players stood in quiet conversation near the lectern, the strivers and climbers circling them like flies, hoping for a nod or an introduction, anything to help the chiefs remember a face.

The good people of the Agency spent as much time on the politics of the CIA as they did on foreign intrigue, and even under normal circumstances, you had to move with care at headquarters. There were plenty of people who would gladly let someone else's op fall apart or leave a source hanging to please the execs and climb over their peers. She could tell the real comers because they never ate alone, scheduling every breakfast and lunch, racking up connections.

Emily had learned long ago, from her mother's advice, that you could resent these people as they got ahead of you or you could beat them at their own game. You couldn't just sit at a desk and hope you would get noticed for work well done, especially not if you were a woman. Someone would always take credit or find a way to stick you with the blame. So Emily had the breakfasts and the lunches, and she outclimbed the climbers. There was no way she was going to let a bunch of careerists who put ambition over principle have the run of this place, bending to whatever politician might give them their next boost. And if that made her seem like the biggest climber of them all, so be it.

She knew what much of the public thought about the CIA. The two friends outside the Agency who had a sense of what she did hadn't been able to hide a certain look when she let them in on the secret. To them, the Agency was all drone strikes, extraordinary renditions, and enhanced interrogations—the weasely committee euphemisms for assassination, kidnapping, and torture. No outsider could possibly disdain those excesses more than Emily, because she had seen them up close and fought them and now bore those sins.

But she still believed in this place—in the mottoes in marble and the heroes in bronze—because the Agency's failures were so often public and its successes secret, measured by what never came to pass, the attacks they kept from happening.

Her grandfather had done four years in a Chinese Communist prison camp, and her uncle was killed in Lebanon in 1984. He was the sixth star from the right, third row up, on the memorial wall that stood behind Emily. She knew as well as anyone that this place wasn't perfect, and half the job was cutting through bullshit, but there was good work to be done here, and someone needed to do it. What she knew about Jones put her at risk, but that's why she was on the inside: to stop men like him.

As she watched him sip from a bottle of water and welcome another to his little circle near the lectern, she wondered how far the rot went. He glanced her way, but his eyes seemed to move right over her. She studied the room, considering his allies, potential suspects. It chilled her to be operating like this here, acting like an officer in hostile territory.

A hand closed on her shoulder. She turned slowly, quieting any nerves, to find Senator Diane Mercer to her right.

"Emily, how are you?" Mercer asked, raising her hands as if about to come in for a hug but holding off. Mercer would normally have hugged her—Emily had known her since she was twelve—but the senator was careful not to play favorites in a professional setting. She was a senator from California and a member of the Senate Select Committee on Intelligence.

Emily had grown up going to church with Mercer's family at St. John's Episcopal on O Street in Georgetown. The summer before high school, she and Mercer's daughter had gotten their navels pierced at a sketchy place on Wisconsin Avenue, an infraction that resulted in a monthlong grounding for the politician's child.

"Senator! I'm doing great." She held her hands out. "How are you?"

"I'm well."

Mercer wore a light blue dress and looked far younger than her age. She swam a mile every morning and was actually the one responsible for forcing the pool in the Senate gym to finally allow women, against the objections—God's honest truth—of two older senators who wanted to keep up the old boys' tradition of doing laps without their clothes. That was in 2009.

Mercer had been a powerful partner at Sidley Austin before she went into politics, and she favored clothes by Akris, the boutique Swiss luxury brand. She was always recommending things that Emily would never be able to afford and kept trying to get her into Pilates. She did private sessions three times a week at the Georgetown Ritz with a trainer, a former New York City ballerina, whom she described as a sadist.

She was an intimidating figure, and Emily was glad that she'd known her for decades, as that took *some* of the edge off it. But Emily was truly happy to see her and to have a potential ally in what was to come. She'd been thinking of approaching her since she'd first noticed her, but if she was going to reach out to her, it was best to do it where no one would see.

Mercer leaned in, her hand going to Emily's elbow, watching her intently. "Everything okay?" she asked. She'd picked up that something was off.

Emily glanced around. No one was close, but she saw Henry West, the deputy director of the FBI, a former D1 football player, and Matt's boss's boss, look toward them, then quickly away. "Working too much. You know how it goes."

"Of course," Mercer said, but there was a trace of doubt in her voice. She had helped look out for Emily when she was younger, especially after her father passed. In later years, Emily would see her every few months, at a dinner with family friends or a reception or the occasional one-on-one coffee. She'd taught Emily, after she landed her first real job in DC, to always buy dresses with pockets and to eliminate *sorry* and *just* from her vocabulary, as in "Sorry, I was just wondering if you'd had a chance to read that memo?" "Don't apologize," Mercer had said. "Don't diminish yourself. Stand up. People may call you a bitch. That's fine. Bitches are the only thing keeping the wheels from coming off this country."

Emily had avoided asking her anything too specific about the Agency. The Senate intel committee was the Agency's watchdog and its purse, and getting too close to it was dangerous for someone at Emily's level. It might mark you as going over people's heads or even selling out the Agency to advance your own career—the intel committees were always looking to recruit their own information sources inside the CIA. There would be a time, when Emily was more senior, to play games of calculated leaks and deals on the Hill, but now that kind of thing was likely to blow up in her face.

Or that's what she'd always thought. The leak changed everything. But she had to be careful. She didn't know what game Jones was playing and who might be involved.

She asked after Mercer's daughter, who had twins now and lived in Seattle. She kept an eye out for Jones, but he was gone. There was no one nearby.

Emily resisted the urge to bring Mercer in and tell her what was happening. She would at least lay the groundwork, set up a coffee date, nothing suspicious. She moved a little closer. "You know, I'd love it if—"

Mercer's attention went over Emily's shoulder, and Emily turned to see Jones strolling toward them with a genial look on his face. "Senator," he said, shaking her hand. "You aren't poaching Emily for the Hill, are you?"

"In a heartbeat, Greg," she said. "Don't give me any ideas."

He asked about her husband, and Emily could barely focus as the small talk went on. She forced herself not to stare at Jones, the anger boiling up as she watched him stand there, not thirty feet from the wall of stars, each a fallen officer, playing some kind of caring uncle after what he had done.

An image came back of Jones speaking at the memorial service for Jeff Parker. She remembered being so moved during Jones's remarks as he paused and cleared his throat, swallowing, fighting back emotion. Had it all been an act? Or had that been the guilt working on him, and he'd managed to play it off as grief?

Jones had comforted Parker's ex-wife and sons that afternoon. Emily had been there. She was Aunt Emily to Parker's boys, and she'd watched as Jones crouched down and told them what a good man their father had been and how he'd kept us all safe.

The thought of it now made her back tighten as Jones stood

three feet away, looking in her direction with that pastor's smile on his face.

Their eyes met. The smile went up a notch.

She could have torn his throat out right there, even as Mercer kept up the pleasantries.

"Caroline and Emily used to love Glen Echo Park," Mercer said, turning toward her.

"Oh, yes," Emily said, wearing her own smile. "The carousel. But I haven't been out there in years."

She felt her phone buzz in her pocket. Maybe Sam. And in that moment, she decided that, no matter what it took, Jones would pay for what he'd done.

31

SAM KEPT HIS speed up as he approached the gray pickup, the license plate clearly visible now. Sam memorized it, but he was in danger of making the tail too obvious and giving himself away.

His phone rang, Emily calling, and he answered. "What's going on?" she asked.

"The meeting happened. I'm on one of them now."

"Where?"

"Tailing him out of Clarendon, driving. How'd you like to be a hero?"

"What do you want?"

"Eye in the sky."

"You're out of your mind. You can't run this solo?"

"Not for long," Sam said. "This guy's a pro. And it's more important to find out where he *was*. I need the eye."

"I can't get authorization, Sam."

"This is it, Emily. There was a computer-to-computer drop. He has the machine on him. He's running an SDR, but I don't think he made me. I lose him, we have nothing. I get too close, he spooks and we have nothing."

Blackshirt turned onto a narrow road at the end of the neighborhood. If Sam tried a tight follow there, he'd be made instantly.

Sam watched him go around the corner, then reached down, flicked through his photos, and messaged her the picture he'd snapped of Blackshirt.

"I just sent you a shot of him. I had to let him out of sight. Can you track him or do I have to take him now?"

"Take him?"

"I'm not going to lose him. And if I stay on him, he'll pick up the tail, so I'll just have to run him down and get that computer myself."

"Sam, hold on."

He rounded the corner.

"There's no time. I'm going." Sam raced after him. There was nowhere for Sam to hide on this road but also no way for Blackshirt to escape.

"Wait. I've seen him before," she said.

"Where?"

"It was a report on a counterintelligence job out of the Washington field office."

"What did they get on him?"

"Nothing. A bleary photo at a suspected drop site, and then he slipped the net for three years. He's a fucking ghost."

"How many people did they have on him when he got away?"

"Full team," she said. "Give me his vehicle. I can use the authorization from the old case to justify the satellite surveillance on him. I'll keep you out of it."

"Gray Chevy Colorado," he said as the pickup came back into view. He gave her the license plate number. "Pulled out of a parking spot in front of the Pinemoor on North Highland Street at four eighteen p.m. Now running south on Hope Road."

"I'm on it," she said.

"Rewind the tape. See if you can map out his contacts and travel before the meeting."

"I'll get someplace I can work and talk and call you back."

"Thanks."

Sam let off the throttle and watched as Blackshirt's truck disappeared around a curve ahead. He didn't think he'd been spotted, but in any case, it was unlikely that Blackshirt would go straight from a risky street operation to see his bosses, not unless he was absolutely convinced he was clear.

But that was the beauty of the eye in the sky. Blackshirt wasn't Sam's real target. He wanted the shot-callers Blackshirt worked for. With the tools Emily had access to, Sam wasn't concerned about losing him. The government's surveillance technology could give him Blackshirt's movements going forward as well as backward. U.S. intelligence had its own kind of time machine, a reconnaissance satellite aimed at the capital.

There was no way Sam could convince Emily to task an individual satellite with watching his man, but he didn't need to. The surveillance system didn't rely on any next-gen technology, just a stroke of inspiration from a retired engineer from the Directorate of Science and Technology. He'd realized that if you put a massively high-resolution camera on a satellite and snapped a shot of a city every thirty seconds, you could track any target backward and forward in time simply by going back and forth through the images.

The technology had first been used in Baghdad to combat roadside bombings. After an explosion, you could go back hours or days to see who had planted the bomb and then go further back in time to follow that vehicle to the bomb factory and see everyone who had come and gone from it.

The DC satellite captured the city and close-in suburbs. There was valuable intelligence to be gained even if Sam lost his target or spooked him so that he disappeared instead of reporting to his superiors. Emily could trace Blackshirt's movements before the meeting and see where he had been and whom he had met with. A lower-level guy like him was much more likely to meet up with high-value targets *before* he made a drop than after, when he might have picked up a tail. With the eye in the sky—as it was known throughout the Agency and FBI—they could then trace where those contacts had gone and whom they had met, possibly giving them the whole network.

Sam wasn't going to simply let Blackshirt run free now, though. The road he was on ended at an intersection with a four-lane highway. Sam turned right, the only way to go, and spotted the gray truck. He sped up until he was running six cars behind him. They neared the edge of Ballston, where the 1960s ranch houses suddenly gave way to glass towers.

After five minutes, they reached a traffic light at an intersection with a two-lane local road. Blackshirt's truck slowed as the light went yellow. Sam looked beyond the intersection to a shopping development with a few malls and parking garages. The highway curved ahead, which meant Blackshirt would be out of sight for a moment. It was a good spot to lose a tail.

As Blackshirt and the cars behind him slowed for the light, Sam left plenty of space between him and the car ahead, knowing what was coming. Blackshirt's truck came to a near standstill, then gunned through the light just as it went red.

Sam had been made, and his target was tired of playing meek. Sam could drop the games now, since there was no concern about spooking Blackshirt from a meetup with his bosses. Sam couldn't afford to let him disappear for another three years. He wanted that computer.

He thought of the satellite overhead. That was the beauty of being able to look back—the future was all yours.

Sam pulled onto the shoulder and drove slowly toward the red light, his eyes going left and right, left and right, tracing the traffic crossing through the intersection on the two-lane. "Come on, come on," he whispered, leaning forward and tightening his grip on the wheel as Blackshirt got farther away every second and his possible escape routes multiplied. The perpendicular traffic to his right cleared—probably stopped by a light farther down—and a stream of cars continued from the left.

He eyed his window, then raced through the intersection, threading behind a BMW as an SUV to his left hit its brakes, still thirty feet off and leaning on his horn, but Sam's Jeep was already through. He followed the curve, looking up at the mall buildings to his right.

Blackshirt had disappeared for the moment, but Sam had a sense where he was going. Those garages meant multiple exits, cover from aerial surveillance, and possibly a second vehicle that he could swap for his pickup.

He sped up the empty street and saw that the garage was free, with no gates. He hit fifty before slowing for the turn and pulling in, tires just at the edge of control.

There was no sign of the truck, but Sam heard an engine revving loud, echoing from the down ramp.

Sam sped after it, skidding on the smooth concrete of each hairpin, scanning the garage for the Chevy truck, his body pressing against the bolsters of the seat from the g's.

He hit the third basement, half empty, then saw the truck in the back corner, its bed sticking out behind a fenced-off piece of HVAC equipment the size of a dumpster.

Sam pulled into a spot, drew his gun, and stepped out. The loud hum from the HVAC pumps washed out any other noise.

Using his own car for cover, he leaned out. No reaction. He circled around to a pillar with a better angle on the truck, showing its empty bed. Its engine was off.

Gun raised, Sam moved in. The driver was gone. Sam checked the cab, then sidestepped, searching the narrow space between the truck and the HVAC equipment. He spun slowly, tracking from one hiding spot to the next with the barrel of his pistol. Nothing.

There were two elevators. Three sets of stairs. A seventy-thousand-square-foot mall overhead with three dozen exits.

Sam walked down the center of the garage, searching every shadow, ready for an attack.

His phone vibrated against his leg and he looked at the screen. Emily was calling. He connected, and she spoke first: "I've got him."

32

EMILY SAT IN a small study room in the back corner of the CIA library, her laptop open before her, its screen covered with satellite imagery. She'd wanted a place where she could work undisturbed and call Sam without being overheard. Scrolling along the map, she followed the path of the Chevy Colorado. She'd picked it up outside the coffee shop that Sam had given her and was now tracing where it had been.

She'd checked in with Sam just after the man in the truck disappeared at the Ballston mall. Sam was searching the vicinity now, ready to roll if she found anything with the satellite. There was no sign of the truck leaving. He had probably fled in another vehicle, but the most important information was in the past. Where had he gone? Who paid him? Who gave him orders and gear?

She went backward in time, watching his gray pickup earlier that morning, seemingly moving in reverse on the highway, out of the snarled density of Northern Virginia and into the hills south of Leesburg. It was a direct route with no indications of any surveillance-detection runs, which meant that the driver assumed he was clear of any watchers. He'd probably done an SDR earlier in the day.

The driver had made only one stop on the way to the Peet's meeting, at a rural park off Route 7. Pretty classic Russian tradecraft for a meeting. She kept going, further back in time, and watched as the truck ran through a long surveillance-detection run—known as "dry-cleaning" in Russian spy slang.

The attempts to lose tails helped flag what Emily needed to look for. It marked the moment when the driver had confirmed he was clear of any surveillance—when he had "gone black," in the lingo. Anytime after that he was operational, and Emily would focus there.

Everything pointed to the park off Route 7 as a meeting site. Had he met someone? Picked up the laptop? She went forward in time and studied the imagery.

The satellite shots weren't detailed enough for her to track him on foot, but she noted only one other car at the park at the same time, arriving before him and leaving after. It was a large black sedan, a Lincoln, from the look of it. Emily leaned in toward the screen.

That could be the shot-caller. She was moving up the chain, breaking through the carefully maintained insulation between the street players and the upper-echelon deep covers.

She focused on the Lincoln now, following its movements over the previous hours, and saw that it had come straight from the foothills and farmland south of Leesburg. Its last stop before meeting up with the driver of the gray pickup was a wooded area, mostly hidden from view by the forest canopy. She could make out a farmhouse near the road at the center of a large property, about five acres of secluded land. Cars were parked at odd angles in the fields behind it, like a junkyard. Two large outbuildings, greenhouses or Quonset huts, stood on the eastern edge of the land, near the trees. The spot didn't fit the profile for someone driving a Lincoln. She could picture an old spook settling down to play gentleman farmer, a cushy life of cocktails, giving orders, and stealing trade secrets, but not at a place like that.

She went further back, but there was no trace of the Lincoln. It must have arrived at the property on one of the back roads shielded from view by the forest cover.

The pickup driver had met with the Lincoln driver, and the Lincoln had posted up earlier at a compound in the middle of nowhere, a place with plenty of room for making bombs or training operatives or God knew what.

Emily was blind to everything but her screen; she was warm now, despite the arctic sixty-six-degree air in the room. The guys in suits set the thermostats.

She lifted her phone and called Sam.

"What do you have?" he asked.

"The pickup driver made one contact this morning. Looks like a superior. I followed him back to a compound out past Ashburn."

"What do you make of it?"

She looked at the land and the outbuildings.

"Not a bad place to start a war."

33

SAM CRUISED OUT of Ashburn on a two-lane road through the woods, heading for the compound Emily had flagged.

"Just a look," he had told her. She was still wary about him going it alone.

It was dark by the time he neared the location. He saw a turn ahead, a winding lane, and picked up his phone.

"Hey," she said.

"I'm getting close. Any movement?"

"Hang on." She came back a moment later. "Still nothing."

"Empty?"

"Or they're hunkered down in there. With those trees, I'm half blind on the place."

"I'll be careful."

"Keep your phone on. I'll watch for anyone coming up behind you."

Sam took the turn and followed a country road for three-quarters of a mile before making a right onto a rough lane of broken-up asphalt; he switched off his lights as he approached the compound. He missed his old Agency rides, BMWs with tuned-up engines that could go dark at the flip of a switch, kitted out with armor and run-flat tires.

Emily had sent him onto a forest road that wrapped around the hill behind the property. He pulled off, bumping over the rough ground between two trees, and parked the Jeep out of sight.

He tapped out a text: "Heading down for a closer look. Off audio. Msg if you see anything."

"Will do. Still looking good."

Sam turned the brightness down on his phone so he could check it without giving himself away. There was no way to know who or what waited on that property. He brought his pistol and two extra magazines.

Blackshirt had been burned. In the worst case, he would alert the rest of the network, and everyone would disappear. There was no time to wait. But there might be an advantage in all of this. His warning might flush them out, force them off their normal, carefully hidden routines.

The woods were thick, but Sam picked his way along a shallow and mostly dry streambed, which gave him a way through. After a minute, he neared the edge of the property and slowed. In the moonlight, he could make out the skeletons of junked cars and an old tower that looked like it had once been a windmill.

A rank smell reached him from the retaining pond. The farmhouse looked abandoned, its roof sagging.

His attention fixed on the two outbuildings, one an old corrugated steel Quonset hut and the other a prefabricated garage with a yellow exterior light. Not a bad place for a bomb factory. He scanned the property again. No signs of anyone. Sam wanted to see inside.

The Quonset hut's windows were boarded up. The prefab building had a side door secured by a dead bolt. He had his entry kit. He eyed the fence. No barbed wire. A hundred feet of good shadow lay between him and the side of the garage.

He glanced down at his phone, shielding the screen, then messaged Emily: "Clear?"

Emily's eyes fixed on the computer. There were only two routes to that compound that she could see. But there must be another way in and out, like a forest road, hidden from view overhead.

She was watching the imagery from the satellite as close to the present as possible, but there was still a three-minute delay required to compress, transmit, and unpack the massive images.

Her eyes went to the doorway of the study room, where she had picked up movement. Matt passed by. She pocketed her phone and waited. Then his face appeared in the window of the door.

She gave him a quick wave that said *Hey, I'm busy.* The door creaked open.

"How's it going?" he asked.

Her phone vibrated in her pocket under the table.

"Good," she said.

A flicker of movement on Emily's screen captured her attention. A black SUV, a Suburban, she thought, had appeared on the road leading to the compound.

"Got something?" Matt asked.

She hesitated, then realized she was sitting forward, all attention.

"No. Just boiling the sea. The usual."

"The bombing?"

"Something else," she said, and the tight line of her lips said enough. You didn't pry about people's work around here. Matt seemed to get the message. He didn't need to know.

"I'm getting a coffee. You want anything?"

"I'm fine. Thanks, Matt."

She wondered if he'd just happened to be walking by. It seemed too convenient.

He shut the door, and Emily looked at her computer. When she played back the images, she saw it clearly: the Suburban was heading for the compound, and the black Lincoln she'd noticed before was following behind it.

She checked the time stamp and pulled up her messaging app to warn Sam, but the cars were probably already there.

Car headlights approached the compound entrance, glowing in the haze. Sam dropped back, away from the fence, taking cover in the darkness, and watched them come: a truck or SUV and a passenger car behind it, rolling along the curving gravel road through the property.

A message came through on his phone. It was Emily, warning him about the new arrivals.

The headlights filtered around the trees beside him. He kept to the long shadow behind one of them as the cars disappeared on the far side of the garage and stopped.

He heard footsteps through the gravel and the clatter of the garage's rolling door opening.

Sam circled around the property to give himself a better view of the two vehicles. Light flooded out from the open garage door. Sam forced himself to slow, picking each step so the noise wouldn't give him away.

He knelt beside a downed log and looked through the chain-link fence. Only the SUV—a Chevy Suburban—was visible, though Sam couldn't see the interior through its tinted windows. The sedan must have parked farther up.

A burly man came out of the garage carrying a black case the size of a ski bag in his right hand. With the light behind him, he was only a silhouette. He opened the liftgate of the SUV and loaded the gear inside.

A bird flew overhead—an owl, Sam guessed from the slow rhythm of its wings. He wondered if it had been spooked by his presence. The man outside the garage watched it go, and the light hit his face.

Sam knew it well. He'd seen it countless times in his mind, lit by the flash of a pistol as that man stood over Alex Clarke and executed him on a Geneva street. It was Shooter Two.

34

SAM DREW HIS gun and stepped forward. He aimed for the man's head through the fence, but he had already started the liftgate closing and moved behind the vehicle on the driver's side. Shooter Two got behind the wheel and the SUV's engine growled as it took off toward the compound exit. The sedan—a black Lincoln—followed a moment later.

Sam ran back to his Jeep, started it up, and headed out. He might be able to catch them on the two-lane. He called Emily as he bucked over the rough surface.

"Hey," she said. "You all right?"

"Fine. Stay on that truck and the car behind it. They came and went. It's the shooter from Geneva."

"What? Here?"

"Yes. I called him Shooter Two in the reports. There should be a sketch in there if you can access them. He grabbed gear from one of the outbuildings and got in the SUV. It could be an op."

"What does he have?"

"I don't know. It was in a case."

"Are you following?"

"Yes. The same route I took here."

"Good. I can pick him up on that. Stay back so he doesn't spook."

"On it," Sam said, taking the turn wide as he hit the two-lane and sped up.

A few minutes later, Emily had picked up the SUV on the satellite, though the Lincoln had taken another route out and disappeared under the tree cover.

He kept his eyes on his speed, forced himself to keep his distance no matter how badly he wanted to corner and kill that man.

Emily's voice guided him through the night: a left, a right at a fork, then back on the highways, moving east toward the capital.

The road thrummed under his tires. "You're still good," she said. "I'll tell you when he exits."

They kept the line connected, and he could just barely hear her, the slow breath, the clicking of keys as he counted off mile after mile on the highway.

He heard the clatter of her keyboard again.

"He's getting off," she said. "Fort Myer Drive south through Rosslyn."

Sam pulled into the right lane. As he neared the exit, she spoke again. "He stopped. Just southeast of the Marine Corps Memorial. Marshall and Meade."

"Did anyone exit the vehicle?"

"The stills show a figure crossing the street toward the memorial and the bell-tower monument."

"One man?" Sam asked. There was a possibility there were others in the vehicle who had waited inside it while Shooter Two grabbed the gear.

"That's all there is on the imagery. He's carrying a long bag, heading for the trees in the southeast corner."

"Got it."

"What's your plan here?"

"Just a look."

"That doesn't sound like you, Sam."

"What do I sound like?"

She dropped her voice an octave and said, "It's on."

"Not bad."

"You want backup?"

"I need you on the satellite."

"FBI?"

"You have anyone there we can trust absolutely?"

A long pause. "Not anymore."

"Then I've got it."

"Be careful."

"Always," he said lightly. He pulled into an empty parking spot farther north on Meade. "Going silent. Message me if you see anything else."

"Will do."

Sam stepped out. This was Arlington's high ground, looking over the Potomac and the District. Down the hill stood the statue of the Marines raising the flag on Iwo Jima. The banner swung slowly in the night. Straight ahead on Meade he could see the rolling grounds of Arlington National Cemetery, an island of stillness.

A delivery van trundled down the street and turned left ahead of Sam, coming between him and where Shooter Two had parked.

Sam ran across the street as it turned, using its bulk for concealment. Sparse trees circled the memorial. Unlike the cemetery, it wasn't fenced or locked down. Busy highways ran along two sides of the memorial grounds, and at night they were deserted and easily accessed.

Sam kept to his right, where a neglected patch of woods stood just uphill from the Netherlands Carillon, a stark modern bell tower. Looking downhill gave him a view almost straight along the National Mall, over the Lincoln Memorial, the Washington Monument, and the Capitol. This spot offered sight lines on the most valuable targets in Washington. What the hell was he carrying?

He crossed to the trees and turned slowly, looking for signs of Shooter Two. All thought seemed to disappear as he concentrated entirely on his senses—the hush of the leaves underfoot, the breeze across his face.

Sam surveyed the Marine Corps Memorial but saw nothing. It was too open.

He looked to his right, where the trees grew thicker, an overgrown patch of forest above the bell tower. It was the best concealment on the hill. Sam went to it, moving slowly, picking his way through the kudzu. He drew his weapon from his holster and started working his way downhill through the terrain, measuring every step for noise.

Once he had gone a hundred feet, he caught movement ahead, closer to the far edge of the woods, downhill from him.

He moved in silently and could make out the figure of a man leaning forward, working on something. Metal whispered against metal. Sam took another step and watched him make an adjustment to a frame, a tripod, just in front of him.

A gun mount? Maybe. Sam thought of the legs of a mortar, a simple but devastatingly effective weapon, essentially a portable piece of artillery, that could lob shells up to three and a half miles with or without line of sight on the target. Or perhaps this guy was spotting, finding ranges for—what, an assassination? Or targeting for a strike from the air?

Sam aimed at the man's center mass. He noticed that he was holding something in his right hand. It looked like a partially folded map or chart.

He was close enough. Three more steps, not worrying about the silence now, and he saw the man go still.

"Hands up," Sam said. "There is a gun aimed at your heart."

No movement. No response.

Pointing the gun at the back of his head, Sam moved in quickly and grabbed the map from the man's hand. The man held it tight, and the paper pulled with surprising strength, then tore. The man spun, elbow coming toward Sam, but Sam was faster. He dodged the blow and drove his boot into the small of the man's back, knocking him forward onto his knees. He rose quickly to his feet, and Sam slid the torn piece of the map into his pocket.

"Don't move!" Sam shouted, aiming at him from behind. The man kept still. "Hands behind your head!"

The figure widened his stance, and Sam's finger tightened on the trigger. Then the man's hands rose and met behind his head. Sam looked for the rest of the map, but it wasn't on the ground. The man must have pocketed it.

"Now move to the side."

He complied, step by slow step. Sam glanced at the tripod and the gear on top: a rectangular box with a lens in the center and a stubby antenna rising from its side. Sam took it for some kind of surveying equipment.

"Turn."

Sam looked into the face of Alex Clarke's killer, Shooter Two. He stood, placid, head slightly tilted to one side, eyes studying Sam.

Keeping the gun steady, Sam brought his phone out with his free hand and took a photo of his face. "Now on your knees."

"I can't do that, Sam." His voice was low and rough. He was over six feet, his neck almost as wide as his head. "Walk away. You're only going to get more of your people killed."

"Last chance," Sam said. The rage ran through him like a shudder, but he kept his voice calm and even.

Shooter Two didn't move. "Fine," Sam said and lowered the

pistol, aiming toward the left side of his belly, feeling a rush of pleasure at the thought of putting a bullet through this man. His fingers tightened on the grip. His eyes focused on the front sight, the tunnel vision of taking aim. He wouldn't kill him, not yet, not unless he had to, no matter how strong the urge. He wanted answers.

The man's head turned to the left. Sam caught the sound of something moving through the underbrush.

They weren't alone. Sam took two long steps back and pivoted toward the noise, searching for a second attacker as he kept moving back and to the side to keep Shooter Two in view.

A fast shadow in the distance. It disappeared behind a tree. The light was stronger there, filling in from the security lamps near the cemetery. Sam made out a dull reflection off a gun.

He focused, aimed, and held his breath for an instant as he pulled the trigger twice, the gun kicking in his hand. A grunt, then nothing. Sam could barely see after the flashes from the shots.

Snick. The sound was close, to his left, Shooter Two racing in. Sam knew the sound—not a gun but a lock-back knife clicking open.

He put his foot back and dodged as Shooter Two lunged at him, holding the knife in a practiced fencer's grip, coming straight at Sam, no wasted motion or slashing arcs.

Sam twisted right and back so the blade passed just to his side. It slit the fabric of his jacket as Sam caught the man's arm in the crook of his elbow, locked it up against his ribs, and cranked on the joint. Sam turned the gun in the narrow space between them, but Shooter Two seized his wrist with his free hand. Sam slowly angled the barrel up toward the man's face. He drove his knee into Sam's forearm, near the elbow, as he wrenched his gun hand out to the side. The pistol flew from Sam's fingers and landed somewhere to his right.

Sam twisted his right wrist free just as Shooter Two jerked his knife arm back, trying to get out of the elbow lock, scraping the blade across Sam's back. Sam grabbed his arm with his right hand, then the left, clamping both down on the wrist, just below the knife, driving his thumbs into the nerves.

A low groan of pain came from Shooter Two's throat, and he punched Sam in the head with his left hand. Sam turned, and the two men stood side by side, their arms in front of them, as Sam tried to pry the knife free.

Shooter Two drove his palm into one of Sam's kidneys from the back, then smashed his knee into Sam's ribs, but Sam held on and bent the wrist back hard, as if he were breaking kindling. The knife slipped from the man's hand into the brush.

A blow from Shooter Two's free hand cracked into the back of Sam's neck, and Sam stumbled, fighting to keep his balance. The man jumped him from behind, knocking Sam forward. He managed to stay upright on one knee as the man's arm wrapped around his throat and clamped down.

He pulled at the arm, trying to pry it loose, as he felt his face going red and warm, his lungs fighting for breath.

Shooter Two cranked the choke down tighter, pressing on his carotid artery, cutting off the blood to his brain. Sparks of white light danced in front of his eyes.

Sam felt hot breath across his cheek. His vision began to narrow. He was almost gone.

Sam put his hand on his knee and pressed off the ground, driving himself up with a desperate strength. It felt like they were both falling back through the air. His body crashed on the other man's as they landed, Shooter Two on his back and Sam on top. A loud breathless wheeze sounded in his ear.

Sam rolled to the side and struggled to his feet, still dazed from the choke, searching for a weapon, for escape. A siren wailed to the north.

He saw the faint reflection—fifteen feet ahead of them, his gun lay in the ground cover. He ran for it, grabbed it, and turned.

No one. Sam scanned the woods slowly, looking down the barrel of the pistol. He stepped through the underbrush and saw the broken branches, the aftermath of the fight.

Then he caught the sound to his right, already far off: a man running.

Legs unsteady, Sam took off after him. An engine started in the distance. A car door slammed. Lights filtered through the trees from a side street as the vehicle pulled away.

He walked back to where he had first seen Shooter Two set up. The tripod was gone.

Sam started moving toward his car. When he neared the edge of the woods, he pulled out the torn piece of paper and turned it to catch the moonlight. It wasn't paper, he realized. It was printed nylon, the corner of a map, drawn at such a fine scale that each building's outline was depicted. It showed the Capitol and part of the Mall.

Along the edge he made out Cyrillic letters: *CCCP*. The Soviet Union. And there was one word written by hand. It was missing a couple of characters because of the tear, but Sam could still identify it. He'd heard Dimos whisper it before he died: HYACINTH.

35

SAM CALLED EMILY as soon as he got back to his car and asked her to track the Suburban. He circled the memorial, looking for it, and saw the police cars coming up Arlington Boulevard. He drove north, and her call came in as he crossed an overpass.

"I picked it up, but now it's gone," Emily said. "He headed north through Rosslyn, then disappeared into an underground garage. I imagine he suspected satellite or just did a nuclear dry-cleaning run after you found him."

"No sign of the Suburban coming back out?"

"No. There are a dozen garages within a few blocks. He could have swapped or gone on foot. You don't sound good, Sam. What the hell happened in there?"

"There were two of them. I shot one and tangled with the second. They both made it out."

"Jesus. Are you all right?"

"I've been better. But I've got something. Where can we talk?"

"I'll meet you at the park from before. Ten minutes."

"See you there."

At the park, Sam rolled through the lot. Emily was already there in her car, an older Lexus RX 350, near the basketball courts. She walked over to Sam's Jeep as he stepped out.

"God, Sam," she said.

"What?"

"Your eye."

He leaned over and looked in the mirror. There was a burst blood vessel in his right eye, a small red stain along the iris.

"What happened in there?"

"I got choked out."

"And that?" She pointed to the shredded side of his jacket.

"He had a knife."

"The same guy?"

"Shooter Two. He's pretty fucking resourceful."

"Are you cut? Bleeding?"

"He scratched up my back, but I don't think it's too bad."

"Get in the car," she said.

"Where are we going?"

"My place."

"Jones was watching it."

"He only checked it twice."

"How do you know?"

She pointed to the sky.

"You tracked him?"

"While I had access. You can't go home. These guys might try to finish the job."

"I'm not going to put you at risk."

"It's fine. I'd rather have the backup, actually. Come on. I'll get you sorted out."

Ten minutes later, they pulled into Emily's garage, Emily driving and Sam crouched in the passenger footwell. She shut the garage door behind them, and Sam rose onto the seat and stepped out of the car. He'd ducked down to stay out of sight in case there was any surveillance on the house. Emily wanted to go home and keep up her normal routines. It was a smart precaution if she was being watched.

He stretched his back and winced. "It's been a while since I pulled that one."

"I used it all the time when I was under diplomatic cover. You remember the cakes?"

He smiled. "Sure."

The Russians watched the embassies and the diplomats who worked there at all times, knowing that some of them were spies. If an officer needed to get clean of surveillance for a meeting, he would carry an ordinary-looking package, often a cake box, developed by the Directorate of Science and Technology, and sit with it in the passenger seat of a car while someone else drove. The driver would go around a corner and stop for an instant, momentarily out of view of anyone following, and the officer would place the box on the passenger seat and jump out. With the press of a button, a silhouette would pop up from the box where the officer had been sitting, the CIA car would take off, and the tails would continue after it none the wiser.

Sam followed her inside. She pulled all the blinds before she hit the lights, and Sam sat on the edge of the living-room sofa. He felt the back of his head—a hard and painful bump was growing where Shooter Two had hit him.

"Where are those cuts?" she asked as she walked into the kitchen.

He touched his ribs and felt the sting. "Here."

She brought back two glasses of water and a plastic storage box full of first aid gear. She put the waters down and gestured for him to take off his shirt.

She sat beside him, and the smell of alcohol filled the air as she opened a prep pad. It burned in the cuts and he set his teeth together.

"Is that all right?" she asked.

"Yeah."

"You said there were two men?"

"Yes. Shooter Two was the one I got up close with. The second had a gun."

"You shot him?"

"Yes, but he made it out too."

"I'm sorry, Sam. I could only see one going in on the imagery."

"It's okay. It was my call."

"Was Shooter Two the man who killed Fin?"

"We don't know. He could have been. He took out Alex Clarke."

"What were they doing there?"

"He had some gear on a tripod. I took it for a weapon at first, but I think he was surveying."

She put a bandage on and leaned back. "Like taking ranges?"

Sam nodded, then did a web search of surveying gear on his phone to find a device that matched what he had seen Shooter Two using. He found an image after a minute and showed it to her. It looked like a high-tech camera in a rectangular frame. An antenna protruded from the top and there was a small keypad at the base. It was all mounted on a tripod.

"I think it was one of these. It's called a total station, standard surveying equipment. They have an extremely accurate version of GPS built in these days."

"For targeting?"

"That'd be my guess."

"Targeting what?"

He reached into his pocket, pulled out a notebook he'd carried in his car, and opened it. He'd placed the torn corner of the map inside for safekeeping, and he showed it to Emily.

She leaned in. "The detail," she said. "I've never seen that scale on an urban map." She put her finger next to the *CCCP*. "These are Cold War. God," she said, and her eyes traced the buildings. "They're targeting the Capitol?"

"Possibly," Sam said. "This was torn off in the fight." Sam's section of map showed the Capitol, Union Station, and part of the Mall. "Depending on the size of the full map, it probably had the White House on it and the State Department building. Have you heard about these maps?"

"In passing. They're for sabotage?"

"Most likely. The Soviet Union sent secret teams of cartographers into the U.S. charting cities like this, with unheard-of levels of detail. Some dissidents told us about them, and a few turned up in the chaos after the dissolution of the USSR, but we were never able to confirm the purpose of the project."

"*Atsint*," she said, pronouncing the handwritten Cyrillic letters along the edge of the map. "Absinthe?"

"*Giatsint*," Sam said. "There are two letters missing."

"HYACINTH?"

Sam nodded. "That's the name of the attack they're planning. Dimos told me just before he died."

"Sweet name. Must be hard-core. Dimos said it would happen by Sunday night?"

"That's right." They had two days left.

"Did he say anything about revenge?"

"No. Though the call I got from Konstantin after the Lincoln Memorial bombing sounded personal. Why do you ask?"

"We've been on alert at Russia House. We picked up some intercepts that suggested the Russian services were increasing their tempo, perhaps preparing for an op against us or the Brits."

"How long have you known?"

"A couple of weeks. We stepped up our activity against them, figuring it would be more cyber or maybe poisoning another dissident. No one saw this coming."

Sam shook his head. "I could have helped, Emily."

"That wasn't an option. But no one could figure out why Russia was getting more aggressive. We picked up one hint: *mesti*."

"Revenge."

"Or vengeance."

"In reference to me?"

"No. More generally, against the West. But we couldn't make sense of it. We haven't done anything to the Kremlin or the Russian services that would warrant it—no new sanctions, nothing."

"Nothing that they could tell you, but who knows what the Agency is hiding?" Sam closed the notebook with the map inside. "I need to talk to Harry Turner."

He was a former Russian intelligence officer, an illegal who'd defected in '89 and settled in the United States under his cover name.

"He's on ice. I don't think anyone's talked to him in decades."

"That's the point. Williams told me about him. He was close to all these programs. He can shed light on this."

She sat back. "Some of his material didn't check out."

"It hasn't checked out *yet*, but what if what he warned about thirty years ago is finally happening?"

"There's a warning on him, potential fabricator."

"I'll take my chances. I'm not interested in the Agency's advice on whom to trust these days. Who knows who put that warning on his file?"

"I can see what I can get at tomorrow morning."

"Are you cool with going back in?"

"Sure. I need to keep up appearances. Everyone in Russia House will be working this weekend."

"Can you follow up on the driver of the gray pickup that I was following?"

"I went back on the satellite and traced him to a house near Annandale where he'd been laying low before the meeting. Classic sleeper profile. I gave it to FBI counterintelligence. They're probably checking it now."

"What?"

"I had to give them something, Sam. You know the Bureau has to sign off on domestic ops. I can't just get up on the satellite and then say, 'Never mind.' They'll kick any info they find back to me."

Sam looked down for a moment. "All right," he said. "Can you get back on the satellite?"

"Very unlikely."

His shirt lay on the table, the side panel torn, small bloodstains on the fabric. "How'd it look?" he asked, thumbing toward his back.

"He scraped you up pretty well. You don't need stitches or anything, though."

Sam took a sip of water. His neck still hurt from the choke.

"You should get some sleep," she said.

"Here?"

"I've got the guest bedroom. They could be looking for you at your place."

"I don't know."

"Just take the help, Sam."

He nodded. "Thanks."

He got up, walked over to the drapes, and looked out in the

narrow space between them toward the park road where Jones had been watching the house.

The lights in the room went out. Emily stood by the switch, a pair of binoculars in her hand. It was easier to see the exterior when it was dark inside.

They spent about ten minutes checking for surveillance, front, back, and sides. They were clear. Sam went up to take a shower and wash away the awful brine smell of a life-and-death fight.

A University of Cambridge T-shirt and a pair of sweatpants were waiting for him outside the bathroom door, men's large. Probably Emily's ex's.

Back downstairs, he found her in the small study off the living room standing on a yoga mat , bent forward at the waist. She touched her toes, then rose slowly, drawing in a deep breath, her eyes closed. Sam left her to it, but as he walked toward the kitchen, he heard her ask: "You all good?"

"Yeah. Don't let me interrupt."

"It's fine," she said and came to the study door.

"Having it all?"

She laughed. "That's right."

"I was hoping we could get into some of that nocturnal gardening, but I guess we shouldn't offer any easy targets." He pointed back to the mat. "That helps you chill out?"

"It does. Everyone looks so Zen with it, but most of us are just doing it so we don't crack up. Too proud to take anything, so *namaste*. And maybe I'll be able to sleep a little."

"I know the drill. That doesn't look too wild. Are you getting upside down or anything?"

"No."

Sam walked closer. "How does it go?"

She beckoned him in and stepped on the mat. "Start with this," she said and leaned forward. Sam followed her, hinging at his hips. He breathed out on her instructions as he stretched down—slowing when he felt a tug of pain from the cuts—then back in as he came up and raised his hands to the ceiling.

She took him through another slow cycle.

"That's it?"

"Let's not get crazy. You're held together with tape." She started another turn, and Sam followed. The whole thing did make him feel more evened out.

"You can keep doing that," she said, then brought one leg forward and did a maneuver where she bent in half, arms outstretched, and tilted to the side like a crashing airplane.

Sam followed suit, mirroring her, trembling with strain as he tried to balance. She seemed to enjoy it as he fought to stay upright, slowly toppled to the side, and caught himself with an outstretched hand.

"It's not all about strength," she said.

He lay on his back as she kept going.

"That's a pose too," she said. "Corpse."

"I've got this one nailed," he said. After a minute or two, he got up. He thanked her and went to do another surveillance check while Emily finished. She went upstairs to get ready for bed.

Sam followed a few minutes later, still carrying the binoculars, and went into the guest room. He put his gun on the nightstand, and Emily appeared in the open door.

"You have everything you need?"

"I'm set. Thanks."

Her eyes went to the gun. "And you're not going to stay up all night on watch?"

"Never," Sam said. He walked over and put his hand on the

door frame. "Seriously," he said. "Get some sleep. After everything you've been through."

"I will."

An easy silence passed between them.

"I guess I *don't* know shit about you," he said.

"That might have been a little strong."

"It wasn't your career that came between us."

"No."

"What, then?"

She looked into his eyes for what felt like a very long time. It seemed like she was debating something. Then she looked slightly down and pressed her lips together.

"I'll see you in the morning," she said. He was looking for a question behind the words, for an invitation, but they were direct. She'd made her decision.

"Good night." He felt a familiar ache as he watched her walk away.

36

EMILY CAME DOWN a little after five a.m. Sam was standing in the living room with a cup of coffee in his hand, doing a scan of the woods in the back.

He turned and saw her in the doorway, her eyebrows rising. "I slept. I swear. Coffee's on."

"Any sign of trouble?"

"No."

Sam joined her in the kitchen as she poured herself coffee and took two yogurts out of the fridge. "I can grab something on my way," he said.

"Sit down." She pulled out a container of blueberries. "Unless you need to go."

"No. That's great."

She put together two bowls of yogurt, granola, and honey with blueberries on top and brought them to the table.

"Thanks," he said. "So you put the eye in the sky on Jones?"

"I did."

"Anything interesting?"

A smile. "You've got a good nose, Sam Hudson. I had time for a quick scan, went back about a week. There was nothing out of the ordinary except for a couple of trips out near Great Falls. The eye lost him in the trees, coming and going."

"Not totally out of profile for him."

"No, but he did a few errands on the way each time. It felt like an SDR."

"Do you want me to follow him?"

"No. You talk to Turner about the maps. He's in the region, I know that. I'll get you an address."

She took a sip of coffee. "We only have until tomorrow night?"

"That's right."

"We're talking about a potential threat to the Capitol or the White House."

Sam waited.

"It's an imminent danger, Sam. We need to take it to someone in government. *I* need to. The chiefs have to know."

"Jones is a chief. We have to be careful. Do you have someone senior you absolutely know is clean?"

"Well, you can't trust the inspector general process. I've seen them retaliate against plenty of whistleblowers, even when they're in the right. But there are people outside the Agency."

Sam turned his cup on the table. "Diane Mercer?"

"You do keep your eyes open. That's our best shot. Go so high profile so fast that no one can make me and the evidence disappear."

"How do you know you can trust her?"

"I've known her for most of my life."

"That's not enough, Emily. Look at Jones. Who would have ever suspected? And she's—well, she's Kissinger in a dress."

"It's a woman thing?"

"No. Come on. She's an operator. She can be ruthless, and we have no idea what she has going on with the Agency leadership."

"She's a knife fighter. Isn't that what we want?" Emily leaned back. "I guess you'd rather run the whole thing solo. I didn't sign up for this cowboy shit, Sam."

"Neither did I."

Emily looked at her phone, checked a message, then shook her head.

"What is it?"

"The FBI. They didn't get anything on the gray pickup from the Ballston Mall garage and nothing from the house I traced the driver to."

"Nothing at all . . . you find that odd?"

"Yes." She rubbed her forehead. "But I'm trying not to be paranoid."

"Paranoia has its moments. We don't know what Jones's game is or who else is involved. There are wars within each nation."

"What does that mean here?"

"Factions. Hidden interests. I don't know. And I'm not bringing anyone else in until I do."

"Not everyone in DC is corrupt."

"No, but enough of them are. You sure you're up to heading in? You're going to keep away from Jones?"

"Uh-uh," she said. "I'm going to ride him and find out what he's doing and how far this goes."

"Cowboy shit."

She raised her mug.

37

LANGE TRAILED A young man, pale and sharp-eyed, up Twenty-Fourth Street through Foggy Bottom, hanging two blocks back on the brick sidewalks. Andrei Pasternak was a second secretary at the Russian embassy on Wisconsin Avenue and an officer in the SVR, Russia's foreign intelligence service. Lange always learned everything about his targets. Pasternak was a Saint Petersburg native with a Jewish grandmother, which was rare inside the services, and he liked to read history late into the night after his wife and daughter had gone to bed.

Pasternak had left the *rezidentura* an hour ago and executed a perfectly competent, if a little obvious, dry-cleaning run on his way here. He was operational.

This neighborhood, between the White House and Georgetown and home to the State Department, boasted expensive corporate apartments that catered to the international NGO set and wasn't totally out of character for a young Russian diplomat.

It was prime terrain for a secret meeting, though, quieter and with fewer VIPs than Georgetown. There were a handful of luxury hotels with overpriced brasseries and steak houses off their lobbies. That made it very easy for a young, ambitious second secretary to meet up with an American diplomat or someone from the White

House or State. They could take separate entrances in and a back hall straight to the private room of one of those hotel restaurants.

It always felt off to be hunting someone from your own service, but Lange had no choice. There were enemies within. Ever since Peter the Great, Russia had lusted to be part of the West, kneeling before Europe and then America, only to be humiliated again and again.

Lange had watched that desire take hold once more as a young officer in the last days of the USSR. The breaking apart of the Soviet empire was not some flowering of freedom but Western subversion, the infiltration and destruction of his homeland. There were those within the secret services who resisted. They put their lives on the line, and in the 1991 coup they sent tanks and paratroopers to surround the Russian Parliament. But they lacked the discipline and the will to go all the way, and in the end, they couldn't hold their nation together against the American spies who backed the reformers and the politicians desperate to enrich themselves and make deals with the United States. They plundered Russia, starved its people, and plunged it into chaos.

That war between the reformers and the hard-liners had never ended, and Lange had proudly walked the hard line for forty years. The fight was about to break out into the open. Russia had only days until chaos swallowed it again. It was the best-kept secret in the world.

Reformers and liberals like Pasternak were on the other side, ready to make a separate peace with the West, to sell out their country and its leaders in exchange for help in seizing power. They claimed they wanted peace, but they would bring Russia's downfall. Lange had to stop them, and if that ultimately meant shedding the blood of his fellow countrymen, so be it.

He watched as Pasternak slowed in front of the fountains of the

Park Hyatt. The restaurant inside, Blue Duck Tavern, was a well-known meeting spot for influential Washingtonians.

Pasternak's eyes went to the right, and Lange could feel him wanting to turn, to look. That was the agony of countersurveillance. The more certain you are that someone is behind you, the more dangerous it becomes to check. The second secretary moved on without another glance at the hotel, continuing up Twenty-Fourth Street, where the crowded luxury of Foggy Bottom's recent development spree gave way to a wooded area along Rock Creek.

Had he abandoned a meeting plan? Noticed the tail?

Lange closed in as Pasternak entered the park, a dell known as the P Street Beach. It was an oddly secluded area at the edge of Dupont Circle, a grass-covered hill that ran down to the water, sheltered by trees. Decades ago, it had been a popular cruising spot—the KGB had used it to ensnare several targets for blackmail—and its hidden corners and underpasses were dangerous terrain after dark, even in the heart of gentrified Washington.

Lange tapped out a message on his phone. The shade under the chestnut trees brought relief from the sun as Pasternak kept going along the path at the edge of the woods, moving faster now, giving up any attempt to act normally. He looked back, and his eyes met Lange's across the lawn.

Lange's identity had long been a state secret. He was a ghost, his goals known only to a few men inside the Kremlin and the intelligence services. Now Pasternak had seen him. That look was fatal.

Lange closed the distance. Pasternak drew out his phone and glanced back again, but before his finger could touch the screen, Lange nodded his head.

Cole, Lange's deputy, stepped out from the woods, sealed his hand over Pasternak's mouth, and wrenched his arm behind his back as he dragged him off the path.

38

AFTER EMILY DROPPED Sam off at the park, he picked up his car and drove back to the compound near Ashburn where he had first spotted Shooter Two. There were no cars, and he could see drag marks on the dirt outside the garage. It looked like they'd pulled up stakes.

A message from Emily came through as he did his survey. She gave him the address for Harry Turner, a house in Chantilly, Virginia, just outside the Beltway, along with his file.

Sam made it there in less than an hour. It was a high-priced neighborhood, all landscaped four- and five-bedroom homes set back among the oaks, about a mile past a Civil War battlefield. Turner's house was the last on the right at the end of a cul-de-sac. Sam pulled over to check it out. Recent construction with a few Craftsman touches, it appealed to Sam a lot more than the standard exurban McMansions around here with their two-story porticos and clear-cut lots. Out front, there was a large flower garden surrounded by rosebushes that looked like they'd taken years to cultivate.

Sam had called Turner on the way, but there was no answer. He saw a couple walking a dog down the block, talking to a third man in khakis and a green polo shirt. The man said something that cracked them up, then turned and started in Sam's direction.

It was Turner. He had a full head of white hair, swept back. That and the loafers made Sam think of a retired investment banker. The guy looked as American as the flag flying off his porch.

He was too far away to intercept easily on the street. Running up on him wasn't a good way to start a dialogue, so Sam watched him go inside, then walked to the house. He did a quick check for threats, then went up the front path and rang the bell.

No one answered right away. As he was about to ring again, he heard someone approaching from the yard and turned around.

"Help you?" Turner asked. He was closer than Sam expected.

Sam moved slowly, keeping his hands slightly out to the sides. Turner had added a golf pullover to his outfit and, Sam suspected, a gun on his belt underneath it.

"I'm a friend of John Stauffer," Sam said. There was no such person, but according to the file, that name served as a parole to confirm Sam was with CIA.

Turner cocked his head to the side, gave Sam a hard look for six long, unsettling seconds, then shook his head. He walked around Sam, opened the door, and went inside.

He motioned for Sam to follow. Sam had expected a bit more of a challenge, but Turner had probably read him as CIA with one look.

"You knew when you saw me?" Sam asked.

"I've had practice."

Turner had spent twelve years working against American intelligence as an illegal. As the Soviet Union disintegrated, he decided to give up spying and simply keep living as his cover. Moscow Center, the KGB's home, was falling apart like the rest of the country, and it only deteriorated further after its sloppy failed coup against Yeltsin. Later, reports came out of officers wandering drunk down the hallways and others ransacking the place for the toilet paper that was about to become impossible to obtain in the post-Soviet chaos.

A half a dozen illegals had defected in those years. The CIA offered them new identities to protect them from their former bosses, but some, tired of change, of running, simply chose to become the lie they had lived for so long. There might be others who crossed over and never showed up on the Agency's radar.

Turner, in his cover, had spent decades establishing himself in the transportation industry with a series of trucking depots—a helpful front for smuggling material and men in and out of the country. He cut ties with Moscow Center in '90, and eventually the Agency found him—there were massive KGB leaks during the breakup. He offered to cooperate with the CIA, detailing what he knew about Russia's deep-cover activities. Many at the Agency believed he was embellishing in order to make himself more valuable. He warned about far-reaching Soviet plots, but none of it was corroborated, and the Agency lost interest. The CIA let him remain in the States in exchange for his cooperation but offered him none of the sweetheart deals—pensions and cushy jobs—that they used to lure other defectors. Not that he needed the money. He'd done well in his cover as a trucking magnate.

Turner led Sam into a study off the living room and flicked on the lights. There was a framed photo on the desk of Turner and a woman by the wheel of a sailboat anchored off a beach in what looked like the Caribbean.

Turner shut the door. After the latch clicked, his manner seemed to change. Outside in public he had been all smiles, but now his face was dour.

Sam knew what a relief it was to drop the mask, if only for a moment.

"So what do I call you?" Turner asked.

"Sam."

"Okay, Sam," Turner said, checking his watch, a twenty-thousand-dollar Jaeger-LeCoultre. "You have ten minutes."

"Until what?"

"Ten minutes."

"You talked with Joseph Williams about a mapping project."

"Yes," he said and leaned against the desk.

Sam raised his eyebrows.

"Soviet military intel put together fifty thousand scale maps of Washington and every other major city and military installation in the United States," Turner said.

"What were they for?"

"Know your enemy. Decapitation, taking out the American leadership and command and control. Or *diversiya*." Speaking his native tongue transformed him for a moment, making him seem even colder. "You're familiar?"

"Yes." *Diversiya* was the Russian word for "diversion." In Soviet doctrine, it referred to sabotage, agents preparing the battlefield for a coming war or sleepers activating after hostilities commenced in order to bleed America from behind enemy lines.

"Were you part of it?"

"No. I picked up a few pieces. We all operated out of cells, illegal residencies, all compartmentalized. I offered what I could to your people a long time ago. They didn't seem very interested."

"They said that none of it checked out."

"That's natural. After I stopped working for the center, they changed everything I knew about. But you're here now. Something finally matched up."

Sam crossed his arms, weighing how much to tell this man.

"The CIA lost interest," Turner said. "They thought Russia was weak, defeated, thought we could all join hands in the glorious pursuit of cash and be happy ever after. They mocked the old hands who tried to keep the Cold War going, claiming we were just trying to keep our relevance. But you know what, Sam?"

"It never ended."

He nodded.

"Did you ever hear about an op named after a flower?"

Turner put his hands down beside him on the desk, as if bracing himself. "Would that flower be a HYACINTH?"

Sam drew a breath. He pulled out the torn section of map, which he'd placed in a plastic bag at Emily's house, and handed it to him.

"Where did you get this?"

Sam didn't answer.

"I see." Turner examined the plastic bag and the state of the printed nylon, then peered at Sam, tilting his head to get a look at Sam's neck. The choke hold had left faint bruises along the sides of his throat, and the redness in his eye was easily noticed.

"It didn't come from a library," Turner said. He put on a pair of reading glasses, studied the section for a minute, then laid it on the desk and took the glasses off.

"Was this being used in an operation? That's how you found it?"

"Yes."

Turner ran his thumb and fingers along his jaw. "God. They're actually using it. Dusting off the old plans." He looked up at Sam. "They're here?"

Sam nodded. Turner walked halfway around the desk, rubbing his hands together.

"That changes things. You know the kind of threat you're asking me to go up against if I help you?"

"I do."

He looked back to the map. "The bombing at the Lincoln Memorial, was that part of this?"

"The opening move."

Turner didn't say anything for what seemed a long time.

"We can protect you," Sam said.

"You can't even protect your own people. You worked under-cover?"

"Yes."

"I could tell." He looked out the window to Sam's side, where there was a trellis and a few roses. "Then you know what it's like to leave your whole life behind like that." He snapped his fingers.

Another glance at the map. Sam didn't press him. Turner was weighing it now, risks and sacrifices and his own interest in stopping these people.

He looked up. "All right," he said. "What do you want?"

"What's the target?"

"I don't know, but just on this map, the full map, you would have the pantheon: White House, State Department, Treasury, Pentagon, Capitol, and the main bridges into Virginia."

"You know this map?"

"Very well."

"Do you have a copy?"

"Wait here," Turner said and walked to the closet on the far side of the study. He went inside and shut the door, and Sam saw a light go on within. The clunk of a safe or vault door sounded a moment later, and Turner came back with a black portfolio.

He undid the string and took out a dozen maps, all sealed in plastic. Sam looked at them and noted the borders. They looked like photographic reproductions.

"Copies?"

"Yes. I gave the originals to the Agency. The price of my green card. Here," he said and slid out one map. Sam looked back and forth between his scrap of nylon and Turner's map. They showed the same area and details, though it looked like two different versions, with changes in the coloring, perhaps from different years.

Unfolded, the full map stretched from Arlington National Cemetery across the Potomac to the Smithsonian and included the White House and Treasury along the northern border and the Pentagon to the southeast. It was eerie to see a map of this place he knew so well marked out in strange colors, the highways running orange, the critical buildings drawn in purple, everything labeled in Cyrillic, as if the Russians had already claimed the territory as their own.

Each potential target was outlined in painstaking detail, down to the individual rings of the Pentagon and the courtyards of the White House complex. Sam leaned over to look more closely. Small numbers were drawn in around the buildings.

"Elevations?" Sam asked.

"Yes," Turner said. "Some of the other maps go into even more detail—every window, every door. How much weight the bridges and the streets can hold."

"Whether they can support a tank?"

"Exactly."

"So these were for an invasion," Sam said, studying the legends, the details on water supplies, pipelines, communications, and transportation links.

"And occupation. They have every house and what each one is made of. They wanted to be ready for everything. Maps are your lifeblood when you have a five-million-man army and your enemy is all airpower."

Everything was hand-drawn, down to the streams in the parks. The scale was listed along the edge of the chart: 1 to 50,000. That was far more detailed than a standard map for navigation. Maps of this scale were for tactical troop movements, house-to-house fighting.

"Why would you use these today? Their satellites are far better."

"The infrastructure is still almost all the same, as are the measurements on the most iconic buildings. There are details here you can't see from the sky."

"They had cartographers on the ground?"

"Oh, yes."

Sam pictured them, hiding in plain sight, silently cataloging every inch of the capital, preparing for a war that would never come.

"Why would someone be using this to survey?" Sam asked.

"Survey?"

"Yes, like taking ranges, measuring distance."

"Targeting, most likely. Or confirming details were still accurate."

"Is this all you have?"

"Physically, yes, but there are others in digital form. After the collapse, a few maps surfaced among collectors. They'd go into the former Soviet Republics and buy up thousands of pages of documents from some starving logistics clerk. I could barely believe it. These were so sensitive when I was working that if they were torn up or burned, you had to bring back shreds or ash. Every one was accounted for."

"You have the scans?"

"As many as I could acquire."

"How many of Washington and nearby?"

"A dozen."

"Can you give me copies?"

Turner opened a laptop on the desk, then reached into the drawer, came out with a thumb drive that said Turner Logistics on the side, and plugged it into the laptop.

Sam looked at the White House elevations again. You could use it for scouting lines of fire or aiming guided weapons. The only scale of attack that made any sense politically would be an assassination. Everything else would be overkill.

The United States and Russia were still nominally allies, even after Russia had slowly undermined America's political system and extended its campaign of killings onto American soil with several assassinations that were never made public. But Russia would never try anything on the scale these maps were suggesting, not unprovoked. At least, that's what Sam had believed before that bomb went off on the steps of the Lincoln Memorial.

Sam noticed Turner checking his watch again, then glancing at the window.

"Sabotage," Sam said. "Bombings. It doesn't make sense. Something on that scale will only blow back on them."

"It may not be the Kremlin's work. There might not be a plan or any authorization from Russia. The men they sent here are a bomb that has been waiting to go off for forty years, maybe more. You know the term *konservy*?"

"'Preserves.' Sleeper agents in the United States who would activate if an all-out conflict broke out."

"They're real. Soldiers in a war that never came, fighting for a nation that no longer exists."

"You were one of them?"

"I played a small part. But you want the man that Williams called Konstantin."

Sam stiffened at the mention of the name. "You knew him? Konstantin?"

"Only by reputation, ghost stories. Nightmare stuff. That's a different breed."

"In what way?"

"You know why I joined the illegals program? Everyone thinks it was to bring the imperialists to their knees, but that wasn't it. It was for peace, to get inside and keep watch on the American machine, to stop another great war like the one that had killed millions of our parents and aunts and uncles. We were to be an early-warning system. That was worth giving up everything I knew and loved to come here and live a lie, hunted every day. For some of the others in the program, though, war becomes life. It's all they have left."

A long look at Sam. "Chekhov's gun," Turner said.

"If you place a rifle over the mantel in the first act," Sam said, "it better go off by the time the play ends."

"Roughly."

"But these plans are for a third world war," Sam said.

"I don't know what goes on in the Kremlin or the White House. I gave up that fight. But I know that there are men on both sides for whom wars have their uses."

"Specifically?"

"I'm too long out of the game, Sam. I gave them everything I knew a long time ago."

"Do you have anything on Konstantin?"

"Nothing. He's a shadow." He took the thumb drive out of the laptop and handed it to Sam, and his eyes went to his watch. "Time's up. You should go."

"Why did you leave the life?"

Turner shrugged. "I came to love this country in spite of its cruelties. I love mowing that fucking lawn and going wherever I want. Back home, the gangsters took over the government. They broke faith with us. But I knew before that. You get tired of the lies. It rots you away. Eventually you have to trust someone. You have to live."

He smiled at Sam, but there was something accusatory about it. "You know what I'm talking about."

Sam heard a car pull up. The other man's face turned grim. Sam took a step to the side. Out the window, he saw a black BMW in the driveway. The door opened.

"Relax," Turner said. "It's my wife."

She stepped out of the car and ushered two black Labs out of the back seat of the SUV. She looked about five to eight years younger than Turner, with dark curls and something genteel about her bearing.

"You have to trust someone," Sam said.

Turner nodded. "Best decision I ever made." He opened the study door. "If you don't mind going out the back."

"Sure," Sam said.

"You know, I used to have conversations just like this with Williams. He tried to warn the others at the Agency." Turner looked down for a moment. "Be careful out there, Sam."

"I will," Sam said. "Thank you." He left the study, crossed through the kitchen, and went out the back door. He slipped across the deck, then circled the house and made for his car.

As he stepped off the curb, he looked back and saw Turner through the living-room window.

He kissed his wife and walked out of view. Then the shade came down.

39

LANGE STOOD IN the break room of an old office complex off a highway outside Gaithersburg, Maryland. Like so many safe houses, it was frozen in its era of first service, the late 1980s, with its steel-framed desks, gray-and-tan-checkered tile floors, and a cigarette smell that would never go away.

He poured a thin stream of rubbing alcohol from a plastic bottle across his knuckles. He didn't react as it flowed over the skin, burning nicely in the cuts. He patted them dry with a paper towel, leaving red traces on it like an ancient script, grabbed the bottle, and walked across the worn linoleum floors into the main part of the office.

A low cry of pain sounded from the far end of the building, muffled by the solid steel door that led to the storeroom where Andrei Pasternak was being kept.

Lange reached the heavy door and hauled it open. A boxy television sat in the middle of an entertainment center straight ahead, its shelves full of old DVDs and VHS cassettes. A few cots were stacked vertically against the back wall. He came around a row of high metal shelves and saw Cole standing over Andrei Pasternak, his chest rising and falling from exertion.

Cole stepped back—those lumbering movements, those thick

arms. He'd nearly killed Sam Hudson last night by wrapping them around his neck. He wore an Ace bandage around his wrist now, but the sprain from the fight didn't seem to be affecting him at all.

Second Secretary Pasternak sat on a metal and vinyl office chair that had been pushed against a support column for stability. His hands and upper arms were pulled back and duct-taped to the chair's frame, and his ankles were bound to its legs. His head drooped forward.

As Lange approached, Pasternak's head rose. Blood trickled from his lower lip, mingling with the sweat coming off his face. He bucked in the chair, but Lange simply raised his hand, as one would when approaching a wild animal. He held up the bottle of alcohol and poured some onto a folded paper towel. Pasternak pulled back, trembling; his head hit the column. Lange moved in slowly and dabbed at the split in Pasternak's lip and the open cut over his eyebrow. A sharp intake of breath came as Pasternak felt the sting, but slowly he relaxed and let Lange tend to the wounds.

This was the dance, savagery, then kindness, taking and giving, establishing total control and winning not only fear but a kind of desperate gratitude—for the moments when the pain stopped, for a sip of water or a glimpse of hope that the subject might see his family or the sun again. There were other reasons to tend to his health. Lange assumed Pasternak would break quickly, but interrogation could last for days or even weeks, and infection needed to be considered. They would bring him close to the line if necessary, but the dead can't talk.

These moments of mercy came easily enough. Pasternak had a toddler and a wife at home in the cramped diplomatic apartments beside the embassy on Wisconsin Avenue. He was thirty-one, younger than Lange's own son, but not by much. This man was following orders, a small part of a much larger faction within Russian intelligence, centered in the SVR. After the Soviet Union fell, the KGB had been split into the foreign SVR and domestic FSB. The latter was the current iteration of Russia's long-feared secret police. The SVR had always been soft, questionable, especially compared to its rivals in Russian military intelligence, the GRU, who now did the real heavy-hitting overseas. Pasternak wasn't leading the traitors, but he would know who was. That's why he was here.

There had been factions within the secret services going back to the first days of the revolution. Pasternak's clique sought closer ties to the West, ways to reopen the economy to Europe and the United States, end the crippling American-led sanctions, and access the cash that so many Russian intelligence officers had hidden offshore in real estate and anonymous accounts. Some of them were even willing to go against the Kremlin itself to bring an end to the more than twenty-year reign of the Russian president, the man who had rescued the motherland from chaos. Lange was going to stop them, and for that they wanted him dead.

They'd come for him a month ago, when he went to the water-front park in Anacostia to collect a drop—an updated burst radio that would help him keep up communication with his allies in the Kremlin. As he neared the site, he picked up a watcher, someone close, too close for an FBI tail, close enough to strike. Lange detoured between a pair of construction sites, condo towers rising. He stepped into the darkness, waited while the man passed. The pursuer carried a silenced pistol, held low beside his left leg as he searched through the shadows. Lange caught him from the right, slamming the edge of his outstretched hand like an ax head into the man's throat, then grabbed for the gun. The two of them struggled for it, and Lange drove the fingers and thumb of his right hand into the man's neck and pinched his trachea while grasping at the gun with his left.

The light caught the man's face as he fought for air. Lange recognized him from the files. He was a young SVR officer who'd graduated from the academy a few years before Lange's son. Lange closed his fingers and held on until the life had gone out of him.

The reformers had sent one of his own to kill him. Lange had spent his entire adult life worming into the heart of the enemy. He would never roll over for some false peace, never humiliate himself before the West. He would stop it at any cost. So they had tried to eliminate him. There was a quiet battle for power in Moscow over who would control the soul of his nation. Lange would damn well make sure the hard-liners won, because if they didn't, if these reformists took over his service and his homeland, he would be a man without a country, and they would never stop hunting him.

Now, as he looked at Pasternak's bloodied face, he felt no pity.

"Andrei," he said as he made a final dab, clearing the blood from Pasternak's cheek. "There are no martyrs. You're an embassy man. You're soft. You can't imagine how ugly it becomes. We already know everything. We know your people are making a deal with the United States to help them take power. Tell me who is leading the operation and when and where they are meeting with the Americans, and you can have your life back. No one will ever know."

Pasternak lifted his head. "You're Konstantin." The words were barely a whisper.

"It can be so easy, Andrei."

"All lies. I know." Pasternak shut his eyes tight. Did he already understand that he wasn't going to leave this place alive? Most at least clung to a false hope. "You say you're fighting for Russia, but you're fighting for your czar. For his cult. For yourselves."

That was the reformers' preferred term for Russia's president, a former KGB man himself, a proud chekist, the hardest of the hard line.

"He robbed this country blind," Pasternak said. "You know it's true. He won't last another week. You can't win."

Lange wondered how many in the services knew about the president's illness, so carefully hidden by the media machine he had spent decades crafting. It was true. He was dying. He had days left, maybe only hours. But he wasn't gone yet.

After more than two decades in power, he was the state. And when he was gone, the war within the services, within the Kremlin, would spill into the open. That was why the reformers were making their move now. But the tanks would roll once more, and this time there would be no compromise with the liberals, no mercy.

"You know the Americans are responsible. We need to answer. They started this war."

"Do you really believe that? Or is that just the truth that will help your side?"

"We make the truth. You should have learned that a long time ago."

"What are you planning?"

Lange said nothing.

"Please. Just stop. No one else needs to die. We can work with the U.S."

For a moment, Lange heard his son's voice saying those same words, a voice he would never hear again. Lange felt a surge of emotion; a mournful half-smile appeared on his face. Then he drove his fist into Pasternak's nose, snapping his head into the column.

Lange leaned over him, took him by the chin, and lifted his head. "Men like you cost us our nation. Now answer my fucking questions."

It took Pasternak a few seconds to gather himself enough to talk. "No. Never."

Even though they were on opposite sides, some part of Lange admired the grit in this officer, a deskman, really not much more than a glorified journalist.

Lange sighed. "Andrei, they always say that at the beginning."

He gave Cole a nod, then stepped back as the other man moved in.

40

COLE HAD SPENT almost two hours alone with Andrei Pasternak. He held Pasternak's nose closed with one hand and braced his head back against the column with the other. A strip of duct tape sealed the man's mouth shut. More than ninety seconds now without air, Pasternak threw himself back and forth in the chair with dwindling power, his restraints tearing at his skin, calling up the reserves of strength that come only at the edge of death, and which most men never knew they had.

Cole held on, watching Pasternak's chest shudder, until he felt the tone going out of his muscles. Cole let go, and Pasternak pulled in a long greedy breath through his nose.

In Chechnya and Eastern Ukraine, Cole would use a gas mask fitted with a rubber tube that he could pinch off at will. Sometimes when he had at last allowed a breath, he would spray tear gas inside and let the subject draw it deep into his or her lungs. Or torture was as simple as sealing someone in a cold hole in the ground in the depths of winter, the skin sticking, freezing to bits of stone among the dirt.

Pasternak had broken, though he'd held out longer than Cole had anticipated. He had given him the names of his commanders and all he knew about the deal they were seeking with the Americans. Lange was in the office, finishing up communications, gathering the operatives they would need for tomorrow night, the final blow.

Cole stepped back and looked down at the wreck of the man in the chair. He had one last question.

Pasternak blinked, looking around the room as the oxygen spread through his body and brain, reviving him.

"One more. And then it's over." A weak nod. Cole ripped the tape off his mouth, and the cut on Pasternak's lip began to well with blood again.

Cole glanced back at the door. He came in close and lowered his voice. "Geneva," he said. "Was there any footage of what happened that night?"

"What?" Pasternak said, his voice weak.

"Tell me what happened in Geneva."

"You know. You were there."

"Who knows who killed Alex Clarke?"

Pasternak closed his eyes against the pain and confusion, surely wondering if this was a trap and what the wrong answer would cost him.

"*You* killed him," he said.

"Does anyone have tape?" Cole asked.

"No."

Cole nodded, a little curl of satisfaction at the corner of his mouth. Pasternak's eyes narrowed with concentration, and he focused on the door.

"He doesn't know," Pasternak said, almost in disbelief. Even before he could shout to get Lange's attention, Cole knew what was coming. He sealed his palm over his mouth, reducing Pasternak's desperate attempts to cry out to nothing more than damp murmurs against his palm.

He was dead by the time Lange returned, hanging forward in the chair, his skin going white. Lange looked at Cole expectantly.

"I thought he would last longer," Cole said. "But I got it."

Lange crossed his arms. "Who's leading them?"

Cole slid him a piece of paper with notes scrawled on it and tapped a name. "You know him?"

"Of course."

"He's the reformers' point man on operations in the U.S., though he's leaving the actual negotiations to other players on his side," Cole said. "He's using the code name TRIBUNE."

"Their deal with the Americans?"

"It's on."

"The deadline hasn't changed?"

"No. Tomorrow night. Ten o'clock."

"Where will they meet to finalize it?"

Cole picked up one of the nylon maps on the table. Sam Hudson had torn off its corner near the Marine Corps Memorial, but that wasn't enough to uncover its secrets: HYACINTH's location and workings. He held it out and put his finger to it. "TRIBUNE may not be there in person, but the negotiators are meeting here."

Lange studied it.

"We won't be able to get in," Cole said. "Or stop them. There are too many entrances, and it's too well guarded."

"We don't have to," Lange said, tracing his finger a short distance over the nylon. He smiled. "HYACINTH will take care of all of it in one shot. I'm going in tonight."

41

EMILY FOLLOWED JONES from twelve cars back in the light Saturday traffic. The man's countersurveillance skills might be rusty—he hadn't been in the field for a long time—but she wasn't taking any chances.

She'd watched him close up his office and take his bag, and she'd given him plenty of space as he left the Agency parking lot at lunchtime. It was easier to tail someone when you had a sense of where he might be going. From the satellite, Emily had Jones's patterns.

Over the past week, Jones had run a route twice toward a neighborhood overlooking Great Falls from the Virginia side. It seemed like he was operational, but every time, the satellite lost him in the trees of the residential area. She wasn't sure if he had been getting clean for meetings or doing trial runs to see if he could make it to a target destination without anyone following him. He had been watching her, and now she could return the favor.

Once Jones turned onto a local road east toward the Potomac, she knew he was on his route again. Checking for tails was slow work, and Emily knew where he was headed. The best way to follow someone was from the front. She turned right and made her way through a neighborhood of high hedges and giant houses. She pulled over two hundred yards back from an intersection that gave her a view of the road that Jones had taken on his previous runs. Easing back in her seat, she waited for her target to appear.

Five minutes, then ten. Had she lost him? Had he spotted her? She could feel her heart drumming against her blouse in the quiet car, and she forced herself to breathe slowly through her nose. In, out, in—

Jones's Volvo flashed by. She counted to five and then pulled out. She caught sight of his car at the end of the block, turning left.

When she rounded that corner, she saw his car turn right and disappear around the tall landscaping. She checked the map on her car's navigation system. There was no outlet that way. She pulled over, brought up Google Maps on her phone, and switched to the satellite view. The street served only one property. Jones had arrived.

She couldn't risk being made by getting any closer, so she pulled a quick K-turn and parked around the corner in the direction she'd come from.

On her phone, she zoomed in on the property, a residence on at least a full acre overlooking the river. From the address, she did a reverse search, looking for any property records or other names attached to that house. It took a few minutes of trying different sites, but eventually she found a zoning adjustment notice with the owner's name.

"Fuck me," she said. She dialed Sam's number and listened to it ring. Three times, four.

"What's up?"

"I'm on Jones. I think I found his source—Sasha Markov."

A pause as Sam absorbed it. "Where are you?" he asked.

"Outside his house. Near Great Falls. It's the route I spotted him on. I'm going to get a closer look."

"Emily . . . be careful. I can be there in twenty-five minutes."

"I've got it."

42

JONES STRODE ACROSS the putting-green-perfect grass of the estate, a showy contemporary mansion whose hard angles made Jones think of a stack of Lego blocks.

A man sat on a concrete platform near the pool, his eyes closed, hands resting in his lap, holding himself with the posture of a yogi.

Jones was surprised at how close he got before the man opened his eyes and noticed him with a start.

"Jesus," Markov said. "How did you get in here?"

"That's my job."

Sasha Markov was an investor who put himself out as a real estate impresario with a sideline producing action and horror films. Although he was born in Moscow, his faintly British English hinted, deliberately, at his early education at St. Paul's in London. Following that, he'd gone to the University of Southern California. He wore a black V-neck tee that offered a partial view of the tattoo on his left biceps—it looked like three blackbirds on a wire, one taking flight—and a quote tattooed in script on his chest, though Jones couldn't make out the words.

With the designer tee, the longish, tousled hair, and the mani-cured stubble, Markov had a very expensive rugged-outlaw thing going that Jones more commonly associated with rockers and actors.

"What's going on?" Markov asked as he rose to his feet. Jones cocked his head to the side and started walking to the other end of the deck, which was built around an infinity pool.

A sheet of water cascaded down the pool's side, lit by the afternoon sun and offering a perfect cover for the sound of their conversation. Jones had long ago learned to love water for its masking properties. If you play music or television to drown out listening devices, then later some enterprising tech can find the exact album or program, subtract its sound waves from the surveillance recording, and get the conversation back. But running water is perfectly random, the sonic equivalent of a spy's onetime pad for encrypting messages.

"Apologies for the scare," Jones said. "There's a little pressure on and I couldn't risk the normal channels." He glanced back to where Markov had been sitting. "Meditating?"

"That's right."

Jones frowned. "You don't seem very relaxed."

"I'm not. Why are you here?" Jones had once seen footage of Markov smashing a rocks glass into a man's face hard enough to shatter them both.

Jones was taking another step, irreversible. But all of this was easier than he had anticipated. He'd been undercover before, had learned how to live a lie. "We need to move this up," he said.

"How soon?"

Jones looked to his left, his eyes drawn by motion deep in the trees. He watched for a long moment. Another gust, and the branches bent. It was nothing. He turned back to Markov. "Tomorrow night."

Markov ran his thumbnail across his chin. "That's tight. You can get me what I need?"

"Of course. You know who I am."

Markov watched the sun glimmer on the surface of the water. "Then I can manage it."

"Where?" Jones asked.

"I have a place."

43

SAM STOOD OUTSIDE his Jeep in a small parking lot off the George Washington Memorial Parkway, high on the Virginia bluffs across from Georgetown.

He checked his phone for the fourth time and watched as a line of clouds crossed from the east.

Emily had messaged him to meet her here at three p.m. That was twelve minutes ago. All he knew was that she had gone in to watch Markov's place.

He dialed her number, listened to it ring, then saw her Lexus rolling into the lot.

He let out a breath of relief as she pulled up beside him and stepped out. "You all right?"

"Fine," she said and swept her hair to the side. Sam looked around, then opened the passenger door of the Jeep for her. After she climbed in, he got into the driver's seat. He wasn't taking any chances on being picked up on audio.

"I saw them," she said. "Jones and Markov."

"Where?"

"Talking in the backyard of Markov's house."

"They didn't pick up on anything?"

"I don't think so. I came in through the rear of the property and hung back. It was pretty heavily wooded. I couldn't hear them, but I got this."

She held her phone out and pulled up an image. It showed Jones and Markov in profile, small figures and grainy because of the distance.

"This wasn't a social call," she said. "He checked for tails before he went, and he could have done the dry runs before to make sure there was no static surveillance on the house. What's your read?"

"Sasha Markov is hard-core, but he's mainly a gateway to the father. The town house, the jet, the offices here and in New York and LA, it's all a front for hiding the family money."

"So Jones is dealing with one of the biggest power brokers in Russia."

Sasha's father, Emir, had amassed the sixth-largest fortune in Russia by plundering the mining sector during the mass privatizations of the 1990s. The son styled himself as an edgy investor, one of these West Coast guys who didn't own a tie, but that was all cover. His job was to launder money for his father and his allies. Emir had sent his boy to the West, the best schools in Britain and the U.S., and now he was the key. He knew how to behave himself at parties—for the most part—knew the right people, even smiled once in a while, and in turn he helped his father park money around the world with all the trappings of class and luxury: art, real estate, sports teams, private investments.

Sasha had been one of the names on the list that Sam had given Emily to check out. He had his fingers in half the dark money flowing out of Russia and potential connections to Gemini and Konstantin's network.

"The Kremlin has been running a lot of operations through the oligarchs for deniability," Sam said. "He could be the connection between Jones and whatever the Russians are planning. I always figured him for a moneyman and facilitator, but he could be in-volved more directly. He's not afraid to get his hands dirty. You think he's operational?"

"I wouldn't rule it out. I tried to tail him after Jones left, but he was watching."

"Can we track him?"

"Not with the satellite. I'm locked out. I'd need another autho-rization."

"You can't use Markov?"

"No. He's not a current counterintelligence target. And we might tip Jones. I may have some alternatives, though."

"I'll pick up the tracking gear I have from my place."

"Did you get anything from Turner?"

Sam pulled out the thumb drive. "A scan of the full map. And a half a dozen others."

She gave him a light punch in the shoulder. "Nicely done."

"They're from the old sabotage campaigns. Soviet. Late seventies or early eighties. He thinks it's probably a long-term sleeper."

"Konstantin?"

"It all matches."

Sam reached behind her seat and grabbed a Clif Bar out of a plastic shopping bag. "You want one?" he asked.

"Sure."

He took out a second one for her and passed it over. "Thanks," she said.

He went over what he'd learned from Turner as they ate. When he finished, Emily sat back and looked out the window, the empty wrapper in her hand. The lot dropped off in a steep bluff with a good view of Fletcher's Cove and the forests along the river on the far side.

He could see her looking over the capital in the distance, the iconic buildings and monuments, each one a target.

"Stay-behind forces? *Diversiya?*" she said, turning back to him and shaking her head. "We need to tell someone, Sam. This is too big. It's an imminent threat. And now we have confirmation on Jones."

"Mercer?"

"Let me feel her out."

Sam ran his hand along the wheel. "We don't know how far this goes. Everything points to it being more than just Jones, a whole faction."

"I think she can go against CIA. She's always sounded critical of it when we talked."

"Nothing is ever simple at that level. She could have been trying to draw you out and turn you into a source inside the Agency."

"I've considered that."

"We have the maps. We have Markov. We're close. We just need more time to understand what's going on."

"I won't tell her what we've found. She's steered me around land mines before. I'll feel her out, see if she knows anything, take her measure. I'm at risk here. It's not your call alone."

He looked straight ahead. Everywhere he turned, it was another ambush.

"Sam?"

He tapped her knee twice with the side of his fist. "I trust you."

She nodded and seemed to understand the gravity of those words for him.

"Can you get to her without anyone else knowing?" he asked.

"I could set up a pretext or—" She glanced at his watch. "Shit."

"What?"

Emily was already moving, grabbing the door handle. "I've got to get to the Ritz."

44

EMILY'S FOOTSTEPS ECHOED off the high brick walls as she approached the doors of the Ritz-Carlton Georgetown. The building was a renovated former masonry factory, a bit of high-low chic. The one-hundred-and-forty-foot-tall smokestack still towered over the property, which was filled with gardens and hidden away on the hilly blocks between the Potomac River and M Street in Georgetown.

As she entered, the weekend bustle and damp heat of Georgetown disappeared, replaced by eucalyptus-scented air and the burble of the full-wall waterfall.

Emily showed her Agency credentials to the receptionist and said she had an urgent message for Senator Mercer.

"This way," the receptionist said, standing almost at attention. Emily thanked her and followed her down a hall the color of slate to a small sitting area looking out over the courtyard garden.

Mercer had her back to her and turned in her chair as she entered.

"Emily?" She smiled. "Are you here for a class?"

"No," she said. She waited as the receptionist left and shut the doors behind her. "I wanted to talk to you in private."

"Ah," Mercer said, growing serious. She closed the two-inch-thick briefing book she'd been reading. The intelligence officer in

Emily couldn't help but steal a look. Mercer was sipping cucumber water and plowing through lethal-drone contracts. After closing the doors to the garden and pulling the blinds, Mercer came back, sat, and gestured for Emily to take the chair across from her.

Emily did. A trace of dampness remained in Mercer's hair from her post-workout shower, and she was wearing her usual Akris power suit.

"I thought you finally gave in on Pilates," Mercer said, and offered her a smile. "Have you been following me?"

"No. You've mentioned your sessions here. I thought I'd give it a try."

"And this is something that couldn't be trusted to my chief of staff?"

"No."

Mercer pursed her lips. "I'm afraid I don't have a lot of time here, Emily. There's a car on its way for me."

"If I came to you with something, would you keep it in absolute confidence?"

"This is about work?"

"Yes."

"There are inspectors general. There is a process at the Agency."

"And if you have reason not to trust the Agency?"

Mercer closed her eyes for an instant as that sank in. "Of course I will help you however I can."

Emily nodded, then put her hands on the table, hesitating.

"You don't trust me?" Mercer asked. It sounded like an accusation, but there was no heat to it, more disbelief than anything. "Jesus. Well. That's good. You should be careful."

"Have you heard anything?" Emily asked.

Mercer's expression betrayed nothing, even as four decades of

Washington survival skills churned behind it. "There may be a leak or a breach in your division, someone working at cross-purposes with the Agency."

She looked for some sign of confirmation from Emily, but Emily held back. She wasn't ready to talk. She was here to read her.

Mercer leaned closer. "Does this have to do with the deaths of Sarah Hassan and Jeff Parker?"

Emily's eyes went wide.

"You're right to be careful," Mercer said. The murmur of voices came from the reception area. Mercer's phone started ringing, and she silenced it. "My aide is here. This isn't a good place to talk. Do you have Signal, the messaging app?"

"Yes."

"You can find me on there with this number," she said and gave Emily the contact information. "I can get away tonight."

Her eyes went down to Emily's hands, clasped together. Emily hadn't realized she was doing it. She felt like she was standing at the edge of a cliff, and her instinct was to pull back. She didn't know what was behind the feeling; perhaps it was going against the institution that had been her life and her family's life or maybe it was Sam's warning not to trust Mercer.

"I know this is hard, Emily. It should be. I'm not going to lie to you. Telling the truth is more difficult than you can possibly imagine. They always go after the whistleblowers. Make sure you're ready for what will come."

"Are you saying I should keep quiet?"

Mercer put her hand on Emily's. "No. I just worry about you. I'll do everything I can."

A knock at the door. "I have to go. You know how to find me."

"Thank you."

"Go out through the rear of the hotel," she said and pointed to a side door behind Emily. "Right, then take the stairs on the left. We shouldn't be seen together. Sometimes I run into Pelton here."

Roger Pelton was the senior senator from Kansas, a hard-talking ex–football coach who never wore a jacket and the last person Emily expected to see in the Ritz spa. Mercer held up her hands and waggled her fingers. "He's in here every week. Manicure and massage. They're all divas, Emily."

Another knock. They stood. Mercer picked up her briefing book and bag. Before she left, she looked Emily in the eye. "You'll be okay."

45

SAM ROLLED PAST Markov's house in Great Falls, catching glimpses of the driveway through the breaks in the landscaping. He counted three cars: a BMW convertible, a Jeep Wrangler Rubicon, and a Hyundai Santa Fe, the last probably a staff member's. Markov usually drove a black Mercedes-AMG G-Wagen. Apparently he needed an off-roader to cruise the cobblestoned streets of Georgetown.

Sam drove to the rear of the property, parked around the corner, and returned on foot. There was a way to at least get eyes on the back of the house through the trees, but as he moved closer to the yard, he saw that there was surveillance everywhere.

The cameras were hardwired, which meant his usual hacking approaches wouldn't work.

He looked over the massive sliding glass doors that opened onto the deck and pool. There were ways in.

Sam shifted his weight from one foot to another, trying to focus as other thoughts crowded in. Images of the faces of the dead—Fin and Clarke, Dimos, Hassan and Parker. He needed to move. He wanted to go in there and stick a gun in Markov's face and get some answers. The house was occupied, but Markov might not even be home. A hot prowl was insanity. It wouldn't get him anywhere but prison or the grave.

After finishing his survey, Sam headed for his car. There were ways to track Markov—his cell phone and his vehicle—but it would take work.

As he drove home, something didn't sit right with Sam. Markov was a dangerous man, no doubt. He'd cut up a guy's face in a London nightclub after he'd tried to stop Markov from hitting on his fiancée. But Markov didn't fit the profile for being part of deep-cover operations. His family was central to illicit Russian money flows but not part of the Russian president's inner circle. The Markovs had bent the knee to him only after he started cracking down on the oligarchs; "Do my bidding or your possessions will be expropriated and you'll be jailed and maybe killed" is a hard offer to refuse.

The president had a small, trusted coterie: the Saint Petersburg set and the *siloviki*—the security-force chiefs turned politicians who ruled Russia and took its wealth for their own.

It didn't make sense that Markov would be in the middle of a plot like the one Dimos had described, one of the Kremlin's most closely held secrets, or that he would be given something as sensitive as handling a Russian mole inside the CIA. Perhaps all of it had been a beautifully arranged cover, or maybe the Markovs were going out on their own, making a bid for the czar's favor. That sort of freelancing had become more common as the oligarchs came under pressure to please Russia's president.

He crossed the river to Georgetown and home. It took him twenty minutes to verify no one was watching before he went in.

He needed the latest footage from his security cameras. With Emily on board, they could run the faces of his watchers through the intel databases and track down more of Konstantin's crew.

Sam walked through his place, gun out, with a sick, alien feeling as he saw every part of his home as a potential threat, a shooting gallery.

He opened up his laptop and started downloading all the footage he would need. While the files moved over, he plugged in the thumb drive from Turner and pulled up the maps.

He put himself in the minds of the attackers. How would you bring this city to its knees? How would you start a war?

They were all hand-drawn, all pre-GPS. There was fine-grained elevation data for so many iconic buildings that it didn't help narrow down targets.

Sam went over a topographic map sketching out every inch of DC's terrain. He noted the detail. The hydrology was marked, the drainages and former marshlands, and there were even notes on the old creeks that now ran hidden under the city's streets—Slash Run and James Creek and Tiber Creek. Williams once told him about a ground-floor dive bar near Union Station where you could actually hear the water flowing on the other side of the wall.

On another map, he found plots of the reservoir that supplied the city's water and the aqueducts and pump stations that fed it downtown. He paused. According to spies who had come over after the fall, the Russians had considered mass poisonings in their sabotage plans.

He went back and checked a map that traced the city's power grid. That had been another target, though much of it would have changed since the Soviet days.

From the Marine Corps Memorial where Shooter Two had been surveying, there were easy sight lines only on taller buildings, like the Capitol and the Washington Monument, but if he was using the GPS to measure something, he wouldn't have needed line of sight.

Revenge. That was the key to all of this, Konstantin's targeting of Sam and the rationale for the stepped-up aggression from Russia that Emily had described. But for what?

"What are you aiming at?" Sam said quietly. He stared at the map. The answer was in front of him, but he couldn't see it.

The transfer of his surveillance footage finished. He shut the laptop and stood up. As he was turning away toward the hall, he caught movement through the window, under the streetlight. Sam stepped closer.

A man stood across the road up the hill on the sidewalk.

He had a fighter's crooked nose, but there was something easy about his posture, entitled. Their eyes met.

The last time Sam had seen him was in Geneva, on the other side of a pistol as he tried to kill Sam but missed by inches.

Shooter One. The man who had covered the far end of the lane as part of the ambush that took Alex Clarke. His beard was gone now. The gunman walked closer, then turned, crossed the street, and disappeared from view.

Sam was out the door in ten seconds. He hit the street where he had seen the shooter.

Gone.

He turned slowly, his gun hand hidden just inside a light jacket he had grabbed on his way out.

They had been watching him for weeks, but they had never come this close, never shown a face. And now a killer was standing in broad daylight.

Was it a distraction? A warning? A provocation?

Sam searched the neighborhood on foot, then ran a box search in his Jeep. Nothing. If the man had had a vehicle nearby, Sam had almost zero chance of finding him now.

He went back inside and cleared the apartment, gun out and ready. He was alone. The rules of engagement were changing, maybe because he'd nearly killed one of Konstantin's people last night. He wasn't safe here.

On his computer, he pulled down the latest shots from his surveillance cameras. One had a straight line of sight to where Shooter One had been standing. The camera was unobtrusive, but still, he was surprised that a pro would let himself be captured on video.

He ran the footage back and saw him, small in the frame but clear enough. Emily would still have access to the Agency's facial-recognition tools. The man just stood there, as if waiting for a friend. It was almost like he wanted to be seen.

Sam screenshot the images and sent them to Emily. He gathered his gear and a change of clothes into a backpack and a duffel and went out to his car. He called Emily as he drove off, scanning the street for any sign of Shooter One.

"What's up?"

"Where are you?" he asked.

"Just grabbed a coffee from Greenberry's. Heading home."

"I sent you a photo of a man. Can you run him through the Agency facial recognition?"

He heard a rustle as she did something with the phone.

"I don't need facial recognition for this," she said. "This is from Georgetown. Jesus. This is outside your place, Sam."

"Who is it?"

"That's Arkady Novik, ex-KGB, a traveling illegal. He's a hitter, Sam. Get the fuck out of there."

"I already have."

"I'll be home in five. You want to meet me there?"

"Do you need to?"

"It's not safe?" she asked.

"I can't be sure. Is there anywhere else you can stay?"

She thought for a moment. "Yes, but if I'm bugging out, I need to stop at home anyway and grab a few things."

"It'd be good to have a bag ready. Just in case," he said. "Watch yourself. I'll be there right after you."

46

COLE STEPPED TOWARD the rear deck of Emily Pierce's home, looking over the vegetable beds, the kale growing between white twine, the yellow squash ready to go. He knelt and touched his fingers to the black earth, admiring her work.

He crossed the deck, dusted with pollen, and stepped up to the back door.

There was no car out front. She lived alone. The place was empty, so he wasn't concerned about the quiet rattle as he worked a piece of foil on a metal bar into the dead bolt. The impressioning tool would open the lock and leave no trace of entry. His wrist still hurt from the fight with Sam Hudson, but he ignored the pain. The bolt yielded after fifteen seconds of work, and he stepped inside.

It was a modest home, one of the older residences in these wooded hills near Scott's Run. Antiques filled the bookshelves, alongside black-and-white photos of family members laughing in the company of American presidents.

Cole moved through a dining room and did a slow circuit of the first floor before climbing the stairs. The carpet muffled his steps as he listened for any sound, like a squealing floorboard, that might betray his presence if Emily Pierce returned home.

The air-conditioning came on and whooshed in the background, fighting against the heat. The windows were closed. That was good. Spring and fall were the hardest seasons for stealth work, when the sounds of surprise or violence could escape a house through open windows.

He turned right and went down the upstairs hallway lined with artwork: ink sketches and watercolors of American landscapes signed by artists whose names he didn't recognize, some dating back to the 1920s and 1930s. On his right was a small bedroom. It had a queen bed, made, with clothes neatly folded on top. Against the wall stood a mahogany desk with half a dozen books stacked on its corner beside a tidy pile of correspondence and files. He spent a few minutes leafing through the pile—all of it personal, bills and investment documents, wedding invitations and thank-you notes—then checked the closet, considering the lines of sight. Cole had a gift for disappearing, for quiet. He could slip behind a trained officer in close quarters without giving the slightest hint of his presence.

He checked the guest bathroom, then moved on to the last room upstairs, the master bedroom. The door was open six inches. He memorized its position and stepped through. The bed was made. A photo on the nightstand showed Emily as a girl in her father's arms on the end of a dock on a rocky shore. A MacBook sat closed beside it.

He walked closer to the bed and touched his hand to the comforter. The house was large enough for a small family, but she lived alone. You had to know your prey like an old friend, and he had Emily's story: a miscarriage, a quick divorce from a British army officer who'd been deployed for all but six months of their two years together. This was once a place of hope, he imagined, and now she was making the best of abandoned plans.

He opened the MacBook and slipped a thumb drive in one of

the ports. It would load malware onto the machine and give him access to it. He watched as code streamed across the display.

A car engine hummed outside, getting closer. He closed the computer, pocketed the drive, and moved back to the doorway, his posture straightening, every sound growing louder as he tuned into the environment. The car pulled into the driveway, and the engine cut out. A door opened and closed.

Cole drew a SIG Sauer from a waistband holster and a suppressor from his pocket and threaded the long black cylinder onto the barrel.

47

EMILY STOOD IN the driveway, watching her house. No movement. She slung the laptop bag holding her work computer across her chest to keep her hands free, then took out a flashlight from her glove box even though it was the middle of the day.

She stepped through the front door, holding the light in an ice-pick grip, ready to blind anyone inside with its powerful beam or use the sharp aluminum bezel around the bulb to attack.

The living room was empty, the back door locked. She cleared the first floor, then went upstairs, first to the guest bedroom and its closet, then the master.

No one was here. She dropped the flashlight on the nightstand next to her personal laptop, then went into the bathroom and drew the door closed behind her. After putting her bag down, she took off her blouse and tossed it in the hamper. She closed her eyes and stretched her neck right and left.

A dull headache pressed behind her sinuses—the stress of the threats all around, of walking the Agency halls not knowing who might be out to get her. That and the Washington heat had left her in need of a shower, but she didn't have time for anything more than washing her face. She just needed to pack a bag and roll out.

She added a few essentials to her toiletries bag, then ran the taps.

Once the water was warm, she leaned over the sink, eyes shut tight, and scrubbed away the salt and sunscreen. She reached blind for the towel that hung beside her shower, grabbed it, and dried her face and neck.

A long look in the mirror, a deep breath.

The light shifted under the door. She took a step to the right, wondering if it was some trick of perception, but no. Something moved out there. She slid open a drawer quietly, took out a pair of scissors, and gripped them in her fist. A long moment passed as she watched for more movement. Nothing.

She took her blouse out of the hamper and pulled it on, then placed one hand on the knob, holding the scissors in the other. She threw the door open and swept into the bedroom, circling.

No one was there. She stepped slowly to the side, looking into the walk-in closet. Clear. She went in and dropped to one knee in front of her gun safe, a small black box on the shelf beside the shoes she never wore.

A whisper from the hallway. Footsteps over carpet?

She punched in the safe code—5731—and hit Enter. It beeped; wrong combination. She tried again, her finger trembling against the plastic, and the bolt pulled back.

Another hushed noise. Was it in the hallway? Or was he already inside the bedroom? She unzipped the gun's case, took out a magazine, and slid it into the grip of the pistol. She turned toward the door as she pulled the slide back until it snapped forward again, chambering a round, the double *snick* of metal on metal loud in the silence. Anyone inside would hear it and would know where to find her.

The lessons of the old close-quarters drills, the shoot house at the Farm, came back to her. Hit the doors fast. She moved out of the closet, covering the room. Empty. Her breath pumped in and out in a fast pattern, and she gripped the pistol tightly with both hands to keep them steady.

Stepping sideways along the wall, she approached the bedroom door, then crossed into the hallway.

Run. But she wasn't about to turn, walk blindly, and take a shot in the back. She went on, clearing the other bathroom and the bedroom she used as an office.

Where the hell did you go?

She took the steps down, following the pistol, passing her aim across the living room and then turning on the landing. A draft of warm air pushed against her.

Crack. Her body pulled tight, and she waited for the pain and shock but felt nothing. The back door creaked open, moved by the wind.

She brought her shoulders back and kept the gun aimed in front of her in a strong isosceles stance as she closed in on the kitchen. The back door swung shut with another gust, banging against the frame but not latching. She stepped carefully through the dining room.

Whoever it was had fled. Or was hiding now, waiting for a chance. She did a quick sweep of the ground floor, then went to the back door. She kicked it open with her left foot and went into the yard, feeling the cold air-conditioned air spill past her out of the house.

The doorbell rang, and she spun toward the open rear door. She didn't go back in, just searched the yard, working her way toward the side of the house.

A long shadow emerged, cast by the late-afternoon sun. She raised the gun, and Sam stepped into view.

His smile of recognition disappeared in an instant when he saw the pistol.

"Get your gun," she said. "They're here."

48

EMILY AND SAM searched the property, clearing it back to the creek that ran in the woods to the rear. Whoever had been inside was gone.

She led Sam in through the back door, and he cleared the house with her as she told him everything that had happened. They ended in her bedroom, and she looked around it in silence.

"He was in here," she said, "while I was in the bathroom."

She shook her head and Sam came to her side. "You okay?"

"Not really. But I'll manage."

Sam looked to the bathroom door. "That was open?"

"Closed. But I could see the light moving under it from inside."

He looked at the sun angling through the window over the nightstand and then the MacBook sitting on top. "That was there the whole time?"

"Yes." Emily walked over and touched her fingers to the laptop. "Warm."

"When was the last time you used it?"

"This morning. After that it would have been asleep."

"How long could he have been in here?"

"A few minutes, at least. I packed my toiletries and washed my face. I was blind in there. He could have killed me." Her lower lip tucked under. "But he didn't."

"He wanted information." Sam went to the Mac and pried the lid open with his thumbnail. "So he could have been here before you got home."

"I might have missed him on the search if he'd managed to get past me."

"And you brought your work machine in from the car?"

"And then into the bathroom. I had my bag with me in there."

"The work computer's good, then?"

"Yes. And we have to consider the MacBook compromised."

"Where did you hear him when you went to get the gun?"

"Upstairs hall, maybe even inside the master bedroom with me."

Sam looked out the door into the hall. "He was going by stealth," Sam said. "Maybe hoping he could get out of here without you knowing. That way he could keep tracking you through the machines."

"Then I slam out of the bathroom. So he knows I know."

"And he comes for you," Sam said, looking to the closet, then walking to the window and peering at the street outside.

"He has doubts after he hears the gun and maybe sees you coming up the street." She went to the closet, grabbed a red quilted duffel bag, and started putting clothes in it.

"You have a Vera Bradley bugout bag?"

"I don't keep a bugout bag when I'm in the United States, in my *home*. At least, I didn't until we started waltzing again. Not everything needs to be nylon webbing and Kydex, all right?" she said as she dropped the gun in, then went to a small safe and pulled out a pair of USB drives.

"What's that?"

"Backups of the data I pulled from the CIA server about Jones deleting DEMETER."

She brought the bag into the bathroom, shut the door, and came out a minute later after changing into a summer dress. Sam moved to the window to watch the street.

"What else do you have on Arkady Novik?" he asked as Emily slung the duffel over her shoulder.

"I'll tell you on the way."

They went downstairs, and Emily led them out the back door. She paused at the threshold and looked over the family photos.

"It might be a while before you can come back here." There was a chance it would be forever, Sam thought, and she knew that.

She put her fingers to the stained oak of the door frame, then turned her head toward the deck. "Let's go."

49

EMILY GAVE SAM an address in Arlington. They got in their cars and headed south, him following her Lexus in his Jeep, then turned onto Old Dominion Road. She pulled off near Waverly Hills, a quiet neighborhood full of brick Colonials.

After a few wrong turns to get black, she checked in with him to make sure they were both clean, then pulled up in front of a Cape Cod with a porch on a dead-end street.

Emily scooped a pair of flyers off the front mat and opened up the house. A neighbor's dog started barking, which Sam took as a good sign. It would tip them to anyone approaching. The stale air inside reminded him of a vacation place. The interior was open to the gabled ceilings and painted a deep pink. Heavy fabric drapes hung from the windows. An oil painting of two young boys, twins, hung over an upright piano.

Sam turned and came face to face with a row of indigenous masks. He took a step back. "Whose place is this?" he asked.

"Family friend. Georgetown professor. She's in Paris, has me check on the place if anything comes up."

An old Gibson acoustic guitar, spruce and mahogany from the look of it, rested on a stand beside the piano.

"It's a sixty-four," she said.

Sam gave her an appreciative nod. He walked on and peered into a bedroom where row after row of antique dolls lined the shelves. "I felt safer with the shooter, honestly."

She worked the screen on her phone.

"What are you up to?" Sam asked.

"Tracking Markov."

"The eye?"

"No. But there are a bunch of shady sources that track cars by their license plates, information brokers. They're mostly used for repo and PI stuff, but the Bureau sometimes taps them in counterintelligence cases. The private sector can actually get away with more than we can. They scan major intersections and shopping areas. I should be able to get his patterns, at least, maybe catch him live. I picked up the tag on his G-Wagen when I was at his house."

She scrolled on her phone. "Nothing yet," she said, then sat on one of the spindly chairs in the living room. She rested her head back, shut her eyes, and took a few deep breaths.

Sam dropped his gear beside the piano, figuring she needed a moment after the close call at the house.

"Arkady Novik," she said without opening her eyes. "He's a center illegal."

That was the term for the MVPs of Russia's deep-cover programs, experienced operators who had spent years, sometimes decades, building covers in Western countries then graduated to working with more freedom of movement. Often, after they faced some heat in their original postings, they would be pulled out and used for one-off missions. In the espionage world, there wasn't necessarily any shame in blowing a cover. It meant you were operating close to the edge, as you should.

Also known as traveling illegals, these officers had plenty of experience and would be dropped into different countries for a high-stakes pitch or an assassination, anything that was too dangerous to risk a deep-cover illegal who needed to blend in for decades with a low profile.

"Wet work?" Sam asked.

"Yes. One of their best."

He sat on the edge of the couch and leaned forward, elbows on his knees, hands clasped.

"You got too close last night, and now they're coming for us," she said. "It's time to break the glass, Sam. Get some help. We have eyes on one of the most-wanted Russian illegals. Let's go to Mercer."

"She was down to meet?"

"Yes."

"What was your read?"

"She hinted, unprompted, that she knew about a potential penetration in Russia House."

"You didn't give her anything?"

"No. And she was reluctant, spent half the time encouraging me not to kick the hornet's nest. If she was part of it, she'd be desperate to co-opt me, to find out how much I knew."

"Or she's good at the soft sell."

"Recruitment 101," Emily said. "But it didn't feel that way."

Sam looked at her. "You said *they're* coming for us. Who?"

"Novik. Russian intel."

"At your place too?"

"I assume."

"What if this isn't about me tangling with Shooter Two last night? What if it's about you reaching out to Mercer?"

"And someone saw me?"

"Possibly."

"Or she tipped them off. That's what you're thinking. She told Jones somehow? Or she's part of it?"

"I don't know, Emily. But you had someone in your house looking for info. Looking for what you know and who you talked to, possibly how dangerous you are now."

"You think it was CIA breaking into my house, maybe trying to kill me?"

"It could have been. Or some of the Russians that Jones is working with. What do we know about Novik?" Sam asked, and he went back through his phone to find the surveillance image of Arkady Novik that he had sent to Emily.

"He's got the pedigree—third-generation chekist, top of his class at the Red Banner Institute. Father received the Order of Lenin for his work in Afghanistan. We have him tied to very high-profile operations in Georgia and Chechnya, but no real proof. We suspected him of working in the United States early in his career, but again, nothing solid."

"Was he ever part of Vympel?" Sam asked. It was a special KGB unit tasked with deep penetration and sabotage, the elite of the secret services.

"Suspected."

"That pattern fits," Sam said and zoomed in on the photo on his phone, studying the man's face, the faint smile. There was something decadent about him. He looked up. "He could be Konstantin," he said. "No one identified Novik from my report, the composite sketches I did after Geneva?"

"If they did, I didn't hear about it. So he went to your house to, what . . . taunt you?"

"He might have come to kill me, and the moment wasn't right. But yes, that's almost what it seemed like. Some eye-to-eye bullshit. I don't know what all this is, but it's personal, back to Geneva and the bombing on the Lincoln."

"Why you?"

"I'd figure revenge, but I didn't kill anyone as far as I know. I've been hammering at that question and gotten nowhere. You still have access to the facial-recognition tools at CIA?"

The Agency had software that could match photos to its databases as well as a stream of real-time cameras at some federal facilities around the U.S. that would ping if a suspect crossed their path. The real-time was buggy and had nothing on the UK's all-seeing network of CCTV, but they might get lucky.

"I should," she said.

"I want to run this photo of Novik, and I have footage of a half a dozen others."

"People watching your place?"

"Or tailing me. The driver of the gray pickup was one of them. That's how I recognized him at the Peet's. I want to find them or see if they've gone near any of the targets from the maps."

"I can swing that," she said. She spent a minute tapping at her screen, then her eyes widened. "There's a hit on the plate. Markov's on the move."

"Where?"

"Georgetown."

50

EMILY LOOKED AT her phone. "He's in the G-Wagen," she said. "Parked in a lot by the canal."

"How long ago?"

"Three minutes. Could be a meetup," she said and showed Sam the screen.

"There are a few industrial buildings left down there under the Whitehurst Freeway that could be good for staging an attack."

"Or he's shopping," she said. "Guy's a clotheshorse. You want to set up on his car?"

"We can tail him if we see him, and if not, I can paint the car," Sam said, using Agency slang for putting a tracker on a target.

"You have the gear?" she asked.

Sam went over to his duffel and pulled out an LG smartphone.

"What's that?"

"It's for tracking cars. Looks like a regular phone for deniability, but it can set up an exploit of the car's own telematics—the satellite radio and the OnStar system—to track it."

"They didn't have that when I was a NOC."

"You should see the NSA catalog these days. Terrifying."

"Can you listen in?"

"Depends on the model, maybe fifty-fifty, but the location data is solid. And there's no beacon to find or extra signal that can give it away."

"Do you have anything for his phone?"

"Sure."

She gave him a disbelieving look. "How much gear do you have cached, Sam?"

"Enough. You can't wait for the grandpas at headquarters on everything."

"How does the phone tracker work?"

"GSM hijack," Sam said. He went back to the bag and pulled out a Samsung phone. It had been developed by the tailored-access operations unit at the NSA and was capable of taking over another phone, following its location, and sometimes even recording audio and video. "But you have to be within a few feet for it to work."

"We'll see," she said and walked toward him. "If we get close, I'll handle that piece. Then we have him even if he gets away from the G-Wagen, maybe get some audio too."

"I'll hit the car and then I can try for his phone."

"Sam." She looked up at him. "Let me do this."

That was the thing about fear. If you backed down, it only got worse. They had violated her home, her safety. She wanted to fight back.

"Nothing crazy, all right?"

"Coming from you?" She laughed and grabbed the phone out of his hand.

Twenty-five minutes later, they drove past the lot by the canal in Georgetown. The G-Wagen was still there, with no one watching it. Emily parked a few blocks away, and they started walking back to the lot along the towpath.

Georgetown was all old mills and warehouses down here. The brick buildings had been converted into apartments and high-end restaurants and boutiques. Today everyone associated Georgetown with money, but this part had been working class and industrial long into the twentieth century.

They climbed a path up to the street where Markov had parked. It ran downhill from M Street toward the river and spanned the canal over a small bridge with railings on either side.

Sam's eyes fixed on the G-Wagen, parked in the last stall of a lot behind a town house and a condo building. He looked up the street toward M, the main commercial drag in Georgetown.

"Let's start with the car," he said quietly. "Head uphill and keep an eye out. I'll hit it."

She nodded, walked past him, and turned right across the bridge while Sam crossed the street and went left, downhill to the lot.

He saw her stop near the end of the block under a restaurant awning and lift her phone.

Sam checked his phone as he entered the lot. She'd messaged him: "He's in Patagonia. Be quick."

He used the text as an excuse to stop a few feet from the driver's door of the Mercedes. Switching to the second phone, the LG, he opened a weather app and held the home and volume-up keys for four seconds. That brought up the software that would let him track the car.

Nearly all modern vehicles are equipped with satellite radios and cellular systems that let owners subscribe to emergency services. In most cases, they're also wired up to microphones. Bugging a car used to be a painstaking affair. You had to break into the target's garage or sabotage the vehicle and then appeal to a patriotic mechanic to let you wire it up while it was serviced. Now, if you had a warrant, it could be done with a single phone call to whatever company handled the car's emergency services link, usually On-Star. It should take Sam only a few minutes with the NSA tools.

He focused on the screen as the app executed long strings of code, pinging the car's satellite system for its unique identifier, then running through a long set of digital handshakes to breach the car's cellular communications. The car's dashboard display turned on, glowing a pale blue.

Sam's phone shook in his pocket again, a new message from Emily: "He's checking out." His heart rate ticked up as he watched the screen, which was stopped on the last line of code, not even a progress bar for comfort.

He kept his head still as his eyes went to the right, and in his peripheral vision, he caught Emily crossing the street, moving downhill toward him. She stopped on the bridge on the same side as the parking lot and the Patagonia store. She was setting up so that Markov would brush past her.

Sam's stomach tightened. He looked down and saw dozens of lines of green text flood the screen. The words *root* and *log-in successful* appeared, followed by a long list of credentials for the vehicle's communications system.

He had him. Sam waited for a car to pass, then crossed the street and started walking uphill. He stopped twenty yards south of the bridge under an elm tree and glanced down at his phone to play for time. All his attention was fixed on the street in his side vision. He watched the door to the Patagonia store, and Emily, who had stopped on the narrow sidewalk on the west side of the bridge facing away from him and the road, looking over the railing at the old lock. Sam brought his hand up toward the grip of his gun and turned to conceal it.

The door to Patagonia opened, and Markov stepped onto the street with a shopping bag in his right hand, the muscles of his arms showing under his T-shirt. He'd be a serious threat up close. The Russian checked his cell and put it back.

Sam watched as Emily lifted her phone, dialed, and raised it to her ear. He moved a foot to the right, mostly covered by the tree, and answered his cell before it even had a chance to vibrate. It was her.

"He's coming," Sam said.

"Can you tell where he's carrying his phone?"

"Right front pocket."

Emily turned slightly, pressing against the railing of the bridge, so that when Markov passed, she would be on his phone side and her back would be to him.

Her left hand went into the pocket of her summer dress, where she had put the hijack device.

"You have five seconds," Sam said.

"That's what I've been telling her the whole time," Emily replied, pretending to be in the middle of a conversation.

Markov approached her, and Sam closed his hand on the grip of his Heckler and Koch. "Not yet," he whispered.

Markov came within inches of her.

"Now," Sam said.

Nothing changed as the Russian passed, but Sam knew that the device in Emily's pocket was hitting his phone with a short-range radio signal, planting spyware.

Markov kept going. Sam let out his breath. Then the man stopped and turned. His left hand went to the railing, and he faced Emily and stepped closer.

Emily saw movement in her peripheral vision. "He's coming back at you," she heard Sam say over the phone.

She at first feigned not noticing the burly Russian as his eyes settled on her. A bead of sweat ran down her ribs as she said, "I know, I told her that."

Markov just watched her, his lips curved with amusement. Behind him, she could make out Sam, his hand reaching under the light jacket he wore.

"Excuse me," Markov said, a light Oxford English accent coloring his speech. She turned her head slightly as if noticing him for the first time but still not looking at him straight on. "Do you know a nice place around here for dinner?"

He took another step, close enough now that Emily could smell a trace of bergamot from the cologne he wore. She looked straight into the green eyes and noted his strength under the black V-neck. She'd seen the photos of the man he'd slashed in a bar fight.

Sam started moving up the sidewalk. She wondered if Markov's line was just flirtation or if it was a way to get her to let her guard down while he moved within striking distance.

Sorry, she mouthed with a faint smile as she pointed to her phone and turned away.

Markov stood his ground and leaned to the side to get another look at her. A grin. A shake of the head. Then he turned and kept walking, down the hill toward his car, as Sam passed on the other side of the street like a stranger.

She kept up the facade of the phone call until she saw Markov turn into the parking lot, then she started walking uphill and crossed the road to meet up with Sam.

They went back to her car and climbed in. Emily exhaled and grabbed the wheel. "Holy shit. I thought he was going to kill me."

"Not happening. It wasn't a bad line, actually. You think that works?"

"Coming from him, the line doesn't really matter. He didn't even see my face before he came up to me."

Sam raised his shoulders. "It's a great dress."

"You know he meditates?"

"I didn't."

"I saw him at the house right before he met with Jones."

"Maybe you guys can sneak in an *ashtanga* before we send him up for espionage and terrorism."

"Right," she said. "Right." She touched her fingers to Sam's cheek and put her lips into a pout. "Jealous?"

He let out a laugh. "I tagged the G-Wagen. I'll have to double-check the app to see how much we can get, but it should at least give us his location."

Emily handed him the Samsung phone. He opened up the tracking app, smiled, and squeezed her shoulder. "Nice."

A buzzing sound filled the car. Emily took her phone out and checked a message.

"What's up?" he asked.

"Mercer. She's ready to meet."

51

SAM GLANCED DOWN at the screen of the LG phone he had used to hack Markov's car. A blue dot had appeared on the map in the tracking app as it picked up the location signal from the G-Wagen. The Russian had taken the Key Bridge out of Georgetown.

"Is it working?" she asked.

The map panned along the river and the dot showed Markov cruising up the George Washington Memorial Parkway, headed toward his own neighborhood.

"Yes. Looks like he's going home. What did Mercer say?"

"She can get away tonight. She wants to meet up near the Tidal Basin. You know the baseball fields?"

"Sure," Sam said as an uneasy feeling took hold of him. That wasn't far from where he had met Dimos, a mile or so north along the river. It was a peninsula of land between the Tidal Basin and the Potomac given over to playing fields, with a good view of the Jefferson Memorial across the basin. All of that turf was popular for clandestine meetups. It was mostly empty at night, and the monuments gave a good excuse for strolling or parking on a bench at any hour.

Spies and fellow travelers are all looking for the same things when it comes to locations. When Sam used to scout for sites around DC, he would often find a smudge or scratch or one of the stickers the Russians had started using—someone had already been there. If you keep your eyes open around the District, they're everywhere.

"She suggested that?"

"Yes. It seemed like she'd met with people this way before."

Sam watched the map on the phone as Markov tracked closer and closer to his house.

"What's wrong? You think she's, what, drawing me into an ambush?"

He looked at her. "They've already taken two of my sources and Fin. I'm not lowering my guard for anything."

Emily looked down at her phone, then back to him. She put her hand on his leg. "You're not a jinx, Sam."

"How much are you going to tell her?"

"I'll start with Jones and DEMETER and how that might be linked with Parker's and Hassan's deaths. Jones probably already knows I'm onto that, so if she is somehow part of it, I won't be giving anything away. And then I'll see what she can offer."

"Keep what we know about Markov and the maps out of it for now."

"I'll save it until we have some good faith."

Sam looked out at a sky of red and purple, the sun setting over the river. He put his knuckles to his chin, felt the stubble scratch.

"Dimos told you the attack would happen tomorrow night," she said.

"Yes. By ten o'clock."

"That's all we know?"

"He was killed before he could give me anything else."

"This morning at work, I heard one of the diplomatic security guys talking about being maxed out for the next forty-eight hours."

"Doing what?"

"They work VIP protection, usually, but they didn't know. They were just called in and had their calendars cleared. That's all I could get."

"Tomorrow night," he said.

"We're running out of time."

He glanced at her phone. "Let's do it. But I'm getting your back."

"It's a one-on-one. She'll spook."

"She won't see me."

52

SAM WALKED ACROSS the packed earth of the baseball field. The Jefferson Memorial stood to the south, peeking out behind the backstop and the trees along the Tidal Basin.

A figure approached: Emily, finishing her rounds. She met him under one of the cherry trees.

"Clear," she said.

"Me too."

They'd come early to the meeting to search the site for any kind of setup.

"You sure you can trust her?"

"Enough to start," Emily said.

The exchange brought him back to Geneva, that apartment, and Finlay's last questions, his doubts before they met with Clarke. "Emily—"

"I've got this, Sam. Keep an eye out."

He checked his watch. "She'll be here soon. I'll be over here," he said. "If you need help, turn my way and run your hand through your hair. I'll be there. And if anything seems off, just walk away."

"Got it," she said, and rolled out.

He pulled back into the shadows among the trees and watched

her cross the fields. She headed toward the roadway on the western edge of the park, along the river.

Sam scanned the surroundings. A couple strolled to his left, near the basin's edge, the spot with the best views of the Jefferson.

A few minutes later, a pair of halogen headlights came up the road: the white BMW SUV. It pulled over and parked.

Mercer stepped out, wearing a dark blue jacket with the collar up in the back—*playing spy*, Sam thought with amusement—and walked toward the bench where Emily was sitting.

Emily rose and greeted her about twenty feet from the bench, near the path along the river. Sam turned slowly, searching the humid night for threats.

Emily and Mercer strolled over the cracked asphalt, moving south, the river lapping against the breakwater and filling the air with a silty smell.

"So what's going on, Emily?"

"I think there's a mole in my division."

"Can you tell me his name? Her name?"

"Will you agree not to do anything with the information before I'm ready?"

Mercer put her hands in the pockets of her coat. "If I have information about a threat . . ." She paused and looked to Emily. "Yes. I will be with you every step of the way. It's someone senior?"

"Greg Jones."

Mercer gave her a solemn nod. "What are you basing this on?"

Emily explained about the missing files and the alterations to the documents related to Parker and Hassan.

"You went looking for this information on your own? Searching for files? Don't tell me whether or not you were cleared for them."

A pained look. "Caesar's wife must be above suspicion. And what prompted you to go after this in the first place?"

"I can't talk about that yet. I—" Emily almost said *just wanted to see*, then caught herself and went with something stronger, as Mercer had taught her so long ago. "I need to know if he might be working with anyone else and if there's anyone we can approach whom we can absolutely trust."

"It's dangerous ground, Emily. He is . . . very well situated in Langley and on the Hill. Do you have anything else? Anything solid?"

"I can document the tampering with the files." Emily hesitated for a moment, then went on. "And I have shots of him watching my house."

"Him personally?"

"Yes. At night."

Mercer breathed out through pursed lips. "There's more," she said.

Emily didn't respond.

"You're holding back. It's fine. I get it. Are you protecting yourself or someone else?"

"Where can we go with this?" Emily asked.

"It's not going to be easy. Understand that up front."

"I know."

"Though if anyone can make it through this, it's you. You were always so willful. Do you remember when your dad brought you to my office?" She looked down and laughed. "And then you lobbied me?"

Emily nodded. She'd been a little intense as a child.

"How old were you?"

"Eleven." She'd done a report on the Violence Against Women Act for school and made sure that Mercer had her facts straight.

"I sent you down the hall to knock on the other senators' doors, and off you went. You talked to everyone in Russell."

"And Dirksen. The security guards showed me the tunnel."

Mercer paused and faced her. "You're so like him, your father."

Emily gave her a guarded look.

"In the best ways. This is going to be hard. No matter what's happening, you know the Agency's instinct is to protect itself, right or wrong."

"I know. I'm ready."

"He'd have been so proud of you, Emily."

Mercer let a moment pass. "I still feel like I'm in the dark here, though."

Sam moved under the trees, tracking Emily and Mercer as they walked along the path, moving closer to where the senator had parked.

A car approached from the south on the low bridge that carried the road across the basin at the very tip of the peninsula. Sam shielded his eyes from its headlights as it took the curve and headed up the road toward Emily. It accelerated and passed her and Mercer, its lights flashing between the trees as it drove on.

The glow spilled out over the woods to his right, and Sam noticed a man moving between the trees on his side of the field, farther north.

It was a good distance and dark, but there was something about his posture, the forward lean of a boxer coming out of his corner, that raised an alarm in Sam. The man turned Sam's way. The face was shadowed, but he seemed to be looking straight at him even though Sam was hidden in the dark.

Sam felt a prickle along his neck and arms. He'd seen that face this afternoon: Arkady Novik, the traveling illegal who'd been standing outside Sam's house. It was another ambush.

He stepped behind the trunk of a maple and tapped out a message to Emily: "Threat from my house is here. Break it off and go."

He drew his gun and started after him, striding over the patchy grass. Sam scanned through the trees. Ahead, they grew thick around the Roosevelt Memorial. Dozens of places to hide. Was he drawing Sam away deliberately? Were there others?

Sam looked back and forth between the woods ahead and the river path where Emily and Mercer walked unprotected. He cursed under his breath, then turned and started moving toward her and the senator.

53

MERCER WALKED JUST ahead of Emily on the path. They were coming back toward her BMW.

"Does this have anything to do with the Lincoln Memorial bombing?" Mercer asked.

Emily said nothing.

"My God," Mercer said. "Emily, is there a threat we need to know about? Something coming?"

Emily stopped and looked down at the gnarled roots stretching through the dirt. She couldn't shake the idea that all of this concern was an act, a trap, but still, the intelligence officer in her had to do something, to raise the alarm. She couldn't live with herself if she let this happen on her watch.

"You don't trust me? Emily, please."

"They are scouting targets in the District, maybe Northern Virginia, within a mile of where we're standing."

Her phone vibrated in her pocket. Emily took it out.

"Whatever evidence you have," Mercer said, "I need it."

Emily read Sam's message and stepped to the side, surveying the park around her, a heaviness growing in her chest. Something was wrong. Had she said too much? Misjudged Mercer?

"Did you hear me?"

"I'm sorry," Emily said. "We need to go."

"What?"

"It's not safe here."

Mercer's brows knit; she looked incredulous and put out for an instant, and then the panic showed in her face.

"Everything will be okay," Emily said, raising her left hand in a calming gesture and drawing her gun with the right. Mercer's eyes were wide open. She'd known only the young woman, not the operative.

Emily lifted her phone and called Sam. "What's happening?"

"A setup. An ambush. I don't know, but get off the fucking X. Get her out of here and go back to the car. Head south. I'm between you and him. I'll cover."

"Sam, are you sure? I can finish this up."

"I saw Novik. It's both your lives. *Move.*"

Mercer took a long step back. "Emily." She spoke with forced composure, trying to get control of the situation. "What is happening?"

"Senator, I'm sorry, but you should go back to your car and leave as quickly as you can."

A man walked toward them on the other side of the road, and Emily saw that it was Sam, moving fast, his pistol out and ready.

Mercer followed her stare. She reeled back, arms rising as if to protect herself at the sight of the armed man.

"Diane. It's okay. He's with me. He's CIA. It's for our protection. I can explain, but you should get back in your car and go. Head south. My friend saw someone coming from the other direction. We'll protect you. Just go."

"Emily."

"Please. I'll call you later. I hope you'll still help us. I'm so sorry."

She nodded, her face pale. "Be safe," she said, and started moving toward her BMW. From the way Mercer looked at Sam, the shock and fear, Emily didn't know if she had lost her trust for good and, perhaps, her only way out of this.

Emily went to Sam's side, and they looked out into the darkness.

"I'll go with her," she said.

"No. She may be part of it."

"After all that?"

"We can cover her from here."

They scanned the fields as Mercer ran to her car. The door slammed, the engine started, and she pulled out.

"Where was he?" Emily asked.

"There." Sam pointed toward the Tidal Basin side and the trees.

"Alone?"

"I don't know."

"You're sure it was him?"

"Ninety percent. Good enough to call it."

She turned, slowly searching the fields. No one. Not a sound.

"You were supposed to stay out of sight, Sam. If she reports this, I'm done."

"You're both alive," he said.

"Do you see anything?"

"No," Sam said.

Emily looked south toward the bridge and saw Mercer's taillights as she neared it. "I know you've lost—"

A white flash filled the night, there and gone in a split second.

A ball of red fire grew, swallowing Mercer's car, and climbed toward the sky, its walls roiling with black smoke.

Sam steeled himself. He'd seen plenty of blasts at a distance and knew this moment, the eerie silence between when the light hit you and the sound.

The shock wave punched him in the chest and knocked his body back an inch. The adrenaline flooded through him and he rode it, used it without letting it take control.

He circled, readying for a secondary attack that would take advantage of the distraction from the blast, a standard tactic. A hail of bullets or another explosion would take out those who ran to help.

The fireball, mostly smoke now, rose into the sky, leaving behind the burning skeleton of Mercer's BMW.

Emily ran toward it, and he followed, the warmth of the flames riding toward him on puffs of wind. As they came closer, he saw an arm, still sleeved in blue, lying on the grass fifty feet from the car, hand to the sky as if demanding something.

The car's frame dropped a foot, and a section of parapet fell off the bridge into the river, sending waves out in perfect circles across the water.

Sam ran faster and grabbed Emily's arm, checking her as they neared the bridge. She looked back at him, freed her arm, and started walking toward the furnace.

"Emily! She's gone!"

She kept going, then turned to the side as a plume of smoke drifted around her. She stopped, the red light wavering over her face. Sam ran to her, put his arm around her shoulders, and pulled her away.

Her face was expressionless, frozen in shock.

"The secondary," he said. "Come on."

Emily's eyes stayed fixed on the car as she moved with him. Once they had gone ten feet, she looked at Sam, nodded, and swallowed. Her steps grew stronger. They started to run back toward the car, Sam in front, covering the darkness ahead with his gun.

54

THERE WAS NO sign of Arkady Novik as they raced to Emily's car. They climbed in and took off, Sam behind the wheel, expecting a shot or a blast from every shadow and every turn, but none came.

He drove along the river and pulled into the lookout off the GW Memorial Parkway where they had stopped that afternoon. Sam could just see the Tidal Basin in the distance and the emergency lights flashing around the bridge. Emily stepped out, and he followed her to the grass on top of the bluff.

An explosion. A dead senator. The DC cops and Capitol Police would already have a dragnet around the park. If Novik could be found, they would find him, but Sam doubted that he would be caught. The man had lived for years as a ghost.

Emily took a step closer to the edge, her arms up, her fingers laced behind her head, pacing slowly.

"Jesus, Sam. What was that?"

"Car bomb," he said.

"It wasn't on the bridge?" Her words were flat, focused, clinging to the work to hold off the shock. She brought her arms down.

"Possibly, but it looked like someone wired up the BMW."

"Novik," she said. "Russian intelligence."

"We're getting too close. He found out somehow that we were

meeting with her and put an end to it. Or he was trying to use her to get us."

"Maybe they were protecting their source, Jones. What if he and Novik are working together? We were about to blow the whistle on him, and they took out our best chance of exposing him and whatever they have him doing." She looked out over the cathedral-like spires of Healy Hall on the Georgetown campus. "Or Jones put it together himself."

Emily shut her eyes and touched her fingers to her temple. "They were hoping I would get in the car with her."

"Or close to it. That was more explosive than you would need to kill the occupants."

"We were walking right toward it."

He stepped over and put his arm around her shoulders.

Emily took a few long breaths, then paced over the dirt.

"I brought her into this." She shut her eyes hard and lowered her head, kneading the palm of her right hand with the fingers of her left.

"Emily. It's not your fault. Don't go there."

She looked up. "How can I not?"

Sam thought of Finlay and Clarke and Dimos. He didn't have a good answer for her or for himself, but he offered her what he could, how he coped: "You keep moving. Come on."

He turned to the car. Emily frowned and reached into her pocket. She took out her phone and looked at a message on the screen.

"What is it?"

"They're calling me in. They want everyone who is working on the bombing at the office."

"Because of Mercer?"

"Two bombs on the Mall. It makes sense."

"Did they call just you, or everyone?"

"The whole team." She scratched at the side of her thumb with her finger.

"Jones will be there. After everything today, I don't know if it's safe."

"It's the one place he can't kill me," she said. "If I disappear, that will only bring suspicion."

"You may already be a suspect. What will you do? What would you tell them?"

"I can find a way to put them onto Novik without giving up what we know. I'll try to figure out what's happening tomorrow night that needs extra security. Maybe that'll give us something on what Konstantin is targeting. And I can get what I need to run your surveillance footage past the Agency files."

"I don't like it."

"You need those files to ID Konstantin's men. They might lead us to him." Emily brought up her hands. "And I might even be able to point the investigation at Jones somehow. This is a United States senator, for God's sake, Sam. It's too big for him to cover up. I plant some bread crumbs, and we let the Bureau find him."

She was talking quickly, pacing. She was still hoping that the world she had thrived in would save her—the world of institutions, authorities, and process. But all of that was gone. There was no ref. No rules. Nowhere to turn. Only survival.

She had just seen a friend, a mentor, torn apart. Sam could understand the shock. The need for order and sense.

"Emily. You can't trust anyone. If this is about starting a war, then we can only imagine how high it goes. We have to do this on our own. We can stop it, but I want you to stay away from Jones."

"We don't even know what we're stopping." She looked back toward the Tidal Basin, and her face fell.

He took a step closer and his hand went to her elbow. It was too much. She needed time.

Emily straightened up and looked at him, letting warmth into her eyes.

"I'm going," she said.

"You don't have to do this."

"I'm not scared, Sam. I'm fucking angry. It's on. Let's go."

55

AS EMILY MADE her way from the tree-lined CIA entrance to the old headquarters building, she felt them staring at her: the guard at the front gate, the snipers looking down from the rooftops, the matronly woman who worked the turnstiles in the foyer every weekend. Her guilt felt as glaring as a neon light. She was withholding information and running an illegal op. She'd just left the scene of a crime. The fact that she was doing it to save the Agency from itself wouldn't mean a damn thing if they decided to take her down. Making the honorable choice had landed plenty of idealistic intelligence officers in limbo or prison. In some cases, the Agency even embraced their cause later but left them to languish.

She'd dropped Sam back at his car on her way in, and now she was standing in the old headquarters lobby, holding her credentials out to the woman at the turnstiles.

"Busy night," she said, looking past Emily to the others coming in behind her. "That's never good."

"No," Emily said.

"Thank you."

"You too." The blast at the Tidal Basin had been all over the radio on her way in, though the press didn't have much. She'd already received a division-wide update stating that Diane Mercer was the only victim.

She took the elevator up to three and walked past Russia House, peering in as the door opened. It was the full crew, buzzing across the open floor plan, and she caught a flash of Jones deep in conversation with someone just outside his office.

The nerves picked up. Her skin was crawling. She kept walking and turned the corner to a dead-end hallway with a bathroom at the end that didn't see a lot of use. She stood before the sink, splashed cold water on her face, and looked at herself. The stress and fatigue showed in her eyes, the anxiety in her flush, but it wasn't terrible.

After drying her face with a paper towel, she took three breaths, counting in for four seconds, holding it for four, out for four, holding for four, and again. It was called box breathing, a technique some jacked-up ex-SEAL had demonstrated for them in training and identical to breathwork she'd been doing in her woo-woo yoga classes for years. It could drop your heart rate and adrenaline levels in a matter of seconds. They taught it to intel officers for operations, to steel any shaking hands that might give you away when faced by hostile forces. She never imagined the threat would be her own superior.

She pushed the door open and stepped into the hallway, moving with confidence. She'd gone about twenty feet when she heard a man's shoes clacking on the linoleum, getting closer. Jones rounded the corner ahead.

Emily quieted her unease and offered him a benign look of recognition.

"Greg," she said. "What's up?"

He walked up to her, came in close enough that Emily caught the whiff of coffee on his breath, and said in a subdued voice: "You've heard the news?"

"Mercer." She nodded and let the pain, real enough, show.

"I'm so sorry. I know you were close."

"Thank you," she said, choking down her disgust at the hypocrisy.

"Emily," he said.

"Yes."

"Is there anything you need to say to me?"

"Like what?"

"What are you working on?"

She put on a puzzled look. "The Lincoln Memorial attack. What is this, Greg?"

"Have you seen Sam Hudson recently?"

"I checked in on him the other night, after the bombing."

"I want you to be careful around him."

She kept up her act as if she weren't following.

"He was at the Lincoln bombing. He was at the shooting on Hains Point. We think he's in contact with Russian intelligence. Please, for your sake, just tell me if you know where he is. I'm worried about Sam, not just what he's doing but what might happen to him."

"You think he was involved with the bombing?" She showed a bit of shock, but she was playing for information, trying to figure out what Jones's angle was here.

"Perhaps. He wouldn't be the first fireman to play with matches. He was deep into these theories. He and Williams had so much invested in them that they just had to be true. You have to be careful, Emily. You can tell me. Have you been talking to him? Do you know where he is?"

Jones was all concern, and everything about it seemed genuine, a perfect performance. It was, in its way, scarier than a straight-up threat, because she saw how insidious he could be, all kind eyes and worry.

He was planting doubts about Sam, trying to turn her against him, accusing him of the things he was guilty of himself.

"I don't know what he's told you, or what you've seen or think you've seen, but if you speak with him, please watch out. He's in a very dangerous place."

It surprised her how strongly some part of her wanted to believe that this was all some nightmare of misunderstanding, that Jones was running an aboveboard operation that she had simply misconstrued as treason. But he knew her. He was playing on her respect for this place, for its mission, for need-to-know.

He moved slightly closer, his eyes narrowing. "Where is he, Emily?" Each word a shard of ice.

She looked back at him squarely, didn't retreat, let a glimmer of anger show. "I don't know, Greg. Now, is there anything you'd like to get off *your* chest?"

That caught him off guard, but then he turned somber, as if faced with an unpleasant but necessary chore. He shook his head, then looked back as if to confirm they were alone. He stepped slightly to the right, between her and the way out, then spoke in the tone of a disappointed father.

"You know, Emily—"

He cut off as a shoe squeaked around the corner, the high peal echoing down the hall. One of the ops deputies came into view.

"Greg," he said.

Jones turned.

"They need us upstairs."

"Sure," he said, his voice bright. Emily was already walking fast around him and down the hall.

She tracked just ahead of them and turned into the Russia House suite, going slowly through the door, long enough for her to make sure Jones was moving on, walking back to the elevators with the deputy.

56

EMILY THOUGHT OF going straight back to the entrance, getting in her car, and running, but she had a window of time now to get what she needed and to see if any intel had come in connecting her with Mercer or the car bombing.

She went to her office, and Matt came up alongside her holding a sheaf of papers in his right hand.

"Emily, are you all right?"

She stopped and faced him. "What do you mean?"

"Mercer . . . I'm so sorry."

"Yes. I'm okay, thank you." She put on a distracted look as if trying to power through. "Where are we?"

"The explosive that took out her BMW looks like a match for the bombing at the Lincoln. We're still waiting on confirmation."

"Do we have any video of the incident? Or of Mercer's movements earlier in the day?"

"Some. We contacted her chief of staff for her schedule. We're pulling footage everywhere she went. I'm going through it now. It might show who had a chance to rig up her car."

Emily felt a stab of fear. Security-camera footage could link her to Mercer, but clearly no one had made the connection yet or she would be in for questioning now.

"Is that on the network?"

"Yes."

"All right. I want to double down on the Soviet angle. I'll go back over the long-term sleepers, the illegals files. We can run any suspects that appear in the footage past those dossiers and see what hits. They were probably watching Mercer. They should show up on tape somewhere."

"You want me to queue up those files for you?"

"I'll handle it," she said. "And check out the dossier on a guy named Arkady Novik."

"The center illegal?"

"Right. The more I looked at the Lincoln bombing, the more I thought of him. Something about the patterns. A hunch, but worth taking another look at the old photo of him we have as you go over the footage."

"I will, thanks."

Emily shut the door to her office, logged into her laptop, and went to the counterintelligence files on suspected Russian illegals and their associates. She started syncing them to her machine so she could look at them later too, away from anyone watching. Her work laptop was set up for classified material, secured by a password and a fingerprint scan.

Next, she opened up the facial-recognition software and began a new query, using tonight's bombing investigation for authorization. She brought up the counterintelligence photo databases—shots of all suspected and confirmed foreign intelligence officers, along with anyone who had crossed the path of the FBI's spy hunters. She wanted to run the images from Sam's surveillance footage past it, but she couldn't risk that here, so she simply cached the images from the database so she could run a search off-line later.

As the files transferred over, she went onto the internal network and began pulling up the evidence that was coming in about Mercer's movements that day.

A lot of surveillance footage had already arrived. It was easy enough in the days of cloud storage; no more running around pulling VHS tapes from the back rooms of stores and restaurants.

She went through the network folders and scanned the videos. They made up a strange, disjointed reel of Diane's last hours in color and black-and-white. Emily watched her walk past the Senate garage entrance at seven a.m. carrying a coffee from Grace Street Coffee Roasters and stopping to talk with the Capitol Police officer on duty. She noticed as Mercer slipped her keys into her pocket.

Always buy dresses with pockets. Emotion tightened Emily's throat as she looked at Mercer's face, frozen mid-laugh.

She went on, searching the video for anything that might implicate her. A shot of the gardens outside the Ritz-Carlton Georgetown froze her in her seat.

Scrubbing forward in time, she caught the moment when Mercer walked out of the spa. Emily kept going and, a few minutes later in the tape, saw herself crossing the camera's field of view in the distance.

Her mouth went dry. She zoomed in on her face, out of focus in the far corner of the frame. She knew what to search for, of course, but still, she had to assume that anyone else scouring those tapes would eventually identify her.

Looking out across the suite, she watched the analysts, and saw Matt staring at his screen, his hand working a mouse.

Emily searched through the other folders until she found footage, recently updated, from the Park Police.

The videos were security-camera footage of the bombing from around the park, and she scanned them for any sign of Novik or herself. This tape was surely going to be scrutinized.

One camera looked northwest along the bridge where Mercer had died. She scrolled through its footage, studying the edge of the fields in the distance. That was near where she and Sam had stood before Mercer went back to her car. She ran the video forward, the dread creeping up as Mercer's car came into the frame and then blew up in a flash of white on the bridge. Emily kept going, but there was no trace of her and Sam on the tape.

Another camera showed the road farther north, and she could just make out her car near the left side of the frame, though the license plate was hard to read in the shadows.

She fast-forwarded until she saw herself approaching her car, then hit Play. Sam was just out of the shot. When Emily opened the passenger door, the interior light hit her face. It would be possible to identify her, and as the car pulled out and made a U-turn on Ohio Drive, a streetlight caught her tags, making them easy enough to read.

Her hand rested on her desk holding a pen, clicking it over and over.

It might have been possible to explain away the Ritz meeting with Mercer. She could have said that she was catching up with her, which would have been an omission of the full truth, not an out-and-out lie, but there was no way she could talk her way out of being spotted in the nearly empty park where Mercer was murdered.

She watched as the facial-recognition software inched toward finishing its downloads—90 percent. The other files were already done.

A knock on her door startled her. It creaked open.

"Emily." Matt leaned his head in. "Sorry."

"Don't worry," she said, playing calm, though she felt anything but. "Come in."

He stepped in and pulled the door shut. She didn't like anything about that move or his posture, a wariness that had him hanging back near the door.

"What's going on, Emily?"

"What do you mean?"

"Were you with Mercer before she died?"

Emily betrayed no reaction, though it felt like all the blood had drained from her veins. She needed to see how much he knew. "What is this about?"

"I saw you on the tape."

"What tape?"

"The park. Your car. You were at the bombing."

"Yes, I was." She sat back and used the armrests on her chair, open, confiding, nothing defensive. Looking out through the narrow glass window beside her door, she saw Jones crossing at the far end of the room. "I was trying to stop all this."

"You knew?" he asked.

"That a bomb was coming? Of course not. But I was talking to Mercer. She was helping me." Matt had her on tape. There was no evading that. She had to justify it, bring him to her side, buy herself time.

"Have you mentioned this to anyone?"

"No. Not yet."

"Emily, you have to tell me what's going on."

"I reached out to her because I wasn't sure who I could trust here."

"What?" She'd never seen him so shaken.

"I think there is a penetration, Matt." That was the only way she could justify her actions, but she wasn't going to give him anything else.

He came in closer and lowered his voice. "Have you shared it with counterintelligence? With anyone?"

"Not yet. I'm not sure how far it goes. I need one day. Let me handle this."

"I can't, Emily."

"I confided in Mercer and then someone killed her. Please don't tell a soul. Anyone who knows about it ends up being hurt. I need to find a safe way to raise the alarm. Do you understand?"

"I can't sit on this, Emily." He stepped toward the door and peered out through the window.

"Matt, please . . ."

"Who put you onto this idea?"

"I can't share anything else, for your sake."

"Was it Sam Hudson?"

"Why?"

"Oh no. Haven't you heard?"

Emily stood, one hand on her desk. "What happened?"

57

SAM DROVE UP Wisconsin Avenue, watching every passerby—the late-night runner, the man with the CVS bag—as he climbed the hill toward his house. He parked four blocks away. Novik was hunting him now, escalating. He might be watching his place.

Sam stepped out of the car and cut between two brick buildings to one of the winding alleys hidden behind Georgetown's facades. He wanted to see if there was any surveillance. If his house was clear, he could get the latest from his cameras and grab some more clothes and gear.

But part of him was hoping it wouldn't be clear. They'd killed one more. They'd brought the same guilt that he carried down on Emily. He wanted to find the attackers, get behind one of them, and draw blood.

He paused, looked between two houses to the north, and saw a Ford Taurus parked on the street leading to his place. A guy sat behind the wheel. Something about him—the number 4 taper cut and the set of his jaw—screamed Bureau to Sam.

Sam went on, slowly, hanging close to the backs of the buildings for cover.

He stopped and scanned the alley far ahead. A man crossed at the next street, wearing a gray sweatshirt, pacing and talking on a cell phone, doing a good job blending in except he had the same haircut as the guy in the car. Foot surveillance. Feds or someone who wanted to look like them.

The law was waiting for him, and he had to assume agents were already inside his place. He swallowed, a bitter taste near the back of his throat, then went back the way he'd come and checked for surveillance on his car for what felt like an eternity. Clear. He started it up and headed east. Once he was sure he wasn't being followed, he lifted his phone to warn Emily.

Emily rounded her desk toward Matt. "Tell me what happened."

"Was Sam Hudson with you tonight at the park?"

"What are you getting at?"

"He was at the other bombing, and he was there when Christopher Dimos was killed."

She waited.

"That was enough to search his place. They found explosives, Emily. They matched the Semtex from the Lincoln Memorial bomb."

"What?"

"It's beyond question."

"The bomber wired up Sam's house too?"

"No. Just trace amounts of the explosives."

"He was hit in the Lincoln bombing. He could have tracked it back to his house."

"No, Emily. It was raw Semtex, not residue from the blast. They picked it up on his tools. It matched the forensics. That's where the bomb was prepared."

"You're wrong."

"If we have a penetration agent, it's him. Off-book meetings with Russians, then his partner gets killed."

"No."

"Emily. This is what he does. He turns people. He uses their trust. Did he get to you?"

"It's not that, Matt. I'm sure. It's not safe for either one of us if I tell you everything and why I'm so certain, but you have to give me one day, please."

"You need to come clean. You know I can't conceal this."

"Was there a tip to search Sam's place? Where did it come from?"

She saw a man pass just outside the door: Jones.

"I can't—"

Matt cut off when he heard the doorknob rattle. Jones opened it and stood in the doorway.

He looked back and forth between the two of them but didn't speak. Pros know how to use silence to draw out words; people will say anything to break the excruciating tension filling a room. Matt's face was tense. You could almost see the stress coming off him.

"What's going on, Greg?" Emily said, her voice calm.

"Am I interrupting?" He looked to Matt, whose eyes were still on Emily. Matt finally turned to face Jones.

"No," Matt said. "Just comparing notes on the video."

"Did you find anything?"

Again, Matt waited an extra beat before he answered. "I'm not sure. I have to go back over it."

"Really," Jones said. "What are we talking about?"

"It might be nothing. Let me fill you in later."

"That's fine," Jones said. "Can I borrow you for a minute? I need a Bureau take on something."

"Sure thing," Matt said and forced a smile. As he followed Jones to the door, Matt glanced back, and Emily whispered, "One day, please."

I'm sorry, he mouthed, real pain in his eyes.

Emily watched them go into Jones's office then checked the progress of the download on her laptop—complete. She grabbed it, went out through the bullpen into the hallway, powered on her phone, and headed for the main entrance. She needed to warn Sam. The FBI might try to arrest him.

She exited through the lobby, turned right off the main path into the darkness among the trees, and called Sam through Signal.

"Where are you?" he asked.

"The Agency. Don't go anywhere near your place."

"Too late, but I'm clear. I saw men staking it out. What's going on?"

"It's the Bureau, Sam. They found traces of the explosives from the Lincoln bombing at your house."

"That's impossible."

"There was residue on tools."

"What tools?"

"I don't know. They said the forensics match. Did you touch anything after you came back the night of the Lincoln bombing?"

"No. There are no tools. Jesus."

"Sam. Make this make sense for me, please."

"You believe them?"

"I believe what they found. Is there anything you haven't told me? Did you bring evidence there, anything?"

"No. It's a plant." She heard him exhale. "We were getting too close, and they had to shut us down. They sicced the whole fucking Bureau on me."

"It sounds crazy, Sam."

"You know the truth. You saw Jones meeting with Markov. You saw the files he purged. They are setting us up, Emily. God, if they can put us at the meeting tonight—"

"They can."

"Get out of there. What do you think is at your house, if they even need more evidence?"

She looked back at the glass doors and the streamlined portico over the entrance, someone's long-ago dream of the future, lit up against the dark. She couldn't imagine leaving this place behind.

"They are cleaning up this mess. Jones, the Russians. Maybe both of them together, but you're not safe. Just go," Sam said.

She could hear the urgency in his voice. It sounded like a stranger's, that note of fear so unlike him.

Jones appeared in the lobby and moved across the marble floor. He went up to the turnstile and spoke with the guard.

She kept going, fast, toward the parking lot. "Where can I meet you?" she said, walking straight to her car. Sam gave her an address as she moved over the wet grass.

"I'll be there in twenty," she said. She got in her Lexus and pulled out, cutting across the rows in the mostly empty lot.

She came to a stop at the exit gate with its mirrored-glass guardhouse. The man inside the hut looked up from a computer terminal and peered out.

Emily's right foot shook against the brake.

The man smiled, and the gate rose.

A phone rang inside the guardhouse, and he turned to answer it.

Emily pressed the gas, rounding the gate before it was fully up, and turned right onto Route 123, watching her mirrors as she sped away through the warm Virginia night.

58

NO CARS FOLLOWED Emily, or at least none that she could see, as she made her way to the address Sam had given her.

She pulled up to a parking garage at the edge of Tysons Corner. She knew why Sam had chosen it. It would break any surveillance from the sky, like the kind she had used to track the gray pickup truck from the coffee-shop meeting.

Emily was the target now, the suspect. It chilled her to see the black sky ahead and the stars of Cassiopeia and to think that her own agency, her own government, might have a camera up there hunting her down.

She entered the garage and drove up the ramps. As she turned onto the third floor, a man stepped out from behind a parked minivan. It was Sam.

She pulled into the next empty spot and met him near the garage's parapet, the wind pushing past them. She looked out over the sparse woods between them and the highway and the sleeping residential developments in the distance.

He didn't say a word, just scanned between the cars as he led her toward the stairs, hugging the wall, avoiding the path of any cameras.

They exited on the street level, and Sam led her across a strip of grass to an access road running along the back of the garage where an aging Ford F-150 was parked.

"Did you steal this?"

They'd all learned how to do it at the Farm. Taking a vehicle was standard procedure when you were cornered. Emily felt numb, unable to believe that she was going black, operating under hard-target rules in her own backyard.

"Borrowed. They won't miss it," he said and got in. The smell of cigarettes wafted out.

Emily climbed in the passenger seat, and they took off.

The steering wheel shook against Sam's palm, rumbling with the old truck's engine.

Emily turned to him as they pulled onto the highway. "Go past my house," she said.

"They might be watching it."

"I have to see. Don't get too close."

He nodded and drove to her neighborhood. He slowed as he rolled past the turn for her street, looking for surveillance.

"Keep going," she said. Sam drove on.

Emily looked stricken. "Unmarked car," she said, resting her head back against the seat. "Just take us to the house in Arlington."

"No one from work knows about it?"

"It's clean."

Ten minutes later, Sam neared the professor's home where they had stopped earlier that day. He did a circuit of the block to check for watchers, then parked.

The neighbor's dog started barking. Emily let them in, and they did a quick search of the house before coming back to the kitchen. She put her keys down on the table.

Sam placed his laptop at the other end, opened it, and started tracking Markov. He was still at home.

He checked his watch. Less than twenty-four hours until the deadline Dimos had given him for the attack. "Did you get the files?" he asked.

She nodded and put her laptop down on the table.

"Great," he said and slid out a chair. "They can't track you with that?" he asked, pointing to her computer.

"Not if I'm careful."

Sam waited for her to open the machine, but she just stood there, looking across the kitchen but not really seeing anything.

"Are you all right?"

"I don't know. Is there anything you haven't told me, Sam?"

"What?" He took a step toward her. "Emily, no."

Her face was pained. She had probably been running on adrenaline since the bombing, and now reality was sinking in. She couldn't go home. Her life as she knew it was over, and Sam was here, just plowing ahead.

"You believe them? That I was part of this?"

She put her hand on the back of a chair.

"I'm sorry you're in the middle of it now," he said, "and I'm sorry about how it went down. But you know the truth here. You're innocent and look what they're doing to you. Trust me, Emily."

"I believe you, Sam. It's just everyone . . . everyone who—"

She broke off, wincing, as if trying to take back the words, but Sam knew where she'd been going: *Everyone who trusts you ends up dead.*

He gritted his teeth.

"Damn it," she said. "Sorry. It's . . . it's a lot."

He moved closer and his hand went toward her elbow.

She held her palm up, and he stopped.

"I need a minute," she said, and she turned and walked out of the kitchen. He let her go. The back door opened. A draft of humid air pushed into the house, and he watched her step into the backyard and stand in the garden with her eyes closed, breathing slowly.

Sam gave her space. Nothing she could say was any worse than the thoughts that dogged him, and he knew exactly how she felt, the shock of finding yourself on the wrong side of the law.

He sat down, double-checked the tracker on Markov, then brought out a small police scanner from one of his bags and put it on the table so he could listen for anyone coming. The FBI would use encrypted traffic, but that couldn't hide everything. A surge in encrypted signals would be an alarm. He started bringing up all the video surveillance he'd gathered from near his house so he could feed them into Emily's facial-recognition software. His eyes went to the window every few minutes to check on her, and finally he saw her looking back, watching him, her arms crossed over her chest.

Sam stood and went out through the back door. The screen creaked shut behind him. The clouds had moved in, promising rain.

"Hey," she said, and walked closer. "Sorry about that. I didn't mean—"

He held his hand up. "Don't be. You weren't wrong. I know how I come off. The crusade thing. I don't want you to feel like I'm using you."

"I don't. It all hit me at once. I needed time. It's not true, Sam, this garbage about you being out for yourself, burning people, trusting the wrong sources because you have something to prove. And I'm sorry if I ever gave you that impression. I know that's not what this is about for you."

"What is it about?"

"Doing right by Fin, by all of them. No matter where that leads. Protecting everyone out there. I saw that with you a long time ago, Sam. You weren't going to stop until you made everything right, until you'd taken down everyone who'd hurt your people. The ego thing was bullshit. It was just because you couldn't stand anyone who got in your way or slowed you down, but you were ten times harder on yourself."

He didn't say anything.

"I see you punishing yourself, Sam. The risks you're taking. You need to forgive yourself. For Fin—for all of them."

"You have?"

"Forgiven you? Yes. Completely."

A silence passed between them.

"Thank you," he said. "But I don't want to be. Not until I make this right."

She thought for a moment. "It's just another cover, Sam, this idea that you have to be perfect, save everyone. It's noble, but it's too much to ask. I saw that with you, that drive. You're human. We all lose people. No one can keep it up. I didn't want to be there to pick up the pieces when that happened, to watch you burn out trying to stop it, or burn out with you. I saw it with my dad. I've been through it myself. I can't do it again." A deep breath. "That's why I walked away after we got together that night. And it killed me to do it."

"So you could have a life?"

"That was part of it."

"And now that's gone." He shook his head, a mix of anger and regret. "I'm sorry I brought you into this, Emily."

"I brought myself into it. I knew what I was doing. Some things are worth it."

"It's going to be ugly now. Alone. Our own people after us. There are ways out."

"I'm not bailing, Sam."

"You could put it on me."

"Nope. You're stuck with me. I'll take the mission over the job any day. Let's get to work."

59

SAM AND EMILY sat side by side at the kitchen table, transferring Sam's surveillance-camera footage to her machine so she could run the facial-recognition program. It took forty-five minutes to queue up and start the search. With the amount of video and the number of candidate images they were comparing it to, the whole process might take a few hours on Emily's laptop.

Since she was under suspicion, she explained, she would probably be locked out of the CIA's access to live camera feeds. That meant she couldn't search for matching faces around the District in real time, but there were other options. "They're not strictly legal," she said. "I'll see what I can do."

She checked the spyware on Markov's phone. It was reporting back its location every minute. "No audio or video, though," she said.

"Can you get anything else off it?"

"Texts and call log. I did a quick look before, and none of it seemed operational. He's probably using something encrypted for that or a separate phone."

"Still, that might give us his network or his patterns," Sam said. Emily nodded, her eyes heavy with fatigue, and looked back to the computer screen.

"I'll go through them," he said. "You want to get some sleep?"

She hesitated for a moment. "I can help."

"I'm wired. We should rest when we can. Who knows what tomorrow will be like?"

"Thanks," she said and stood. She put her hand on his shoulder and kissed the top of his head. "You have everything you need?"

He put his hand on hers. "I'm good."

Emily went up, and Sam lost himself in the work, waiting for matches from the facial-recognition software and looking for any connections between Markov and the other players or signs of what he and Jones were planning, but the messages were routine: hookup texts to a string of women, calls to restaurants and college friends.

On his laptop, Sam studied the maps again, examining the torn piece he'd taken off Shooter Two and the digital copies of the maps he'd gotten from Turner, tracing every building, every target, looking over the Cyrillic text and the classifications along the edge. A light rain started to fall, drumming against the windows.

After twenty minutes, he pushed the computer away. He pictured Shooter Two's face and Arkady Novik's. They were out there. One more day. And he still couldn't see it. His options were running out. He pulled up a map of Jones's house. His eyes went to his gun on the table. Soon.

Sam got up, did a last check of the locks and windows and alarm—though nothing would do better than the wound-up dog next door—and went upstairs, bringing both laptops with him, his closed, Emily's still running. He brought them into the second bedroom, which had pale pink walls and stuffed animals on the shelves, and put them on a small white desk.

He pulled off his boots and clothes and got in the twin bed to catch a few hours of sleep. As tired as he was, he couldn't rest. His mind raced, fitting together every lead, the flash of the bomb flickering over and over in his mind.

The door opened, and Sam went for the gun on the nightstand but stopped halfway there. Emily stood in the doorway, wearing a tank top and pajama bottoms, silhouetted by the yellow light in the hall.

"Everything okay?"

"Fine," she said.

He held his arm out and she climbed into bed beside him. He brought her in close, her head resting on his chest. They lay like that for a long time, their breath coming and going together. Then her hand brushed his cheek, and he felt her lips on his, tentatively at first, then strong.

Her hand slid down to his neck, pulling him in. Sam let out a quiet sound of pain.

"God," Emily said. "I'm sorry."

"Don't be." He laughed and felt her body press against his.

60

LANGE MOVED FORWARD on his hands and knees over the wet floor of the tunnel, his shoulders brushing against the ceiling with every advance.

His flashlight cast a red glow down the narrow space, a long concrete coffin. Above him, he could hear a rushing sound like wind blowing underground.

Every ten meters or so, the tunnel narrowed under a thick concrete arch that looked like far more than was necessary to support the ceiling. Lange flattened down to pass under one of them.

He felt a faint stream of air rushing against his face, pushing away the stale smells, then double-checked the nylon map. After six meters, the tunnel ended.

Lange trained his light on the wall and made out a small metal grate set against the ceiling. He moved close to it and listened, feeling the air flow out. He shone the light through and could see the contours of another tunnel, about two meters tall and one meter wide, lined with insulated pipes on all sides.

They carried steam and chilled water from the Central Heating Plant to the federal buildings along the Mall, everything from the Capitol to the Treasury and the White House.

Lange took out a small tool, a black plastic box a little larger than his hand, and began passing it over the concrete, watching the LEDs on its face. Red, green, red. Something had been buried in the wall between this sewer and the steam tunnel.

He moved back to the nearest concrete arch and scanned it. The light went red, green, red near the top as he traced the hidden work of the saboteurs who had stolen down here nearly thirty-five years ago.

His left hand was braced on the floor, sunk into a layer of grit. No one had been here in decades.

Red, green, red.

He put the box down and ran his fingers over the rough surface of the arch.

It had been here the whole time, buried beneath the most well-guarded sites in America, at the place where all of the District's unseen tunnels ran within a few meters of each other. HYACINTH.

He brought the light back to the map and traced another route. Then he turned, pulling his knees tight to his chest to get around in the narrow space, forcing the breath out of his lungs, and started back.

The spaces grew larger and older as he progressed into the deeper layers of the city's history, concrete giving way to red brick.

Forty-five minutes later, his shoes soaked with water, his body damp with sweat, he came to it, the center of the labyrinth. He climbed out from a tunnel and lowered himself down a brick wall.

His light moved over the uneven masonry. It was a chamber ten meters wide and twelve meters long with a large brick pillar in its center. Along one wall, a stream of water ran in an open sewer.

He moved slowly, taking it all in as one would a cathedral.

The Americans and Soviets had long waged war underground. The U.S. had spent millions of dollars to build a tunnel under East Berlin to tap East German and Soviet military communications and hundreds of millions to burrow under the Russian embassy in DC. Both were ultimately failures, betrayed by moles.

But the HYACINTH work, built by hand over a decade, had never been discovered. Even if certain elements of it had been found, its true purpose would have been difficult, if not impossible, to discern. It turned the very foundations of the city into a weapon that Russia could use to attack at will.

His light stopped and fixed on what looked like a sealed-up window frame in the brick. He moved closer, his pulse rising tick by tick.

The seal in the frame appeared to be solid concrete, but with the right pressure on the bottom and by prying with his fingers at the top, he was able to pull it out, a one-centimeter-thick shell. He eased it to the ground, and then looked inside the recess.

A dull metal panel stood out from the brick in the back. Lange studied it. This was the heart. His eyes fixed on the small circle of chrome with a hole at its center near the top: a lock. He smiled.

His hand went into his pocket and closed on the smooth steel of the six-sided key.

61

RAIN PATTERED AGAINST the window. It was still well before dawn. Emily was already moving beside him. He stretched his neck and felt a twinge of pain.

"You okay?" she asked.

"Fighting form."

"It would have been ironic if I was the thing that finally killed you."

"Worth it," he said and ran his hand along her thigh. "So that's living?"

She nodded slowly.

"Then I'm all for it."

"Right?"

"We get through this and I'll make a habit of it." He settled his head back on the pillow. "Though it may need to be in a nonextradition country."

"As long as it's warm," Emily said and sat up on the edge of the bed.

"You know, at the beginning of all this, I thought you were playing me or working for someone. I thought you could be the mole."

"I was," she said. "Not a mole, I mean. I was working for myself."

"Coming by my house to check on me?"

"I wanted to make sure you were all right, but I was also interested in finding out whether you were behind any of this."

"Undercover. When did you change your mind on me?"

She ran her thumb over his cheek and gave him a sweet look. "Who says I did?"

She got up, walked a few feet away, then glanced back. "It was last night. Now, come on. Game day."

They went downstairs. Emily set up her computer on the kitchen table beside his. Sam made coffee, and she found some frozen waffles in the freezer and put them in the toaster.

He turned on cable news in the background and started checking the headlines on his phone. The bombing was the lead story everywhere. Diane Mercer had been identified as the victim, and the press was already tying it to the Lincoln Memorial blast, the graphics packages screaming "Terror on the Mall."

"That's what Konstantin wants," Sam said. "The fear."

On the TV, a congressman speaking gravely to a white-haired host suggested that both attacks were foreign plots and that America was ready to answer them with force.

"The hawks are circling," she said, standing over her computer. "He's been after the Russians since Star Wars. If the evidence tying this to Russia gets out, it's going to escalate fast."

"And if Konstantin does something massive tonight, it's over. Why would he want a war?"

"You know the reformers were building power, possibly trying to mount a challenge against the Kremlin."

"There's always someone angling."

"While you were on leave, we picked up intel that it's been growing into a serious threat. The Russian president's opponents think he's getting weaker. He's hunkered down at Novo-Ogaryovo." It was an estate outside Moscow, the Russian leader's capital-city refuge. "If there was a conflict with the U.S., the hard line could use it to lock up power. The people would rally around the leader."

Sam ran his hand along his jaw. "That has to be it. But the scale of these attacks still seems out of proportion."

"I don't know," Emily said.

Sam muted the TV and put on the captions. "Any hits on the facial recognition?"

"No," she said. "I can try to tweak a few settings. I heard back from FBI counterintelligence last night on the house in Annandale that we tracked the gray pickup to. It was totally clean, no evidence, no traces."

"It looked like they cleared out the compound near Ashburn too," Sam said and went to the coffee machine.

She looked at the maps on his laptop. "Did those give you anything?"

He shook his head, then came up beside her, gave her a cup of coffee, and took a sip of his own.

He walked to the window on the side of the kitchen and looked out through the drizzle, rivulets of rain streaking down the glass. In the distance, the water ran in a stream along the curb at the edge of the street, then dropped into the sewer.

"Is there something out there?" Emily asked.

"No," Sam said, turning and going back to the table. He looked at the torn scrap of map he'd taken from Shooter Two, tracing the outlines of the structures, some of them barely more than dots of ink on the page.

On his computer, he brought up the digital map from Turner that showed the same area. Then he switched to another scan, one that laid out the water systems, aqueducts, and sewers under the District.

"Look at this," he said, pointing to the nylon map. A black dot indicated a structure along Constitution Avenue. It was small enough to be a phone booth. Then he showed her the map of the same area on the computer.

"It's missing," he said. "It's only on Shooter Two's map."

She looked them over. "They're not identical. They could be from a couple of years apart."

"They are. I checked when some of these buildings went up. But that doesn't explain these." He pointed to four more dots, one near Union Station and the others along Constitution Avenue. "They're only on Shooter Two's map. The HYACINTH map."

"Targets?" she asked as Sam pulled up Google Maps and switched to a satellite view.

"Not likely. They're in the middle of the street, not high-profile buildings." He stared at the satellite imagery.

"What am I looking at?"

"They're manholes," he said, tapping the screen, "and small pumping stations."

"The Soviets were always playing games with maps," she said.

The party was paranoid about invasion or attack, and the only maps available to the public in the Soviet days were almost impossible to navigate with. Anything of military or intelligence interest on them would often be mislabeled or put out of place: a factory standing on the wrong side of the river, an airstrip shifted ten miles from its real location. Sam's older sources often talked about the strangeness of it, seeing paranoia embodied in something so basic and landmarks out of place, part of the unreality of Soviet life.

"But they're both military maps," she said.

Sam pointed to the mark in the corner of the digital map.

"*Sovershenno sekretno*," he said. It was the highest general level of classification in the Soviet system, equivalent to *top secret* in the United States. But Turner hadn't been read in on HYACINTH.

No one was. He showed her the scrap of torn map and pointed to the letters in the corner: *SS/OP.* "The HYACINTH map is *Sovershenno sekretno/osobaia papka*." That meant "top secret/special folder" and was used only for extremely sensitive information that was more tightly held than top secret. The U.S. had an equivalent: TS-SCI, for "top secret/sensitive compartmented information."

"Shooter Two had better maps," Sam said. "With details particular to HYACINTH."

"The sewers."

"It has to be."

"As access points?"

"Here," Sam said and brought up the digital map of the DC water system. "These all match up with the route of the old Tiber Creek." He traced it on the map. "It came in from the northeast, near where the rail lines to Union Station are now, then curved around the foot of Capitol Hill. From there, it was channeled into the Washington City Canal, running due west where Constitution Avenue is today, on the northern edge of the National Mall. Then it drained out into the Potomac and the pools and marshes just south of the White House."

"Wow. It was as big as Rock Creek?"

"If not bigger. They paved it over and built Constitution Ave. on top. You can drive a bus through the underground tunnel where it runs now."

"It was all water," she said, looking over the map where the Washington Monument and Lincoln Memorial now stood.

"John Quincy Adams used to take a daily swim in Tiber Creek in front of the White House. It used to be waterfront property. The Mall is all landfill, but the creek is still down there, enclosed."

"What made you think of it?"

"I was looking at the water-system maps, thinking that they

might even be considering the old mass-poisoning plans. I remembered Williams once talked about a dive bar called the Tiber Creek Pub on Capitol Hill. You could hear the creek running on the other side of its walls."

One corner of her mouth curled up. "You think he was onto it?"

"Maybe he was getting close."

Emily traced her finger across the screen. Tiber Creek and the old canal tunnel crossed almost the entire city. "That's, what, five miles of tunnel?"

"At least. Not counting everywhere it branches off."

"It would take an army to search it all." She looked back and forth between the maps. "What's the best access point?"

"Here," Sam said, pointing to one of the markings on the torn section. "There are probably others, but we're missing the full HYACINTH map."

"It's near Union Station. That could be a target. Not too far to the Capitol either."

"The tunnel the creek runs through is like a highway under those landmarks," Sam said, tracing Constitution along the Mall. "They set up at the Marine Corps Memorial to survey, so what does that give us?"

"It points to State. The White House. The other monuments."

"There are dozens of old tunnels under there, packed on top of each other. Corridors for steam connect all the federal buildings from the Capitol to the White House, even the Smithsonian."

"So you would use the tunnels for access?" she asked. "Plant explosives under a target?"

"That's my assumption. There might be a way into a secure area, a weakness that's been hidden for a long time, though it's hard to imagine something that would get them inside the White House complex."

"They searched and secured all those tunnels after 9/11, spent years on it. If there was a way into a sensitive site, they would have found it."

"You know half of that was theater. We're talking miles of tunnel, some as old as the city itself."

He looked back at the torn piece of map.

"You're going to check it out?" she asked.

"They're planning something for tonight. There has to be a sign. I want eyes on those access points."

"Together?"

"Can you stay on Markov?"

"Absolutely."

"What will you do for a car?"

"Steal the professor's," she said and nodded toward the Volkswagen in the driveway.

"Borrow."

That got a smile.

He walked to his bag and went through his gear. Emily watched as he checked his flashlight.

"You're going in?"

"If I see something."

"I thought you hated tunnels."

Sam remembered the taste of the dry Afghan dust in his mouth. "I do."

62

THE RUBLYOVSKOYE HIGHWAY runs west out of Moscow through the forests along the banks of the Moskva River. Once called the Czar's Road, it has led to the dachas of a long line of Russia's rulers, from the father of Peter the Great to the Romanov czars, Lenin and Stalin, Khrushchev, Gorbachev, and beyond. Russia's current leader was no exception, opting out of the Kremlin residence for the past seven years and gifting himself the state dacha at Novo-Ogaryovo for his private villa.

It stood among the other mansions in Rublyovka, as the district was known. Long home to the nation's elite, the area had become a kind of Russian Beverly Hills where the oligarchs and the *siloviki* competed over the most expensive real estate in the world, dotted with the garish trappings of kleptocracy—architectural arms races behind high gates and dealerships selling Ferraris and Maseratis. Many of the luxury stores were now empty and the chateaus half finished, suffering under the weight of American sanctions, evidence of an empire in decline.

The president's neo-Baroque villa was forty minutes from Red Square by car, though he always went by helicopter. It stood behind six-meter-high fences guarded by hand-picked soldiers from the presidential security service.

On the third floor of the main residence, a large bedroom had been converted into an intensive care unit for a single patient.

Soft light angled through the curtains. The blue silk chairs of the sitting area had been pushed to the side to make room for the hospital bed and equipment, all standing opposite the original four-poster with its red and gold drapery.

Russia's president lay on his back. Two doctors stood near the nightstand, and his longtime mistress leaned over the bed and clasped his hand. She said his name softly again and again.

He hadn't spoken since before they put him on the ventilator, his last words something slurred about riding horses, the name of his favorite Arabian the only part easily understood. His eyes were open but unfocused, glazed with moisture.

She put her hand to his cheek and whispered the diminutive form of his name. She was the one person in the world who could call him that. He didn't answer.

Her hand pulled back. "He's so cold," she said to the doctors, her voice breaking as she looked down at his flesh, a hint of blue showing under the skin.

One of the doctors whispered something to her and walked her into the corridor. When she was safely gone, the other one touched a button on the ventilator. Its pumps slowed to a stop and its monitors went silent. He unhooked the ventilator tube from his trachea and watched for the Lazarus sign, the spasm of the arms that even the brain-dead can sometimes muster when removed from support. But there was no response. He held his hand over the throat, feeling the breath from the tracheostomy, and counted the seconds on his wristwatch.

No air came. The president was dead.

He reconnected the tube and walked to the door, where the prime minister stood next to the head of the president's private security division. The PM, who was second in line to the presidency, had bright, hooded eyes and a studied neutrality to his face.

"He's gone," the doctor said.

The president's security chief watched it all, clenching his jaw as he heard the doctor's verdict. The prime minister was unreliable; there were rumors he was secretly in league with the reformers.

Soon the storm would come. Russian succession had long been a bloody affair—Stalin's death, perhaps by poison, then Beria's rise, followed by his quick execution for treason by Khrushchev. More troubling was the 1991 transition, which ended with tanks in Red Square and the reformers narrowly stopping a KGB coup. The security chief could not give the president's enemies time to gather strength and lay plans to take control. Many of them were in this compound now, and there was no way to know who was faithful.

The head of security had long been trusted with the president's ugliest tasks. He came from the hard-line camp in the secret services, men who claimed the chekist mantle going back to the bloody campaigns of Iron Felix against all enemies of the revolution. This time they wouldn't fail. They needed to galvanize the nation, the world.

In a few moments, his message would go by trusted courier to Khodynka Airfield, headquarters of the GRU, Russia's military intelligence agency, where it would be shared among the small constellation of men who knew what it took to keep this nation strong. From there the word would go to a satellite that passed in orbit over Washington, DC, every ninety minutes and be transmitted in an encrypted radio burst to a man who went by the name Michael Lange.

The president was gone. Now the war began.

63

SAM WALKED PAST the Kimpton George on E Street, one of the first boutique hotels to open in DC. Formerly called the Bellevue, the hotel had housed the Tiber Creek Pub on its ground floor. Now that space was Bistro Bis, an upscale French restaurant a short walk from the Capitol that served as the go-to gathering spot for fundraisers and lobbyists.

Sam passed by the front doors and saw the brightly colored pop-art portraits of George Washington inside. He kept going. After a minute, he stopped at the mouth of an alley and peered down it. Behind the facades of glass and steel, these alleys were lined with aging brick and filled-in warehouse windows, the remnants of old DC.

He'd checked two other sites from his map on the way into the city, both manholes in the open. This was his primary target, a pumping station hidden in the alleys north of E Street that he'd scouted by satellite. It offered the largest, most well-concealed route into the old Tiber Creek tunnel that he could identify on the HYACINTH map.

Sam stepped slowly down the alley, his hand hovering near his gun.

A manhole might provide access, but for a sabotage mission you wanted lots of cover and an easy way in to bring down gear and weapons. If you were going to hit something from belowground, you would need an enormous amount of explosive. There was a chance that it was already buried down there and had been for years, but a cache that large would surely have been discovered by now. If it were radiological, it would have been even easier to find.

Perhaps the whole plan was about access, not a buried weapon. The Soviets had somehow carved a way into a sensitive target like the White House or the State Department, and the particulars of that route had been kept secret for decades, but that was even harder to imagine than a hidden cache of explosives.

There were a few other ways into the tunnels, but they would have been on the parts of the HYACINTH map that he was missing, so Sam started by zeroing in on this station.

He listened for any movement as he walked, but it was hard to pick up anything over the hum of air-conditioning units gearing up for the day and the banging of trucks unloading behind one of the buildings farther down the block.

He turned the corner into a larger alley running east to west between E Street and Massachusetts Avenue and saw it, just ahead: a concrete structure about head-high with a padlocked steel door. It stood in the shadow of a crumbling brick Irish bar and an eight-story office tower.

As Sam moved closer, he saw a steel grate in the ground next to it.

He crossed the alley, looking for threats, and he walked back under a dome security camera near a loading dock. It looked down on the approaches to the pumping station. He brought out his phone and set to work hacking the feed.

Once that was finished, he walked toward the station along a line that kept him just out of the camera's sight. Standing on the grate, he could hear the sound of water rushing below. He looked down, unable to see the flow, though he could pick up a musty mineral smell.

He checked the padlock on the structure's steel door—an American brand. Harder than most, but with a few minutes, he could handle it.

He stepped back, reached into his entry kit, and brought out a pick and tension wrench. As he lifted the lock, his phone vibrated.

A new message had come in through Signal—a voice recording from a number Sam didn't recognize. He spun around slowly, looking for any sign of a threat, but there was nothing. Sam hit Play and held the phone to his ear.

"They died because of you, Sam, because they trusted you."

The sound of the voice turned his stomach. He'd last heard it on the Mall just before a blast ripped across the steps of the Lincoln Memorial. It was Konstantin.

"So sure of yourself," the message went on, "but you have no idea what you're in the middle of. How does it feel to be hunted by your own people? You gave your life to them and now you're the enemy, right by my side. I want you to know that the blood is on your hands. I'm going to take everything from you. I know how terrified you are. I can see it in your face."

Sam turned, drawing the gun as the last words sounded in his ear. He searched the windows above, dropping back to cover.

I'm going to take everything from you.

He raised the handset, called Emily, and listened as it rang and rang.

There was no answer.

Sam started moving fast toward his car, and another call came in. Emily. "Are you all right?" he asked.

"Yes," she said. "What's up?"

"I heard from Konstantin. He may be coming after us. Are you where I last saw you?"

"No. On the move. Following our yoga friend."

"You need backup?"

"I don't know that he's operational yet, but you should get here."

"What's happening?"

"I got a hit on the facial recognition."

"Who is it?"

"You need to see for yourself."

64

EMILY WAS PARKED in the back lot of a dated but high-end shopping center in McLean. Sam pulled up in the row opposite and went to her passenger door. She took her computer off the seat, and he got in.

Half a sandwich wrapped in wax paper sat in the center console. She caught him looking at it. "All yours," she said.

"Bless you." He picked it up—turkey and avocado—and ate as he scanned the stores and restaurants, mostly empty after the lunchtime rush. "Where's our boy?"

"The day spa. Going on ninety minutes. It's a massage and acupuncture place."

"Stressed."

"Right. He should be done soon."

"Tracker good?"

"Five by five."

He smiled at her breaking out the military lingo for him, and she passed him the computer. The facial-recognition software was open.

She tapped a window on the right side of the screen. It showed a photo of Alex Clarke. Sam remembered those sincere eyes, and his mind went back to the execution on that Geneva street.

"Where'd you get this?"

"From your reports to HQs for his assessment."

"Why are you looking at him again?"

"I wasn't. That's the hit from the facial-recognition search."

"Wait. What did it match?"

"Your surveillance footage down the street from your house."

Emily tapped the track pad and pulled up a still. It was from one of the cameras at the coffee shop on Sam's street. A man had been captured in shadow by the edge of the frame next to a wrought-iron fence, possibly following Sam. A blue square highlighted the man's face, indicating a match.

"When is this from?"

"Nine days ago. Five thirty a.m."

"I was heading out for a run," Sam said and stared at the image. The man was far from the camera and in the dark, but once Sam had been primed to see it, there was no mistaking the contours of Alex Clarke's face. An ill feeling flooded him.

"What's the confidence on the match?"

"Eighty-five percent."

"He's dead, Emily. I saw it."

"There are false positives," she said.

Sam looked at the face again and suddenly felt cold. "That looks like him, Emily."

"I'll run it again."

"How many times have you done it?"

"Three."

Sam shook his head. "I watched him die."

"Is there any way he might have made it?"

"Seems impossible. They shot him twice in the head from three feet away. Though I didn't see his body after." His fingers went to his ribs. "I got hit, went down for a minute or two, max. When I looked back, he was gone, along with the shooters."

"Could it have been a setup? Blanks?"

"No. I saw his face. I saw the bullets hit."

"Or he survived somehow. It happens."

"And then he comes to the U.S. and is watching me and doesn't make contact?" Sam stared at the dead man following him. "What if it is a setup?"

"Everything going back to Geneva?" she asked.

"And even before that. It all could have been a way to draw me out, maybe part of their plot to identify NOCs or use me."

Sam's eyes went back to the screen. "The same side," he said.

"What?"

"It's something Konstantin said."

"You talked to him?"

"No. He sent a voice message through Signal, trying to provoke me. He said he would take everything from me, that I had no idea what I was in the middle of, and he almost made it sound like we were on the same side."

"Why does he keep coming after you?"

"Because I'm getting close, but there's more to it. It's personal."

"Revenge. Just like with the Lincoln bombing. But what did you do to him?"

Sam put his sandwich down. "Traded gunshots with his men. Nothing to warrant this. What if they have been using me somehow, trying to manipulate me?"

"Then can you trust what Dimos told you?"

"It all checked out. The map. HYACINTH. Finding a mole. Jones. Dimos died to get me that information. It was no act."

"I saw it, Sam. Jones and Markov. That's real. Mercer confirmed they're worried about a mole. They tried to kill you at the Marine Corps Memorial. It can't all be a setup. We're close."

"Why does Arkady Novik, after years in the shadows, let me see him twice?" Sam asked.

She thought for a moment. "I don't know." She straightened up and looked through the windshield. Markov was coming out, crossing the lot toward his G-Wagen.

"If this is a trap, Emily, I don't want you anywhere near it."

"If it's a trap, you need someone watching your back," she said and started the car.

She gave Markov a lead and then pulled out. Sam tracked him using the malware they'd planted on his phone and car, following his progress on a map.

They stayed back, just out of his sight, as he made two turns and then a left into a subdivision.

"Checking for surveillance," Sam said. "He's going black."

65

MARKOV WORKED HIS way through the surveillance-detection run like a professional. Sam and Emily followed him into the District heading toward H Street, north of Capitol Hill.

Sam felt the rush building. The longer Markov worked to make or drop any tails, the more Sam grew convinced that this was the moment they had been waiting for. Sam glanced to the east and saw the classical facade of Union Station. All of this area was on his section of the HYACINTH map.

"He stopped," Sam said, looking at the tracking app on the phone. "Fourth and Neal."

"The warehouses?"

"Right. Get us closer."

They turned across Florida Avenue and entered a district of one- and two-story warehouses full of Asian and African wholesalers.

"Not Markov's usual scene," she said.

"There are a few spots that make sense, but I don't think he's shopping."

One of these warehouses had been developed into Union Market, a trendy food hall that presaged the gentrification of the neighborhood, Ivy City. It had long been a dumping ground for trash and seedy clubs, isolated and neglected because it was surrounded by the Union Station rail lines and Amtrak yards.

"There used to be a racetrack back here," Emily said. "Turn of the century. My dad told me about it. Then Congress banned gambling within a mile of the Capitol."

"A monopoly on vice. Makes sense." He directed her closer to where Markov had parked, still staying out of his view.

They stopped two blocks away, and Sam stepped out. The place was mostly eighty-year-old warehouses, mom-and-pop places run by immigrant families that sold ethnic specialty foods and the tourist kitsch that vendors hawked from vans on the National Mall. He went to the corner and looked toward the spot where Markov had parked. The G-Wagen was there, empty, beside a vacant lot.

Sam looked for Markov, but he was gone. He went back around the corner and met Emily. "You have his phone?" he asked.

"It's in the same location as the G-Wagen." She looked toward the train tracks. "We're close to Tiber Creek?"

"A tenth of a mile."

They walked back to the corner. "This is all wrong for a meetup," Sam said, looking down the street. If Markov was connecting with someone, he would have picked a neighborhood where he could blend in and have an excuse for being there, cover for action. But there was no good reason for Markov to be back here among the vacant buildings and wholesale butchers.

"You'd come here if you needed a lot of room and seclusion," he said, eyeing the bricked-up windows of the warehouses.

"An operation," she said, and looked south to the dome of the Capitol.

He started walking in that direction, away from the wholesalers loading their minivans with souvenirs and T-shirts. An Amtrak train rumbled by in the distance.

Sam crossed an intersection, then paused. Next to the tracks, there was a warehouse typical of the area, a two-story brick classical revival with a bunch of shoddy storefronts tacked on the front. All of them were closed and boarded up. It was mostly cut off from the rest of the markets by a parking garage and truck depot. Soon it would be carved up into shops that liked to dress themselves in the urban grit they'd replaced, but for now it was the only fully boarded-up building in sight.

Emily looked to it, then him, and he nodded.

Her posture changed, her shoulders going back, readying for the fight. He led them closer and gestured for Emily to go check the front of the building. He circled to the back, where an alley ran beside a chain-link fence.

Walking through the overgrown grass, he avoided the patches of gravel to stay quiet. The place was sealed up tight with new locks and steel doors, which could have been a sign of a new investor or of something far more sinister. There were no cameras, which was odd, given the other security, but maybe someone wanted no record of who was coming and going.

The loading docks on this side were filled in with cinder blocks covered in graffiti. A one-story structure jutted off the back of the building, perhaps an old office. Sam examined a steel door in the structure's side. There were faint tracks, still damp, in the gravel leading up to it, and the weeds beside it had a few broken stems. Someone had gone in there.

He went on past the one-story structure and checked the windows along the main part of the building, all boarded up. One was more weathered than the rest, the plywood delaminating at the corner. He went and put his ear to it. The wood was warm from the sun. He heard nothing.

Sam looked around, then dug his fingers into the corner of the board and pried it back. It creaked softly, and he went still, but there was no reaction from inside. After a moment, he put his eye to the gap and peered in.

A few rays of light fell on the main floor of the warehouse, where stacks of debris were piled up next to the columns and along the walls.

The stale air from inside hit his nose. He saw no one and picked up no movement. He would have liked more intel on the layout, but there wasn't time. He was going in.

The rasp of footsteps sounded on the gravel behind him. His hand went to his gun and he began to turn.

"Not another inch."

Sam knew that voice. He checked himself, fingers on the holstered weapon, and looked to his right to see Greg Jones's eyes locked on him over the iron sights of a Beretta.

Sam ran the odds—the distance between them, the confidence of Jones's grip and stance. He moved slightly toward him and watched the barrel go steady, aimed straight at Sam's head, the finger ready against the trigger. Another move and Sam was dead.

"You traitor," Sam said.

"What?"

"I know, Jones. It's over. You'll only make it worse by killing me."

Jones's eyes narrowed, and Sam read his face, looking for doubt or for the steel that came before the shot, in which case he'd just have to draw and dodge and take his chances with that bullet.

A shadow moved behind Jones, a shooter's silhouette. Emily came around the corner of the building, sidestepping, her gun up and fixed on Jones's center mass like a compass needle to north.

"Lower the gun," she said to Jones with unmistakable command, a pause after each word.

"Emily, listen—"

"Fuck your *listen*. Put it down. Now."

Sam used the distraction to pull his gun and take aim. He watched the muscles in Jones's face tighten, his knuckles going white on the grip.

66

JONES FORCED A breath out between his lips, then brought the Beretta down to his side, his finger moving from the trigger to rest along the frame. He looked back and forth between Sam and Emily.

"What are you doing here?" she asked.

"Meeting with a source."

"Where is he?"

"Gone."

"Bullshit," she said.

"Someone is going around killing sources." Jones looked at Sam. "You always seem to be nearby when it happens. I had reason to be cautious, so I told him to get the hell out of here."

"How did you make us?" Sam asked.

"I taught you. I can find you."

"Apparently not," Sam said, and nodded toward Emily. "What's inside the warehouse?"

"Nothing. It was just a place to meet."

"Put the gun on the ground," she said.

"How do I know you won't kill me?"

"I haven't yet," Emily said.

"And Diane Mercer wasn't so lucky?"

Emily's arms went rigid, her face twisting with anger.

"No," Jones said, reading her reaction. "I didn't think it was you. Let's all put them down and talk, okay? You want to know what's happening?"

He eased down, laid his pistol on the ground, then stepped away. Sam met Emily's eyes. They gave each other a subtle nod, and Emily lowered her gun.

"Where is Markov now?" she asked.

"I don't know."

Sam checked the tracker. Markov's phone was still with his car. He must have left by another route and ditched his cell. Emily looked to Sam, and he shook his head.

"Open it up," Emily said, cocking her head toward the warehouse.

"It's empty," Jones said.

"Open it."

"Fine," Jones said. "We need to get off the street before we're all in handcuffs anyway."

He leaned toward his pistol, and Emily raised hers again. "Let me get that for you." She picked up his gun and slipped it into her pocket, the grip sticking out. She stepped to the side, and Jones walked back to the steel door where Sam had first noticed the signs of entry.

Jones took out a key attached to a small numbered tag and unlocked the dead bolt.

Emily stayed back to watch Jones, and Sam went in first to clear it, moving quickly through the door into an empty office area. Its windows, the glass missing, overlooked the whole warehouse floor. He turned, sweeping the vast space, then went to a panel and started switching on the lights. Lamps high above came on.

He saw no one and edged out through the open door of the office onto the warehouse floor, the changing angles giving him a view behind the three large concrete pillars running down the center that supported the ceiling. There were various piles of junk pushed together—banquet tables, torn-out shelving, old Formica desks stacked on top of each other—but as he moved farther in, he confirmed there was nothing behind them.

The warehouse was mostly one open space, though both long walls, the east and west sides, had concrete partitions that came out perpendicular to the wall about fifteen feet, running all the way up to the ceiling to support the girders overhead. They created a series of bays, and Sam worked his way through them until he was satisfied that there was no one lying in wait.

"We're clear," he called out and started checking the floor, searching for any grates or signs of underground access. This warehouse would have been good cover for transporting matériel into the tunnels on a massive scale. The Russians could simply have bought the building through a cover business. That was how the Americans set up their tunnel projects.

He worked his way back toward the entrance. Emily led Jones in, and he walked across the warehouse floor and stopped next to a large folding table with a few mismatched rolling chairs around it.

Sam looked over the dust on the table. It had been smeared off the edge and one of the seats. "You already met with Markov?"

"Yes," Jones said, sitting down. "Though we didn't get very far before you showed up."

Sam stood to the side of the table, and Emily faced Jones. "We want answers," she said.

"What's the question?"

"What are they planning?" Emily asked. "We know you're working with the Russians."

Jones leaned back and looked up at her. "I wish I had known that."

67

SAM MOVED CLOSER to Jones and stood over him. "Tell us what's going on."

Jones pressed back in his chair. "What are you going to do?" he asked, looking from Sam to Emily.

Emily stared at him.

"We are running out of time," Sam said. "Everything is on the table."

Emily stood there with her gun at the ready, and Sam watched her, her nostrils flaring with every breath. She had just seen Mercer get blown apart, just had her own life and everything she stood for shredded. She was liable to do anything.

"My God," Jones said to Emily. "Look what he's done to you. What he's turned you into."

"You turned me into this," Emily said, her voice grim.

Jones swallowed, the fear showing. "I'm going to tell you what happened, because you should know I had nothing to do with their deaths or any of this."

"What is this place?" Sam asked.

"It's only a spot to meet, really."

"A whole warehouse?"

"Markov's. But there is no way to trace it back to him."

"How did he get out? We didn't see him."

"There's an exit in the corner back there. It goes out through one of the storefronts."

"And what is he doing with this place?"

"Developing it. Laundering money through it too."

"What were you two doing here?" Sam asked. "What the fuck are you planning?"

"Nothing. I'm just trying to get information out of him on who is behind these bombings. I'm working a source. As simple as that. I'm trying to stop all this."

Emily stepped in. "You're senior intelligence service. You're stateside. You don't have sources. We saw you running an hourlong SDR before you met with him to hide it. We know. We have evidence. You deleted any reference to DEMETER. You followed me. You tampered with the reports on Parker's and Hassan's deaths. Did you get them killed?"

Jones looked down.

"Answer me."

"In a way."

"What happened with DEMETER?"

Jones avoided their eyes.

Sam put a firm hand on his shoulder, a silent threat.

"I'm on your side here," Jones said, pulling away. "It was a recruitment op. I was developing a source who claimed to have access to the support networks for Russian illegals in the United States. Money and gear and orders flowed through Cyprus and Spain, places where Russians liked to hide their cash offshore."

"What does that have to do with Parker and Hassan?"

"My source was a Belarusian banker who resettled in Spain and went by the name Peter Borodin. He was gold, and he started laying out all the tools that the Russians used, the way they stole Western identities to get past customs and how they moved the money. Everything he gave us checked out, so I brought him in and came to trust him. We would meet in safe houses. Parker and Hassan came to some of them so they could help run down his leads."

Sam felt his stomach drop. He started to see where this was going.

"One day Borodin sent a signal for an emergency meeting. I went, but he wasn't there. He wasn't at home or at his office. He'd taken nothing from his apartment in Valencia, and the door had been forced. We assumed that he'd been taken by Russian intel, probably killed. Then we started losing other sources. Two of them disappeared about three months apart. And then Parker, and then Hassan."

"They all used the same safe houses?" Sam asked.

Jones nodded gravely. "We knew we had some kind of leak or penetration. Counterintelligence worked it, but that went nowhere. I kept asking myself if I had missed something, if I had fucked up somehow, or if we had just been outplayed by Moscow again. That's where it stood for a long time, until I saw your reports on Gemini, before Geneva. The leads you were working—the fronts in Spain, Switzerland, Panama—matched Borodin's patterns, sometimes even the same addresses. Everything I knew about Borodin, you connected to Russian intel. It seemed like he was still out there, operating."

Emily looked to Sam. "He was a dangle," Sam said. "You let him in, showed him the safe houses, and he used them to track down your whole network, the sources, Parker and Hassan. Then he posed as the Russians' first victim in order to make his exit."

Jones didn't speak for a long time. "I wasn't sure. I needed to understand what had happened myself."

"You covered it up and hid the files before anyone else could put it together?"

Jones looked over the filthy table. "I just needed some space to get my head around it. I had to know what I was dealing with, give myself time to prepare. If I had found the proof, I would have given the right information to counterintelligence."

"While keeping any trace of your culpability out of it?"

"If I could."

"What did he look like?" Sam asked. "Borodin?"

"Hard. Seemed like he should be working with his hands."

"Heavy brow? Lines along the sides of his mouth? Scar near the temple?"

Jones nodded.

"Did you look at the composite sketch I did in the report on the Geneva ambush?" Sam asked. "The man identified as Shooter Two?"

"I saw it."

"Was that him?"

"It could have been. There were similarities, but that was just a sketch."

Sam took out his phone and showed him the photo he'd taken of Shooter Two at the Marine Corps Memorial. "And this?"

Jones looked at it, his face going pale. He put his head in his hands, then looked up. "That's him. Borodin."

"He's behind these bombings. I thought he might even be Konstantin, but he would never risk himself as a dangle." Sam slammed his hand on the table. "We could have found him and stopped this if you weren't trying to cover your ass."

"I wasn't sure. He looked so different."

"Or you didn't want to see it," Emily said, glaring at Jones as she moved closer to him. "You just made a few mistakes and tried to save your skin? You expect us to believe that? You were watching me. I warned Mercer about you, and a few hours later she was dead."

"Emily, that wasn't me."

"You set up Sam to take the fall. Planted evidence at his house. You were going to kill us or turn the whole damn state loose on us to do the job."

"I had nothing to do with any of that."

"Then what are you doing here, and why are you meeting with Markov? And what the hell is this?" She lifted a thumb drive. "I found it when I searched him," she said to Sam.

"Markov knows these networks. I went to him for help, to use him as a source. I was trying to find Borodin myself and figure out what was happening, trying to see if there was some way I could stop it or get the info back to the Agency without destroying my career."

She shook her head. "You could have just come clean to counterintelligence, told them everything, and started this investigation months ago."

"Just say, 'I'm sorry, I may have accidentally fed our whole network to Russian intel and gotten two of our people killed, but I swear it was an honest mistake and I'm definitely not turned'? I would have been lucky to stay out of prison."

"You're a traitor," Emily said.

"That's what you want to believe. Black and white. After thirty years, I switch sides and all of a sudden I'm planting bombs on the Mall. Does that make sense?"

Sam could see the doubt in Emily's face.

Jones went on. "How about a story where a guy fucks up and then does his best to fix it without ruining his own life?"

"What did Markov give you?" Sam asked.

Jones licked his lips, then straightened up. He was calculating, and he'd gained back a little confidence, a man drawing a needed card.

"Is he part of Konstantin's network?" Sam asked.

"No. But he pays attention. There isn't much he doesn't know or can't find out."

Sam moved in and tented his fingers on the table. "And he was going to give up information that would put him at cross-purposes with Russian intel out of the goodness of his heart?"

"I have my levers."

"You have dirt on him?"

"There was a deal to be made."

"If the Agency had leverage on him, we would have used it years ago. What did you offer him? What is this?" Sam banged the table next to the drive. "If this doesn't start making sense, you're done."

Jones turned his eyes to Sam. "I would help him, give him information on the other oligarchs, offer the occasional favor in hurting his competitors. Nothing that would go against U.S. interests. It's what we do with the cartels—have one in your pocket and the rest under your heel."

"Who else were you working with at CIA?"

"No one. The whole point was to keep it hidden."

"You sell out your agency, your oath, to save your ass. So what did he give you in exchange?"

"A lead. GRU surveillance activity. Very out of the ordinary. Possibly preparation for an op."

"Where?"

"We can help each other out here."

"You're trying to bargain?" Sam said. "The attack is happening tonight. It'll be mass casualties, orders of magnitude worse than what they've done so far. Stop thinking of yourself for a goddamn minute and tell me what you know."

"Hear me out. You're both under suspicion. Even if you find out what's happening, no one will believe you. I told you the truth because I wanted you to understand that I had no part in these bombings. I'm trying to stop them—my way. Work with me. Let me handle everything that happened with DEMETER. If you let me keep my involvement out of it, I will vouch for you and help clear you in the deaths of Finlay and Mercer and in the Lincoln bombing. You were there for all of them, Sam. It doesn't look good. I can cover for you, but not if I lose my job. If you want to be a martyr, fine, but you're not in this alone." He looked at Emily.

"I don't need a rescue," Emily said. "I don't need anything from you. Don't use me for your sordid shit."

"Do you want a merit badge, or do you want to stop these killers?"

Emily sneered. "You're everything wrong with CIA," she said to Jones. "And you're bluffing. How do we know all of this isn't another lie?"

"I guess you don't. But I think you want to know what Markov gave me bad enough that you'll say yes."

"The location?" she asked.

"And he can give us a source inside Russian intel who can help us stop the attack. Their service isn't a monolith. There are those who want peace, who will work with us. Markov can connect me."

"Who is it?"

"He's close to the illegals program. All I have is the crypt he's using." Jones pushed his chair away from the table. "TRIBUNE."

Sam covered up any reaction, but the name hit him hard. That was the source that Dimos had been trying to connect Sam to before he died.

"We don't talk about it a lot in training, Emily," Jones said. "And I'm so fucking sorry about how this happened, but sometimes this is how the deals get done up on seven. It's Washington. Welcome to the top."

She looked at Sam and then gestured with her head to the side. He followed her across the warehouse floor, both of them keeping watch on Jones as they moved out of earshot. She stepped close to Sam and whispered, "He's playing us."

"Yes. But I think he's telling the truth too." Sam was still rattled by the photo of Alex Clarke outside his place and looking for traps everywhere, but this seemed clear. "That's the world I know, where people are more shabby and weak than they are diabolical. Dimos was going to put me onto a source close to Konstantin, same crypt, TRIBUNE. He's on the right track. He has a location. We combine that with what we know about the tunnels and we can stop this thing."

"There are other ways to get it out of him."

"I wouldn't mind making him hurt," Sam said. Jones had let Williams take the blame for his own failings. "But it won't work. He's trained, and we need him to get more from Markov."

"You think he can clear us?"

Sam looked at Jones, his fingers laced on the table. "Probably. But that means playing along, helping him hide what happened. Can you live with yourself, knowing you made that kind of pact?"

"Can you?" she asked.

"I'll do whatever it takes to stop this. We're innocent. But I don't think that matters anymore. We need him. But I'm not going to push you down that path. You were closer to Parker. They're your people. It's your call."

"Parker's wife, his kids. They deserve the truth. We can just play along for now. Get the information we need and then do it right later."

"Once you go down this path, Emily, it's hard to come back."

"It's the Agency, Sam. I know. But we have only six hours. Dimos said the attack would happen by ten p.m. Can we count on that?"

"We can't risk not to. He died to get me that info."

"Then that's it."

"You're sure?"

"I am," she said.

He nodded, and she walked back to Jones.

"Fine," she said. "What do you have?"

"See?" Jones said. "You understand. If you were in my shoes—"

"Not another word," she said, standing next to the table. "Now tell us about this GRU surveillance."

"How do I know you'll keep up your end of the deal?" Jones asked.

Sam turned his head and listened. The faintest rasping sound came from the far side of the warehouse.

He raised his gun. Emily followed his gaze.

"What is it?" she asked.

"Watch him," Sam said, and stepped forward.

The lights cut out.

68

"**WHAT IS THIS**, Jones?" Sam said, drawing his gun and moving toward the table, waiting for his eyes to adjust to the dark.

"I don't know. Who followed you here?"

A chair scraped over the floor. "Don't move," Sam said, aiming toward Jones's voice.

A clank of metal came from ahead and to the right, the north end of the warehouse, near where they had entered. Sam took a few steps toward it, zeroing in on the noise.

A powerful beam of light switched on and swung toward him and Emily as a red muzzle flare jumped out again and again—the softened blast of a rifle fitted with a suppressor.

Sam heard fast footsteps behind him and then a grunt as someone fell. It sounded like Emily's voice. He moved toward the sound as the light swept over him and lit up Emily, on her feet again and moving at a flat-out sprint toward him and then past, crossing the floor and taking cover behind one of the partial concrete walls on the eastern side of the warehouse. He raced after her, firing off three rounds on the move toward the source of the light. He didn't expect to get a kill at fifty yards on the run, but it would back off the shooter.

Pressing against the concrete wall, he felt the grime against his neck. "You okay?"

"Yes," she said, short of breath. "But I lost Jones's gun when I tripped."

A second light came on, and the attackers moved closer, covering the warehouse floor. She and Sam had ducked behind a wall a third of the way down toward the southern end of the space. The shooters, at least two, were working their way from the north, hunting behind the columns and piled furniture. He could make out a whispered command: *"Bezopasno. Preuspevat."* It was Russian: "Clear. Go ahead."

Sam looked across the floor and saw Jones, lit by the glow of the attackers' lights, standing behind a partial wall on the opposite side of the warehouse but five yards farther north, even closer to the gunmen. His face was set with a mix of determination and fear. He held his Beretta in both hands.

Sam pointed him out to Emily. Jones had taken cover against the shooters himself. He looked their way. Sam was close enough to the edge of the partition that Jones had an angle on him and could have fired. Sam was ready to take him if he tried to shoot, but Jones only stared back, his chest rising and falling. He wasn't in on the attack. He pointed to the southwest corner of the warehouse, where he had said Markov exited. There was a way out. Jones touched his gun and gestured to the advancing shooters, then to Sam and Emily and that corner exit. He had the better angle on the attackers. It was an offer—he would give suppressive fire while Emily and Sam ran. The exit was behind another partition on Jones's side of the warehouse, farther south, and Jones wouldn't be able to get around that concrete wall without exposing himself to shots. When they made it there, they could cover Jones in return.

Sam could hear the gunmen coming closer, in short runs between concealment that showed they were well trained. He and Emily had only seconds until they were open to fire. Sam nodded to Jones, reached for Emily, and pointed out the exit. "He shoots. We go," he whispered.

"Got it."

Sam watched as Jones took a few short breaths, finding the courage, then came around his wall and shot—*crack-crack, crack-crack,* well-aimed double taps. Sam went in the lead, taking aim, closer to the fire, and they sprinted over the worn concrete floors. The lights swung their way and bullets split the air just behind them.

Time seemed to slow. It felt like they would never make it to the far partition. A light fixed on Emily.

Crack. Another shot from Jones, and the light jerked away.

They reached the safety of the last partition. In the faint light, he could make out the door. Sirens wailed outside, though they sounded distant. "Go," he said, pointing toward the door. He sidestepped to the edge of the partition and the open floor. From there, he could give Jones cover to make it to them.

She shook her head no. He glared at her, but she didn't move. There was no time to argue. The lights moved closer. The attackers must have been coming around Jones's cover by now. Sam leaned out and sent two shots at the left beam, then two shots at the right.

A groan of pain came as the light on the left dropped to the ground, and the other one fixed on him. Sam dropped back as the muzzle let out a lick of fire. The concrete next to Sam shattered, throwing out shards. He heard Jones running, leaned out again, aiming toward the light tracking Jones, and fired two shots.

Another blast came from deeper in the warehouse, a third shooter. The flash lit up the man's face, and Sam froze for an instant as he recognized the blue eyes. It looked like Alex Clarke, but something was off—the cheeks were drawn, the face lined.

There was no time to think as Jones took a wild step, stumbled, and crashed down on his hand, then his stomach. Hit. Eight feet away. Sam kept firing as he lunged toward him.

Gunshots rang out behind him—Emily bringing more suppressive fire. Sam grabbed Jones's shirt by the collar and hauled him behind the wall with his left hand as he kept up the fire with his right. Another cry of pain from one of the attackers. Another hit.

The sirens grew louder.

Sam took a knee beside Jones and patted along his back, searching for the wound. Then Sam felt dampness on his own knee. Blood pooled on the floor. He turned Jones over gently and found the exit wound just below his chest on his left side. Sam covered it with both hands and pressed down. Jones moaned and Emily held a position at the edge of the wall, gun out.

Jones's voice creaked, and Sam leaned close to him. "Fifteenth and Constitution," Jones said, barely finding breath.

"That's where the surveillance is? The op?"

He nodded and gripped Sam's sleeve. "After dark."

Sam glanced over his shoulder. The lights were gone. He turned back to Jones and kept the pressure on the wound, the blood welling between his fingers, feeling the faint rhythm of his heart. "How do I connect with Markov?"

The quietest sound of breath. Sam could barely make out the words: "I'm sorry."

They were back in the dark now. Another clang came from deep in the warehouse, the north side. He could hear Emily shuffling closer. She crouched beside him, her hand on his shoulder. "That was the door. I think they're leaving."

"Jones," Sam whispered. "Jones."

Emily reached for Jones's neck and felt for the pulse. A siren screamed outside. "He's gone, Sam." Jones's chest was still beneath Sam's hands. Emily squeezed Sam's shoulder. "We need to go."

69

THEY EXITED INTO one of the storefronts, passed a counter topped with a quarter of an inch of dust, and stepped through a steel door to the outside.

Sam squinted against the afternoon light after all the time in the darkness. He covered the street to the north and heard the police closing in from that direction.

They ran across. Markov's car was still parked in the same spot.

"Come on," Emily said, looking ahead to where she had left the Volkswagen. If they circled around the buildings and worked their way back to it, they could probably stay out of sight of the cops.

Sam kept looking north, the way he thought the gunmen had exited the warehouse.

"What are you doing?" she asked. "If the shooters don't get you that way, the police will."

"Konstantin was there."

"What?"

"In the back, the third shooter."

"How do you know?"

Before he could answer, blue and red lights painted the storefronts at the far end of the street. Sam's eyes kept searching between the warehouses for any sign of the attackers.

"Sam," she said, waving him toward the car. "Look at yourself. Let's go. You can't win this from prison."

He lifted his hands—covered in red from trying to save Jones. A last look to the north, then he turned, and they ran for the car.

A half hour later, they were back at the professor's house in Waverly Hills. Sam cleaned himself up in the kitchen, the blood swirling down the stainless-steel sink, then found Emily in the living room, shifting foot to foot as she looked out the front window from beside the blinds.

"You okay?" he asked.

"I'll be fine," she said. "It's just . . . Jones." She ran her hands back through her hair. "And Parker and Hassan. I was so angry at him for what he did, and then . . ." She closed her eyes. "It's awful. Seeing him like that. After he helped us."

She opened them again and walked across the room. "I need a minute. Have you ever felt like you were going to shake out of your skin if you didn't move, do something?"

"Every day for the past seven weeks."

She put her hands behind her head and started taking deep breaths.

Sam opened up his laptop and checked the camera on the pumping station. No movement.

"How did you know it was Konstantin in the warehouse?" she asked.

Sam looked at her. "Let me see your laptop."

She pulled it from her bag, opened it on the coffee table, and logged in.

"Can you bring up the match from this morning?" he asked.

"Alex Clarke?"

He nodded. Emily opened the facial-recognition match that showed Clarke near Sam's house.

"I saw him," Sam said.

"Clarke! Taking shots at us? Are you saying he's Konstantin?"

"That's not Clarke. The man I saw looked so much like him but twenty-five years older."

Emily thought for a moment. "His father?"

"That's my bet. It's family. Could be an uncle or maybe a much older brother. But father makes the most sense."

"That would give a false match. Parents and twins can throw off the system."

Sam sat down and stared at the grainy image. He remembered the voice on the phone, the anger, the hate.

"That's why it's so personal," Emily said.

"Yes."

"But you didn't kill Clarke. Why would he go after you for revenge?"

"I developed Clarke. He was going to work with me, for peace, he said. That sounded so goddamn soft when I first heard it, I nearly laughed. He said he was trying to stop a faction that wanted a conflict with the U.S."

"His father."

"Konstantin. If he thought that I had somehow turned his son against him and his homeland, seduced him to the American side, there would be no greater betrayal."

"He's angry with you for turning him. But the Russians killed him."

"It was Shooter Two. He and Konstantin are working together."

Emily took a step back and crossed her arms. "You think Konstantin had his own son killed for going against him?"

Sam looked at the photo, studying the shadowed figure. It was absolutely the man who had shot at him in the warehouse. They had finally come face to face.

Sam had seen him murder innocents on the Mall, but a son? The coldness of it staggered him. He remembered Alex's last words before he was killed: "How could he—" He'd been betrayed.

"I do. And he would have to blame me for forcing him to do it. Imagine the anger."

"God. If he's capable of that," Emily said, "what would he be willing to do tonight?"

"We can't have him running loose with the key to whatever the hell the Soviets set up."

"Do you believe what Jones told you?"

"Yes. He had every chance to take us down in that warehouse, but he backed us up."

"And now?"

"Fifteenth and Constitution," Sam said. "That's right over the Tiber Creek tunnel, the old canal. We don't have much time."

"Until?"

"Sunset. Jones told me the surveillance patterns were after dark. It all matches up with the timeline from Dimos, the attack coming tonight."

He picked up his computer, brought up a map of Fifteenth and Constitution, then switched to a satellite view. It was in the heart of monumental Washington, at the southeast corner of the Ellipse, the large park that lay just south of the White House.

Emily stood beside him as Sam tapped the screen. "White House. Treasury. Washington Monument. All within a block and a half."

"You think that's their way into the underground?"

"Or their final target." Sam zoomed in. "There isn't much good access to the tunnels at that spot based on what I saw before. There's an old converted gatehouse that might connect and some grates beside the Commerce building. We can't rule out a surface attack either—breaching one of the buildings, a sniper, even a mortar or rocket."

"It's not line of sight on the White House, but it is in range for a mortar."

Sam's eyes kept returning to the Washington Monument just after that intersection, a fragile icon that had been threatened by an amateurish vehicular attack in the 1980s, though the White House would be a far more critical target. "If they're pulling the trigger tonight, they'll already be prepping."

"You want to go in?"

The question surprised Sam. "Of course," he said.

"You're not afraid? They've used bombs so far. We don't know how big HYACINTH might be. They could be targeting one man, the White House, or the whole damn city." Emily's fingers drummed against her leg.

"Then we get out of there by nightfall," Sam said. "Listen—"

She held up her palm. "Don't. I'm going."

Sam gave her a half-smile, raising his hands. "I know better than to try to tell you what to do. You walked into the fire, and you saved me back there, Emily. I need you. And yes, I'm . . . wary. But we're close. Williams was right. This is it. And one way or another, it ends tonight."

"Then you get back to life?"

Sam let out a dark laugh. "Depends on how tonight goes."

He took a few steps toward the piano and the old Gibson acoustic on its stand. When he turned back, he saw Emily watching him. One corner of her mouth ticked up.

Sam plucked the strings one at a time just below the headstock.

Still in tune. He picked it up and hit the riff from "C'est la Vie—You Never Can Tell."

Emily started laughing.

"You know that one?" Sam asked.

"I think I might," she said.

He put the guitar back on its stand. "Let's go get these assholes."

70

FORTY-FIVE MINUTES LATER, Sam and Emily were walking down the tree-lined pathways of the Ellipse heading toward Fifteenth and Constitution with the White House behind them. They'd left the Volkswagen a few blocks north.

The elms cast long shadows in the last light of day. Emily wore sunglasses and Sam a cap pulled low as he chose a route to keep them far from the cameras on the federal buildings nearby. They'd scouted the area first by car and picked up no signs of surveillance, but Sam was still ready for an ambush at any moment, eyes moving and hand close to his gun.

"There." Sam pointed across the lawn to what looked like a small limestone temple standing in the southeast corner of the park.

"I've never even noticed it before."

It was an odd structure, with its decaying carved stone and worn fascia, a Greek ruin dropped in a city park. About twelve feet square and ten high, it had windows on the north and south sides and a heavy paneled door facing the street.

"It's one of the original gatehouses for the Capitol," Sam said. "Bulfinch designed it. They moved it here in the 1880s after Olmsted redid everything." He pointed across the street. "The old gateposts are over there." On each of the southern corners of the intersection, a squat limestone column stood, twelve feet high, parts of them almost black from car exhaust and age.

"It's the way in?"

"Possibly," Sam said. "Though it doesn't line up with any of the other sewer accesses." It stood out like a kind of forgotten portal at the edge of the park. "Seems too obvious and open this close to the White House." He looked across the street, studying passersby for any signs of surveillance or threat. "We should check that grate next to the Department of Commerce steps too."

As they came closer, he looked up and saw the Washington Monument rising to the south, red lights flashing in the windows of the pyramid at the top, off and on, off and on. Sam had always thought there was something sinister about them, like the all-seeing eye on the dollar bill at the peak of this strange Egyptian obelisk commanding the capital.

Taking down the greatest icon on the Mall would humiliate the United States and prime it for war. Sam surveyed the tourists on the hill leading up to it.

"Everyone will be looking for the two of us together," Emily said.

She was right. Some part of him was reluctant to send her out on her own, but he could still cover her.

"Head across the intersection," he said. "Keep watch. I'll get a closer look at the gatehouse. Keep the channel open."

Emily nodded, peeled off, and put a pair of wired earbuds in. Sam stepped next to a tree, pulled out a wireless set, and placed the buds lightly in his ears so he could still hear what was happening around him.

She called him, and he answered the phone without a word. "All set?" she asked.

"Good to go." The less talking, the less attention. She would raise him if she saw anything. To anyone watching, they were just two random pedestrians drowning out the sounds of traffic.

She crossed Constitution Avenue going south, then Fifteenth Street going east, and settled into a stroll along the south sidewalk of Constitution, sweeping for any static surveillance. She stopped outside a museum and set up watch on the gatehouse.

The sun dropped low in the sky, turning red through the haze behind the monument. Night was coming soon. He was standing at the heart of the attack, a wanted man in the shadow of the most well-guarded real estate in the world.

Sam moved through a grove of elms at the edge of the park. He paused until the sidewalk was clear and then walked straight and fast the short distance to the gatehouse. The glass of the windows was wavy with age. Inside, he could make out a smooth concrete foundation covered in dust with no sign of any kind of access or even a seam.

"Eyes on you," Emily said through his earbuds.

"How far?"

"Around the corner on Constitution, behind the bus shelter. He looks homeless—boots, canvas jacket over a gray hoodie. Now he's moving."

"Which way?"

"East. Slow walk."

"He's in the game?"

"Eighty percent sure. It's pretty classic." Surveillance teams often opted for cover as homeless people. You could sit in the middle of the city for hours, and almost everyone would pass you with a practiced blindness. The gatehouse wasn't the way in, but it seemed like they had the right spot.

Emily had disappeared around the corner to keep up with him. "Did he make you?" Sam asked.

"Never looked my way, but he could have seen you."

"He's fleeing?"

"Or going to call it in or meet with someone. I'm crossing Constitution," she said. "Staying with him on the north sidewalk."

"I'll be behind you." Sam scanned the street for other watchers, every contour and color brightening as the adrenaline rushed through his system. They had to cut that man off before he could call in backup. Sam was going to get some answers out of him.

He reached the corner and could see Emily in the distance at the end of the block. Crossing Fifteenth, he kept following her on the north side of Constitution.

Emily went through the intersection ahead as Sam closed the gap. He broke into a run, but even a sprint wouldn't have gotten him there in time because the light changed, and six lanes of traffic crossed through the intersection in front of him.

"You good?" Sam asked. "I'm blocked at the light."

"Fine," she said. "Still on him. No sign he's picked me up." A box truck pulled up in the crosswalk, blocking his view. Sam paced north to look behind it. Emily was gone.

This block and the next were dominated by connected federal buildings with long classical facades and massive columned entrances, all modeled on Paris's monumental avenues. The whole complex, a labyrinth known as Federal Triangle, spread over seventy-five acres between Constitution and Pennsylvania Avenue along the north side of the Mall.

Downtown DC was quiet on the weekends, except for tourists, and there were fewer and fewer of them as night approached and Sam moved east away from the major monuments.

"Lost him," she said. "Van pulled out of a parking entrance, and he might have used it for a screen."

"Where?" Sam asked, watching the light go yellow.

"Right after the Mellon Auditorium. He could be close. I'm going quiet."

"Wait for me."

Sam ran through the crosswalk as soon as the light changed, playing chicken with a Toyota Tacoma trying to sneak through a late right turn.

He looked ahead to the steps of the Mellon, an enormous hall for galas connected to the federal buildings. On either side of it there were archways that led to pedestrian arcades. They ran through the buildings, giving access to small courtyards and passages and the center of the Federal Triangle complex.

"I think he went up the passage," she whispered.

"Hang on," Sam said. "I'm almost there."

No reply. A rush of air. A loud clatter. Sam listened for breath, for the sound of an open connection, for anything, but only silence came back. He started sprinting.

71

EMILY MOVED TOWARD the arcade, passing between the heavy concrete planters, part of the ubiquitous post-9/11 security landscape of the capital. She stepped to the side, scanning the entrance to the passage, a high limestone archway with a black and gold lantern hanging from its center.

Pressing against the stonework, she slipped her pistol from its holster and held it in front of her thigh, out of view. She leaned out slightly and looked down the passage for her man. It opened into a small cobblestoned courtyard with streetlamps that looked like they could have come out of Edwardian London. At the far end, the passage narrowed before going on to the grand central plaza between the Reagan and Wilson buildings at the heart of Federal Triangle. No sign of her target.

She crossed into the open for a better view. "I think he went up the passage," she said quietly.

"Hang on," Sam replied. "I'm almost there."

Emily heard hard steps coming behind her. She turned, hoping it was Sam but raising the gun just in case. The attacker was already in too close, a powerfully built man of medium height with his jaw set and deep creases along the sides of his mouth.

He lowered as he charged, wrapped his arms around her—a

bandage on the right wrist—and hauled her deeper into the passage. Her earbuds ripped out. With her arms pinned to her sides, she put her feet down, trying to slow him. His full strength pushed her back, but she braced herself, driving with her legs, stopping his advance.

The side of his boot scraped down her shin, a brilliant ribbon of pain, then drove her left ankle to the side. A low crack echoed in the archway, more heard than felt; Emily's ankle alive not with hurt so much as numbness and a sense of something profoundly wrong.

Time slowed. She stumbled, pain like lightning from her broken ankle. The man kept her upright, crushed her against him as he stood behind her. She tried to bring the gun across her body to get a shot off at him, wriggling her arm free, but his right hand clamped down on her wrist. The strength felt more mechanical than human. As he wrenched her hand to the side, the gun dropped from her fingers and skittered across the cobblestones. He reached around her chest with his left arm, pinning her left arm to her side, and grabbed her right forearm with his left hand, tying up both of her arms with just one of his.

His right hand was free. A quiet snick. She saw the knife flash toward her face.

A drop of sweat came off the man's chin and dripped down her neck.

"Shhh," he whispered, lips to her ear, as the cold blade pressed against her throat.

72

SAM HEARD A woman call out in pain. He wheeled around the entrance to the passage, raising his pistol as he stepped into the darkness under the archway.

In a courtyard at the end of the passage, a man held Emily to his chest, a knife to her throat.

Sam raised the pistol and took aim at his head. He recognized the face of Shooter Two. He kept Emily in front of him as a shield, and Sam traced around her with his sights, looking for his shot, but it was too close.

She snapped her head back, driving it into the man's face. He flinched to the side and Sam fired, the only clean shot he had, opening a hole high on the man's chest near the shoulder. Emily grabbed at his knife arm, pulled it away from her neck, then slammed an elbow into his chin while he was thrown by the shot. He staggered, and she shoved him to the side, out of Sam's field of view down the passage.

Emily took a step, then fell, groaning, her ankle bending all wrong. She pushed and dragged herself along the cobbles toward a gun on the ground, wrapped her fingers around it, and rolled over, firing as she turned, four shots flashing, her lower lip tucked in.

Shooter Two appeared at the mouth of the passage, stumbling, knife in hand, as Emily took another shot.

He missed a step and fell to one knee. Sam shot him in the head, and he collapsed onto his face three feet from her. Sam ran in and kicked the knife away.

Emily raised herself up on her left hand, and Sam took a knee beside her.

"My ankle. It's broken," she said, eyes wide, breathing fast. Her hand went to her throat. A thin red line, like a paper cut, ran across the skin. Sam looked closely to make sure it wasn't any deeper. She checked her fingers. They came away with a trace of blood. "It's not bad?"

"It doesn't look it. There might be others coming. I'll get you out of here."

She let her head down and exhaled in relief. Sam helped her up on her good foot, bringing her right arm around his neck and supporting her from the waist. He started moving south toward the passageway, back to the street where they had entered, the gun in his free hand. She limped along beside him, her pistol in her left.

"I knew he was done once you bit that lip. You're a fucking sniper, Pierce."

She let out a laugh, but it wasn't much more than a hitch of her chest. Her eyes were narrowed against the pain.

"You're going to be all right," he said. Her hand gripped his shoulder, and he pulled her in tighter as they stepped into the shadows of the passage.

She looked back. "Sam!"

He turned and saw movement on the far side of the courtyard, fifty yards off, in the shadows of the passage that led out to the north. He raised the gun, turning awkwardly as he supported her.

A flicker of movement, then nothing. It could be the watcher she'd followed here, the one posing as a homeless man, or other backup. Sam kept going, looking over his shoulder to the north as he led them through the archway, ready to fire at the first sign of another attacker.

He only had to get to the sidewalk and turn the corner, and they would have cover. Eight feet from the mouth of the passage, he heard Emily curse and looked forward to see a gun rising, the black barrel and silencer pointed straight at him, and behind it a face he would never forget.

It was Arkady Novik. His aim passed over Sam and Emily, and Novik waved them to the right with his free hand. "I'm on your side," he said. "Go."

Sam raised his Heckler and Koch toward him, but Novik was already moving beyond them into the passage, the gun tracking past Sam.

The whole space flashed red twice, then a third time, echoing back the snap of silenced shots.

Sam kept his gun aimed at Novik. Beyond him, in the courtyard they had just left, the man who had been coming for them fell forward on his knees out of the northern passage, two holes in his chest and one in the center of his forehead, then collapsed facedown on the cobbles.

Sam looked back to Novik, two paces from him, the man who had shot at and missed him that night in Geneva. Novik's gun was at a low ready, pointed away. Sam looked beyond him to the attacker he had just put down with three perfect shots from fifty yards. He understood at last: Novik didn't miss.

73

SAM AND EMILY moved deeper into the passage behind Novik. He wore a light linen jacket over a blue button-down open at the neck, the look of a contented financier, a jarring juxtaposition with the violence he'd just calmly committed.

He turned to face them, his eyes glancing back and forth, covering both entrances to the courtyard.

"There are more coming," he said, "and the police. Let me help you. I was working with Alex Clarke and Christopher Dimos."

"Prove it," Sam said.

"TRIBUNE."

Sam had seen enough to believe him, but that confirmed it. "Which way?"

"To the street," Novik said.

Sam helped Emily move toward the exit, and Novik came around them, taking point at the end of the passage.

"In Geneva?" Sam said.

"There was a man coming for you from behind. I was shooting at him. Then more approached from the other direction."

Sam had understood it as soon as he saw Novik make those three shots in the courtyard. Novik had been an ally that night as well.

Novik pointed to a black Audi double-parked about twenty feet down. "I can get you out of here."

"In exchange for what?"

"Nothing. I want what you want. But I need you alive to stop this."

"He's SVR, Sam," Emily said into his ear. "What if this was a setup? What if all of it has been? It's treason."

"That's right. For both of us," Novik said.

Sam looked back at the dead man in the courtyard. He felt the doubt, the weight of all he'd been taught, of headquarters' simple blacks and whites.

Fuck doubt. Sam's instincts were good. Geneva was an ambush, not some trap he'd rushed into. It was the first step on the trail of a killer. And this was the last.

"This was the source Clarke and Dimos were trying to put me onto," Sam said. "We need him."

Emily pulled herself up on Sam's shoulder, looked at the Russian, then back to Sam. "You're sure?"

"Yes."

"Then let's go."

They stepped into the street. A few people watched them curiously from down the block.

"It's all right," Sam bellowed in a tone of command. "Everything's under control. Get back. Get back."

People are inclined to obey authority. Novik, Sam, and Emily looked like two trained officers and a victim, and the bystanders kept their distance as Sam helped Emily into the back of Novik's Audi, then climbed into the passenger seat.

They pulled out as the police lights flashed farther up Constitution.

Emily watched Novik in the rearview mirror.

"The night Diane Mercer died," she said. "You were there."

"As a warning. I knew they were watching her. I didn't know how they were going to hit you, but I needed to raise the alarm."

Emily said nothing as she considered this. Novik's presence had led Sam to call the meeting and kept her away from that car bomb.

"You're our guardian angel?" she asked.

He met her eyes in the mirror. "Avenging."

A black SUV sped east past them, sirens wailing. The feds were here. Novik drove west on Constitution, passing the museums, as the sun set behind the trees along the Potomac.

Sam turned around to check on Emily. Her ankle was already swelling, as thick as her calf. "How are you doing?"

"Fine," she said, her hands stabilizing the joint, her lips tight with pain.

"You should be in a hospital."

"I'm not dying, Sam. The FBI will pick me up there. We need to finish this."

He looked up and caught Novik glancing back at her with a faint smile of appreciation.

"Why is the SVR helping us?" she asked Novik.

"Konstantin, you call him?"

"Yes," she said.

"He's rogue."

"Your service can't stop him itself?"

"We've tried, but there are powerful people who want him to succeed."

"In what?" Sam asked.

"Starting a war. Or the closest thing to one he can manage."

"How?"

"HYACINTH. A decapitation strike of some kind."

"Nuclear?"

"No. But we don't know much beyond that. HYACINTH was the great secret of the KGB's First Directorate. We know that it will be massive. We know it involves caches buried near Washington decades ago, weapons for sabotage, we assume."

"Where?"

"We've been trying to track down the caches for years. We suspected there was one in rural Virginia, near Gilberts Corner. Four days ago an off-duty police officer disappeared in that area. The sheriff's deputies found what they initially feared was a shallow grave nearby, but it was empty and too small to bury a man."

"He found one of the caches," Sam said.

"That's our assumption. The cop discovered it or came across Konstantin while he was recovering it, and Konstantin took him out."

"What does that give us?"

"Nothing. There are no leads, and knowing Konstantin, there never will be."

They drove across Arlington Memorial Bridge and Robert E. Lee's former mansion rose on the hill ahead.

"Why would he—or anyone in the Kremlin—want an open conflict with the United States?" Sam asked. "Your president has been winning the spy war."

"Our president is dead."

Emily's breath caught.

"What?" Sam said.

"Early this morning eastern time, the president of the Russian Federation succumbed to his illness," Novik said.

Sam looked to Emily.

"We knew he was hiding out at Novo-Ogaryovo," she said. "There was speculation something was wrong, but nothing solid."

"It's true," Novik said. "He went more quickly than anyone expected. Power passed to the prime minister, but he doesn't have the support of the hard-liners in the secret services. He won't last. We're heading for a war of succession, another coup, blood in the streets. It's a matter of hours, maybe days. The hard-liners are nothing without their leader. He was the state. They need a crisis, an external enemy. It's always the same playbook."

He glanced at the mirrors, watching for anyone following.

"Head south," Sam said as they entered the circle after the bridge. Novik eyed him.

"South," Sam said. "We're not going by your script."

He eased the wheel to the left. Sam believed what Novik was saying so far. It explained why Russia would be willing to provoke the United States. But he wasn't going to let Novik take them wherever he chose.

"The hard-liners think a conflict will cement their power?" Sam asked.

"The strength of the state has been built on fear of the invader for centuries, going all the way back to Ivan the Terrible."

"They wouldn't attack on that scale unprovoked."

"They have their provocation. The Americans killed the Russian president."

"No," Emily said. "We absolutely did not. We didn't even know for sure that he was sick. The hard-liners really believe that?"

"It doesn't matter if it's true. The people will accept what they're told. The president was strength itself. A god. The easiest way for the public to conceive of him dying would be foul play. The *siloviki* need a conflict, a threat to scare the country into giving them absolute power."

"The attack is tonight?"

Novik nodded. "We believe it will happen by ten p.m."

Exactly what Dimos had said. "Pull in there," Sam said. "The park."

The Russian gave him a guarded look and then steered into the right lane.

"What's the logic on the timing?" Sam asked.

"There is a faction working against the hard-liners—reformers and those who simply want to avoid chaos and bloodshed. They're reaching out through back channels to the American president and the secretary of state to negotiate a new path."

"Have you heard of this?" Sam asked Emily.

"No. But that would explain the stepped-up diplomatic security."

"Konstantin needs to stop it," Novik said, "to derail any chance for peace. If there is a massive attack, any hope of a deal will vanish."

"It could just blow back on the hard-liners," Sam said. "And build up support for the other faction."

Novik let out a grim laugh. "Think about what happens if a Russian deploys a weapon that the Kremlin built and hid under your capital for thirty-five years. The hawks in Congress are already out for blood. There are those on both sides who stand to profit from a conflict with a great enemy. Think about the last time America was attacked. Imagine what will happen if Konstantin destroys Washington—the overreaction, the lashing out."

Novik gestured toward the lights of the city across the river. "There will be a response, and the hard-liners will get what they want. Frankly, it doesn't matter what the truth is. The strategy has always been simply to flood the zone with chaos and noise until no one believes anything. Then they win."

"Pull up there," Sam said, and Novik drove through the lot and took a parking space looking across the river toward the Tidal Basin and the park where Diane Mercer was killed.

"You're willing to work with your enemy?" Sam asked.

"You're not my enemy in this. You may not believe it, but my mission has always been about advance warning, keeping the balance, keeping the peace. That mission is what led Alex Clarke to you, and Christopher Dimos."

Even as he said it, Sam could only think of those who'd died screaming in the basement of the Lubyanka prison at the hands of Russia's secret police.

"If Konstantin and his allies take control," Novik went on, "there will be no country, no home left for me to return to. Not after I've crossed them."

Sam looked out the windshield at the lights of the Capitol dome. "Why is Konstantin so hell-bent on coming after me personally?"

"Because of Geneva."

Sam didn't say anything for a moment.

"You already know."

"Clarke was his son. And I turned him."

Novik ran his hand along the leather of the steering wheel. "Konstantin thinks that you killed him."

Sam leaned toward the man and watched as the Russian's muscles tensed in the face of the threat. "You know I didn't."

"I know that now. The hard-liners killed Clarke. Konstantin's own deputy ran the operation, the same man you two shot dead in that passage. We were able to reconstruct his movements."

"Without Konstantin knowing?"

"That's right. Clarke was the one person who might have been able to bring his father back from the brink, toward peace. Once

Konstantin's deputy saw that Alex was ready to treat with the Americans, he took him out."

"And blamed me."

"To push Konstantin over the edge. It's not just politics for him. It's revenge. Against you. Against this nation that took his only son."

"You're sure the Geneva ambush was strictly the work of Konstantin's deputy?"

"You think you might have been betrayed by your own side?"

"Possibly."

"No. That didn't play into it. It was all internal maneuvering."

"They really believed Alex could have talked him out of it?"

Novik nodded. "His son was all he had."

"You could have come to me sooner."

"I didn't trust you. Two of our men, Alex Clarke and Christopher Dimos, went to you and were killed. I needed time to see what side you were really on and make sure you weren't the one leaking CIA information to Konstantin. I'm still not certain that trusting you is a good idea, but Alex was. You had more access and more freedom to maneuver in the States than we ever would. He thought you were the only person talented enough and reckless enough to go against your own service and stop Konstantin no matter what it cost or which side you had to take. Your actions have borne that out. So I'm here."

"And I'm listening. How do I stop him?"

"What do you know about the attack?"

Sam caught the veiled look of alarm in Emily's eyes. This could all be a ploy to find out what Sam knew in order to outflank him, or even a way for Novik to locate and take control of the weapon himself.

"You want to help me, help me," Sam said.

Novik pointed to the windshield and the black surface of the Potomac in the distance, wavering like mercury under the dying light.

"The river?" Sam asked.

"Yes. That's what we've gathered about the specifics of the attack. They're coming from the river."

Sam thought of the maps. He studied the Washington skyline, remembering the Marine Corps Memorial with its expansive views up and down the Potomac.

"A boat? Poisoning the water?"

"From the river. That's all we know."

Sam retraced every access point to the Tiber Creek tunnels in his mind. Then he saw it, and he was certain. He looked at the time, and an overwhelming need to move took hold of him.

He glanced at Emily without saying a word, and when he turned back, Novik's eyes were on him.

"You know what it means."

Sam said nothing.

"Let me help you."

"You already have. I'll handle it."

"You don't trust me with it. I understand. Just tell me what you need."

"Your car," Sam said.

Novik tilted his head to the side. "I can drive you."

"No."

"You think I'll follow?"

"I know it."

"You're not wrong." A smile as Novik opened the driver door and stepped into the night. Sam circled around the hood.

The Russian dropped the keys in his hand, then wrote an e-mail address on a piece of paper and passed it to Sam. "Let me know where you leave the car."

"You'll be all right?"

"I'll find my way. *Udachi, tovarisch.* Good luck, comrade."

"You too," Sam said.

Novik moved to the side and Sam stepped into the car, shut the door, and took off. The Russian shrank in his rearview, still with that untroubled air, like he was out for an evening stroll.

Sam looked back to Emily, and she pointed around the interior of the car. He wanted to tell her what he'd understood, but they couldn't risk the car being bugged.

He drove back into the city, toward the center of the attack, parked Novik's Audi, and helped Emily into the passenger seat of the Volkswagen. He grabbed a road atlas out of the back seat to improvise a splint for her ankle. "I'll handle that," she said, taking it. "Just drive."

Sam got behind the wheel and pulled out, Emily looking his way. They were finally alone, clear of Novik's car and whatever audio and tracking it might have.

"There's only one entrance to the old canal from the river," Sam said. "The Potomac Pumping Station. It's big, perfect for staging an attack."

"How do you get in?"

Sam glanced at her injured ankle—the left—then the holstered pistol on her hip. "How many rounds are in that?"

74

LANGE CROSSED THE open bay of the Potomac Pumping Station, a garage-like space lined with large-bore pipes and winch lifts hanging from the ceiling.

His fingers closed on the key in his pocket as he approached an open manhole surrounded by a yellow railing. He grabbed the rail and lowered himself down, rung by rung, through the narrow shaft. The air grew damp and cool, and the concrete gave way to brick.

He had been in these tunnels before, but that was only a trial run. This was the moment he'd been building to for ten years.

At the last rung, he dropped. The sound of his boots hitting the walkway echoed back from what seemed impossibly far off. The tunnel was four and a half meters wide, and its rounded brick ceiling five and a half meters tall at its highest point. One-meter-wide walkways ran along both sides just above a river of gray water flowing through the center, moving fast after last night's rains. The light receded as he started moving east, toward where the tunnel ran under the State Department.

In his last moments aboveground, he had looked that way, to State's historic buildings and, beyond them, the drab concrete blocks of its modern headquarters. In a secure room somewhere on that campus, the reformists were selling his nation's soul for a false peace. They had no idea what was coming.

One of Lange's men guarded the entrance to the pumping station above. Any more would risk drawing attention to his design. He'd trusted no one with the details of HYACINTH, and now Cole was gone.

They were closing in. Lange had long ago learned to savor the pressure, the rush, to use it to make himself sharper. It was the only way to survive.

He walked in darkness, his hand tracing the rough brick wall. Every so often, a light broke through from the city above, a manhole cover or storm drain.

His mind went back to an all-white hospital room, the Central Clinical Hospital in Kuntsevo, the facility reserved for Moscow's elite. He remembered the way the frost drew stars on the window and the warmth of his boy's body by his side.

His only child, Pavel, had been weak from birth, with a cleft in his mitral valve and a hole in the atrium of his heart. A nurse had discovered it when she heard the murmur. Lange was so broken by the loss of his wife in childbirth that it almost seemed right that fate would take his boy too. Pavel was two years old when they were finally able to arrange the operation, and Lange's profession gave him access to the Kremlin hospital at Kuntsevo. That privilege alone justified everything he had done in the shadows.

He remembered when the day came for the open-heart procedure. The surgeon came out after, a confident Ukrainian who simply said, "I fixed him."

That night, Lange climbed into the hospital bed where Pavel lay in a daze from the anesthesia and held him until the dawn came. He took four months off while Pavel recovered, the longest he had been home since he began work as an illegal. For those months, he wasn't Michael Lange or George Malek or Karl Stadler or any of the other covers. He wasn't a killer. He was a father helping a curious toddler relearn how to walk.

The boy's grandmother, the only family Lange had left, raised him. Lange could see him only once or twice a year, if that, and he was always amazed at how much stronger his son was with every visit, working ten times harder than the other boys, playing football in that Valeri Karpin jersey for hours every day while his grandmother urged him to slow down and go easy on his heart. He never relented. Later in life, Lange would caution Pavel against joining the secret services, but Pavel was as stubborn as his father.

The Americans had murdered his boy in Geneva. Pavel was the one weakness Lange allowed himself, and now he was his strength. It gave him the resolve to pull the trigger even as he thought of the thousands of souls, of families, walking overhead. Lange's rage had grown inside him like a tumor since that day. Now, finally, he could release it.

Tonight, they would answer for Pavel's death. It was the last gift he could give his son. HYACINTH would be his monument.

75

SAM CROUCHED ALONG the side of a highway on-ramp just south of the Kennedy Center. The night air was cool, but he could still feel a light sweat on his skin, his pulse beating hard.

This part of Foggy Bottom had once been nothing but gasworks and breweries and swamps. Now a tangle of highway overpasses and on-ramps dominated the land along the Potomac, feeding the hundreds of thousands of Virginia commuters who came over the Roosevelt Bridge every morning onto the streets of the District.

Sam held still as a truck flashed by, its slipstream hitting him like a wave, then sprinted across the road.

He ran to a ragged triangle of grass and trees between the three-lane ramps that served the bridge, ducked behind a stack of concrete barriers covered in kudzu, and waited, watching for sentries, his gun out.

A break in the traffic and the glow of headlights gave him a chance to move unseen to the guardrail at the edge of the grassy area.

He looked down; he was standing on top of the Potomac Pumping Station. It had been one of the sewer entry points he had marked on his map this morning to investigate.

The station was built into the earth that supported the bridge and on-ramps. To access it, you turned off one of the feeder roads onto a downhill driveway into a large sunken area with a parking lot and grass and trees on either side. That sunken area ended in a wide stone wall where the land had been built up to support the bridge. Sam now stood on top of the wall, looking down at the parking lot.

Steel doors set into the stone wall below him allowed entrance to the pumping station and the sewers beneath it, what had once been the Washington City Canal and the route of the old Tiber Creek.

He moved to the left, toward the end of the wall, where the ground sloped up from the lot below and he could manage an easy six-foot drop to the grass.

There was one car parked down there, a white pickup. At the far end of the parking lot, a man stepped out from the shadows and walked toward the steel doors.

Sam pulled back into the brush as the man came closer, stopped by the truck, and checked his phone. He wore jeans, a visibility vest, and a hard hat. He was either a utility worker waiting for the boss or one of Konstantin's guards working a thinly veiled patrol. The man turned and started walking past the other doors. With the headlights from the highway, Sam could just make out the bulges under the sweatshirt: gun on the right side, extra magazines on the left. There was no one else around.

Sam lifted his phone and tapped out a message. Then he slipped toward the edge of the wall, drew his gun, and waited.

The man turned and walked toward him. Sam shifted his weight onto the balls of his feet and readied the Heckler and Koch.

A Volkswagen rolled down the driveway toward the sunken lot. The guard's gun hand drifted toward his right hip; his left went to his pocket and came out with a black object, a radio.

Sam dropped the six feet and moved toward him, the car's engine covering the sound of his approach. Emily was behind the wheel, blinding the guard with her headlights.

The man drew but kept the gun hidden out of view by his right thigh as he lifted the radio.

Sam took aim. "Federal officer! Drop the weapon!"

The guard spun, raising his pistol.

Sam squeezed the trigger twice, the gun bucking in his hand, and sent two rounds into the man's chest. The guard kept turning. The gun trembled in his fist, and he fired, sending the bullet hissing to Sam's left as Sam kept his aim and finished him with a third shot to the head.

The man collapsed to the ground. Sam ran to him and kicked away the weapon, then faced the doors to the pumping station, ready for any others.

He glanced back to see Emily leaning out of the open door of the Volkswagen. She was holding her gun next to the car's A-pillar, covering the entrances. "Are you hit?" she asked.

"I'm good," he said as he searched the man's pockets. His wallet held a license and DC Water credentials, all most likely forged. On his waist he carried four extended magazines for his SIG Sauer.

His keys were clipped to his jeans. Sam pulled them and walked across the lot to the door at the center of the stone wall. Even out here, he could pick up the earthy smell. He eyed the keys until he found a match, then slipped it into the dead bolt. If there were more guards inside, they most likely would have come running at the sound of the gunshots. But they could have been waiting behind that door, ready to defend against a breach.

Sam turned the key. The lock squealed. He raised his gun, then pressed against the wall beside the door and threw it open. No shots. Not a sound. A glance back. Emily covered him from the car.

He went in, running through the door, moving left to right, making himself a hard target. The place was empty except for pipes and machinery. Sam circled, listening for any sign of others, though all he could hear was the turn of the pumps and the rushing water coming from below.

At the far end of the station, a yellow railing blocked off a manhole. Sam looked down and saw black water.

He made his way back out, hauled the body inside, and met Emily at the car.

"He was the only one," Sam said.

"This is it?"

Sam nodded.

"What about Fifteenth and Constitution?"

"The tunnel runs under there. This is easy access. We could have had the right location without knowing the way in. I'm going in. It's time to raise the alarm."

He and Emily had already gone over it. Now that they knew that Jones had been working on his own, there was less risk in going to the Bureau. He and Emily knew the threat and the scale and had a good sense of the location. Sam would go after Konstantin, but those sewers were a labyrinth, and they would need every agent available to find him and whatever lay hidden down there. Emily couldn't walk, but she could get the word to the Bureau.

"I'll call Matt Wilkinson. He's the FBI liaison in Russia House."

"You trust him?"

"As much as I trust any of them. He'll be straight with me, at least. And he has a line to Deputy Director West."

"Be ready, Emily. They may treat you like a criminal, a traitor."

"I don't care what they think. I'll get it done."

"How is that?" He pointed to her ankle, wrapped in a splint she'd put together from the road atlas and her belt.

"A bastard, but I'll be fine." Emily looked to the door. "Are you sure? You're walking into the heart of this thing."

"We can't wait. And he's not on a suicide run. He must be setting it up. There's time for me to get out."

She checked her watch. "You don't know that. Sam, you don't have to get yourself . . ." Her lips pressed into a line. "You don't owe this to Williams, or Finlay. You've got nothing to prove."

"Thank you, Emily. I know. It's not that. I've got this. I'll find him."

She took his hand, and he bent down and touched his forehead to hers.

"I'll see you in a few," he said, as casually as if he were stepping out for coffee.

She took a breath, then let go.

"Yes, you will," she said. "Go get him."

Sam turned and walked to the pumping station. He gave her a last look and stepped inside. It was twenty feet to the manhole. He put his foot on the top rung and started climbing down into the dark.

76

WITH THE LIGHT shining down the manhole from the station above, Sam could make out the contours of the tunnel. It was a redbrick archway nearly twenty feet high with a walkway running along either side of a ghostly gray river.

He'd expected an overpowering odor of sewage, but it was manageable, the musty smell of wet basement and behind it something like a camp latrine.

He turned east and looked down the tunnel. Here and there, faint rays of light came down from manhole covers and drains, and he could pick out a slight turn about four hundred yards ahead.

He moved carefully, letting his eyes adjust, his fingers tracing over the bricks. At odd intervals, holes opened up in the wall, high and low, draining water from pipes and leaving slick blooms of rust and mold.

His footsteps weren't too loud over the grit and muck of the walkway. The rush of the water would cover them.

As he came to the bend, he saw the section of the tunnel where the canal had once run. It was two miles long, straight all the way to Capitol Hill. A few minutes' walk would put him right under the target Jones had given at Fifteenth and Constitution.

He entered a long section of pure dark, the tunnel feeling more and more like a grave with every step. His heart beat faster, his senses sharpening.

His foot splashed through a cold stream of water, and far ahead he saw a red light spill across the bricks.

Sam pressed against the wall, and the damp seeped into his clothes. He saw a figure in silhouette holding the light. As it turned, Sam could see the face in the distance and just make him out: Konstantin.

Sam pulled his gun, though it was way too far for an accurate shot, then the light cut off.

Sam went after him, closing the distance, caution and calculation giving way to the single-mindedness of the hunt.

After a minute, Sam saw him, still far ahead, by the glow from above. The red light flickered on, then turned left and right, illuminating two smaller tunnels off the main route. Konstantin disappeared to the right, going south.

Sam fixed what he had seen in his mind—a round tunnel, waist-high, branching off—and raced toward it. He slowed as he approached the junction, barely able to see by the light from a storm drain about thirty yards ahead. He looked down the small tunnel to the south, but there was no sign of his man, and no sound of him splashing through the water that ran along its bottom. Sam needed to get closer.

He checked his watch and figured his pace, then looked up to the grate of the storm drain. He was probably halfway between the White House and the Washington Monument, close to Fifteenth and Constitution where that limestone gatehouse stood. The tunnel Konstantin had taken would lead toward the old foundations of the Washington Monument, buried deep under the Mall.

There were grooves in the silt along the bottom of the pipe, a sign of recent movement. Sam carried a flashlight but didn't want to give himself away. He crawled in headfirst. It was just big enough for him to fit, though to move, he had to proceed on his hands and knees.

After a few seconds, he was in absolute darkness. It brought a kind of vertigo. He could have been crawling straight up or straight down, lost in space.

He heard water pouring ahead, and after a moment a small stream splashed down on him like an open faucet. It soaked into his clothes, weighing them against his body as he pressed on. After that, the path was dry, though it seemed to narrow slightly, his shoulders and elbows brushing against the walls of the pipe. A low rushing sound came from ahead, like a slow-moving stream, and the next time Sam planted his hand, it slipped through empty space. Water moved below him. This pipe ended and dropped into some kind of pool or channeled stream. He reached down and touched the surface.

A red glow appeared to the right, light filtering through the water. Sam pulled back so as not to be seen, but from the light he could make out his surroundings. His pipe dropped into a rectangular concrete junction box filled halfway up with the water he had just touched.

It flowed to the right, entering and completely filling another sewer, a round brick tunnel about three feet in diameter, another pipe.

He waited, his pulse pounding in his neck and deep in his ears.

The light was coming from that pipe. It must give access to another chamber, but the only way through was to drop under the water and commit to that tunnel.

The light moved away, then disappeared.

Something was hidden on the other side. Konstantin was there.

77

EMILY WAITED IN her car, backed into a spot along the riverbank, watching the entrances to the lot. It was a strip of asphalt hidden among the trees by the Potomac, the parking area for Roosevelt Island, a short drive from the pumping station. The branches creaked overhead as a gust of wind moved through, rippling the water.

A black Ford Explorer pulled in the northern entrance and took a spot fifteen feet from her car.

Matt Wilkinson stepped out, wearing a light windbreaker that the weather didn't warrant. Armed. Made sense.

She had summoned him here with a short phone call. She flashed her lights and opened her door. With her right hand on the wheel, she waved him over with her left, keeping both hands in plain view: no threat.

Matt came up to her door and did a quick visual search. His eyes paused on the cut across her neck and the splint around her swollen ankle. "What happened? Are you all right?"

"Don't worry about it. We don't have a lot of time, Matt. There is an attack coming. It could be any moment now. Sam and I have been trying to stop it. You may not believe all of that, given what's happened. It doesn't matter if you do. But you told me you would help if I turned myself in. So I'm here. Now, listen—"

"Why did you run, Emily?"

"Because there was no time. I had to find out what was going on and now I'm coming back to you and the Bureau to stop this. I know I'm in trouble. I'll take whatever's coming, but for now, just listen to me. The man who triggered the Lincoln Memorial bombing is planning a much larger strike. He and his people are using the old sewer tunnel under Constitution Avenue. They accessed it through the pumping station just south of the Kennedy Center. Sam went in after them, but you need to back him up on the search. We don't know how many attackers there are or what they're working with. You need EOD." Explosive-ordnance disposal—the bomb squad.

"I'll bring you in, and you can explain all of this."

"There's no time, Matt. Get on the phone to Henry West right now, and get those teams in to stop this."

He glanced to the left, and Emily noticed another truck, blacked out and parked past the entrance Matt had used. She turned her head and saw another pull up at the southern entrance.

His posture went rigid, anticipating a reaction.

"I expected it, Matt," she said, with only disappointment in her voice. "I'm coming in willingly. I'm alone. I'm innocent. But no matter what happens to me, you need to get the word up the chain. Evacuate all of downtown. Everything within three blocks of Constitution Ave."

"What are they planning?"

"We only know that it's a mass-casualty event, the same people behind the Lincoln and Mercer bombings. They were just warming up. It'll happen by ten p.m., maybe earlier. We spooked them, so they might push up the timing."

"You're talking about clearing out the White House? State? Bureau headquarters?"

"Everything," she said, fighting to stay calm with the pain flaring in her ankle and the seconds ticking away. "It's an old Soviet plan, a decapitation strike. A lot of people are going to die. Get them the hell out of there while you can."

His eyes went to the lights of the city on the far side of the river. There were bodies all over this town. Emily knew how suspicious she seemed.

"If this is a setup, Emily"—he glanced down at her leg—"if he got to you somehow, just tell me. We can protect you."

"That's not it, I swear. I know how everything looks. The Bureau can do whatever it wants to me, but deal with the threat first."

She still believed in the CIA and the FBI, in the people who worked there, still believed that in spite of it all, they would find their way to the truth.

He put his hand on top of the car and looked off toward the trees. Then he pulled his phone. "All right."

Emily sat back and took a breath. He believed her.

Before he could dial, the other headlights switched on, and they accelerated toward the lot.

Matt looked left and right, surprise on his face as the vehicles sped closer and boxed them in, the glare of their headlights in Emily's eyes.

Men swarmed from both trucks, and Matt stood between them and Emily.

"What is this?" he shouted as the men circled the car. Two came for her from the back, guns out, and another pulled him away as he turned to her.

She kept both of her hands on the wheel and looked at Matt. "I knew this might happen. The Potomac Pumping Station." Her voice was calm and commanding even as they grabbed her arms and pulled her from the car, her ankle raking over the sill, sending out a stab of pain. "Clear those buildings, and get your people in there, now!"

78

LANGE LOWERED HIMSELF down the brick wall and dropped to the floor. He scanned the chamber with his red light, going over the pillar and the water running in the open sewer along one wall. To his left was the sealed-off panel framed in brick—HYACINTH's controls.

He had to crawl the final passage here, a high vent that no one would ever find unless he knew where to look.

From a small bag that he carried across his body, he took a coil of detonation cord and two bricks of explosives, the same Semtex he'd used in the Lincoln bombing and Mercer's killing.

He crouched and set to work, priming the explosives with the cord, then crimping it into a small electronic detonator that would handle the delay. As he seated the last piece of cord, he noticed a faint tremble in his left hand. He looked at it, smiled, and stilled his fingers.

Lange moved to the side and regarded the two blocks of Semtex in the red light. Less than a kilo, barely enough to take out a large SUV, though tonight they would burn out the heart of a city. They were only the trigger.

He walked to the other side of the chamber, pried out the concrete seal, and rested it on the ground. His light shone on the gray powder-coated panel at the back of the recess.

It had lain here hidden and still for thirty-five years. At the top there was a small hexagonal hole for a key, and at the bottom there were two wheels. Flecked with corrosion, they still moved smoothly. Lange would use them to set the delay. They had marks around their edges, but no numbers. The operator had to know how the mechanism worked.

He kept the hours at zero, then set the minutes. He had planned to give himself more time, but Hudson was closing in, and he allowed only enough for him to make it out of these tunnels before the blast came.

Stepping back, he took the key from his pocket and held it in front of him, the light flashing off the six-sided steel.

Saboteurs had come before him decades ago, working by night, navigating the crumbling underground of the city. They laid a series of explosive charges under the supports for the gas pipeline that ran just north of Constitution Avenue. The charges were small and buried well beneath the line, designed to physically rupture it without igniting the pressurized gas. That was surprisingly easy, since gas must diffuse and mix with air before it becomes explosive. For the same reason, a match dropped in a bucket of gasoline simply goes out.

Those men, all engineers, had placed the explosives at critical points in the city's underground infrastructure so that the broken main would flood gas into the sewer tunnels of the old canal and Tiber Creek, as well as the steam tunnels that ran under the White House, the Treasury, and the State Department. They didn't need to cart down tons of explosive or risk an easily detected radiological device. Their work was never discovered because the main weapon lay in plain sight: tens of thousands of cubic meters of natural gas flowing underneath the city every day.

HYACINTH worked on the same principle as a thermobaric

bomb, a fuel-air explosive. The first blast disperses the fuel without igniting it, and once it has spread out, a second charge sets it off. Such weapons are the most powerful conventional explosives known to man, with yields comparable to a small nuclear blast. The American version, the GBU-43/B Massive Ordnance Air Blast, was called the MOAB, or "the mother of all bombs," and the later, larger Russian version, the Aviation Thermobaric Bomb of Increased Power, was nicknamed "the father of all bombs."

The control panel on the wall would trigger the first charges, rupturing the cast-iron gas main and diffusing the gas. The Semtex charges in this room would go off on a delay once the gas had spread, turning the foundations of the capital into a massive explosive centered between the White House and the Washington Monument.

What Lange started here would end with his allies taking the Kremlin and absolute control. He could finally return to his home for good, to the place of power he had rightfully earned, to his true name.

He stepped forward and slid in the key.

79

SAM LOOKED DOWN at the water. The red glow was still gone. From the angles the light had been moving, that pipe couldn't have been very long.

"Fucking tunnels," Sam muttered and eased down the wall of the junction box into the water.

The current pulled him toward the pipe where he had seen the red light. His boots found the slick bottom of the junction box, and he fought against the flow, his treads sliding back.

Three deep breaths, and he lowered himself down, felt the water rise over his ears, mouth, and nose, then dove forward with the stream into the pipe.

With his ears submerged, Sam heard his pulse banging like a bass drum inside his skull. He dragged both hands along the walls of the pipe for control.

Time seemed to slow. As his shoulders squeezed against the brick, and the water pressure built behind him, the panic pushed in—it was narrowing down; there was no exit; he would run out of breath, and the water would never give him up.

His fingernails scraped along the grimy brick and then suddenly his right hand was free. It rose from the surface of the water into the air, and he grabbed the edge of what felt like another walkway.

He opened his eyes to bloodred light and pulled himself up. The stream of water that carried him ran in an open sewer at one end of a large brick chamber. He stayed low, head just above the surface, almost eye-level with the floor.

The space was maybe thirty by forty feet, with a large square brick pillar in the center. The red light was coming from behind it, and it blocked Sam from the view of anyone on the far side.

Hungry for air, he filled his lungs as he drew his gun, then tilted it down and to the side, drawing the slide back a quarter inch to clear any water from the chamber.

He held himself against the current, waiting, scanning. The sounds of rushing water filled the area, flowing past him and behind the walls. It should have covered any noise he'd made.

He hauled himself up onto the bricks, moving slowly, inch by inch, to keep the sound down. After crossing to the pillar, he slipped to the side, closing in on the source of the light. Leaning out around the corner, he saw a shadow projected on the wall like a giant. Sam edged out and saw the figure: a man standing by the wall. In front of him there was a recess, a waist-high opening the size of a window. The man's right hand pulled back from it. He held a thin piece of metal between his fingers, a tool or a key.

Sam aimed at his back, his heart. "Hands out to the sides!" he shouted, his voice like thunder after all the quiet. The man froze.

"I have you covered. Hands out or I kill you."

The hands rose, and the man turned slowly. He had a rancher's face, broad and strong and weathered. The same blue eyes as Alex, though older. It was unsettling, as if Alex Clarke had managed to live another twenty-five years, though there was no tranquility to this man.

"Drop it," Sam said.

The piece of metal slipped through his fingers and jangled against the ground. It was a hexagonal key.

"Step back."

He moved slowly, arms up, untroubled, almost amused, a caricature of surrender. He had a natural arrogance typical of successful sleepers.

After all these years, Sam had him. Looking into his face, he felt anger like a pure blue flame and a strange sense of lightness and clarity.

Sam stepped to the right, closer to the recess in the wall. Then he noticed the charges on the floor—two bundles of plastic explosive, the telltale orange of Semtex, already primed and linked; the detonation cord ran somewhere behind Konstantin, though there was no sign of any trigger.

Sam aimed at the man's head, as he had been trained to do when facing off with bombers. His hands were clear, and there was no sign of an explosive device on him, no vest or belt.

"Keep your hands up. Move them one inch toward your body, and I shoot."

"I understand. Sam, is it?" Konstantin tilted his head slightly to the side, studying him. "It's good to finally meet you."

He smiled warmly, a man used to drawing people in with a look, and Sam could begin to understand how he had managed to manipulate and move through this country unseen for so long.

Konstantin was dry except for the hems and knees of his work pants. There must be another way in and out, but Sam couldn't see it. He nodded toward the recess in the wall. "What is that?"

"You know what it is."

Sam took a step closer. At the back, there was a sheet-metal junction box dotted with rust, like an old fuse panel. It seemed at first to be some kind of lock, with two wheels like safe dials at the bottom, though they had no numbers, and a small chrome keyway near the top that matched the six-sided key.

Sam assumed it was a triggering mechanism. The wheels could be for entering a combination or setting a timer. He kept the gun aimed at his head, crouched, and picked up the key with his left hand.

"How do I stop this?"

"You don't. It's too late."

Konstantin stepped forward an inch, and Sam tightened his finger on the trigger.

"All you can do is run," the other man said. "That's what you do, right, Sam? Always running. Look out for yourself. Let the others die."

Sam looked at the explosives as he felt the blood rising in his face and neck, sweat mingling with the drying water.

It didn't add up. Why have only two small charges here? That was enough to destroy this room, possibly blow a crater through to the streets above, but nothing more. It wasn't enough to take down the deep foundations of the monument. Why have those explosives out in addition to whatever was hooked up to the panel? He considered trying the key, but that might arm or set off the device.

"How does it work?"

"Run, Sam. If you start now, you might make it."

Sam had never spoken to this man face to face, but he knew him well. With his ego, a suicide mission would be his last choice. They had at least a little time. Sam didn't move. He wasn't afraid to die in this hole if need be.

"Shut it down," Sam said, and his resolve seemed to shake Konstantin. He took another step closer to the panel, eyeing the dials, picturing the inner complexity. A quiet buzz sounded from within.

There was no way to open it that he could see, and one wrong move could trigger a detonation. He needed this man to disable it.

"We know everything already—your faction, your plan," Sam said. "It won't work anymore. We know exactly who's responsible. This will just rally the U.S. to your rivals' side. We'll destroy you and your allies. It will be for nothing."

"Leave the politics to me, Sam. It's not your strength. I'm ready for the end, and it will be worth it, not least to watch you burn for what you did."

"I didn't kill your son. He wanted peace. Stop this. Do him that honor."

Konstantin's eyes narrowed to slits as the rage took hold. His face went hard, and his smile changed to a killer's grin, the cover dropping at last.

"Do not talk about my son." He shook his head as he spoke, barely restraining himself.

Sam kept his aim, eyes on Konstantin's across the sights. Every instinct pushed him to pull that trigger, to take his revenge, but there was a chance Sam could convince him to stop this or at least buy more time. He had found the raw nerve. He would try it, and if that failed, then the bullet.

"Geneva. I know who shot your son."

A flash of doubt, then Konstantin moved to the side, away from the wall with the panel, the look of satisfaction returning to his face.

"Lies," he said.

Sam steadied his aim. "You—"

A loud click came from the panel, then the blast hit, swallowing Sam's words.

80

THE FBI AGENTS drove Emily back into the city along Constitution Avenue, moving toward the heart of the attack. No protest, reasoning, or threat could stop them as they passed the White House, the Ellipse, and Fifteenth Street, then pulled a U-turn to park along the north side of the street.

They left her locked in the back of the Chevy Tahoe, alone with the driver, who kept his eyes ahead, ignoring her. The side of her fist ached from banging on the partition.

A half a dozen Bureau and Metropolitan Police Department vehicles blocked off the street, a cordon around the passageway beside the Mellon Auditorium where she had killed Shooter Two, now a crime scene.

Looking through the SUV's windshield, she could see the Washington Monument rising into the night sky past the tall trees around the National Museum of African American History and Culture.

Ground zero. She leaned to the side and saw Matt talking with a man in a suit with close-cropped white hair and a lineman's build: Deputy Director Henry West. West held his hands out in front of him as if telling Matt to stop, then turned and walked toward the Tahoe.

Two agents flanked him; one of them was the man who had dragged her out of the car near Roosevelt Island.

West signaled for them to stand back, then opened the door.

"Emily, we need some answers here."

"Of course. That's why I came in. But——"

"No." He leaned over to her. "Listen to me. First you tell me about the dead man in the passage."

"He's a Russian illegal. He killed a source of ours in Geneva named Alex Clarke. And he tried to kill me in that courtyard two hours ago. He broke my ankle and did this," she said, pointing to the cut on her neck.

"You shot him?"

"I defended myself, yes."

"And killed Greg Jones?"

"No."

"And Diane Mercer?"

"No."

He watched her for a moment.

"An attack is coming, and we are standing on top of the target," she said. "It could go at any second. You need to clear this whole area, Constitution back to the Potomac."

"Matt briefed me. You want us to evacuate everything. Get the president on the move. Shut down anything that might be happening tonight, no matter how important, get those people into cars, out in the open."

She felt sick. He was wondering if she was still part of it, if this was a ploy, a step in the attack. "It's the truth. I came to *you* with this. We need to move off this spot or we're going to get hit."

He didn't respond, just looked at her, a cold intelligence churning behind a passive face, the purest expression she knew of the national security bureaucracy.

He turned away without a word, and one of the men slammed shut the door.

"Wait!" Emily pounded her fist against the glass as he walked off.

She looked out the window at the old stone gatehouse of the Capitol and the American flags circling the base of the Washington Monument.

Boom. A low and powerful explosion shook the ground beneath them. Car alarms started screaming.

Boom-boom.

The blasts cracked off in quick succession, closer and louder each time.

The driver leaned his head to the side, listening to his earpiece, then dropped the Tahoe into gear. They took off down Constitution to get away from the explosions.

Emily squeezed the door handle and watched the long classical arcades of Federal Triangle flash by as the truck picked up speed, heading east.

A cloud of dirt blew into the air from the grass just north of the monument, drawing a chorus of screams from the pedestrians on the Mall. An elm toppled, its roots tearing from the broken earth as it crashed down, and the tourists took off running.

"Faster!" she yelled, watching as the blasts raced toward them.

81

A BOOM SHOOK the tunnel chamber, felt as much as heard. A second followed, then a third, the blasts punching Sam in the lungs, moving closer, ripping toward him from deep underground.

A last explosion enveloped him in a deafening pressure. Hard blows struck Sam in the back and then the head as a cloud of dust blacked out the room.

Sam fought to keep his aim and his balance, but the wall to his right tumbled onto him, the weight building, threatening to crush his legs and hips as it pushed him down onto his knees and his left hand.

Dust plastered his mouth and tongue. He choked, then held his breath as the grit settled. Fighting to free his gun arm, he dragged himself forward, the bricks tearing at his pinned legs. He was buried up to his thighs, leaning slightly ahead. His ribs, only just healed from taking the shot in Geneva, burned with pain.

The beam of a flashlight panned toward him, almost solid through the swirling cloud, as Konstantin picked his way over the rubble holding a knife by his side.

Sam freed his right hand, though he didn't draw it out. He felt among the bricks for the gun, but it was buried.

Cool air streamed through the cavern, turning the dust into swirls like rising smoke.

A rank cabbage smell overpowered him. Natural gas. It was pouring into the room from the destroyed wall, streaming out between the wreckage, filling the chamber and the tunnels that led to it.

He tried to concentrate despite the ringing in his ears. Those first blasts must have started a gas leak, and the charges in this room would set it off once the gas had spread. So would a gunshot. The whole place, and the tunnels beyond it, were a bomb. Those explosions were only the beginning. If the gas ignited, it could take down the city.

Sam tried to pull himself free, fingernails scraping against the debris, but his legs were still pinned down by the bricks. He turned them and hauled himself forward despite the pain as they scraped against the broken edges. He felt the left move, but the right was still stuck.

Konstantin approached Sam, shining the light into his eyes, seeming to savor his weakness.

Sam pulled again and felt the rubble around his right leg loosen. He eyed the pile for anything he could use as a weapon. Konstantin flipped the knife into an ice-pick grip and stood over him.

Sam raised his head and looked him in the eye. "Your own men killed your son," he said. He breathed in, tasting the bitter dust.

The Russian paused, his face a mix of anger and wariness. "Mind games won't save you."

"It was your partner, the man you sent to survey from the Marine Corps Memorial. He knew your son was against this and that he could convince you it was wrong. He killed him in Geneva, shot him twice in the head, then put it on me to push you over the edge."

Sam shifted his weight onto his knees. "They were using you— for this."

The light dropped a few inches. Sam pushed himself back, his torso straight up now.

A man of Konstantin's talents surely could see that he was telling the truth. Spend enough time in a world of lies, and you develop a heightened sense of what's real, a hunger for what you lack.

Konstantin didn't speak. Did he know it was right? Could he trust anything anymore? Or was he so deep in the lie he could only go deeper?

"You know it's true. His last thoughts were that his father betrayed him. But you can stop this."

Konstantin's face pulled into a brutal scowl. He seemed about to speak but said nothing, only clenched his jaw. A low growl sounded from the back of his throat. He was close to breaking.

Sam wanted him to believe, to stop the attack, but he didn't expect it. He was a rigid man and could live any lie he chose. It was the only way to survive for so long in cover. Throwing him off for a moment was all Sam needed.

He closed his hands on a broken-off piece of concrete two feet long and a foot across. Konstantin's fist tightened on the knife, and he rushed in. Sam lifted the concrete as he drove himself forward with both legs, drawing on every ounce of strength he had built over the hard weeks in exile, all his anger over the lives this man had taken and would take. He put it all into this strike, unhesitating even as Konstantin lunged, and the blade slashed across Sam's forearm.

The block of concrete cracked into Konstantin's cheek and temple. He groaned and staggered back as Sam closed in.

The Russian found his footing and stabbed the blade straight toward Sam's heart. Sam pivoted, grabbed his wrist, and wrenched the knife free. He drove his other elbow into Konstantin's chest, lifting him off his feet. He came down hard on his back on the jagged debris.

Sam looked down at him, the knife warm in his hand. He could see the faces of the dead once more: Jeff Parker, Sarah Hassan, Christopher Dimos, and Finlay, taking his last breaths on that marble floor in Geneva. He wanted to make everything even at last, to drive the blade into Konstantin's chest and say their names as the life went out of him.

But stopping the bomb came first. The Russian tried to lift himself up twice but didn't seem to have the strength. The right side of his face twitched. He reached behind his back, and his fingers came out streaked with blood.

Sam stepped to the side, dizzy from the gas, and looked at the rubble along the wall, trying to see where the detonation cord led. He held the knife out while he pushed through the bricks with his boot. "Where's the trigger?"

"Pavel," Konstantin said, struggling for the words. "He thought I gave the order to kill him?"

That must have been Alex Clarke's real name. He said it so softly. Sam remembered Clarke's last words: *How could he—*

"Yes," he said.

Konstantin's eyes closed. His face twisted in agony. "No," he said, drawing out the word, his voice breaking.

"It's the truth. Tell me how to shut it down."

After a pained breath, the Russian spoke. "You turned him, corrupted him. His blood is on your hands. Nothing changes. Our lives don't matter. Only the mission. Only history. There's justice in it, though." A sick smile crossed his lips. "We all deserve to burn."

His eyes went to the broken bricks by the wall. Sam reached down and pulled them aside, looking for a trigger, a way to stop it. He could make out a faint green light flashing, hidden in the debris. It was an LED. The detonator.

He focused, fighting against the effects of the vapor, choking on its overpowering smell. The LED lit up again, then again, the interval halving each time.

"I told you . . . you were too late," Konstantin said, gasping.

The light flashed faster, blinking now.

Sam was fifteen feet from the surface of the water that had brought him into this room. He dug through the rubble with his bare hand and his fist still closed on the knife. The fresh cut on his arm throbbed. The light was almost solid green. He drove his hand down toward it, the bricks scraping his skin, closed his fingers on the detonator and cord, and hauled it out. The long white wire dragged from beneath the stone, tearing free from the explosives.

Without them, the Semtex wouldn't go off, but the detonators and cord would put out a small blast on their own, more than enough to ignite the gas.

Sam threw himself across the room, dropped down, and shoved the cord and detonators under the surface of the water. He let go as the current took them, and they disappeared into the outflow pipe.

He stepped back, feeling the room spinning because of the gas, and ran toward the pillar. The detonator and cord blew when he was still three feet from them. The water flashed red, and a muted boom filled the chamber as a surge of water burst out from the sewer pipe.

Sam braced for ignition, for the swallowing fire, but none came. He moved toward Konstantin—his eyes open and blank, his chest still—then reeled to the side, almost losing his balance as the gas overwhelmed him. There was no time for anything but escape.

Sam turned back, guided himself along the wall, and dropped into the water to get out the way he had come in.

The current was running against him now that he was backtracking. He lowered down, bringing his head below the surface, and fought against the flow. Then he let go of the knife and dragged himself underwater toward an opening that seemed like it moved farther and farther back with every inch he gained.

He felt his strength leaving him, his lungs shrinking in his chest like crumpled paper.

Then his hand rose through the surface of the water. He was out.

Sam stood up, pulled in a deep, hungry breath, and broke out coughing. The water flowed past his waist. He brought out his light and trained it on the wall to his left, the way he'd entered. The gas was everywhere, the smell growing stronger, bubbling through the surface.

He climbed into the sewer that led back to the main tunnel. The slash in his forearm burned, but he had no time to give it any thought. Crawling, angled down now, he worked his way to the exit.

After a minute, he reached the end and turned left onto the walkway, the high brick tunnel of the old canal now feeling as open as an atrium. But there was no escaping the gas as it filled this endless hall and poured out under the foundations of the capital.

He moved along the walkway, taking shallow breaths, his head growing lighter with each step. Running his hand along the wall, he steadied his steps, his fingers passing slick flows of water. A stumble. He caught himself, but thirty feet later he went down again, the vapors overwhelming. He rose on one knee as the blackness moved in.

Bright lights focused on him, and behind them he could make out men in masks running toward him in tactical gear, all black with FBI patches on the plate carriers, M4 rifles at the ready.

He raised his hands. The last thing he remembered was calling out, "Gas! Gas! Don't shoot."

82

SAM HUDSON OPENED his eyes and white light flooded in. Stretching out his hands, he felt the stiff linens of a hospital bed.

One bandage covered his forearm and another the shin of his right leg. His ribs ached with every breath. He checked his wrists for handcuffs. He'd seen men shackled in hospital beds, had questioned a few of them himself. But his hands were free. He lifted his head and looked around the room.

Emily leaned forward in the visitor chair and smiled at him.

"I'm not dead, huh?" he said.

"No." She reached out and put her hand on his arm. "You're at Sibley."

"Even better," Sam said. They'd put him in DC's rich-people hospital. His mind still felt hazy, as if wrapped in warm cotton, but he could see those tunnels, feel the damp, and remember Konstantin's body laid out among the bricks. "It didn't go off."

"No. They evacuated downtown and cut off the gas mains. The hazmat crews and a National Guard unit are down there flushing out what's left."

Sam put his hand on hers, nodded, and laid his head back on the pillow. "I wouldn't have made it out if you hadn't gotten the Bureau down there. Thank you."

"Of course. They found a body with a fractured skull underground."

"Where?"

"A kind of overflow chamber. It had a panel connected to the charges that took out the gas main."

"That was Konstantin," Sam said. "They're certain he's dead?"

"Yes."

He felt a heaviness lift from every muscle in his body. The weight of what he'd been carrying surprised him. He lay there for a moment, just feeling the warmth of her hand under his palm and the promise of rest like he hadn't known for years.

A soft knock, then the door opened. Sam looked over to see a young man lean his head in. He had short blond hair and looked like he'd stepped off the cover of a Boy Scout manual.

"Sam," Emily said, "this is Matt Wilkinson from the Bureau."

Sam nodded to him. He guessed that Matt had been just outside, standing guard and waiting for Sam to wake. He wasn't carrying any cuffs or trying to look like an authority. Sam imagined they'd send someone, or more likely a team, with a little more command presence if they were going to arrest him.

Emily gave Matt a kind look. He was an ally. "The CI team is here," Matt said. Counterintelligence. "They need a statement if you're feeling up to it."

"FBI?" Sam asked.

"And CIA. Joint."

They were asking his permission, Emily was here, and he wasn't hidden away in a military hospital, all of which were good signs that the brass had begun to see the truth. Tipping them to HYACINTH had probably proved which side he was on, but just because he was in the right didn't mean he was in the clear.

Over the next month, with the information Sam and Emily provided, the investigators were able to trace the movements of Konstantin and his men, linking them to the killings of Jones and Mercer and to the bombing at the Lincoln.

Markov would corroborate Sam and Emily's account of what had happened with Jones in the run-up to the gas attack. Sam did the approach on Markov himself, not that the Russian had much choice. He had already cooperated with the Agency against the GRU, even though Jones had been working on his own, and if his betrayal became widely known within the Russian secret services, there was a good chance he would end up dispossessed or dead. He needed protection, and Sam brought him to the Agency.

Sam went back to visit Harry Turner, the defector, to flesh out the story on HYACINTH and the maps and see if he could get him some recognition from CIA for his assistance in stopping the attack. But all Sam found was an empty house and a For Sale sign. Harry had put himself at risk in helping Sam, and Sam remembered those photos of him and his wife on a sailboat anchored in pale blue waters. A new life somewhere. He'd be fine. He'd done it before.

Five weeks after the attack, Sam was called into the Agency for a meeting. It took place in a mahogany-lined office on the seventh floor of the old headquarters building with the number-one man in the directorate of operations. Sam had been cleared. The exec told him that there would be no criminal or in-house sanctions for his pursuit of the Konstantin matter.

The suit seemed to expect nothing but gratitude from him, but Sam saw things differently. "What are you doing about the Greg Jones leaks, the compromised safe houses, the leaders who missed it, and the NOCs who have been exposed?"

The number one didn't seem to like that, and the meeting ended soon after. Sam didn't mind. He had the leverage: the truth of a failure that would bring the Agency low.

Emily met him in the lobby on his way out. She'd just come off administrative duty and graduated from a cast to a walking boot for her ankle.

"How'd the doghouse treat you?" Sam asked her.

"I'm impressed you only went half-crazy when you were on leave."

He told her he was in the clear. She looked at him, measuring his expression. "Isn't that good news?"

Then he told her about the rest of the meeting.

"That's about how mine went," she said. "We'll get it done."

Two more stars had been carved into the marble of the CIA's Memorial Wall, for Parker and Hassan, just next to Finlay's.

The agency finally recognized that they had fallen in the line of duty, but the executives were keeping a tight grip on the facts of what happened, including Jones's role and their failure to stop him. The full story was still secret, like the stories of some of the other officers on that wall, classified for the good of the nation, or sometimes just the good of the Agency, a way to bury its sins while holding up its heroes.

They walked out under the inscription from the Gospel according to John that greeted officers every day and night as they passed through these halls: *And ye shall know the truth and the truth shall make you free.* Allen Dulles had insisted on having that quote engraved in stone in the lobby, a strange motto for a place that operated by deception and lived on secrets. Sam looked down to see Emily's eyes on him, a bit of devil-may-care behind them. She pointed to the inscription. "It's worth a try."

(He would go with her the next week when she visited Parker's and Hassan's families and told them what had really happened, however much the Agency wanted to keep it in the dark. They deserved the truth.)

From the CIA entrance, they walked outside, past the statue of Nathan Hale, the Memorial Garden rising on the hillside to their right.

She held her phone out to Sam and showed him the front page of the *New York Times*, a photo of the new president of Russia, the former prime minister, walking with his American counterpart during a multilateral summit meeting in Berlin. They strolled past the Brandenburg Gate late in the evening, just the two of them with no interpreters or aides.

After the attack, there were months of rumors and whispers of conspiracy. Some suggested that the gas leaks, contained blasts, and evacuations along the Mall that Sunday night were the result of something much more sinister than a failing pipeline and likely linked to the memorial bombings. A few of the hawks in Congress even claimed it was the opening salvo in a full-scale foreign attack, but those ideas didn't get very far on the Hill. Sam and Emily's actions that evening remained a closely held secret. Like all of his best work, it never happened, and he wasn't there.

The new Russian president seemed blessed at every turn, a step ahead of the rivals who plotted to unseat him. He uncovered and neutralized a coup attempt from within the secret services, a last desperate strike from the ultranationalists. Now he was leading the reset with the West, walking back Russian aggression and taking steps against the *siloviki* who had swallowed up so much of his nation's wealth.

"Strange how that worked out," Emily said as they entered the gardens.

"Yes, it is." Sam smiled. "Still, trust but verify."

He looked to the southwest, toward the capital. Few would know how close it had come to disaster. He thought of Finlay, and Alex Clarke, and Diane Mercer, and Christopher Dimos. They hadn't died in vain.

The Agency called Sam back to headquarters again weeks later for a meeting in the same seventh-floor office, though the old number one was gone, and the man who had taken over his job had a very different tone. Half a dozen execs had gone down for letting Jones get away with what he had done, one of those periodic blood-lettings the Agency used to try to move past its mistakes. They offered him his old job back. He looked around the mahogany box and said he'd think about it as long as they never tried to promote him back here.

The day after Sam had gotten out of the hospital, he sent a message to the encrypted e-mail address Arkady Novik had given him to let him know where he could pick up his car.

They never met in person, but Novik provided Sam with intelligence through drops that helped the U.S. and the new Russian administration outflank the hard-liners.

One night when Sam was keeping an eye on a longtime fixture of the Russian *rezidentura* he suspected of working with the ultra-nationalists, he picked up movement on the far side of the property, a farm estate in Potomac, and trained his binoculars at the woods beyond. It was Novik, looking back. He gave a salute, then pulled into the shadows. Sam never saw him again.

Sam kept up running the long miles, but it was different now, his mind clear from the first step. A week after the Agency asked him to return to duty, he went out to the Potomac just south of

Great Falls, the river trail on the Virginia side, where the water ran dark green between granite cliffs dotted with lichen. It was where they had scattered Williams's ashes. He sat on the edge, his feet hanging twenty feet above the surface, his palms on the cold stone.

"We got him," he said to the water. "You were right."

Sam took out Williams's pocket radio, set it on the rock beside him, and watched the river flow.

"Bottom of the sixth. Nationals ahead four to two, and Yan Gomes at the bat. A high fast one, driven out to center field."

Emily went to his house that night. He was having a few people over. He met her at the door, and she handed him a bottle of wine.

"Wise," he said, "though I keep a few around now."

Sam took her coat and she hugged him. "What's that?" she asked, looking up. A rich smell drifted in from the kitchen.

"Chili," he said. "It'll be ready in a half hour."

Voices and music came from the backyard. She walked in without so much as a limp now and looked around. Sam had repainted the place. He told her about being called back to CIA. They'd offered him a chance to run field ops in Europe.

"What are you going to do?"

"I may take it," he said.

"After everything they did to you?"

"Someone's got to look out for our people."

They went into the kitchen, and he poured her a glass of wine before they went into the backyard. A couple of kids ran behind a circle of chairs and benches, and Sam's friends sat near the firepit.

Sam introduced Emily around. Here, she was just another Washingtonian, and if anyone asked what she did, she gave them a job title that sounded just as boring as Sam's. But no one asked. She loved that about the people he brought together.

Ryan, Sam's old friend from Pennsylvania, brightened up when he saw her.

"I remember you," he said. "Madam's Organ. 'C'est la Vie.' You brought the house down." He looked to the Martin guitar resting against one of the chairs. "Are you going to sing tonight?"

Emily held up her hand, laughing. "Let me have a couple drinks first."

She sat next to Sam by the fire. They all talked for a while, and the conversation drifted on.

"How long do you have to decide on the job?" she asked him.

"A while. I'm going to take some time off. I'm starting to think I could use a break," he deadpanned.

That got a laugh out of her. She shook her head, then sipped her wine.

"Katahdin, Acadia," he said. "Get out in the trees. Let all of this go."

A bittersweet look touched her eyes. "Did Fin tell you about that?"

"Yes. It sounded like paradise."

"It is."

"I could use a guide. If you're up for it."

She flexed her ankle. "I can manage," she said. "Parts of it. And there are some great diners up there."

He put his arm around her shoulders. "Deal."

ACKNOWLEDGMENTS

A huge thank-you to my family for all their help while I was writing this book. Their love and support really carried me through. A special thanks to my wife, Heather, the best copilot I could ever dream of, and to my mother, Ellen, who is a blast to talk to about plots and an invaluable reader at every step.

I am enormously grateful to my agent, Dan Conaway, and editor, David Highfill. It's hard to imagine a wiser or kinder pair, and I'm so lucky to have them on my team. The folks at Writers House, William Morrow, and HarperCollins are the absolute best; thanks to Peggy Boulos-Smith, Lauren Carsley, Jennifer Hart, Kaitlin Harri, Brittani Hilles, Tessa James, Andy LeCount, Liate Stehlik, and Evangelos Vasilakis. Tracy Roe, as always, did a fantastic job copyediting the manuscript. And thank you to Shawn Ryan, Seth Gordon, Jamie Vanderbilt, William Sherak, Paul Neinberg, Nicole Tossou, Will Watkins, Peter Nichols, Tiffany Graddick, and Netflix for working magic in L.A.

I drew on a variety of sources for this novel. Ishmael Jones's *The Human Factor* and Amaryllis Fox's *Life Undercover* are terrific reads about the lives of non-official cover CIA officers. Gordon Corera's *Russians Among Us* offers an excellent overview of Russian sleepers in the U.S. from the Soviet days to the present.

The tunnels and hidden waterways under DC in the novel are real, though I took a few liberties with their layout and particulars to suit the story, as I did with the broader DC geography in a couple of spots. Thanks to Elliot Carter for his fascinating project documenting the underground world of the capital and for helping me with research. You can find his work, including many photos and illustrations of the tunnels featured in *Red Warning*, at washingtontunnels.com.

Thanks to KC Higgins for his vast knowledge of hidden DC and guidance in urban spelunking and to Peter Higgins for tipping me off to the old Tiber Creek Pub and being an indispensable resource on the District as well as all things FBI and CIA. And thank you to John MacGaffin for sharing insights from his career in intelligence. (I should note that I made up the snipers on the CIA rooftop for dramatic purposes. The "eye in the sky" technology described in this book is real, though it relies on drones rather than satellites and isn't, to my knowledge, used over DC.) Tom Lee and Julian Sanchez pitched in with technical advice, though any tech snafus in the text are on me. Dr. Steven Davis was so helpful with medical details, and a big thank-you to Tisha Martz and Chris Holm for their early reads of the manuscript and excellent notes.

The general contours of Soviet sabotage plans and hidden weapons caches also come from real life (though the HYACINTH plot is wholly invented). Anyone interested in reading more should take a look at the defector Stanislav Lunev's congressional testimony and memoir, though some of his claims are a matter of debate.

I first came across the hyper-detailed Soviet military maps of the United States in a *Wired* article by Greg Miller, and we all have John Davies, Alexander Kent, and their colleagues to thank for collecting them and making them available publicly in their book *The Red Atlas*.

The power struggles during and after the fall of the Soviet Union make for a fascinating and complex story, greatly simplified here. For the full history, I recommend *Putin's People* by Catherine Belton, a brilliantly done book.

I'd also like to thank Dr. Welton Gersony, my pediatric cardiologist, and Dr. Frederick O. Bowman Jr., the surgeon who operated on my heart when I was a toddler. I took the happier particulars of Pavel's story ("I fixed him," as our family remembers the surgeon's line) from my own experiences and owe my life to those doctors.